She swallowed the _____ at and reached for the door _____ e front parlor Carson was standing in the bay window, his arms folded across his chest as he gazed out at the passing traffic.

Something strange, light, and breathless fluttered in Katherine's heart at the sight of his broad shoulders and clean, handsome profile. Something inside of her longed to be near him, touched by him, though instinct told her that she must not allow that. His touch would melt the reserve she'd built to protect herself from fortune hunters.

When he turned from the window, a smug smile played across his lips. "I won't waste time with preambles. I have taken time to consider your condition on the proposal I offered last night. I have come to a decision."

"So quickly?" she asked, afraid to guess what he might have decided.

Still smiling, he reached into his coat pocket, pulled out a half-sheet of white paper, and unfolded it. With a flourish, he held it up for her to read. "Take a good look at this."

Puzzled, Katherine stared at the tall lettering on the paper: BILL OF SALE. She sucked in a startled breath. The significance of the document sent a shock and something akin to relief through her. Heavens, he'd gone and done it.

Quickly he folded up the bill of sale and tucked it into his breast pocket. "I won't patronize you by dropping to my knee to propose," he said. He took her by the elbows and drew her close. Her honeysuckle scent reached him, and she felt so soft and tempting with her body pressed against his that he almost forgot what he wanted to say. "Our marriage is a matter of practicality. But your acceptance of my plan means a great deal to me. How about a kiss to seal the bargain?"

"I suppose a kiss is appropriate," she said, her voice hesitant with confusion. Her gaze went to his mouth and she licked her lips in anticipation. . . .

BOOK YOUR PLACE ON OUR WEBSITE AND MAKE THE READING CONNECTION!

We've created a customized website just for our very special readers, where you can get the inside scoop on everything that's going on with Zebra, Pinnacle and Kensington books.

When you come online, you'll have the exciting opportunity to:

- View covers of upcoming books
- Read sample chapters
- Learn about our future publishing schedule (listed by publication month *and author*)
- Find out when your favorite authors will be visiting a city near you
- Search for and order backlist books from our online catalog
- Check out author bios and background information
- Send e-mail to your favorite authors
- Meet the Kensington staff online
- Join us in weekly chats with authors, readers and other guests
- Get writing guidelines
- AND MUCH MORE!

Visit our website at
http://www.zebrabooks.com

BRIGHTER THAN GOLD

Linda Madl

ZEBRA BOOKS
KENSINGTON PUBLISHING CORP.
http://www.zebrabooks.com

ZEBRA BOOKS are published by

Kensington Publishing Corp.
850 Third Avenue
New York, NY 10022

All Kensington titles, imprints and distributed lines are available at special quantity discounts for bulk purchases for sales
promotion, premiums, fund raising, educational or institutional
use.

Special book excerpts or customized printings can also be created to fit specific needs. For details, write or phone the office of
the Kensington Special Sales Manager: Kensington Publishing
Corp., 850 Third Avenue, New York, NY, Attn. Special Sales
Department. Phone: 1-800-221-2647.

Zebra and the Z logo Reg. U.S. Pat. & TM Off.

First Printing: October, 2000
10 9 8 7 6 5 4 3 2 1

Printed in the United States of America

A Marriage Ring

The ring so worn as you behold,
So thin, so pale, is yet of gold:
The passion such it was to prove;
Worn with life's cares, love yet was love.

—GEORGE CRABBE

Chapter One

Denver, 1890

"Let's kill off your wife," suggested Randolph Hearn, the lanky editor of the *Rocky Mountain Sentinel*, as he lounged back on Dolly Green's drawing room sofa.

Before Carson Fairfax could respond, a malicious smile formed on his best friend's lips. Randolph gazed up at the ornate ceiling of the House of Sphinxes and raised his voice in a theatrical tone. "First, the dear lady would die a sad, poetic death, described dramatically in her obituary. Then I would write a front-page follow-up about the funeral. Something suitably impressive for the wife of one of Denver's richest men—*and* the third son of the Earl of Atwick.

"You know—fog settling over the city as though the elements were weeping along with us mortals for the passing of one so young, so beautiful, so beloved. Dozens and dozens of black-plumed horses would parade through the streets, mounds of lilies would cover her casket, and a throng of mourning dignitaries would march behind the gleaming hearse."

Fired by his vision, Randolph sat up and leveled a long index finger at him. "And you'll be speechless in your profound grief as the bereaved husband. What inscription do you think I should quote for her gravestone?"

"Do shut up, old chap," snapped Carson, avowed bachelor and the Fairfax family black sheep.

"Come now, Carson, where is your sense of humor?" Dolly asked from her favorite chair by the fire. Amid the late afternoon gloom, the firelight set silvery glints dancing in the white hair of the society matron and brought a rosy luster to her five-strand pearl choker. In her lap lay the telegram he'd just received.

"I see the irony, madame, but I do not think it at all funny." Too apprehensive to sit, he leaned against the marble mantel, closer to the crackling flames, attempting to warm himself against the disbelief—and the cold October wind—that had chilled him to the bone. The fictitious world he'd built to please his mother when she'd been on her deathbed, *and* to thwart his father, who had forbidden him to return to England, was about to tumble down around him. "And I'd appreciate it, Randolph, old chap, if you'd offer some constructive ideas, not ridicule."

"Now, now, gentlemen, let's not turn on each other when the going gets rough," Dolly counseled. "Carson, you must admit, this is good news. Your mother has not only recovered from her illness but is strong enough to travel. The bad news is, she wants to spend Christmas with you—and your *wife.*"

"I'm delighted about her recovery, of course. There's never been any question of that," Carson countered, and he meant it. He'd thrown a party months ago at the Gentlemen's Respite to celebrate the day his brothers had sent confirmation of their mother's miraculous recuperation.

When the three days of partying had come to an end, the reality of what he'd done had set in. How could he tell his mother he'd lied? So he'd begun to add to his string of falsehoods. Now, a year later, it was time to pay the piper.

"I think we should keep the solution simple—whatever we

decide to do," he said to his partners in crime. He spread his hands toward the roaring fire, but the heat still failed to banish his chill. He disliked dishonesty. Even as a gambler he seldom practiced it.

"Easy to say, Carson, dear, but not so easy to do," Dolly replied. "Since this all began, we've woven quite an intricate set of tales for you and Kitty. By the way, I keep forgetting to ask, how did you come to name your wife Kitty?"

"Lucky jumped on the desk while I was composing the letter to Mother," he said with a shrug. "And it seemed like a good American name."

"Lucky?" Dolly frowned and cast a questioning glance toward Randolph. "The Respite's cat?"

"Even the cat bears guilt in this," Randolph admitted, his malicious mockery slipping away into a worried frown. "Lord, how did we get into this mess?"

Carson remembered all too well how he'd begun to build his house of cards. First, he'd learned he was about to lose his mother. With bitter clarity he recalled the exact wording of the three telegrams he had received within a few short hours on October 7, 1889.

First the telegram from his father had stunned and infuriated him.

Carson stop Physicians give your mother less than a fortnight to live stop Do not return stop Wire your farewell stop Your Father full stop

Grief-stricken and rebellious, he'd immediately started to pack for the trip to England. *A pox on you, Father,* he'd muttered to himself as he crammed shirts into a small valise. Animosity, like an iron wall, had long separated him from the earl. The terse command not to return home only made him more determined to reach his mother's bedside before it was too late. If he traveled fast and alone, sleeping on the move, he could be home in two weeks. Ignoring his father's instruction, he'd sent Jack Tremain to buy a ticket for him on the next train headed east.

His father, the rich and influential earl, had always insisted on having the finest medical men in the realm attending whenever Mother so much as sneezed. Who could have guessed that this time they were wrong?

Carson was about to leave for the train station when the second telegram had arrived, this one from his brothers.

Carson stop Mother's end near stop Do not return stop Father anguished stop Strain between you would only worsen matters stop Mother wishes to hear from you stop Write words of comfort stop We will read them to her stop Your brothers John and Neville full stop

Even now he could envision John, the stern, humorless Atwick heir, so like Father, and Neville, the much-decorated army officer, bent over the telegram form, carefully choosing each word they wrote. But they had made a good point.

He didn't give a damn how Father felt. Mother's feelings, however, were another matter.

If he went to England, he had little doubt that he and his father would quarrel. How would that effect his mother? What good would his visit do if their conflict upset her? Carson set his valise aside.

Yet what words of comfort could he write to her? What could he say to ease her discomfort?

Then his mother's telegram had arrived.

Dear Son stop Bed rest for my current malady has given me time to reflect on past stop What a fine life your father and I have had stop I so wish you and he would come to terms stop It troubles me that you remain far away and alone stop Life offers no greater happiness than a loving spouse stop It would put my heart at ease to know that you are settled and happy with a wife stop But know

*dear son that you remain ever in my heart stop Your
loving mother full stop*

The anger and grief stirred by his father's telegram vanished.
His mother's message flooded Carson with warmth and tenderness. Tears had ached in his throat. When he closed his eyes,
he could feel her caring hand on his four-year-old head, an
unforgettable gesture of love that lived inside him still. Father
had just given him a particularly harsh set down for misbehaving
in church. His mother had touched him with love and reassurance—then later, when he was supposed to be out of hearing,
he had heard them arguing.

He'd known since his father had locked him in the cellar for
refusing to serve as altar boy at St. Paul's that there was no
pleasing the earl. By then he'd already spent the entire twelve
years of his life trying. Though he had nothing against the
church, parading along behind a cleric was the last place he
belonged.

As the earl's angry footsteps had faded on the cellar stairs,
he'd seen with dazzling, youthful clarity that his father would
never accept him for whom and what he was. He was meant
to be an adventurer, an entrepreneur, a creature of the secular
world.

From that day forward he'd made no more attempts to be
what his father wanted.

Whenever things looked impossible, the memory of his mother's hand on his head had given him faith in himself. Her love
had remained constant. Evidence of it glowed in her eyes, in
her touch, and in her voice. Even when he'd been dismissed
from school for winning all the other boys' pocket money at
cards. Even when he'd been sent down from university for
trying to prove to the fellows that card-playing was a mathematical science. Even when he'd been escorted out of his father's
London club because he'd won against the Duke of Deander
too often for just good luck or skill—and he was labeled a
black sheep.

Even when he could see in his mother's eyes that she suspected he enjoyed being the Fairfax black sheep—it was the one thing he did well—the shining brightness of her love had never diminished.

"Tell us again, Carson, what you wrote to your mother," Dolly urged, jarring him from his memories. "Whatever we do, it must be true to the story we've already created. I don't remember exactly what you said."

"I remember." Carson turned from the fire and quoted the telegram he'd sent to his mother almost a year earlier.

Dearest Mother stop Do not fret over my future stop I send happy news of engagement to lovely woman stop Wedding date to be set soon stop Will reside among Denver elite stop Only concern is your health stop Focus on recovery stop Though the sea separates us I remain near you in my thoughts and heart stop Your loving son Carson full stop

"Well, that certainly would comfort any mother," Dolly said, smiling benignly at Carson. "Did you ever think that easing her mind allowed her to get well?"

"No, that thought never occurred to me," he said honestly, surprised by Dolly's suggestion. He'd never doubted that he'd been more trouble to his mother than he'd ever been a cure. "I just didn't want Mother leaving this world troubled over me. She deserved better."

"And so we gave it to her," Dolly said with a nod. "Mr. and Mrs. Carson Fairfax, complete with a Denver society wedding."

"Notable dignitaries attended the nuptials." Randolph, the streetwise reporter, smiled with childlike pride. "I reported it all with Dolly's assistance in describing everything from the wedding gown to the guests' hats."

"As well as the food on the reception table," added Dolly. "It was quite an event."

"And I thank you." He still had a copy of the wedding story from the *Sentinel* filed away in his desk at the Respite. Randolph had never revealed the lengths to which he'd had to go to get the story and the fake wedding invitations printed. Carson had sent the newspaper clippings and keepsakes to his mother, and he would be eternally grateful to Randolph and Dolly for their help. "Mother was terribly disappointed that she was unable to attend. But she is well enough to travel now and our problem remains. She is going to be here in less than eight weeks."

Randolph shrugged, "Well, like I said, if you want to keep it simple, let's kill off your wife and I'll write up the funeral. You'll wear a black armband for mourning and—"

"Please cease this murdering of poor Kitty," Dolly scolded as she twisted in her chair to face Randolph.

"Kitty's death doesn't solve anything, Randolph," he said. During a year of nursing lie after lie, he'd grown skilled in recognizing the complications each additional fabrication created. "What if Mother wants to see Kitty's grave? And there's our story about the house on Capitol Hill . . ."

"Mmm, the house." Randolph glanced toward Dolly, as if housing was her responsibility. "I don't suppose you could lodge your mother in Horace Tabor's hotel? I'm sure the silver king would be delighted to have a countess in residence at the Windsor."

"No, no. That will never do," Dolly said, shaking a warning finger at Randolph. "Nor will Carson's apartment over the Respite be adequate. He is one of the richest men in Denver. The countess must stay in the comfort of his opulent mansion so she can return home to tell his father and brothers what a luxurious place it is. Am I right, Carson?"

The truth of Dolly's statement struck so unexpectedly close to home, he almost winced, though he deplored displays of emotion. In his business it was foolish and weak. Even more, he disliked people reading his true feelings. He cast the grande dame of Denver society a look of respect. "I wouldn't care to face you across the poker table, madame."

"Few can keep secrets from me," she said, rearing back in her chair to regard him with a regal expression that would put a duchess to shame. "The fact is, I don't think we can afford to indulge in simplicity. I think we're in too deep for that."

"Too bad, old chap." Randolph sat back, stretching his arms along the sofa back and crossing his grasshopperlike legs. "That means between now and December sixth, when your mother arrives, you need to find yourself a wife."

"I'm not keen on the idea of marriage," he said. Long ago he'd vowed to himself that he would never marry. That he would never be a husband and, especially, never a father. He would never be guilty of ruining another's life as his father had his.

"For one reason," he explained for Dolly's sake, "gamblers don't make good husbands. We're too restless and irresponsible."

"The way you've managed to duck every matchmaking mama in Denver made me suspect as much," Dolly said, her lips thinning as if she was concerned about something of great importance. Finally she spoke with reluctance. "Would it help if I told you that I happen to know of a good candidate for your wife?"

"Who?" asked Randolph, sitting forward on the edge of the sofa, his long face with its pointed chin alive with curiosity.

"I doubt there's such a candidate," Carson said, uneasy with Dolly's revelation. He'd watched her matchmake more than one happy couple, which was all well and good for them. But he did not intend to fall prey to her skills.

"Not even Katherine Tucker?" Dolly asked, watching him closely.

Carson covered his surprise by reaching for another log to put on the fire. He'd been aware of the girl since he'd first seen her ten years earlier sleighing with her father. But he'd never revealed his interest—to anyone.

"Denver's ice queen?" exclaimed Randolph, bouncing off the sofa. "You must be kidding. She's turned a cold shoulder to at least a dozen suitors."

"Katherine is not an ice queen," Dolly corrected, her steady gaze making Carson increasingly uncomfortable. "She's just a little reserved and misguided after what happened to her father. And don't forget, she is Denver's most notable gold mine heiress."

"She's Denver's reformer extraordinaire and a snob," Carson declared, unable to keep antipathy from twisting his mouth into a frown.

Strangely, her recent petition drive against drinking and gambling establishments had proven to be a boon to the Gentlemen's Respite. Curiosity seekers never failed to show up when she stood on the corner across from his club soliciting signatures. People would obligingly sign her paper. Then, eventually, they strolled through his doors.

But the mention of Katherine Tucker, socialite—snob and heiress—was enough to make him reconsider Randolph's plan for killing off his fictitious wife.

Suddenly Carson's hands and feet were toasty warm from the fire. He stepped away from the blaze.

"I hardly think Katherine and I are a match, Dolly," he began, certain he could reason himself out of this predicament. "My personal feelings about marriage aside, why would Katherine Tucker have any interest in marrying me, the owner and operator of the Gentlemen's Respite?"

"Because you are handsome, rich, and well connected," Dolly said, smiling up at him with a gleam of mystery in her eyes. The mistress of the House of the Sphinxes—named for the stone likenesses of the Egyptian monument guarding the walk to her house—loved to be cryptic. "Besides, I have reason to believe that mitigating circumstances are about to develop that might make her consider such an offer."

"Mitigating circumstances?" Carson glanced across the

room at Randolph, wondering if the newspaperman had an inkling about what Dolly meant.

Randolph admitted his ignorance with a shrug.

"Before you get yourself convinced that this is a silly idea, think of the Elms," Dolly continued. "You were at the Tuckers' Christmas tree decorating party last year."

"Half of Denver was at that party," he said dismissively, but the image of Katherine Tucker filled his head: her lacy gown of red velvet clinging provocatively to her hourglass figure, a single string of pearls lying around her graceful neck, her full lips glistening tantalizingly in the candlelight.

He'd thought more than once that it was a crime for a woman known as the ice queen to have lips that luscious.

"You know how beautifully Katherine decorates that house every Christmas," Dolly continued. "Fresh greenery, satin ribbons, hothouse flowers, colored candles in silver candlesticks. And the Elms is so spacious. Plenty of room. Your mother would be well entertained in surroundings as elegant as any London home. Think of the stories the countess would carry back to your father."

"Ummm?" Mention of his father jarred Carson from delicious thoughts of Katherine's small-waisted figure. He glared at Dolly.

"She's well traveled and well educated." Dolly smiled at him wickedly before continuing. "She has met royalty, and you know how she loves to playact in amateur theatricals. So she's unlikely to become flustered about having a countess in her house. You do see the picture?"

"I see it," Carson muttered, and he did, all too clearly.

The Elms—the three-story angular Italianate house—stood proud and elegant (not unlike its mistress) on Pearl Street in the heart of Capitol Hill, the most prestigious section of Denver. Ornate brass and crystal gaslit chandeliers hung from intricate plaster ceiling medallions. An array of antique and imported furniture cluttered the rooms in the modern style. From the tall windows cascaded lace and jewel-toned damask draperies to pool on the floor.

There were three bathrooms with hot and cold running water. Four different imported woods created the parquet design of the dining room floor. Dozens of the namesake trees shaded the yard and lined the drive.

But its most unique feature was the palm- and fern-filled, twenty-foot-long heated glass conservatory, which boasted a fountain and an Italian marble floor—the ideal place for a lady to stroll even in the cold Rocky Mountain winter.

No expense had been spared. No detail had been overlooked.

The Elms was perfect: from the superb John Singer Sargent portrait of Benjamin and Amanda Leigh Tucker that hung in the drawing room to the stately black cast-iron columns and the delicate wrought-iron fretwork at its entrance. The house represented exactly the sort of exuberant, sophisticated American wealth Carson longed to show his mother.

And . . . what a charming hostess Katherine Tucker would be—if she chose to serve as such.

"And just how do you propose we make this all happen?" he challenged, warming to Dolly's idea but unable to imagine Katherine offering him any kind of cooperation. She was barely polite enough to dance with him when he asked at social functions. "Do I just call on Miss Tucker and say, 'Katherine, dear, may I live in your house and call you wife for the month of December? And by the way, we'll be having a countess as a houseguest, along with her maid and traveling companion'?"

A victorious smile spread across Dolly's face as she waved away the details. "I'll leave that up to you, Carson. You're the man with vision. The gambler. But also a man of honor. You'll figure out how to handle the marriage thing. By the way, I'm having a little soiree at the house on Saturday night, after the opera. A few select guests are invited, and I believe Katherine will be there. Do come."

"You'd better accept the invitation, old chap," Randolph

advised with a laugh. "You're going to have to work fast if you're going to have a wife by Christmas."

Carson hardly heard his friend's taunt. Hypnotized by the fire, he was already turning over ideas in his head about how he could get out of this mess—and the ideas all centered on Katherine Tucker.

Chapter Two

A fierce October wind blustered down the Denver street, kicking up dust, snatching at men's hats, and thrusting an icy finger down the neck of Katherine Tucker's fur-trimmed coat. Clutching the soft collar closer, she ducked her head against the gale and marched on, undaunted by the wintry assault.

"We need only five more signatures. Then our petition will be complete," said Opal Shaw, the part-time girl in Mr. Bradley's bookshop and her partner that day for the Ladies' Moderation League. Opal was a plain girl about her own age with mousy hair and faded blue eyes, but her speech was educated. She loved books, and she had a good heart. Katherine liked her. As they trudged against the wind, Opal also clutched at her coat, a threadbare dark wool garment with sleeves too fitted to be fashionable.

"I know. Victory is near," Katherine said, glad to be out and busy, glad to be focusing her efforts on making Denver a better place. Glad to escape the burdens that had developed since the accident at the Clementine last spring. She leaned into the windy gusts and struggled on, her satchel flopping against her side, her free hand grasping her coat collar.

She didn't stop until they reached the corner of Fourteenth and Curtis—across from the Gentlemen's Respite.

With her gloved hand on her fur hat, she raised her head to study the red brick building. Opal beside her followed suit.

"Look at the place, sitting there as innocent as a sleeping baby," Opal said. "From the outside, one can hardly tell that it's anything more than a respectable hotel. Red velvet curtains at the windows. That uniformed doorman at the entrance. No loud music. No drunken louts in the street. No fights. But we ladies of Denver aren't deceived, are we?"

"No," Katherine replied, remembering Fairfax's description of his establishment, offered last time they'd danced together. "Mr. Fairfax claims he offers a fine restaurant, a vintage wine cellar, and a smoking room filled with enough books and newspapers to compete with the library. But we are not deceived."

"It's still nothing more than a saloon," Opal said. "And if that isn't bad enough, the playing cards are imported from Europe with kings and queens on them, and I heard . . ." She trailed off, then leaned closer to whisper in Katherine's ear. "The female dealers wear low-necked gowns! I mean so low their bosoms almost fall out."

"Yes, the necklines are very low," she agreed, even though she'd seen lower during her trip to Paris four years earlier. Her gaze drifted to the second-story floor-to-ceiling window where Carson Fairfax usually sat.

Opal followed her gaze. "Glory, he's not there today." But the disappointment in her voice contradicted her words.

Contrary to the fabled sit-with-your-back-to-the-wall philosophy of Wild West gamblers, the dark-haired, blue-eyed Englishman had a habit of sitting in full view in the window. From there he watched the street, waved to friends, and admired passing horseflesh—and the ladies, it was rumored. She knew that he often watched her while she was soliciting signatures.

It was most disconcerting. Thankfully, today the draperies were drawn.

"No, he's not there *yet.*" Pleased, Katherine reached for her satchel. "And I hope the draperies stay closed. With five more signatures, Carson Fairfax may be looking for a new place to set up his disreputable business. Five more signatures, and the future of the women and children of Denver will be more secure."

"Yes, won't that be nice," Opal said with a smile, but then she frowned. "But I do admit I'll be sorry not to see his handsome face so often."

Another gust of wind ruffled the pages of the petition notebook Katherine pulled from her satchel. Tightening her grip on the precious endorsements, she pulled out her ink bottle and pen, all in readiness to begin their work.

A movement in the second-story window caught their attention. They glanced up to see the draperies open. Carson Fairfax, the owner and operator of the Gentlemen's Respite, seated himself at a table near the floor-to-ceiling window.

"Drat," she muttered. Guilt and surprise fluttered in her belly.

He slouched negligently in his straight-backed chair, his long legs stretched out before him, his thumb hooked in the pocket of his bright burgundy red waistcoat, and his fistful of playing cards resting on the table.

Aware that he'd caught their attention, he grinned, unhooked his thumb, and waved a greeting to them.

The heat of a blush rose in Katherine's cheeks despite the cold wind. He did this every time she stood on his corner, sitting in his window and watching her. He smiled. He waved. He sometimes pointed out gentlemen he apparently thought she should approach. He was thoroughly irritating.

"Arrogant scoundrel," she muttered, longing to turn her back on him, even if it was impolite.

"Should we ignore him?" Opal asked, her gaze still fastened on the man in the window.

"Of course we don't ignore him. That would be bad breeding." Besides, it would give him too much satisfaction, which, Katherine knew, was exactly what Fairfax wanted.

With her nose in the air, she acknowledged the gambler's greeting with a slight nod combined with drawing her coat closer.

"That's true. We mustn't look ill-bred." Opal grinned and returned an enthusiastic wave.

A fine partner the girl was. One smile from the opposition and she was half willing to go over to the other side. Katherine glared at Fairfax, wishing he was fat and smug, like the other saloonkeepers, instead of handsome and charmingly conceited. Then her job would be easier.

She turned back to her petition. Dealing with Carson Fairfax, she'd come to realize, was the awkward—and frustrating— part of her mission. He was the pet of Denver society, entertained and fawned over at all the important social events. She suspected that was exactly why the ladies of the League had asked her to work on the Gentlemen's Respite petition. She'd just as soon work on eliminating other taverns where her father might have been drinking the night he stepped out in front of a wagon, in a drunken stupor, and later died of his injuries.

But the ladies of the League thought that because she moved in the same social circle as Fairfax, she might have sway over him as well as the influential members of Denver society. The ladies did not understand that the movers and shakers of the city simply ignored the fact that the Englishman was a gambler and a saloonkeeper.

Rich was rich. It was its own definition, its own standard. Denver's elite had made their fortunes through a variety of risk-taking ventures. They saw little wrong with Fairfax's chosen profession. Besides, he was kin to a British earl. Denver wanted to regard him as a royal and one of their own. How could you fight that?

When she furtively glanced up at Fairfax again, to her relief, he had returned to his cards.

"That's better," she murmured, allowing her gaze to linger on him.

"Glory, he is a handsome fellow in that refined English way of his." Opal sighed.

Silently, Katherine had to agree. There was no denying he was attractive, for an older man. He was tallish, broad-shoul-dered, and lean of hip. Nearly every mama of a marriageable daughter had tried to match her darling with Carson Fairfax. At Denver's social functions, everyone from the young misses to the matrons practically drooled over him. They even whis-pered prayers that he would ask them to dance. She had heard them. He was a fine dancer; she knew from personal experience.

But she was not so easily impressed with fancy footwork on the dance floor or with royal connections. Those socialite mamas shouldn't be either, Katherine thought. She'd been to London and had been entertained in the finest aristocratic homes. She knew that a third son was the heir to nothing and hardly merited a lady's notice.

Dragging her gaze away from the bane of her existence, she took advantage of Fairfax's disinterest. With her petition in hand, she and Opal began to solicit signatures. Opal soon gained one signature from a passing clergyman.

Requesting names had made Katherine a bit uncomfortable when she'd first begun to work with the ladies of the League. But she believed so deeply in her cause, she'd soon learned how to catch the eye of a passerby and to explain what she was seeking without giving offense.

Still, this morning, though there was no lack of men on the street, her first solicitation attempts were unsuccessful. One passerby smiled indulgently at her, tipped his hat, but shook his head when she offered the petition. Then he crossed the street and entered the Respite.

She refused to let the rebuff discourage her. Another gentle-man ducked his head and hurried by. He, too, crossed the street and entered the men's club.

At last two well-dressed older gentlemen came tottering down the walk and stopped before her.

"Why, Mr. Wagner, so good to see you again," Katherine greeted the elder of the two, gratified to see a familiar face—yet disappointed, too.

"I'll sign your petition." Mr. Wagner offered her a wide, yellow-toothed smile.

"That's so kind of you, sir," she said, speaking up because she knew he was hard of hearing. She introduced Opal to the gentleman, then reminded him, "But you've already signed this petition once, Mr. Wagner."

"I haven't signed it," said the other man, a younger though graying version of Mr. Wagner.

"This is my son, John Junior." Mr. Wagner clapped his hand on the younger man's back. "I brought him down here to have a look at you—uh, I mean at your petition. Johnnie, Miss Tucker is Ben Tucker's girl. You remember Ben and the Amanda Leigh mine? Yes, sir, Johnnie will sign for you."

"Wonderful. I'm delighted to meet you, Mr. Wagner." Katherine handed the petition notebook to John Junior and dipped her pen in the ink bottle sitting on the flat top of the hitching post. She'd never met the younger Mr. Wagner, but she knew that the Wagners had made their fortune in outfitting prospectors and had sold off the business long ago. Yet Mr. Wagner, Senior, had never given up his concern for the city of Denver.

As the man signed a bold signature with a shaky hand, she explained the purpose of her campaign.

"Yes, yes, worthy cause. Very worthy," he mumbled, returning the pen to her.

"Thank you, both of you, for your support," she said when the man had finished.

"Our pleasure, my dear," the older man said, tipping his hat.

Then, of all things, the pair stepped off the walk and tottered straight across the street toward the Gentlemen's Respite.

Katherine stared after them in astonishment.

"That's one more signature," Opal was saying as she pored over the petition.

"But look where they are going," Katherine exclaimed.

In the middle of the street, Mr. Wagner turned to his son. Speaking loudly, as though everyone was as deaf as he was, he said, "Didn't I tell you she's a looker?"

"You're right about that, Pop." John Junior nodded. "A real looker. But I think she'd be purtier if she would smile. I like my women to smile."

"Yep, a smile is nice," the older man agreed with a nod of his grizzled head.

"Glad you brought me down here, Pop," John Junior continued. "You going to try the faro table today or the roulette?"

"Roulette, I think," Mr. Wagner said as the pair was about to disappear through the door held open for them by the Gentlemen's Respite's doorman. "I like the way the roulette gal's dress falls off her shoulder when she leans over to spin the wheel."

"Well, I never!" Opal cried with a gasp.

Katherine huffed and slapped her skirt with the petition. "How can they sign our petition, ogle us as if we are nothing more than prize horseflesh, then patronize the very establishment they have just endorsed forcing out of town?"

In exasperation, she glanced up at Fairfax's window.

He was watching her again. This time he offered her a mock frown, shook his head, and raised his free hand in a gesture of helplessness.

"As if you can't keep them away, you scoundrel," she muttered, her eyes narrowed. She shook her head at him. "You ought to be ashamed."

"From that grin, I don't think he is," Opal supplied. A chuckle escaped her as she added, "He's a devil, isn't he?"

Katherine shot the girl a scowl. Opal hung her head.

At that moment, the Respite's doors swung open with a bang. A man emerged, carrying a huge tray set on a small table and covered with white linen towels. He wore a slouch hat, a red-

and-green-plaid blanket coat over orange-and-green-plaid trousers. She recognized him immediately as Fairfax's right-hand man, Jack Tremain. Papa had always declared that retired Cornishman Jack Tremain was one of the best miners in the Rockies.

At the edge of the wooden walkaway, Tremain waited for a horse and buggy to pass, then he crossed the street, the china and silver on the tray clinking as he picked his way around the horse manure. When he reached Katherine and Opal's corner, he set the table down on the walkway and straightened to face them.

"Good day, Miss Tucker." He touched the brim of his brown hat. "Miss Shaw."

"Hello, Mr. Tremain." She inclined her head, curious about the man's mission.

"Mr. Fairfax observed that the day is cold, and he thought ye ladies might like a spot of tea to warm yerselves." Tremain lifted the white linen napkins to reveal a steaming silver teapot, a hot milk pot, a bowl of sugar cubes, a dish of lemon slices, two china teacups, and a plate of dainty sandwiches.

Katherine bit her lip. Anger welled up inside her. *The gall.*

"A genuine English tea," exclaimed Opal.

"Or if ye'd rather, yer both welcome to come inside the Respite to warm yerselves as Mr. Fairfax's guests," Tremain said. "But Mr. Fairfax thought ye might prefer to take yer refreshment out here, with the Respite being a men's club and all."

"I think we'd prefer to stay out here," Opal said, glancing at her for confirmation.

She immediately turned to the window to see if Fairfax was watching. He was. A small questioning smile curved on his lips. The devil was trying to buy them off. She turned back to Tremain. "We will not be distracted from our purpose, Mr. Tremain. You can tell Mr. Fairfax that."

"But I wouldn't want to see this go to waste," Opal said, staring at the inviting plate of delicacies.

Tremain's eyes widened in surprise. "I don't think that Mr. Fairfax intended to influence yer purpose, Miss Tucker. He just thought ye'd like something to warm yer insides on a cold day."

"Well, he is mistaken," she said.

"He is?" Opal asked, gazing from Katherine to Tremain. She looked just as confused as Tremain did. "Are you sure?"

"Yes, he is," Katherine repeated, certain Fairfax's hospitable gesture was less than genuine. Gamblers played every angle of a game, didn't they? She turned to the window and spoke directly to the Respite's proprietor. "If you think my position on gambling and drinking can be softened by tea and sandwiches, then you have little understanding of what the true issues are here."

"And just what is the true issue?" questioned a deep voice that Katherine instantly recognized.

She whirled around to find Randolph Hearn looming behind them. A sigh of pleasure slipped from her. At last, an ally. She'd visited with the *Rocky Mountain Sentinel*'s editor at several social and charity events around town. He was a loose-limbed man with sharp gray eyes and a cynical smile. She liked him. He seemed to be one man who had a sincere interest in improving Denver's moral climate. "Mr. Hearn, hello. Are you here to report on our petition campaign against Denver's gambling halls?"

"No, though I support your effort," Hearn said, reaching for Katherine's notebook. "May I sign your petition?"

"Yes, please do," Opal said, clapping her mitten-clad hands. "Having your name on the petition, Mr. Hearn, will be a great coup. The League ladies will be thrilled. And that will be three signatures today, Katherine."

She thrust the book toward him and dipped her pen in the ink. "Thank you."

"Are you having much success?" Hearn asked as he added his name in a tight, unreadable scrawl at the bottom of the signature column.

"Yes, but the strangest thing just happened," she began, then related the morning's encounter with the Wagners to him. "Then, like the others, Mr. Wagner and John Junior walked into that—that *place*. And then Mr. Fairfax sent out this tea tray to mock us."

"Seems a little hypocritical, doesn't it?" Hearn said, looking toward Fairfax's window. When he saw the Englishman, he waved. The gambler returned the greeting.

"What on earth?" she blurted in bafflement. "Not you too? Have you no sense of propriety? I should think you'd be here to learn about our effort to improve the moral spirit of our city."

"And you have my newspaper's support," Hearn repeated and smiled indulgently as he handed the petition back to her. "However, it's not the Gentlemen's Respite that this city needs to get rid of, Miss Tucker. The minimum stake at one of Carson's tables pretty much weeds out any small-time gamblers. I assure you, the men who play at the Respite can afford to be foolish with their money."

"Whose side are you on?" Katherine demanded, mystified by his attitude.

"Decency's side, but I'm late for lunch with Carson," Hearn said, stepping toward the street. "Join us. I'm sure Carson would be glad to offer you a meal. He loves having you out here."

Hearn's words shocked Katherine speechless.

"You're great for business." Hearn nodded and grinned. "He told me so. Every time you're out here on the corner—*you*, not one of your League sisters, no offense, Miss Shaw—but when you're around, Katherine, the Respite's trade picks up."

She glanced up at the window again. Fairfax was shaking his head and mouthing something. "What is he saying?" she asked.

"I think he is saying 'Don't believe a word he says,' " Opal offered.

Hearn just laughed, touched his hat, and started across the street, the winter wind flapping his coattails as he went.

Stung by the newspaperman's revelation, she whirled on Jack Tremain, who had remained silent throughout her exchange with Hearn.

"Is it true?" she demanded, leaning across the tea tray toward the Cornishman, her hands braced on her hips, her elbows akimbo.

Opal retreated.

"Tell me, Mr. Tremain, does Mr. Fairfax want me out here on the corner?"

Tremain cringed. "I couldn't say, miss. I just brought the tray out like the captain asked me."

"Well, take it back," she ordered. Fairfax's motivation was even more sinister than she'd suspected. He wasn't just trying to influence her opinion of him and the Respite. He was using her to improve business. How humiliating!

"All of it?" Opal asked with yearning as she studied the tray once more.

"We'll have none of it." Katherine waved the food away. "We're not about to accept anything from Mr. Fairfax."

Without another word, Tremain picked up the table and tray and retreated across the street.

"I can't believe we've been taken advantage of." Overwhelmed by a sense of shame and smouldering anger, she capped her bottle of ink and shoved it and the petition—still wanting two names—into her satchel.

"Perhaps, but we did get three more signatures, and one of them is from the editor of a newspaper," Opal consoled.

"Yes, and thank you for your help," she said, suddenly aware that her anger with Fairfax was making her rude to poor Opal. "You've been a big help to me. Now, off to your job. We don't want Mr. Bradley to be angry because you're late for work."

After saying good-bye, Opal departed.

As Katherine was about to leave, she glanced up once more

at Carson Fairfax's window. He was standing there, his frock coat pushed back and his hands shoved into his trouser pockets, the fine tailoring of his clothes impossible to miss. When he caught her eye, he frowned and shook his head slowly.

"As if you're so disappointed that I wouldn't accept your tea tray," she muttered between clenched teeth. "Opal's right. You *are* a brash devil." She turned her back on him without feeling the least obligation to be polite. She hated being used. It wounded her pride and made her feel as if she had no control over her life.

She was no one's pawn. Deciding that *brash devil* was too polite an epithet for Carson Fairfax, she marched away searching for something more appropriate.

"Craven coxcomb. Roguish lout," she murmured, allowing the words to roll off her tongue and resonate in her ear. She was drawing from her favorite source: Shakespeare. Mama had always declared that the Bard had the best ear for the truly elegant disparaging name.

"Warped varlet." Pulling her coat closer against the cold, she repeated the name, listening to the syllables critically. "Yes, that has a nice, dark, poetic sound for an Englishman. Warped varlet."

Katherine was still muttering the slur, turning it into a little singsong, her mind's eye full of the image of Carson Fairfax smiling mock disappointment, when she turned the corner and collided with a bony, masculine body.

The collision knocked her off balance. But not before she caught the scent of Owen Benedict's pomade. He grabbed her shoulders to steady her.

"There you are, Katherine," he said. Then, as if she were a red-hot horseshoe, he released her before she had regained her balance.

"Uncle Owen," she gasped, bracing her feet to keep from teetering into the street. Owen Benedict had been Papa's trusted business partner and Mama's dear friend for as long as she could remember, and she'd always known him as "uncle."

Once steadied, she straightened her hat and gazed into the austere countenance of her legal guardian. He had a long face and a weak chin. The wind whipped his Benjamin Franklin, shoulder-length white hair into a wreath around his face. "I wasn't expecting to run into you, but what a pleasant surprise," she said with a flustered smile.

The tall, spare man stepped back from her and touched the brim of his top hat. "Mrs. Dodd told me you were out with your petition drive again," he said.

There was no dismissing the disapproval in his tone, but she chose to overlook it. On more than one Christmas Day, he and his shy wife, Edna, had shared dinner with the Tuckers. Though the Benedicts were neither warm nor demonstrative people, they were the closest thing to blood relatives she and her sister, Lily, had. She respected, admired, and trusted them completely.

She noted Uncle Owen's creased brow and suddenly wondered what had brought him in search of her. "How is Aunt Edna? Is something wrong?"

"No, nothing like that." He spoke in a low, urgent tone. "I just had word from Nolan Stuart. He needs to see us in his office right away."

Taking her firmly by the arm, he steered Katherine around toward Nolan's office.

"He probably has a draft for the money I requested," she said, resisting his strong grip. Uncle Owen was an intense man who took everything far too seriously.

"What money?" he demanded. "You said nothing of a request for funds to me."

"Because they're for the annual Christmas party," she said, finally extricating herself from her uncle's grip.

Uncle Owen blinked, obviously having forgotten about one of the biggest social events in Denver. She could hardly forget it. Since her financial difficulties had begun, the Christmas party was the one thing that she and Lily had anticipated with pleasure.

"Oh, I doubt the party is the issue," he said, frowning. "I think this is about something more serious."

"I hope not," she said, dismayed by the thought of more bad news. The accident at the Clementine mine in the spring had caused more problems than she'd dreamed a gold heiress could have.

"Where is Willis with the buggy?" Uncle Owen asked, looking up and down the street. When he saw no waiting vehicle, he turned to Katherine. "Surely you did not walk."

"I had to let Willis go last month," she murmured, tugging on her fur-trimmed hat again, drawing it further over her ears. She had no wish to solicit Uncle Owen's pity. "Why do I need a buggy to take me everywhere? The Elms is quite close to town. The exercise and fresh air are good for me. If I tire or have packages, I simply take the cable car."

"But the cable cars are hardly reliable in bad weather," Uncle Owen stammered and stepped back.

"Then I won't be out in bad weather," she said.

"I didn't realize things were so dire, my dear."

"Willis found a position with Dolly Green, who promised I could have him back whenever I need him," she said, thankful for her godmother's help, and eager to smooth over the awkwardness of the moment. "I suppose we must go find out what Nolan wants. I love walking in this crisp air, don't you?"

Without waiting for Uncle Owen to reply, she tucked her hands into her coat pockets and led the way down the walk.

At the office of Whitman and Whitman, Attorneys at Law, she and Uncle Owen were immediately ushered into Nolan's office, where the lawyer sat behind a massive desk stacked with papers and law books. Despite the wooden paneling and the rich carpet, the room smelled like a library of well-used leather and musty paper.

Nolan rose, solemnly greeting Katherine and extending his hand to Uncle Owen. He was a handsome man, only a few years her senior, with a full head of sandy-colored hair, intelligent hazel eyes, and a slightly crooked nose that gave him a rakish look.

It was rumored he was to be the next partner in Whitman and Whitman, if and when the gentlemen decided to take a partner. Half the unmarried ladies of Denver had their caps set for him, but he seemed to think he and she were a couple. She indulged his notion—most of the time. He was a pleasant enough suitor who, as partner to one of the most prestigious law firms in the city, would be unlikely to have designs on her fortune.

Greetings exchanged, Katherine seated herself in the chair Nolan had indicated and smiled at him, hoping her smile would win one from him in return. When it did not, she let her expression fade. He must, indeed, have bad news. "What's this all about, Nolan? Has there been another mine accident?"

"Oh, no, nothing that awful," he said, resuming his seat behind the desk. "However, my news is significant."

"Well, out with it, man." Uncle Owen spoke from behind Katherine's chair, where he stood. Impatience resonated in his nasal voice.

"I am so sorry to be the bearer of such news," Nolan began, his gaze on Katherine's face.

"Well?" She tried to prepare herself for the worst, but she had no idea how alarmed to be. What could be worse than the accident at the Clementine, where two men were killed and several injured?

Nolan continued, "I learned this morning, unofficially, from Ray Jones at the Cherry Street Bank, that the bank board has voted to call in the mortgage on the Elms."

Chapter Three

"What did you say?" Katherine asked, her heart pounding. She leaned forward and prayed she'd heard Nolan incorrectly.

He pressed his lips together in obvious distaste for his words. "Katherine, I'm sorry to tell you that Ray Jones told me this morning that the board of directors at the Cherry Street Bank is calling in the mortgage on the Elms by October thirty-first. You won't receive the official notice for another week. But you will have to pay back the loan or lose the house."

"But I thought we had until January first," she said, flabbergasted. "There must be some mistake."

"Unfortunately there is a provision in the contract that allows the bank to call in the loan sooner if the board deems immediate repayment necessary," Nolan explained with a pained expression.

"I don't remember reading that." She searched her memory of the long document she had signed when it had become necessary to borrow money on the Elms to cover expenses caused by the mine accident. There had been so many indecipherable phrases and strange paragraphs about nearly impossible circumstances she could recall few details of the contract beyond the deadlines. She turned toward Uncle Owen. "Do you remember that part?"

"Yes, well . . ." He stopped to clear his throat. "It's something of a standard condition in most bank documents."

Katherine faced Nolan, her hands suddenly cold and damp in her lap. Something seemed terribly wrong, but for the life of her, she didn't know enough about business to know what it might be. She barely knew the questions to ask. Regardless, she was not about to lose the Elms. She was willing to give up many things if she must, but she was not giving up Lily's childhood home.

"But I don't understand," she persisted. "How can Lily and I be so incredibly rich and yet so absolutely poor that we're about to lose our house?"

"It's a simple matter of cash on hand," said Nolan. "With your gold mine, real estate holdings, and railroad investments, you and your sister are very wealthy ladies." He leaned forward, elbows on his desk, and spoke slowly and, she thought, patronizingly. "But Katherine, there simply is not enough cash to pay off the bank, let alone for you to throw an ostentatious party."

Katherine's bewilderment shifted into indignation. She gathered herself on the edge of her chair. "The annual tree-decorating party is not an ostentation. It is a yuletide tradition in Denver. For the past ten years the Tuckers have entertained the schoolchildren as well as the cream of society at Christmas time. Furthermore, the Elms is Lily's and my home. Papa built it for Mama, and he intended us to have it always. There must be some way to settle with the bank without endangering it."

"Now, now, Katherine," Uncle Owen soothed. "No need to kill the messenger. Nolan is no happier about this turn of events than we are. The truth is, with all the mine accident expenses and because of your father's drinking and gambling before he died, you're a little short right now."

"I'm all too aware of the shortfall." She pressed her lips together impatiently. Just last week she'd sold off the Chippendale table from the upstairs hall to have enough money for Mrs. Dodd's trip to the market. It had been a humiliating experience. She lived in dread that Mr. Moro, the furniture dealer, might forget his promise and let slip to some bargain-seeking gossip that the Tuckers were selling off their fine pieces.

"I think I might have a solution to this," Uncle Owen said. "Sell off the Amanda Leigh and its equipment."

"But the Amanda Leigh is worthless." The suggestion surprised her.

"However, its equipment is worth a great deal," Uncle Owen countered. "And remember, it is your only holding that produces no income and holds no prospects of ever doing so."

"It is the only holding I promised Papa I would never give up," she reminded her uncle. Aching memories of her father's deathbed scene poured through her. It had been two years since he'd died, but she still missed him terribly. "I promised before Papa, Lily, God, and the Reverend Blake that I would keep the Amanda Leigh."

"And it was a generous vow for a daughter to make to her dying father." Uncle Owen placed his hands on her shoulders. He'd never been the kind of man who took children onto his lap or brought gifts for no reason—like other girls' uncles. But for a man who'd never been doting today his touch was oddly warm and sympathetic.

"Your father was attached to the Amanda Leigh because it was named after your mother, and it was his first strike. But it's mined out. There is no room to be sentimental in today's business world. I'm certain your father never foresaw this unfortunate circumstance, which forces cruel choices on you. If he had, he would never have asked you to make that ridiculous promise."

"No, I'm sure he never foresaw this," Katherine echoed. The Amanda Leigh had indeed been Papa's first strike. It had made him and Mama rich and brought them happiness—for a while. Now the Amanda Leigh only stirred memories of her father's dying request.

Never give up the Amanda Leigh, Kitty girl. It still holds riches. Promise me. Never give it up. And with tears streaming down her cheeks, she'd promised him just that. And she would keep her word.

"There must be another way," she said, surprised and suddenly uneasy with Uncle Owen's advice. He'd never advised her to go against her father's wishes before. "There must be other options to keep Lily and me solvent and living in the Elms."

"I've explored everything," Nolan protested. "If you sold the mine and its equipment, you could pay off the bank and have the cash you need for the Christmas party, or even to take a trip."

"Plan a wedding, perhaps," Uncle Owen added with a hopeful smile.

"All I want to do is keep the Elms for Lily," Katherine said, disregarding Uncle Owen's remark. He'd been hinting that she should get married since she was sixteen, before she'd gone to school in the East seven years earlier. She'd been an independent woman for two years, since Papa's death, and secretly she'd rather come to like having control of her life. Marriage was something she would do one day, but never out of necessity. "I'm not going to give up the Amanda Leigh to keep our home. There must be another way."

Uncle Owen's smile vanished. "At least promise us that you'll consider the possibility. You have few other options."

Abruptly, Katherine rose. Something was wrong, though she couldn't see the error in what they were telling her. The room was suddenly oppressive, and the need to escape was powerful. "I will consider the sale of the Amanda Leigh. But I make no promises. Excuse me, gentlemen. I have other errands to attend to."

"Katherine, I am sorry about this." Nolan rose from his chair, his eyes dark and wary. "Shall I pick you up for the opera on Saturday at about seven?"

"Yes, seven," she confirmed over her shoulder.

"I'll walk you out," Uncle Owen said, opening the office door for her.

On the street she sucked in a breath of cool, fresh air as he closed the door behind them.

"This is bad news." He looked away, down the street. "I'd be glad to help you out with a little loan, but as your partner in the Clementine, I find that I, too, am short of cash after the repairs. That's why I think you must reconsider your stand on the Amanda Leigh. Perhaps if you were married to Nolan, there would be no problem at all. I'm sure he'd come to your rescue."

"Nolan and I have agreed we will not be rushed into marriage by outside influences," she said, finding herself tired and irritable.

"Umm," Uncle Owen murmured without looking at her. "I think Nolan would propose to you in a heartbeat if you gave him encouragement."

"I know you mean well, Uncle Owen, but I'm quite satisfied with my relationship with Nolan." She was content with being called on by the young lawyer. He was a thoughtful, handsome, well-behaved escort who knew his place in society. As a couple they were invited everywhere, greeted with warmth, and entertained with cordiality. "I'm happy with things as they are."

"But nothing remains the same, Katherine," he warned. "It may not be easy to have your cake and eat it, too."

"I know," she said as she turned toward home. "I must be off, Uncle. Good-bye."

Her step was firm and quick in spite of the fear and loneliness gathering in her heart. Despite her outward determination, she felt as if she were walking in quicksand, her feet sucked down into a quagmire, leaving her helpless and confused. The flicker of mistrust that had been instilled in her by the meeting was insidious: If she couldn't count on Uncle Owen and Nolan to help her find another way to save the Elms, who could she count on?

* * *

As soon as Owen Benedict was certain Katherine had disappeared around the corner, he turned on his heel and reentered the law offices of Whitman and Whitman.

The interview with her had not gone the way he wanted, and he wasn't going to allow Nolan to think otherwise. He marched through the outer office without a glance at the busy law clerks and into Nolan's office and slammed the door. Without removing his hat or delivering any other preamble, he dropped into a chair.

Nolan, who was still seated behind his desk, looked up from the document he was writing. He appeared surprised to see his client again but made no protest.

"We must put more pressure on her," Owen announced.

"She's more resistant that I expected her to be," Nolan acknowledged.

"Resistant? I think stubborn is the word for it." He kept his voice low so no one would overhear them. "How long have you been courting her? Isn't it time to romance her more? Force things a little. Win some influence over her."

A furrow formed between Nolan's brows. "Just what are you implying?"

"Think about it, you fool," he said, growing nearly as impatient with the young lawyer as he was with Katherine. He leaned forward and quirked a brow. "You're a red-blooded male, aren't you? You're the one who has her to himself in a dark buggy on opera night. Compromise her if you must."

At the sound of the word *fool,* Nolan drew himself up and set his mouth in a thin line. "In case you haven't noticed, Katherine's reputation as ice queen happens to be deserved. When she walked in here, she didn't even offer her cheek for a kiss, and we've been seeing each other for over a year. All that aside, she's a respectable young lady, and I'm a gentleman, Mr. Benedict. If anyone is the fool here, it is you for promising that mysterious company you won't reveal to me that you could get Katherine to sell the Amanda Leigh and its equipment."

"You'll not think it so foolish when you're her husband and have influence over millions of dollars," Owen said, beginning to wonder if Nolan was going to be as cooperative a partner as he needed. These youngsters who had no memory of Denver in the rough-and-tumble days tended to be soft—but at least they were greedy. "Do you have the balls for this or not?"

"I have the balls for it," Nolan said, his youthful face grown stony. "But remember, this isn't like dealing with some dance-hall girl. Katherine is a lady with a reputation and connections."

"I watched Katherine grow up and I know exactly who she is," Owen said, annoyed at having a whelp like Nolan Stewart tell him what was what. "She's the spoiled, snobby, overeducated, vain daughter of Benjamin A. Tucker. Her Achilles heel is her family. She will cave into anything that threatens her domestic bliss, just like her father did."

"I don't see her caving," Nolan said, his voice harsh and angry. "I don't think you know as much about her as you think."

"If compromising her offends your sensibilities, then for gawd's sake, get down on your knees and follow her around until she agrees to marry you," he said, impatient with the young lawyer's lack of imagination. "Do I need to remind you how much money is at stake here? A lot. A fortune. You wouldn't be apple-polishing for old Whitman and Whitman in the next office and praying for a partnership if you married her. You could set up your own law practice or just retire."

The hard, angry lines of Nolan's expression fell away as the thought of missing out on this lucrative deal took hold. He blinked at Owen.

Owen allowed a smile. "I didn't think you needed reminding. Show Katherine how much you care for her. Be passionate. Lord, she's twenty-four and the daughter of a two-bit actress. Don't let her cool facade fool you. There's hot blood running through her veins. She can't keep up this virginal ice queen role for much longer. Turn on your charm, Nolan boy, and convince the lady to marry you—one way or the other.''

Katherine heard the piano music as soon as she turned up the walk to the Elms. She loved hearing her sister play, even when Lily was working her way through scales or exercises. Her little sister had a gift for the keyboard—the touch, the ear—and Katherine did everything she could to encourage development of that gift. But today Lily was playing a piece she'd mastered several weeks earlier, a Chopin polonaise.

It was a welcome sound after the disappointments of Katherine's morning.

All the way home she'd considered who she might turn to for a loan to save the house. Uncle Owen had made it clear he couldn't help. Nolan wasn't even a partner in the firm yet. They were not and would not be engaged. He was in no position to help her. A loan from another bank was no solution to the problem; she'd just have another payoff date to worry about. She couldn't bear to think of admitting her problem to Dolly. Call it pride, but she preferred that as few people as possible knew about her troubles.

Trying not to despair, she stepped lightly onto the porch so as not to disturb Lily's playing. She stood listening, allowing the music to lull her worries into the background before letting herself in.

The music ebbed and flowed, almost lovely enough to make her forget about the irritating Carson Fairfax and the even more troubling threat of losing the house. Inside, she dropped her satchel and gloves on the hall table, glad to be home, and began to strip off her coat and hat. She was about to hang them on the hall tree when she noted a silver-headed cane and a high-quality black bowler already hanging there.

So, they had a visitor. Who did they know who wore a bowler? The style was usually preferred by salesmen and gamblers. But a guest explained why Lily was showing off her new repertoire piece.

Smoothing her hair and shaking wrinkles out of her skirt, Katherine composed herself to enter the music room and welcome their guest. She wasn't in the mood to be sociable, not after her interview with Uncle Owen and Nolan and her silent exchange with Carson Fairfax. But her mother had always told her that a guest must be received and made to feel welcome. Though Lily loved to play hostess, she couldn't leave her twelve-year-old sister to fill the role alone.

As the polonaise came to an end, Katherine placed a smile on her face and stepped into the music room prepared to offer a congenial welcome. "That was lovely playing, Lily. Who are you entertaining . . . ?"

Their caller rose from the settee by the window and grinned at her.

She froze, her words trailing off and her smile fading.

"Katherine, Mr. Fairfax has come to call," Lily said, still at the piano. "Isn't that nice of him?"

"Good day, Miss Tucker," Fairfax said, inclining his head in that aristocratic manner that made a girl feel as though he'd bowed low over her hand. The man was always more impressive at close quarters than he was from a distance, Katherine realized, fighting off the giddy flutter in her belly. His manners were impeccably gallant. His face was handsome—but just barely, she decided—with sharp, aquiline features and a strong jaw. But it was his smile that was devastating—wide and instant, dazzling with white teeth and a spark of devilishness in his eyes. Was it any wonder he was such a favorite with the society hostesses?

In the dull daylight, his short, curly hair gleamed black. His bluest of blue eyes fell on her, keen and clear, with an interest that made her feel as if she was the most important woman in the world.

She retreated a step under the intensity of his appraising gaze.

"It's so nice to see you near at hand where we can speak to each other rather than making signs through glass," he observed without any display of awkwardness.

"Mr. Warped—" Katherine bit her tongue. That's what she deserved for repeating that epithet to herself for a block down Curtis Street. "Ahemm. Mr. Fairfax. Excuse me. But frankly I'm surprised to see you here. What can I do for you?"

"Mrs. D is preparing tea for us," Lily said, easing off the piano stool and making her way across the room to the settee by the window, perfectly at ease. Visitors would hardly suspect that she was blind.

That was why, Katherine reminded herself, that she must never lose the Elms. It was the only home Lily had ever known. She would never allow it to be taken away from her little sister.

"I don't think Mr. Fairfax called to have tea," she said, suddenly realizing the significance of what Lily had said. Mrs. Dodd thought even less of gamblers and saloonkeepers than she did. "You said Mrs. D is making tea?"

"Oh, yes," Lily said. "She agreed it was the least we could do for Mr. Fairfax, calling on such a cold, miserable day."

A guileless expression spread across Fairfax's face. "I could hardly refuse such a generous offer while I waited for you."

"Of course not," she said, puzzled by the reason for his call. Mentally she steeled herself for a debate about the petition. Obviously that was what he'd come about. She met his gaze with a steady, stubborn stare to warn him that if he intended to change her stand on the petition, he could save his breath.

His smile broadened as he studied her, as if he guessed exactly what she was thinking. Then he returned to his seat next to Lily. "I quite enjoyed your playing, Lily. You were an excellent accompanist last Christmas for the carol sing at the tree decorating party. What else are you working on for your repertoire?"

Lily began to chatter about a Bach two-part invention she wanted to master.

Only Katherine remained standing, stiff, awkward, and

ignored. It felt as though someone had sucked the wind out of her sails.

Before she could decide how to proceed, Mrs. Dodd bustled into the room bearing a huge tray of tea and sugar cookies. Katherine moved aside.

With a glower that would have withered a cactus, the housekeeper placed the tray on the tea table in front of Fairfax and Lily.

"About time you got home, Miss Katherine," Mrs. Dodd said, backing away, her glower still in place. The housekeeper had been with the Tuckers as long as Katherine could remember, since Mr. Dodd had gambled away their savings and left her destitute. Mama had taken pity on the woman and hired her. Mrs. D was more a member of the family than a servant. "I made the tea hot and strong just the way you said Mr. Fairfax likes it, Lily. There's a pot of hot milk for you, sir. I know you English gents take milk in your tea."

"Exactly right, Mrs. Dodd," Fairfax said, smiling appreciatively. "You've done an admirable job."

The downward turn of Mrs. D's mouth eased a bit.

"A splendid spread," Fairfax added as he studied the tray. "You are a treasure, Mrs. Dodd."

"Oh, well, it's kind of you to say so, sir," Mrs. Dodd demurred. A pink blush colored her round face. "Very kind indeed."

Astonished, Katherine stared at her housekeeper, whom she'd never seen blush. The woman was sixty years old, for heaven's sake.

"I'll be back in a few minutes to see if there's anything more you need," Mrs. Dodd said and left the room, her glower gone.

In the silence after the housekeeper's exit, Katherine realized that Fairfax was watching her expectantly. When she did not move, he reached for the teapot.

"Well, if you ladies promise you won't tell the rest of Denver, I'll be mother today."

Lily laughed. "We won't tell, will we, Katherine? Do sit, Sis. Ooh, I smell sugar cookies, my favorite."

"Yes, there are sugar cookies." She moved from behind the chair and seated herself in it. All the while her gaze was locked on Fairfax's large, capable hands as he served tea from her fragile rosebud china tea service.

He poured deftly through the silver tea strainer, his long, tapering fingers managing without the least awkwardness. Agile fingers, no doubt, whether holding silver or porcelain—or a deck of cards. Fascinating.

An odd chill raced through her. The skin on the back of her neck tingled.

"One lump or two, Miss Katherine?" Fairfax asked, his long fingers squeezing the silver sugar tongs in a manner that absorbed her.

"Katherine?" Lily prompted.

Katherine started. She glanced up at Fairfax's face, wondering if he read anything in her gaze.

"May I call you Miss Katherine?" Fairfax continued, one hand poised over the sugar bowl as he held a full teacup in the other. "It's confusing with two Miss Tuckers in the room."

"You may call me Miss Lily."

"Thank you," Fairfax said, turning to the twelve-year-old. "Please call me Carson."

"Thank you, Carson," Lily said, grinning with delight at being allowed the adult familiarity.

"Yes, of course, call me Katherine," she said, attempting to regain her accustomed poise. "I take one lump, please."

"One lump for Katherine." Fairfax dropped a sugar cube into the teacup, then stirred it using hands that undoubtedly had plucked many a marked card from a sleeve or under a table. What quick, sensitive fingers he must have, she thought.

He offered the cup.

She accepted it without comment, careful not to allow their fingers to touch. Any contact with him would burn, from her fingertips right up her arm and into her body and . . . She was certain of it, though she didn't know how or why. Purposely, she avoided his gaze and wondered when he was going to bring up the petition. She longed to get the ordeal over with.

Instead, he chatted about piano works including the Bach two-part invention as he served tea to Lily, then to himself. Lily was charmed. Fairfax's attention seemed genuine. No remark was required from Katherine, so she sat back in the chair, sipping her tea without tasting it, and offered none. Suspicious as she might be of Fairfax's motives, for the moment she was reluctant to deprive her sister of the pleasure she seemed to be taking in the Englishman's attention.

She found herself reappraising him, calling up the things she'd heard. Things like his near legendary skill at the card table and his wealth. Though he liked fine horses and owned several, he never wagered on horse races or fights of any kind— human or animal. A curious kind of gambler. Rumor had it that he owned the better part of one of the largest banks in Denver, a prosperous insurance company, and a fair amount of respectable downtown Denver real estate in addition to the Gentlemen's Respite.

Just then, Mrs. D reappeared in the doorway and cast her a knowing look. "Sorry to interrupt, but it is time for you to feed Max, Miss Lily. That dog is whining like he's starved."

"Oh," Lily groaned. "Must I?"

"Yes, do as Mrs. Dodd says," Katherine said, grateful to the housekeeper for understanding that she and Fairfax needed to talk alone.

Lily set down her teacup without spilling a drop, stood without upsetting the tray, and extended her hand in Fairfax's direction. "And you must call again, Carson. I promise to play the Bach for you."

"Yes, I'd like that." Fairfax stood also. Taking her hand, he showed Lily the same courtesy he would have shown any adult lady. His thoughtfulness touched Katherine.

Lily and Mrs. Dodd left the music room.

In the ensuing silence, Katherine leaned forward and set her teacup on the tray. "All right, Mr. Fairfax, it is time for you to explain yourself."

"Katherine, please, I thought we agreed you would call me Carson," he said, a look of disappointment on his face as he settled onto the settee again. "I thoroughly enjoyed your performance in the last theatrical the Thespians performed in the spring. You're a very good actress. Are you going to perform with them again this fall?"

"Don't press your luck, *Mr. Fairfax*," she said, finding that her poise had returned, along with a measure of impatience. But at the moment she didn't feel like a good actress. "If you've come here to argue the Respite's case with me, you are wasting your time and mine."

Fairfax's expression remained bland. "The reason I called has nothing to do with the Respite's case, as you call it. I have called today to apologize. I fear my invitation to tea at the Respite this morning offended you."

Surprised that he cared, she sat back in her chair. "Well, yes, I was offended."

"I thought so."

"But it wasn't just the offer of the tea that I found offensive," Katherine continued. "It was what Randolph Hearn told me."

"I thought he might be telling tales when you frowned at me." A shadow of discomfort passed over Fairfax's face. "Dare I ask exactly what Randolph said?"

"He said that you like to have me out there on the corner because it improves your business," Katherine said, her anger returning. "Is that true?"

Fairfax shook his head, but he did not keep a small smile from his face. "Randolph told you that?"

She nodded. "Well? Are you using me?"

"I never asked you to stand out there on the corner," he said, an edge of annoyance creeping into his tone. Now she'd offended him. "But you are a beautiful woman. If you insist on knowing, your presence does draw more men to the Respite than usual. As far as I'm concerned, you can stand out there on that corner with your petition all winter if you like.''

Outraged, she jumped to her feet. "So you sent Cornish Jack out to offer me tea to encourage me to stay?"

Fairfax also stood, moving with slow, sleek grace, no trace of anger in his expression. "Yes, partly, and partly because you looked like it was colder than the North Pole out there on the corner. I thought some strong, hot tea would do you good.''

He seemed so forthright. She took a deep breath, her anger slipping in spite of her reluctance to give it up. "It *was* cold out there.''

His grin returned. "Your lips were turning blue.''

"Were they?" she asked, her fingers flying to her mouth. "I must have looked a fright.''

"But the wind put a nice blush in your cheeks," he added, his full, jaunty grin returning.

She could feel another blush rising. Drat the man. He was practicing his charm on her and she wanted none of it. "I appreciate your call," she said stiffly, without meeting his gaze. She turned to lead the way out into the entry hall.

"And I enjoyed visiting with Lily," he said, following her. "I haven't seen her since the Christmas party last year. She is maturing into a lovely young lady.''

That irresistible smile of pride returned to Katherine's lips. "Yes, hasn't she?" She snatched his bowler and silver-headed walking stick from the hall tree and held them out to him. "You know this doesn't change anything about the petition.''

"I didn't think it would.'' He took the cane with one hand and put his hat on with the other, tipping it back on his head in a manner that gave him an incredibly classy, rakish look.

Unaccountably, butterflies fluttered in her belly again.

"I'd like to ask if I might call again," he said. "Just social.''

She blinked at him in total astonishment. Why on earth would the elusive bachelor, Carson Fairfax, want to call on her? He'd never shown any interest beyond asking for an occasional dance. "Aaah. You know Nolan Stewart and I are . . .''

"Engaged?" he asked, eyeing her with a look that said he knew perfectly well they were not.

"No, nothing like that," she stammered. There it was again, that sense of being under appraisal. He was eyeing her, from the top of her head to the hem of her skirt. What did he want? "But there is the petition drive and all . . ."

He shrugged, as if the petition was of no significance. "Then I may call again at the Elms?"

"Yes, well, I think Lily would like that," she finally said, finding it easier to commit her sister rather than herself. Drat the man. Disconcerted, her hands fluttered uselessly in the air.

"Excellent," he said, clearly pleased. "Thank you for the tea."

With that he let himself out the door and walked down the brick walk, tall, elegant, and utterly confident—wielding a walking stick he plainly had no use for.

Katherine watched him from behind the lace-covered glass door.

Now, what had that been all about? Despite their discussion, she still did not know what Carson Fairfax had wanted. He'd only spoken about the petition when she'd brought it up. She didn't believe for a moment that he just wanted permission to make social calls.

When Fairfax disappeared down the street, Katherine strolled across the hallway into the drawing room as she did from time to time to be certain that everything was in its place—or to talk to Mama and Papa's portrait.

The day had been an exhausting one, full of twists and turns. The fine carpet whispered comfortingly beneath her kid shoes. She sank down onto one of the damask-covered chairs and gazed up at her parents' portrait over the fireplace.

"So what do I do now, Papa?" she asked. Her father, dressed in a dark suit, smiled back at her, his face full of the warmth and humor that had been his until the last two years of his life. Her mother—the actress who'd always loved the audience— costumed in a red and gold Elizabethan gown for her part in

Taming of the Shrew, admired her husband with fondness. The pose was very like the way Katherine remembered them.

The happy Tuckers before Mama died when Katherine was only eighteen and Lily barely seven. Before the world fell apart and Papa started drinking and gambling because he couldn't bear the pain of life without Mama.

She couldn't blame him for that. Mama had been a big presence in all their lives. But she did blame the drink and the gaming tables. She did blame the saloons and taverns. And they'd known her wrath ever since she'd started supporting the Ladies' Moderation League after Papa's death.

She studied her parents. Sometimes just sitting in the room with the portrait made her feel as if they were still here, in the Elms, watching over Lily and her—with love. Of course, they knew all of their affairs.

"The house is threatened and a gambler is knocking at the door, though heavens knows why," she said. "Unless . . ."

Another idea occurred. Perhaps Carson Fairfax could lend her the money to save the Elms. The ridiculousness of that solution struck her immediately. No, never. Not a loan from a saloonkeeper. She could never accept that. Why would a loan from him be any better than one from a bank? And what would her friends of the Ladies' Moderation League say?

The funny thing was, she did like Carson Fairfax better than she had before his call. How could you not like a man willing to pour tea when one hostess was unable to do so—and the other too rude?

"Then what, Papa?" she asked, gazing fondly up at her parents. "I'm fresh out of ideas for keeping the Elms."

The answer came. Softly, but clear.

Wait and trust your instincts, Kitty girl. Papa had always told her, *Trust your gut.* The words were so distinct in her head, she almost thought she'd heard Papa's voice.

It was only a longing, she knew, to hear his voice again. But Papa had always been right.

So trust her instincts she would.

Chapter Four

"You're working late tonight," Owen said, when Ray Jones let him in the back door of the Cherry Street Bank after dark. The high-ceilinged lobby of the bank was dark and empty. They were alone.

Jones, a large man with a jolly, fleshy face that belied a shrewd temperament and a penchant for underhanded dealings, shut the door behind him and locked it. "Just going over a few figures. How did it go today with the Tucker girl? Is this threat to call in the mortgage on the Elms going to work?"

"I don't know." He walked into Jones' office hardly noting the desk laden with open ledgers, and sat, though he hadn't been invited to do so. He'd been here often enough after hours to make himself at home. "She feels pretty strongly about that promise she made ol' Ben."

"I suspected she might not be so easily persuaded as you thought," Jones said, opening a cabinet behind his desk and bringing out a bottle of good whiskey. He poured each of them a drink. "Tucker let her have her head too often. She's too independent to fall for every idea that's put to her."

"And she hates the thought of her blind sister being turned out of the only home she's ever known," Owen said, accepting the drink. "Give her time to think about the consequences. And I haven't given up on Stewart yet. He knows life could be a lot easier for him if he makes her Mrs. Nolan Stewart before she comes into the full fortune on her next birthday and I'm out of the picture as guardian."

"Stewart has had over a year to make this marriage happen," Jones said, savoring the whiskey. "She turns twenty-five in six months. He hasn't even put an engagement ring on her finger yet. I tell you, Owen, I can see those two Tucker girls staying in that house forever, turning into strange old maids doing charitable works for the rest of their lives."

"What a waste of good money," Owen mourned into his glass.

"What a waste of a good fuck," Jones said with a lewd laugh. "Know a man who hasn't had that fantasy about her?"

He frowned. The profanity offended him, but he refused to show it. He didn't like Jones, but the man had the connections he needed to achieve what he wanted. "She's probably too cold for that."

"No such thing," Jones snorted. "I don't believe in that ice queen nonsense. As long as a woman with a figure like that is alive . . . Stewart should at least be interested in bedding her. But we do stray from our goal. You think there's any chance she's going to agree to sell the Amanda Leigh?"

"Yes, I do," Owen said. "But we, Nolan and I, must convince her that she has no other choice. I've been doing my best, but she's as sentimental as her father. She doesn't want to break her promise to him."

"Her birthday isn't the only time limit we have," Jones said. "Do I need to remind you that if you really want to launch yourself into politics, we have to get the machinery moving soon? It takes time to lay the groundwork, and you're not getting any younger."

Silently he cringed inside as he studied the whiskey in his

glass. At fifty-five he hated any mention of his age. He liked to think he still had a future ahead of him. Maybe not one as long as younger men had, but he still had things to do, accomplishments he wanted to claim. A place in the statehouse would please him just fine.

"But let me ask the really important question," Jones said, leaning back in his leather chair, the buttons of his shirt straining to keep his belly covered. "How badly do you want to get into politics? It takes money and commitment, not just pretty words and a lot of glad-handing. Do you want it badly enough?"

"I know what it takes, Ray," Owen said, still studying his glass. "I know the clock is ticking. Trust me. I think things are going to fall into place soon. We just have to allow Katherine to realize how dire her straits are. We have to let Nolan press his suit. Then we'll see how quickly Katherine puts the Amanda Leigh mine on the block."

By Saturday Katherine had no more idea what she was going to do to keep the Elms than she'd had on Wednesday when Nolan had given her the bad news. But it was opera night, and she loved the opera.

"Mr. Stewart doesn't seem quite himself tonight," Mrs. D said as she and Katherine searched for the evening wrap she wanted to wear.

Nolan, immaculately garbed in a tuxedo and top hat, was awaiting her downstairs in the hallway.

"He seemed fine to me," Katherine lied as she shoved the garments in her wardrobe back and forth. She, too, had sensed a change in him the minute he'd walked in the door. It had made her uneasy, but she didn't want to encourage Mrs. D to speculate. She could handle Nolan.

"Maybe I'm just getting old and fussy," Mrs. D said, pulling a jacket from the wardrobe. "Here it is. This is the black velvet one you wanted, isn't it? I just wish your father was here. He wouldn't take any nonsense from these young men who come to our door.''

''And what makes you think I do?'' she asked, donning the velvet jacket. With a smile she gave Mrs. D a quick peck on the cheek. ''I have to go. We're late.''

But as she hurried down the stairs and felt Nolan's gaze on her, she had to agree with Mrs. D about the subtle shift in his behavior. There was a certain new ardor in his gaze. An undue pressure on her hand when he helped her into the buggy. It didn't frighten her, but it was worrisome. She hoped he'd not gotten the notion in his head to propose or anything serious like that.

In the buggy, he sat closer to her than usual, his thigh so near hers, she could feel his heat through her skirts. At the opera when the lights went down he leaned near, his arm draped across the back of her seat, so near that she could almost feel his breath on her ear.

She and Nolan had been seeing each other for a long time, and she was accustomed to his polite touch: his fingers at her elbow when they walked, his hand brushing hers when he handed her a cup of punch, the pressure of his palm at the small of her back when they entered a ballroom. But this fervent hovering was unnerving.

Did it have anything to do with the house business? Surely not. But what did Nolan think about her financial situation? Pity? That thought made her back stiffen. Responsibility? A need to sway her about the Amanda Leigh? None of those motivations was agreeable. With effort she made herself concentrate on the performance on stage.

During the intermission, Nolan excused himself. As she scanned the crowd, she spied Carson Fairfax and Randolph Hearn sitting in a box across the theater from them. She found herself staring at him. He looked incredibly elegant in his black formal wear.

The fact that there was no woman in his escort secretly pleased her. Hadn't she heard some whispers about him having a mistress? That was several years ago, shortly after she'd been introduced to society—and the adult rumor mill. It had also been rumored that in addition to being the third son of an earl, he was the Fairfax black sheep, a title that only added to the man's mystique in a city like Denver.

And there had been an even darker—though vague—observation about how people who clashed with Carson Fairfax disappeared. An early partner of his had abruptly vanished shortly before he'd built the Gentlemen's Respite. However, in recent years she'd heard nothing bad about him—beyond the League's outrage over the gambling at the Gentlemen's Respite.

As if he'd known she was watching, Carson looked up from his opera program and gazed at her. A thrill curled in her stomach. She met his gaze, astonished at her own boldness. Unable to look away, she felt as though he'd drawn near, sitting next to her in Nolan's place. Or was that just some strange wish? she wondered guiltily.

He nodded to her, a discreet greeting seemingly undetected by Hearn. Clandestinely, she returned it, then forced herself to look away. Why on earth did this man fascinate her so? Snapping her fan open, she frantically attempted to wave away the heat from her cheeks. Just then Nolan returned, and she made a show of turning to speak to him about the wonderful costumes.

When the opera ended, relief swept over her. Nolan was smothering her with his attentions. She seriously considered claiming a headache to beg off attending Dolly Green's soiree. But she liked Dolly, and she always enjoyed social events at her godmother's house. Perhaps the company of acquaintances would distract Nolan.

Once again she and Nolan were sitting close in the buggy, their legs pressed together under the lap robe he'd spread over them. Traffic near the theater was congested right after the performance, but Nolan maneuvered the buggy through it quickly. Above, stars sparkled in the cold October sky. The horse's breath plumed into the night air.

"There's something I've wanted to talk to you about for some weeks," Nolan began soon after they had exchanged brief comments about the opera. Katherine became alert. Was he going to explain his strange behavior now?

"Maybe this isn't the time or the place," Nolan continued. "I mean, in the buggy and all. But otherwise the timing is perfect. And I do have the courage. That's important."

"Courage?" Katherine repeated, her unease increasing. "If you are concerned about the business over the Elms—"

"No, it's not that," he hastened to say. "Not that I'm unconcerned. And what I have to say has something to do with that, but what I want to talk to you about is . . . well, we've been keeping company for how long?"

"About a year and half," she supplied, frantically searching for a way to turn the conversation away from their relationship.

"I know we talked about there being no need to rush into an engagement—"

"I still feel that way," Katherine announced. Thankfully, it was impossible to see Nolan's face in the darkness. If she saw disappointment in his expression, she knew she'd feel guilty and her resolve would weaken. She did not love him and she'd known that for some time. But she'd allowed their relationship to go on because . . . well, it was comfortable.

"But if we were engaged or married, it would be very simple for me to give you a loan," Nolan said. "As it stands—well, as unfair as it would be, you know society's eyebrows would be raised if I was the one who paid off the house mortgage. It would not look good at all."

"Your offer to help is very generous." She chose her words carefully. Nolan was hardly a pauper, but she doubted his resources were sufficient to help her. And instinctively she knew that kind of personal financial involvement would be a grave mistake.

"Wait, hear me out," Nolan said, pulling the buggy over, just beyond the gate to the House of the Sphinxes. He turned to her and seized her hand. "Katherine, say you'll marry me.

Consent to an engagement and we'll announce it tonight at Dolly's party. Monday morning, I'll make arrangements with the bank to take care of the mortgage. I can even make arrangements for you to have enough funds for the Christmas tree party. You'll have everything you want. But most importantly, you won't have to give up the Elms.''

"This is all rather sudden, Nolan." She attempted to free her hands from his grasp. If she did not marry him, she lost either the Amanda Leigh or the Elms. If she married him, she lost nothing—but her freedom forever. She did not like the choices. "Marriage was not among the options I've considered."

"Well, there you are," Nolan said, victory in his voice. He squeezed her hands and leaned closer, slipping his other arm around her shoulders. "See how simple the solution is? Just say yes and all your troubles will go away."

She took a deep breath and forcefully pulled her hand from Nolan's grasp. "I'm afraid it is not that simple."

He moved away fractionally. "What do you mean, it's not that simple?"

"Nolan, I am flattered by your offer of marriage," she began, sorry that she had not considered how she would respond when he proposed. She'd depended too much on their agreement not to rush.

His arm remained around her shoulders. "I can hear the 'but' coming."

"We've been such good friends and companions, Nolan, but I don't love you," Katherine finally managed to say.

His silence was icier than the night air.

"So you see, marriage would not be fair to you," she added, praying he would see.

"You would rather risk losing the Elms than marry me?" he demanded in a low, growling tone. When he moved to face her, light from the streetlamp revealed the harsh, angry lines of his face.

"I'd rather be honest," she said, shrinking into the corner of the buggy seat.

With a suddenness that shocked her, Nolan locked his arms around her and shoved her deeper into the corner. His body pressed heavily against hers.

Momentarily she was too surprised to struggle. His breath was hot and heavy against her throat. He smelled of sour liquor and stale cigar smoke. She realized he must have taken a drink when he'd gone out during the opera intermission. She pushed against his chest, but he did not move. Without warning she felt the sudden icy touch of his bare hand inching its way up under her skirt.

"Stop it," she ordered, more outraged than frightened.

His fingers clawed upward between her knees, then between her thighs.

"Honesty be damned, Katherine," he said, his voice husky with lust. He pushed at her so, she could hardly move. "And what does love have to do with it? Or romance, for that matter? What is it you want? Tell me. Want me to talk dirty to you? Is that it?"

She attempted to clamp her legs together. But his body was pressed so tightly against hers that she could hardly move. His hand worked relentlessly toward her private place.

Horror blossomed. She'd never had reason to fear Nolan. His assault was unthinkable. Desperately she fought him and the panic that threatened to send her into hysterics.

The evening had turned into a jumbled nightmare. With all her strength, she pushed him away. But he was stronger than she. His hand tore at the sensitive skin above her stocking. His fingernails scored across her bare flesh, stinging.

"You're crazy!" Terrified by his assault, she struggled harder, determined to thwart him.

"Oh, Katherine, haven't you ever wondered what it would be like to lie beneath me? Your thighs open, me inside you. Haven't your married girlfriends told you about the thrill a man's cock can give when it works down there? Marry me,

Katherine. Let me show you how good it can be. I'll see that you have everything you want. Your sister, too. Just say yes.''

"No. Stop it.'' She panted from her exertions. His hand slipped up beneath her drawers. Linen ripped.

She opened her mouth to scream. He slapped her. The blow stung.

"Evening, sir,'' came a voice out of the darkness. "Are you come for Mrs. Green's party?''

Katherine recognized the voice. She swallowed her screech and went still. For some unknown reason Nolan's hold on her slackened more. Her former driver's footsteps crunched on the gravel as he came walking out of the darkness toward them.

"Willis, it's me, Miss Katherine,'' she called, trying not to sound as hysterical as she was. "Willis?''

Nolan's clutching beneath her skirt ceased. He sat back in the buggy seat, cursing softly.

"Miss Katherine? Is that really you?''

"Yes, it's Miss Katherine and Mr. Stewart,'' Nolan said, sounding astonishingly normal. "We're here for the party, but we've decided not to stay.''

"I'm staying,'' Katherine cried, gathering up her skirts and launching herself out of the buggy—and nearly into Willis's arms.

"Trust a woman to change her mind,'' Nolan said with a laugh as if they'd had nothing more than a lover's quarrel.

"Would you like me to park your buggy in the stable with the others?'' Willis asked.

Katherine didn't wait to hear more. Turning, she ran on trembling legs toward the house. She didn't care if Nolan stayed or not. She just wanted to reach safety within her godmother's brightly lit mansion.

Grateful the ladies' withdrawing room was empty, Katherine sank onto a pink overstuffed boudoir chair and waited for her shivering to subside. Dolly had been so busy greeting guests that she'd managed to slip by with a quick hello and an excuse that she needed to freshen up. What she wanted was time to gather her wits and come to terms with what had just happened.

She glanced into the mirror. A white-faced, dry-eyed girl in a wrinkled gown and with mussed hair stared back at her. For a moment she hardly recognized herself. Creases marred the smooth taffeta of her plum-colored gown. When she tucked a loose tendril behind her ear, her hand still shook.

She felt swept up in a nightmare. One of the most trusted men in her life had just betrayed her. If Friday's interview with Nolan had raised doubts about his true motives toward her and Lily and their inheritance, tonight in the buggy had confirmed them.

Maybe if I pinch myself, I'll wake up. But she knew no pinching, regardless of how painful, was going to deliver her from this ugly dream.

Clearly Nolan had his own plans for the Tucker fortune. She didn't understand exactly what he wanted, but if he'd succeeded in becoming her husband, he could have persuaded or forced her into anything he wanted with her and Lily's assets. She had trusted him completely, just as Papa had. The realization was frightening.

"Ooh!" She glared at the ceiling and fought back tears of anger and humiliation. She'd allowed him to convince her and Uncle Owen to sign the mortgage on the Elms. "How could I have been so blind?" she groaned.

Then she lost her battle. Tears coursed down her cheeks.

Worse than betrayal, the threat of physical danger had shocked her beyond words. She closed her eyes against visions of those terrifying moments in Nolan's buggy. If Willis had not interrupted, Nolan would have forced himself on her. Once compromised, she would have felt obligated to marry him.

Putting her hand to her throat, she willed herself to take a deep, calming breath. Safe, she repeated over and over to herself. She was safe.

There was a rapid knock, and then the door swung open.

Dolly's face appeared in the gap. "Are you all right?" Taking in the fact that the room was empty, she added, "Do you want some company?"

"Come in." Katherine braved a smile. She could hardly snub her hostess. Dabbing her eyes with a handkerchief from the stack on the dressing table, she added, "I'm afraid *La Traviata* always makes me cry."

"That's strange," Dolly said. Satin rustled as the regal dowager seated herself across from her. "Nolan said you had something in your eye. In any case, what happened out there in the street? I noticed you didn't exactly arrive on Nolan's arm. Did you two quarrel?"

"You could say that." Katherine surrendered to a partial truth, but purposely avoided meeting Dolly's gaze.

"I know it's none of my business," Dolly said, scrutinizing her so closely that she feared the older woman guessed more than she cared to have known. "But I'm your godmother and too old to care about those niceties. Propriety is dashed dull. I'd guess from the whiteness around your mouth and the bleakness in your eyes that this was a serious difference of opinion."

"I'm afraid so," she admitted. She yearned to confide her shock and dismay in someone. But the entire nightmare seemed so unreal, she needed to examine it in the light of day before she told anyone about it.

"You don't have to tell me anything," Dolly continued. "But you don't want to go home with Nolan, do you?"

"No!" The word escaped Katherine before she could catch it. She hadn't wanted it to be obvious that she and Nolan were finished just yet. She didn't want to cause an embarrassing stir at her godmother's house. But the thought of once more climbing into the buggy with the lawyer terrified her. Never again would she trust him. "Can we tell him I've taken ill and must stay here tonight? Then after everyone is gone, Willis can see me home."

"I think we can do better than that," Dolly said, rising from her chair and reaching for Katherine's hand. When she grasped

Katherine's cold fingers in her gnarled ones, she gasped. "My gracious girl, your hands are like ice. You have had a shock. Come rest in my room. A fire burns in there already and I'll send Hollis up with some medicinal brandy. Then I'll send Nolan home, none the wiser. Leave this to me."

Relieved to have someone so capable and warm take charge, Katherine gladly allowed Dolly to have her way.

Carson sipped champagne and eyed Nolan Stewart from across the room. Something was wrong; he could smell it. He hadn't been the consummate gambler all these years just because he had an excellent memory and understood mathematical probability. His opponents' faces were like an open book to him. Tonight, on the surface, Stewart was his usual cordial, cocky self. But underneath the man was shaken and angry. Why?

The lawyer moved around the room, shaking hands and acknowledging people. Stewart knew who he must ingratiate himself with and who he could snub in a room full of Denver's elite. But his greetings were off-key. He kept looking over his shoulder, as if he expected someone to join him. Katherine? She was nowhere to be seen.

Carson had seen her rush in, her luscious mouth small and tight. To his surprise and disappointment, she'd immediately dashed off toward the ladies' withdrawing room. He'd been looking forward to talking to her this evening after they had made an uneasy peace over tea at the Elms.

The more he thought about Dolly's idea of Katherine posing as his wife for his mother's visit, the more he warmed to the idea. He'd had his eye on Katherine Tucker since he'd first come to Denver, almost ten years earlier. She'd only been a girl then, her womanly beauty just beginning to emerge from her pretty child's features. The dark-fringed turquoise eyes. The thick chestnut hair. That mouth.

She'd been so young, and she'd affected him so strongly,

he'd feared for the first time in twenty-one years of life that he had perverted tastes. The memory made him smile now. But the next day he'd gone out and established himself with a mistress.

Over the years, he'd refused to contemplate the possibility of a relationship between them. There were a number of reasons against it. Her youth, obviously. Her schooling in the East. Her problems with her father's drinking and gambling. The Ladies' Moderation League. His profession as a gambler and owner of the Respite. Nolan Stewart.

Still, as attracted to her as he was—and as wrong as Stewart seemed to be for her—Carson had his doubts.

The woman who was going to pose as his wife needed to be bold, courageous, and subtly original. She would have to have a quick wit and be an accomplished actress. In short, Katherine needed to be everything that her stage-loving mother was said to have been.

Besides that, he wasn't satisfied that she was desperate enough to possess the kind of nerve the role of his wife was going to require.

Yet the question begged, why had Katherine deserted her lawyer so quickly? Was her absence the reason why Nolan seemed to be suffering? Carson wondered. No doubt Dolly would know.

"Under other circumstances, I'd say you are the gosh-darned-luckiest man I've ever met, Carson," Dolly said from behind him, tapping his shoulder with her fan.

"I've enjoyed my share of Lady Luck's favors," he replied, with little interest in guessing at Dolly's meaning. "What's going on? Where is Katherine?"

"Upstairs, unnerved and tearful," Dolly said. "That's the unlucky part."

"A lover's quarrel?" he asked, pleased.

"Worse than that, I'd say." Dolly's face hardened. He was reminded that she had earned her way as a washerwoman in the mining camps before she'd become the grande dame of

Denver society. She'd seen much, and beneath the flash and dazzle of her wealth, she was a tough lady. "The poor girl isn't hysterical—small wonder—but she's badly shaken. Her clothes seem to have suffered from some mishap that she won't explain. She is adamant about not being escorted home by her beau. Draw your own conclusions."

Pleasure gave way to anger. "I've never liked Stewart, but surely he wouldn't be so ungentlemanly as to . . ."

"I learned a long time ago, boors infest all stations of life," Dolly said, studying the lawyer just as Carson had. "But I've seen Katherine's face. I don't think anybody will get her into a buggy with Nolan Stewart again. She seems to have her reasons."

"The bastard," he muttered, his eyes narrowing as he watched Stewart shake hands with Ray Jones, president of the Cherry Street Bank, which competed with Carson's own. The two were always as thick as thieves, an analogy he suspected was more apt than anyone guessed.

"Forget Stewart," Dolly said. "Katherine is important now. If we handle this right—well, everything will fall perfectly into place. One step at a time. I'm going to take Nolan aside and tell him that Katherine has fallen ill and is going to spend the night here. After everyone has left, you'll be a knight in shining armor and escort her home."

"Knight in shining armor is hardly my sort of role," Carson pointed out. "Especially in Miss Tucker's eyes. Why don't I go over there and knock that smug smile off Stewart's face, drag him out the door, and dump him in the gutter where he belongs?"

"Not at my party, you won't." It wasn't until Dolly laid her hand on his arm that he realized how truly prepared he was to carry out his threat. "Listen, you told me that you visited Katherine the other day, and she agreed to let you call on her."

"Yes, but that's hardly the same thing as getting in a buggy with me after a bad experience," he said, wondering how distraught she was. "If she won't allow Stewart to take her home, why would she let me?"

"Because I'm going to remind her of what a gentleman you are," Dolly said. "Kindly don't contradict me."

Chapter Five

"But I'd rather Willis took me home," Katherine said directly to Fairfax's face when Dolly's guests had deserted the mansion and the servants were dousing the gas jets. He regarded her blandly. It was Dolly's soft repetition of her name that warned Katherine of her tactlessness.

She was feeling somewhat restored after a brandy and a two-hour nap on Dolly's huge bed. The numbing effects of her nightmarish experience with Nolan had faded.

In a quiet house Dolly had walked her down the sweeping staircase, explaining that Nolan had left almost immediately after he'd been told that she was ill and that Carson Fairfax would see her home.

"What did you tell him?" she asked as arm-in-arm they descended the stairs.

"Only that Nolan was called away and that you need an escort home," Dolly whispered in reply. "Nothing to be embarrassed about."

At the foot of the stairs, where Fairfax awaited them, Katherine had blurted out rather heedlessly what she really wanted.

"Katherine, Katherine," whispered Dolly with a shake of her head.

Her face warmed as she realized how rude she had sounded. "I mean—it's just, well, I'd rather not impose on you, Mr. Fairfax," she stammered. "I don't mean to offend, but the Elms is out of your way, isn't it?"

"No great distance," he said, offering that disarming little bow of his. "It would be my pleasure to see you safely home."

"Willis has his hands full in the stable after seeing to all the guests' horses." Dolly took Katherine's hand and put it on Fairfax's arm. "You understand. And I know Carson doesn't mind in the least driving you home."

"You can be assured, Dolly, that Miss Tucker will be safe with me."

Oddly, Katherine agreed as she met his innocent gaze. Beneath her hand his forearm was warm and solid. How dangerous could a man be who willingly played "mother" at a tea party? "All right, then, Mr. Fairfax. Let's go."

"Carson," he said, offering her an enticing smile. "Remember? You agreed to call me Carson."

"Yes, that's right, Carson." Though she was in no mood to be charmed, she was unable to resist returning his smile.

He helped her on with her coat, his fingers brushing her neck as he helped her smooth the collar. His touch burned, just as she'd suspected it would, but he did not seem to notice. She stepped away. He took up his cloak, hat, and cane and ushered her out the door, past the sphinxes to his waiting buggy. They were soon driving through the deserted Denver streets.

They spoke little during the ride. Though she was restored enough to face the world, her emotions were in too much turmoil to allow her to make small talk. Carson seemed to expect none and, thankfully, he asked no awkward questions. He appeared as satisfied as Katherine to let the echo of the horses's hooves on the empty street fill the silence.

The first thing Katherine noticed when they turned into the curving drive up to the Elms was the darkness. Mrs. Dodd always left the outside porch lamp burning when she was out late. She thought she glimpsed a lamp burning in the family parlor behind the heavy draperies. But tonight, the entrance was shadowed. Unreasonable though she knew it was, she clutched the side of the buggy in apprehension.

As they drew up to the front step, the light of the buggy lamps chased away the darkness.

Katherine relaxed. She didn't know what she'd expected. The entire evening had been so unsettling; her nerves were overwrought.

Carson looped the reins around the buggy whip, leaped to the ground with his cane tucked under his arm, then turned to reach up for her. Katherine allowed him to place his hands on her waist and swing her down. His hold was powerful but nothing improper. His strength and nearness were so reassuring, she was tempted to lean against him for a moment. It had been a long time since she'd leaned trustingly against a man. Papa had been dead over two years. But the instant her feet were firmly on the ground, Carson released her. She swayed slightly before regaining her balance.

"Are you all right?" he asked, holding his hands out on either side of her shoulders to catch her, but without touching her.

Embarrassed, partly for her earlier outspoken rejection of him as an escort and for her weakness, Katherine shook her head. "Yes, I'm fine."

Determined to appear collected, she started toward the door.

She'd only taken a couple of steps, her gaze on the stones, when a figure appeared from the shadows. Surprise sucked the breath from her. She halted.

"Well, look who we have here," Nolan said, blocking the front door. His hat sat askew and a lock of hair lay plastered across his forehead. His bloodshot and frenetic eyes told Katherine he'd been drinking heavily. "You look surprisingly well, Katherine, after taking sick at Dolly's. Recovered enough to give yourself to a gambler now, are you?"

She opened her mouth to defend herself.

"Shut your mouth, Stewart," Carson ordered, his voice calm but authoritative, as if he made such demands every night. At the same time he moved forward, easing himself between her and Nolan. "Remove yourself from the premises immediately."

She clutched at Carson's arm to drag him from between them, but he was immoveable.

"*You* get off the premises, Fairfax." Nolan slurred his words. "I came to apologize to the lady. You see, I knew she wouldn't leave her dear sister and Mrs. Dodd alone all night." Nolan stepped closer and shook a finger under Carson's nose. "Your company is unwelcome here."

Beneath her hand, Carson's arm tensed, but he made no move to leave. Despite his outward calm, the tip of his cane tapped impatiently on the stone step.

"Please leave, Nolan," she pleaded, her heart beginning to pound as she realized that the Englishman was probably far more adept at dealing with hostile drunks than Nolan was at dealing with a sober gentleman. She had no desire for anyone to be hurt on her doorstep. "Go home, Nolan. Get some sleep. In the morning, if you wish to apologize, write me a letter."

"But—" Nolan began, angry bewilderment contorting his handsome face.

"You heard it from the lady's lips," Carson said, a quiet, no-nonsense tone in his voice. "Leave. Miss Tucker does not wish to see you."

Nolan drew himself up. "You'll agree to speak to me alone, Katherine, or you'll kiss your precious Elms good-bye."

She went cold and still inside. Fear slipped away. "How dare you threaten me!"

She tried to step out from behind Carson to speak to Nolan face-to-face. But the Englishman edged his way between them again. No matter how firmly she attempted to shove him aside, Carson did not budge.

"Say what you have to say, Katherine," he instructed without taking his gaze from Nolan. ''Then Mr. Stewart will be on his way.''

''The hell I will.'' Nolan lurched at her. His hand lashed out, grazing the puffy leg-of-mutton sleeve of her velvet jacket. Startled, she twisted away, backing down off the porch, her heart pounding in her ears.

Carson's cane came up under Nolan's outstretched arm. The lawyer grunted in pain. He swung a fist at Fairfax's head. The Englishman ducked, his bowler tumbling to the porch floor. He launched a blow to Nolan's midsection. Air whooshed out of the lawyer. Bent double, he staggered backward, his left arm pressed against his stomach. He thumped against the side of the house, his breath hissing through his teeth. His hat fell forward off his brow and rolled down the steps.

It happened in little more than the blink of an eye. All Katherine could do was stand frozen. She longed to stop the melee but was too stunned to move.

Carson backed away but remained between her and her attacker.

A string of curses spewed from Nolan's mouth the likes of which she'd never heard him utter. With his right hand he began to fumble in his coat pocket. She watched him in bewilderment.

Carson's eyes narrowed. ''Don't do it, Stewart.''

From nowhere a rapier flashed in the lamplight. Where Carson had carried a cane, he wielded—with deadly grace—a long, shiny rapier.

Shock coursed through Katherine. She stepped backward, allowing him room to maneuver.

''Take your hand out of your pocket,'' Carson ordered with the same deadly cool he'd used earlier. ''If you fire that gun through your coat, I can still skewer your liver before I die. I don't care to think of how Miss Tucker will finish you off. At the moment I suspect your cries for mercy will go unheeded.''

Nolan froze. His gaze shifted from her, then back to Carson. His face paled, suddenly devoid of violence, haggard with defeat.

"Mercy, indeed," she scoffed, the pounding of her heart now slowed to a rapid flutter. "Get your sorry hide out of here, Nolan," she added, surprised at how easily her father's vocabulary came to her lips.

He withdrew his hand from his pocket. Uneasily his eyes shifted from Carson to her and back again. His drunkenness had vanished. He held up both hands, palms open to show that he held no weapons. "No need to get violent, Fairfax."

"I quite agree." Carson dropped the point of the rapier to the porch floor. "On your way, then."

"Not so fast." Nolan was cold sober and worried now. "You're not going to say anything about this to anyone, are you, Katherine?"

"Oh, do you fear for your reputation now?" she asked, with little sympathy. "You should have thought of that before."

"I wouldn't be the only one to suffer if this came to light, you know," Nolan said, mustering what little was left of his dignity.

She knew he was right. The last thing she wanted was for all of Denver to know that Nolan Stewart, her beau for the last year and a half, was no better than the rest of the city's fortune hunters. "I'll say nothing, as long as you do the same," she said out of pride, not leniency.

Nolan glanced at Fairfax. "And you, sir?"

"I shall defer to the lady's wishes," the Englishman said, returning the rapier to cane form.

"But there's nothing I can do about what the bank has demanded," Nolan continued, apparently anxious about his earlier threat. "You understand, Katherine?"

"No, I don't," she said, suddenly weary and longing for him to be gone. "You were my lawyer. I trusted you to look out for my and Lily's best interests. Apparently I expected too much. But what's done is done, and I don't care to discuss it with you any more tonight."

Carson nodded his head in the direction of the dark drive. "You heard the lady. On your way, Stewart."

Without another word, Nolan slunk off into the darkness.

Silently Katherine thanked heaven that she'd not come home with Willis. He would hardly have been able to stand up to Nolan. She opened her mouth to thank Carson.

But the Englishman had already picked up his hat and returned to place a hand at the small of her back. He gently urged her toward the door. "In the house. We'll talk there. I expect a full explanation."

The elation of sending Nolan on his way dissolved into apprehension as Katherine led Carson into the family parlor, where a lamp glowed in a dim but friendly welcome. How much could she explain to Carson without getting into the intimate details of what had happened with Nolan earlier, or the embarrassing fact of the mortgage on the Elms?

The sight of the parlor's burning lamp sent her mind racing back to the moment when they'd turned into the drive and she'd noted the darkness. "Nolan must have put out the porch lamp. Mrs. Dodd always leaves it on. Just as she leaves the parlor lamp burning."

"So his ambush was plotted, then," Carson said, following her into the room.

"Apparently." The maliciousness of Nolan's intent finally struck her with full force. Her knees turned to rubber. She had to sit down.

Carson glanced at her, then began pulling off his gloves and looking around the room. "Where do you keep the sherry?"

"What? Sherry? There in the sideboard." Katherine gave a bewildered wave toward the cabinet. Her exhilaration withered as realization of the danger they'd just faced took ugly shape. Someone could have been seriously hurt out there on the porch.

"Drink up." Carson shoved a glass into her hands. "It will clear your head."

Katherine doubted that, but she did as he ordered. "Do you always carry a sword with you?"

"Yes," he said, sipping from his own sherry and restlessly pacing around the room. "A necessity of my profession."

"And you were certain that Nolan had a gun in his pocket?" Katherine continued, longing to believe better of Nolan's intentions.

"He was showing it off around the club just last week." Carson seated himself across the table from her. "It was merely a two-barrel derringer with a pearl handle that he thought was quite clever."

Horrified at the thought of Nolan holding a real gun on her and Carson, Katherine forgot the sherry and stared at him. "Does Nolan patronize the Respite and show off guns often?"

"He is a member and stops by from time to time, mostly for supper," Carson said without looking at her. "He gambles little and, if it's any comfort, I seriously doubt he really intended to use the gun."

She shook her head. Her hand still trembled as she set her glass on the side table. "That's not much comfort."

Carson drained his glass and set it on the table. "Now," he began, rising and walking to the center of the room where he faced her with the lamp between them. The shadows cast on his stern features and dark hair made him look more like a warlock than a saloonkeeper. The image wasn't difficult to believe after seeing him draw the rapier out of nowhere and level it at Nolan.

A shiver passed through her as she wondered what dark magic Carson might practice beyond his unholy luck at the card table.

Suddenly he seized a chair and set it down in front of her. He sat, facing her. He took her free hand in his and began to chaff it, as if rubbing away frostbite—or fear. "Tell me what Nolan was babbling about out there," he demanded softly, concentrating on her fingers. "He was carrying on worse than a jealous lover."

The strength in his hands steadied her nerves. His warmth sent a current of awareness through her. The man sitting across from her was much more than a dandy at the card table or a society pet. He was virile, courageous, and discerning.

For a moment she considered glossing over the ordeal. She didn't care to share the sordid details of the Tuckers' financial affairs with the preeminent gambler of Denver. But he'd come to her rescue at some risk to himself. He deserved to know the truth.

"Well?" he prompted, his left brow raised in query. His thumb stroked the back of her hand.

"You will hold this in confidence, of course." She looked away in embarrassment. This was almost worse than having the high and mighty of Denver find out that she'd been selling off the furniture.

"I already agreed to confidentiality outside, Katherine. What's going on? What did Stewart mean about you kissing the Elms good-bye?"

"He was so exquisitely articulate, wasn't he?" she muttered, twisting the stem of her glass between the fingers of her free hand.

"Tell me what's going on. Maybe I can help."

"I doubt it, but remember the terrible shaft cave-in at the Clementine last spring?" she began, the woebegone faces of the dead miners' families still painfully clear in her mind's eye. She'd donated as much food and money to them as she'd dared and was planning to send them Christmas baskets.

Carson frowned, obviously not seeing the connection. "Yes, most unfortunate. But the mine is almost cleaned out and producing ore again, isn't it?"

"Almost." As briefly as possible, Katherine told him the entire story about how Nolan had arranged the mortgaging of the Elms to finance repairs because the estate was short of cash. Uncle Owen had seemed to think it a legitimate way to acquire the needed money. This time the tale roused real anger with herself and with the Cherry Street Bank, with whom she had dealt so trustingly.

"How does Owen Benedict fit into all of this?" Carson

asked, a disapproving frown on his lips. "Isn't he your guardian? Wasn't he looking into these things?"

"I think he was as trusting of Nolan and the bank as I was," she said, still too embarrassed by her imprudence in the matter to face the Englishman. "Doesn't it all sound like something right out of a melodrama on the Palace's stage? The dastardly villain. The helpless heroine." She couldn't resist pressing her forearm against her brow like a despairing actress. "I do so hate being helpless. And I'm so embarrassed that you had to be dragged into this sordid affair."

She chanced a glance at him. He was watching her, a frown still on his face. "You do have my gratitude, you know."

"Actually I was just thinking that there is no need for you to be helpless," he said, as if he'd heard none of her words of appreciation.

"How is that?"

"Perhaps we could pool our resources and help each other."

What did that mean? Mystified but curious, she leaned closer to get a better look at Carson's face, but now he was the one avoiding her gaze.

"Just what do you mean?" Katherine asked. A touching look of hope—then suspicion—crossed her pretty heart-shaped face.

It was Carson's turn to avoid her eyes, hiding his pleasure. He took a deep breath. So losing the Elms was the mitigating circumstance Dolly had spoken of? It was almost too sweet— too perfect—to be true.

As Katherine's suitor, Nolan Stewart had taken unfair advantage of her situation. When she didn't agree to marriage to save the Elms, he'd attempted to compromise her.

With his gambler's discipline, Carson kept his pleasure and appreciation of the situation from reaching his lips.

The question remained—was she angry or desperate enough to defy convention to get what she wanted? Either way, he was certain that she was entirely too bright—and too spoiled—to remain anyone's victim for long.

He faced her. "What I mean is that I'm in a position to take care of your mortgage problems in return for a favor."

"What sort of favor?" Katherine asked. The glimmer of distrust that clouded her eyes stung his pride, though he didn't understand why. She had every right to be suspicious.

"Hear me out. Don't agree to this until you've heard the entire plan," he cautioned before forging on. "It's a business favor. In return for paying off the mortgage, you will marry me."

After a shocked pause—but no gasp, no threat to faint—she said, "Go on."

Ignoring her growing paleness, he told the entire story of receiving the telegrams a year earlier regarding his mother's impending death. He explained with as little mention of his father as possible—Katherine didn't need to know every vulgar detail of the Fairfaxes's dirty laundry—how he'd lied about being engaged, hoping to put his dying mother's mind at ease.

"But your mother recovered," she interrupted, a furrow of confusion forming between her elegant brows. He found her attention heartening. "I remember hearing about the celebration of the countess's recovery at the Respite almost a year ago. So what is the difficulty?"

"The difficulty is that I'm *not* engaged or married," Carson concluded, glad to have the problem on the table. But when he looked at Katherine she merely stared back at him, obviously perplexed. "And my mother is coming for a Christmas visit and expects to meet my bride."

"Surely you've told her the truth by now."

"How was I to tell my mother that I'd lied to her on her deathbed?" he asked. *Why would I give my father another failing to lay at my door?* he bit back. Suddenly he was impatient with her lack of comprehension. And he felt exposed and vulnerable. Dolly Green and Hearn already knew more about his life than he liked, and here he was confessing all to the self-righteous Miss Katherine Tucker.

"You see, when Mother was able to reply to my telegram, she was absolutely overjoyed that I was engaged. She was ecstatic. What could I say? I couldn't shatter her happiness, not after all she'd been through."

"Yes, I see the problem." Katherine looked away, those luscious lips pursed in thought.

He was about to turn away when he saw her brush something from her eyes. "I do understand about deathbed promises," she said, her voice low, barely audible.

When she looked up at him, her eyes glistened, but he saw no tears.

"I made a promise to my father before he passed—about the Amanda Leigh—and he looked so relieved when I agreed to do what he wanted. . . ." She paused, staring off into space. A hiccup escaped her—or was it a sob? "Anybody who wants me to break the promise I made to him will have to drag me behind wild horses first."

A whisper of relief—and sympathy—breathed through him. She understood. She'd made a vow to her father. He'd lied to his mother. But they'd each done it to offer comfort to a dying loved one. Funny that they would have a thing like that in common.

Encouraged, he took her other hand. "There's more."

Her eyes grew wide as she listened to Carson detail an astonishing plan for them to marry and live together in the Elms during the countess's Christmas visit.

"Acting as husband and wife, we can entertain her for a month or however long she wants to stay," he said, speaking so quickly that she could not possibly interrupt him. "It would be like acting in one of those amateur theatricals you like to do. Hostess, a natural role for you. Mother will love the Denver social life and the Elms. She will be delighted to have a look at the shops and be received at the best homes. After the New Year celebration, she'll be on her way back to Atwick Manor.''

Carson paused to look at her.

All she could do was stare at him in speechless amazement. His story about the exchange of telegrams and his ultimate fib about having a wife to comfort his mother had to be true. No untruth would be so bizarre.

Finally she tried to reply, but her mouth moved without making a sound.

''I'm offering a legitimate marriage,'' Carson said, as if to reassure her of honorable intentions. When she still said nothing, he hurried on. After his mother departed, he would procure a quiet annulment. They would both be free again. He would move on to San Francisco. He was involved in a business enterprise, something even grander than the Respite, with Alice Johnson in the Bay City area. Moving west had been his intention before all of this had come up.

But before he left, he would be certain she and Lily owned the Elms and would be as secure as ever.

''I will gladly sign whatever agreement you and Owen Benedict want to protect your Tucker inheritance,'' he finished. ''See, it's simple. I provide all the expenses for a wife and a house at Christmas.''

For a moment the silence in the parlor was deafening. He gazed at her steadily. Other than the hurriedness of his speech, he seemed supremely confident that she would agree to his outrageous proposal.

''I realize on first hearing this must seem overwhelming,'' he concluded.

''Alice Johnson—isn't she the . . . ?'' Katherine began.

''Yes, she is a former madame whom I've taken on as a business partner,'' Carson said. ''Despite what the Denver gossips say, I swear we are business partners only. She has a great head for business and is already setting up things for our venture in the Bay City.''

''I see,'' she said, at last mastering her voice but feeling quite overcome. Everyone in Denver knew exactly who Alice Johnson was. It was difficult for her to imagine what kind of business arrangement the madame and the saloonkeeper had. "It is rather extreme, don't you think? What you propose appears to be a marriage of convenience with a new twist— until annulment do us part?"

"Precisely." A hopeful smile tugged at his lips. "I knew you were mature enough to understand. We will share the Fairfax name and the house. Of course, we must appear to be married. You'll have the prestige of having royalty stay at the Elms. I know Mother will take great pleasure in your annual tree decorating party."

"Oh, yes, the tree decorating party," Katherine muttered, bemused. "When her visit is over, she returns to England and you leave for San Francisco?"

"And you may want to take Lily on a long trip until gossip dies down," Carson said. "I'll have the annulment taken care of quietly. When you return after a few months' absence, the Elms will be yours and you can carry on as Katherine Tucker or however you like. I'm certain Dolly will help you smooth things over with Denver society."

"Dolly?" Katherine exclaimed, remembering her helpful godmother. "What does she have to do with this? How much does she know about Nolan and the Elms?"

"Rest assured Dolly only suspects you have problems. After Nolan's behavior this evening, how can she not suspect? But I assure you, she will be discreet."

"Who else knows?" she demanded, suddenly feeling as though Denver society knew more about her reduced circumstances than she did.

"No one, but me," Carson said, touching her hand. "Your secret is safe. Dolly and Randolph have helped me keep up this farcical front for a year. They are willing to help us with this. Trust me."

"But your mother thinks you've been married for almost a year," she said trying to make sense of his insane proposal.

"And so will Denver when we're finished," he said, clearly prepared for this point. "We will have a quiet civil ceremony with an informal announcement of our marriage. Then we will be seen all over Denver together—shopping, driving, at parties, theater—until everyone is thoroughly tired of us. Dolly will be helpful with society invitations. We'll put a photograph of us as bride and groom on the mantel. I'll move a few things in to make it look as if we've been living under the same roof. By December when Mother comes, we'll be old news."

Her head swam with confusion. She rose from the chair and paced across the room to the bay window overlooking the dark, winter-bare rose garden.

And the Elms will be yours, he'd said.

Her mind raced ahead. No more selling off furniture. No worry over how to pay Mrs. Evans, Lily's tutor. She could bring Willis back, and the buggy and horses. That sounded good, very good. And when it was all over, she'd have her freedom, too.

But she must proceed carefully here. What points hadn't been covered? Where was the fine print?

"What about your father, the earl?"

"He won't be coming," Carson said, a sudden harshness edged his voice. "Father prefers to stay in England."

She said nothing more. Something really troubled her about what he proposed.

"May I take your silence to mean you are considering this proposal?" Carson asked, watching her with a sidelong gaze. "I realize this is a rather sudden presentation of an unusual scheme, especially after your unpleasant experience with Nolan. But I also think it's something you should consider as a benefit to both of us."

"You do seem to want to do this for the right reasons— your mother," she said, her back still to him as she thought quickly. How serious was Carson Fairfax about this scandalous scheme? There was a way to find out.

"You're a gambler and a saloonkeeper," she said, thinking out loud.

"I've made no denial of that," he said.

Trust your gut, Kitty, girl, Papa had said.

She turned to Carson. "I can't marry the proprietor of the Respite, you understand. What would I say to the ladies of the League? Granted, Dolly will be able to smooth things over with Denver society, but what about the League? To wed an infamous gentlemen's club owner would be completely out of character for me."

Carson stared at her briefly then looked away, his eyes suddenly hooded. Was this how he appeared to other players at the game table? Katherine wondered.

"Good point," he acknowledged, sounding studiously reasonable. "I'm sure the good ladies will wonder what you're up to."

"I might consider doing what you suggest. As you say, it would be beneficial to us both," she persisted, her thoughts taking form as she spoke. The opportunity was almost too good to be true. She might lose everything, or she might gain everything. "But I have one condition."

"And what would that be?" Carson asked, his smile guarded.

"It's simple," she said, casting him a virtuous smile. "I'll become your wife and hostess for Christmas if you sell the Gentlemen's Respite."

Chapter Six

Carson studied Katherine, careful to keep his surprise and indignation from his face. Silently he reproached himself for not foreseeing this game play. She might be down, but she wasn't witless. If she was going to ask for a condition, of course, it would have to do with the Respite. Where was his head? Admiring her ankles.

He rose from his chair. Unwillingly, he found himself respecting her audacity. No half-baked I'll-thank-you-not-to-play-cards-in-my-house condition from her. She wanted him to sell the very club he'd sweated and labored for years to build.

How was he to play this gambit?

Circumspectly. She had not refused him. Accomplishing his goal was not out of sight—just farther down the road than he'd expected.

"If my mother can accept that I'm a saloonkeeper," he said as evenly as he could, "I don't know why you and the League can't. But a concession can be arranged. How about a sizable donation to the League?"

"Bribery!?" Katherine said, her voice low with outrage. "Do you truly expect me to risk my reputation with a scandalous annulment and Lily's future in exchange for money alone? What you do is illegal in Denver and it affects the lives of too many innocent people."

"May I remind you that the Gentlemen's Respite is a perfectly legitimate club that conforms to the city's laws, holds all the necessary licenses, and pays taxes."

"You mean, pays bribes."

Carson's eyes narrowed. One moment she was shrewd beyond her years and experience. The next she was as innocent as a babe in the woods. He did business the way Denver business was done. He shrugged. "I don't make the rules. I merely comply with them."

"How virtuous," Katherine quipped. "Is that what you tell the starving families of Denver?"

"I tell the starving I meet to see my cook in the Respite's kitchen," Carson said, his patience with her virtue beginning to grow thin.

"And generous, too," Katherine replied, her tone laced with sarcasm. "As moved as I am by your desire to make your mother happy, I must ask for the sale of the Respite in return for helping you."

"You'd rather Nolan moved into the Elms?" he threw at her, though he'd already decided Stewart's days in Denver were numbered.

"You'd rather tell your mother that you lied about having a wife?" she tossed back.

Carson managed to cover his wince. Perhaps one cruel threat deserved another, but his control was crumbling. He turned away from her and paced around the table once more before stopping to stare distractedly at the glowing remnants of the coal fire. She had not refused him, but he didn't like her condition on his proposal. It wasn't just the loss of the Respite; she was trying to change him, make him over into something she found acceptable—just as his father had. He resented it. He wanted to marry her and have the Elms, but there had to be another way. For the life of him, he could not see it at the moment.

He turned to her, scrutinizing her expectant face. "I think we should sleep on these decisions before we make any commitment."

Katherine's heart sank, but she fought to keep her disappointment from showing. Had she gone too far with her demands? She drew a long, wary breath. Perhaps nothing was solved at all: Not her problem with the Elms. Not his problem with his mother. She had to be certain of what he meant. "Do you wish to withdraw your offer, sir?"

Carson met her gaze. His expression chilled her.

"I withdraw nothing, madame. The offer is on the table with your condition. I spent a good deal of time and effort in building the Respite and its reputation," he said in a low and icy voice. "It means a great deal to me. I wish to have time to consider the condition you have placed on my offer."

Without further comment, Carson took up his hat, cloak, and cane and started toward the door.

Wringing her hands, Katherine followed him, trying not to regret her demands. Had she held the solution to her problems in her hands then foolishly thrown it away? No, she would not allow herself to believe that. "I'll hear from you tomorrow, then?" she asked.

"Lock the door behind me," he instructed as he donned his hat, his back to her. "I doubt Nolan will cause any more trouble, but don't chance it." He turned slightly but would not look at her. "Tomorrow."

Then he was gone, the sound of his horses and buggy vanishing into the night.

Katherine locked the door behind him as he'd instructed. A clear image of Carson's face and the sound of his voice lingered in her head. She berated herself for not understanding how much the Respite meant to him.

"Well, Papa," Katherine muttered as she paused in the drawing room door to look up at the Sargent portrait of her parents. Though there was only a dim glow from the parlor lamp, she could see her father and mother's beloved faces forever captured on the canvas. Mother's smile proud and haughty, Papa's smile benign and loving. "What do you think of my instincts now?"

With the single-minded concentration that he often used at the game table, Carson set Katherine's condition on his proposal aside and set about doing what had to be done before the night was finished.

He mastered the lock on Nolan Stewart's boarding hotel room door in a few seconds. Even in the wee hours of the morning, when only one gaslight burned in the dim corridor, the mechanism was easy to pick.

He smiled to himself when the final click announced his success. Defeating a locked door never failed to satisfy him, to give him a sense of triumph. He would always be able to thank his father for this skill at least, though he knew it wasn't what the earl had intended for him to learn when he'd been locked away for refusing to abide by his father's dictates.

Soundlessly Carson let himself into the lawyer's room and shut the door. By the light of the street lamp outside, he found Stewart's coat on the coatrack and removed the gun from the pocket. Slipping the weapon into his own coat pocket, he strolled leisurely toward the bedroom, where he could hear the lawyer snoring—no doubt sleeping off the corn liquor courage he'd consumed earlier in the evening.

When he reached the door to the bedroom, a floorboard creaked underfoot. Stewart, who appeared to have dropped onto his bed fully clothed, ceased snoring.

Carson moved on into the room.

"Who's there?" Stewart called. He tried to sit up, but he sank down again with a groan.

Taking pleasure in whatever pain the man suffered—the

lawyer deserved nothing less than agony after what he'd done to Katherine—Carson found a lamp on the desk.

"Identify yourself, dammit, or I'll shoot," Stewart called, struggling to rise again, one arm groping for something on the bedside table. When he found nothing, he cursed again.

"I daresay you won't shoot, unless you have another gun besides the one I took from your coat pocket," he said, unconcerned. If Stewart was so proud of his little pistol that he'd brought it to the club to show it off, he probably didn't own many other weapons.

Carson pulled matches from his pocket, struck one, and put it to the lamp wick. Light flooded the room.

"Fairfax? How'd you get in here?" Stewart finally levered himself into an upright position and attempted to focus on Carson. The man's waistcoat had ridden up over his ribs, his necktie was untied, his collar was askew, and his coat was quite wrinkled.

"I'm a man of many talents, Stewart." Without relinquishing his walking stick or removing his hat, he turned the desk chair around and straddled it so he faced the bleary-eyed lawyer. "I think it's time you and I had a talk."

"I don't think we have much to say," Stewart said, attempting to straighten his waistcoat. "I'll resign my membership in the Respite tomorrow, if that's what this is about."

"Splendid, but that's the least of my concerns," Carson said, eyeing his foe and wondering what he might be able to learn from the man. "Where are you from, Stewart?"

"Ohio. Cleveland, to be exact." To his credit, the lawyer's eyes suddenly cleared—the seriousness of the conversation apparently sinking in. His mouth thinned belligerently. "Look, Fairfax, I've heard the rumors about how people who oppose you disappear. But this time you're not dealing with someone of questionable connections. If anything happens to me—"

"Not after tonight," Carson interrupted quietly. "Not if Miss Tucker should press charges against you. What would Whitman and Whitman think about that? Their promising partnership candidate accused of assaulting a fine young woman with an impeccable reputation. It would not do. No, not at all. Have you ever thought of returning to Ohio?''

Stewart's mouth snapped shut. Then he said, "No, I haven't. There's nothing there for me. My folks died in a house fire a while back.''

Carson made a mournful face. "Sorry to hear that. So you'll be interested in moving west?''

Stewart sprang up from the bed, blustering. "See here, Fairfax, you can't just—''

Carson was on his feet in an instant. Metal sang. The walking stick's rapier blade flashed in the lamplight. "You can go willingly or I will personally escort you out of town.''

Stewart's eyes widened, his gaze glued to the lethal weapon. He sagged against the edge of the bed and began to stammer, spittle splattering his chin. "Surely you understand, I didn't mean any harm. Lord, man, I've been courting Katherine for over a year. I asked her to marry me.''

"I don't give a bloody damn what you intended or proposed.'' He could feel his fury growing hotter and more difficult to hold at bay—and he didn't really care. The rapier flashed again. He wanted to see Stewart cower—at least. "Your attentions were unwanted. What you did was intolerable. If I wasn't a civilized man, I'd cut your throat here and now and leave you for the porters to carry out with the rubbish.''

Stewart's trembling hand strayed to his throat as he gazed at the blade—bloody visions of his own demise obviously dancing in his head.

"So what will it be in the morning?'' Carson continued, quietly sliding the rapier back into the ebony walking stick, then sitting astride the chair once again. "The train east or the train west?''

Stewart took a deep breath and his shoulders slouched. "Actually I've always wanted to go to San Francisco.''

"Truly?'' Carson asked, surprised by the coincidence of the

lawyer's interest in the Bay City, where he had plans to go himself.

"Or maybe not," Stewart hastened to add. "Maybe some other—"

"Perhaps we can come to a mutual agreement," he said, deciding to move on to what he really wanted to know. "But you must do me a favor first."

"Agreement?" Wariness echoed in Stewart's voice. "Favor?"

"First, it is understood that you will leave Denver and never return to trouble Katherine Tucker again."

"Agreed," Stewart said without hesitation.

Carson nodded. "Secondly, tell me what you know about the calling in of the mortgage on the Elms."

"How do you know about that?"

"Katherine had some interesting things to tell me this evening," Carson said. "And I want to know more."

"The details of my client's affairs are confidential, you know," Stewart said with a shake of his head.

Maybe the man was an idiot. He gave his walking stick a twirl. "Surely you can see your way to sharing some details about the mortgage with me."

Stewart caught the gesture and began to nod rapidly. "Yes, a few details perhaps. At the time, after the accident at the Clementine, the mortgage Ray Jones from the Cherry Street Bank offered seemed like a reasonable solution to Katherine's problems. I had no reason to think that they'd call it in early. It's highly irregular, but within their rights."

"Did he give any excuse?" he asked.

Stewart shook his head. "Nothing specific."

"Tell me the name of the company that has shown interest in buying the Amanda Leigh," Carson said.

"I honestly don't know anything about it except that Owen Benedict came to me with the information that they'd approached him. He didn't even give me a name, but I believe it was a Georgetown firm."

"Georgetown?" he repeated. "Interesting. The Amanda Leigh is near Georgetown, is it not?"

"Yes, so it makes sense that they'd know about the equipment there," Stewart said. "And perfectly reasonable for them to purchase it and move it to a nearby mine."

Carson nodded. "Here's my proposition: I want to know the name of this company and who the officers and shareholders are. Go to Georgetown and find that out for me. You will keep me informed of your activities with a weekly report."

"I can do that," Stewart said.

"When you've concluded your investigation to my satisfaction, you will go on to San Francisco," he said. "You will not return to Denver. I'll see to it that you have entrée to a respectable job on the coast. Agreed?"

"Agreed," Stewart said, his face brightening, as if he thought the offer too good to be true. "That's it?"

Carson rose from the chair. "If Miss Tucker is troubled by you in any way, all bets are off. Is that clear?"

"Perfectly," Stewart said. "I'll be on the train to Georgetown tomorrow morning. The officers' names should be easy enough to learn. A matter of public record. But shareholders' names can be more difficult to come by."

"I have great faith that you will find out everything for me," Carson said. "I'll expect your first report in a week."

"Yes, sir," Stewart said, coming to his feet also. He appeared as eager and earnest as a freshly scolded schoolboy. "I'll keep you informed of everything I learn. And I won't trouble Katherine again."

"Excellent." Carson had no reason to doubt the lawyer would do what he said. Satisfied, for Katherine's sake, he left Stewart's room without saying good-bye. He'd hear from the lawyer again soon enough.

"Sis, you haven't heard a word I said," Lily complained at the breakfast table.

Katherine started guiltily. "Yes, I have."

But she had indeed been woolgathering—about Carson Fairfax and his offer, and about the two letters she'd already sent out that morning, one to Nolan and one to Uncle Owen.

Still, she hated for Lily to think she wasn't listening. Frantically she searched her memory for her sister's last words. "You've found a new arrangement for 'Come All Ye Faithful' that you want to try for the Christmas tree decorating party."

"And? What else?" Lily prompted.

"Uh," Katherine stammered, unable to recall anything more. Her mind was not sharp this morning. She'd hardly slept all night. Each sound in the house or out in the yard had reminded her of Carson's warning about Nolan returning. But he hadn't. Thank heavens. "I'm sorry, Lily. I'm hardly awake this morning."

"I knew it," Lily said with a laugh. "You're thinking about the opera last night."

"Well, yes," she said, glad her sister suggested the topic. "It was a superb performance. All of the singers were in great form."

"Tell me about it," Lily demanded, placing her elbow on the table and resting her chin in her hand.

Katherine did her best to describe the production of *La Traviata*—the sights and sounds of the bejeweled audience parading in and out of the gilded Tabor Opera House. She recounted colors and textures vaguely remembered by her little sister, who'd lost her sight at the age of four. But Lily loved to hear the descriptions, and Katherine told as much as she could.

"Honestly, I think all the ladies there last night were wearing lavender scent," she finished. "And the orchestra was in fine form, too."

"It sounds too wonderful," Lily mused, a frown marring her pretty face. "When will I get to go to the opera?"

She touched her sister's cheek. They'd had this conversation before. She thought it unrealistic to take a twelve-year-old to a formal theatrical performance intended to entertain adults. But sometimes Lily seemed so mature. "We'll see when something appropriate comes to town."

Mrs. Dodd bustled into the breakfast room. "Mrs. Evans is here for your lessons, Lily."

"Run along, dear," Katherine said, kissing her sister's cheek. "We'll talk later." Lily rose, her sweet smile returning to her face as she left the breakfast room, counting the steps into the hallway, then into the music room.

As soon as she was gone, Mrs. D turned to Katherine again. "Mr. Benedict is here also. He arrived the same time Mrs. Evans did. That letter you had me have hand delivered this morning must have set a fire under the man."

"Indeed," she said, surprised that Uncle Owen was already on her doorstep. "Show him in."

He stormed into the breakfast room, a fierce frown on his face and his white hair standing out from his head like fuzz on a dandelion.

"Katherine!" He carried her letter in his hand and shook it at her. "Katherine, what is this nonsense about releasing Nolan as your lawyer and finding a new one?"

"I mean exactly what I said in the letter," she said, suddenly hesitant to go into detail with her uncle about the indecent liberties Nolan had taken the night before. "I sent a letter to Nolan dismissing him. It seems to me that he has not served our interests well, and I believe we need a new lawyer. One who will steer us clear of unfortunate little problems like foreclosure on a mortgage. Won't you sit and have some coffee?"

"What did he do to offend?" Owen drew back and seemed to make an effort to calm himself. "What did he say to set you on your high horse? I'm sure he'll want to clear up any misunderstanding."

"There is no misunderstanding," she said. The choice of Nolan as a lawyer had been Uncle Owen's, so it was only natural for him to defend the man. "Nolan behaved in an unforgivable fashion in the buggy last night. I have reason to suspect his intentions."

"I find that hard to believe." Uncle Owen grasped the back of the chair across the desk from her. "Nolan Stewart is a gentleman."

"He wasn't a gentleman last night." Annoyed with her uncle's skepticism, she let her voice turn cold. "I wasn't going to tell you, but perhaps you should know. When he put his hand where no man but a husband should—well, there was no mistaking his ungentlemanly intentions."

"He dared to—?" Uncle Owen stared slack-jawed at her. "How dare he touch you? I did not mean to doubt—"

Releasing the chair, he paced to the window, his back turned to her so she couldn't see his face. He was embarrassed, of course, just as she was.

"The fool," he muttered. "Who would have thought such a thing of Stewart?"

"Now you see why I find myself questioning whether his advice was given solely for Lily and my benefit or to profit other designs," she said, relieved at her uncle's indignant reaction. "There is nothing Nolan can say to change my mind. No apology. Nothing will be enough to satisfy me."

"Of course , I understand how you feel," Uncle Owen said, still without looking at her. "We could press charges, if you like." he added hesitantly.

"No, I promised not to speak of it," she said, with every intention of keeping her promise to Nolan, for her own sake and Lily's. "It is just too embarrassing. I know you will keep this unfortunate incident in confidence."

"Yes, of course, that is best," he agreed with a strange, furtive eagerness. "You are right. And we must secure new legal representation."

"I'd like several prospects to choose from," she said, reciting the steps she'd plotted during the sleepless hours of the night. "I'm nearly twenty-five and will be coming into my fortune. I'd like to select this lawyer myself."

"Several prospects?" Uncle Owen repeated in a tone of

disbelief. "Select him yourself? Katherine, this is still my responsibility. Why don't you allow me—?"

"But I want to do this myself," she continued, warming to her newfound authority. She had little idea of how to manage the tangled fortune that would become her responsibility in a few months. But Uncle Owen seemed as easily duped by lawyers and bankers as she was. Yet there had to be a way to keep the Elms. And she was going to find it.

Even though she had no husband to help her—she could hardly expected to see Carson Fairfax again after the abrupt way he'd left last night—there had to be a way.

"The successful candidate will be one who can help us immediately," she said.

"I'll see to it right away," Uncle Owen agreed with a nod.

"I'll need your advice, naturally," she said, aware of his silent disapproval of her taking a hand in her own affairs. "But I will conduct the interviews. Thanks to the bank, we have no time to waste."

"True," he agreed with a distracted frown. "There's no time to waste."

Chapter Seven

"I'm not going to do it," Carson announced to Dolly the next morning when he strolled into her breakfast room, brushing past Hollis with only the briefest of greetings—quite unlike himself. "She asks too much."

Dolly looked up from spreading honey on her toast to see Carson immaculately dressed and groomed, and his gambler's cool cooler than ever.

"And good morning to you, too," she said, laying her knife down and regarding him with mild irritation. She'd expected to see him this morning because she'd asked him to let her know how things went. Apparently they had not gone well.

"Charming soiree last night, Dolly," she continued without asking what he was *not* going to do. She had no need to ask. Nor was she particularly surprised that Katherine had demanded something. Her goddaughter had a mind of her own. "You look lovely this morning, Dolly. Why, thank you, Carson. So glad you enjoyed the gathering. Do sit and have some tea."

Her conversational prompts drew no smile from him, but he seated himself in the chair to her right.

"Why don't you pose as my wife?" he suggested calmly. "Then Mother can stay here at House of the Sphinxes."

"Don't tempt me, dear boy." She offered him a naughty smile as she nibbled on her toast and studied him over the crust. *That worldly sense of humor. How like Timothy he is,* she reflected for the umpteenth time. Ah, her Timothy, who had died before he could make his mark in the world, before he could select a life's mate, and make his own happiness. What had happened to her only son had been so maddeningly out of her control—his sudden illness, then his death. But with Carson and Katherine, she might make a difference.

"Tempted though I am, I don't think a match between us would work," she continued. "For one thing, I'm older than your mother. No one would take us seriously as a couple." She touched his hand briefly. "Now, tell me what happened."

While she poured his tea, he described the scene at the Elms the night before. She listened with only half an ear. She'd taken an instant liking to Carson the moment they'd met on the train ten years earlier. He'd been so young then, and clearly not ready for marriage. Something deep inside him had been wounded—whether it had to do with a woman or something even more fundamental, she'd never been certain.

But over the years he'd matured into quite an intriguing man: a flamboyant yet refined gambler and saloonkeeper who was charmingly arrogant in a curiously understated manner that only an Englishman could master. The Denver women—except for the Ladies' Moderation League—adored his obvious elegance and risqué profession.

Despite his appeal to the ladies, he'd kept all—even his mistress, as far as she knew—at a distance. She'd been unable to sort out exactly what kind of woman would make the perfect wife for Carson. She'd nearly given up trying until about a year ago. That was when she'd noted the way he and Katherine looked at each other across the room.

Their gazes only rested on the other for a brief but profound moment. She'd been surprised. They were not a pairing she would have thought of on her own. Yet, unlikely as it seemed, something was right about the two.

Over the past year she'd noted that Carson never failed to ask Katherine to dance at balls and she never refused. Their touch on the dance floor was excruciatingly decorous. At receptions, soirees, and picnics they always spoke, their conversation brief and courteous, their treatment of each other painfully polite.

There was no surer sign of attraction.

But Carson was devoted to the Respite.

And Katherine had joined the Ladies' Moderation League, those well-meaning ladies with a misbegotten, misdirected cause.

Nevertheless, Dolly was fairly certain that all she had to do was get them together for long enough. When Carson had told her of the countess's visit, she'd thought—in the best mining vernacular—Eureka!

"That blackguard Stewart has taken advantage of his position as Katherine's lawyer," Carson was grousing. "But he won't be bothering her again."

"I had no idea she'd been forced into a mortgage on the Elms," Dolly said, concentrating on Carson's words. Hearing about the pressure put on Katherine dismayed her. No wonder the girl had been so unnerved by Stewart's advances the night before.

"I thought Nolan was more of a gentleman than that," she muttered, recalling Katherine's pale face and trembling hands when she'd entered the house last night. Naturally the poor girl was shaken. And she was too proud to tell her godmother about her financial problems. What the hell was Owen Benedict doing to help?

But the most outrageous news of all was that Nolan had appeared later and hinted that he had a weapon. That news actually made Dolly's eyes narrow. "I'm sure that only frightened Katherine more."

"She recovered quickly enough," Carson said in a dry tone.

"By the time he threatened us, she was beyond shaken. She was angry. I nearly had to hold her back."

"Good. But I hope she wasn't too angry to be receptive to your proposal," Dolly said, watching Carson carefully.

"I hoped it would make her more receptive," he said, seemingly unaware of his tea. "And when she wasn't shocked by my offer, I thought we might come to some agreement."

"But you didn't?" Dolly busied herself with another slice of toast. She decided on the imported lemon curd spread this time. "Just what did you propose to her?"

Carson explained the details. She was unsurprised by his offer of marriage; he was an honorable man in his gambler's way. But the annulment?

"An offer of a marriage followed by a quick annulment never fails to charm a lady," Dolly dryly pointed out as she slathered lemon curd on her toast. "No wondered Katherine demanded a condition of her own."

"Annulment is the only fair thing to offer," Carson said, pushing his teacup away. A slight defensiveness crept into his voice, but defiance gleamed in his eyes. "I've no intention of staying in Denver. You know that. Giving Katherine her freedom when I go to San Francisco is the only *fair* thing to do."

"But it hardly warms a girl's heart." Dolly refused to let his annoyance trouble her. "So, she asked for something in return?"

Carson told her, his voice low, his emotions in obvious turmoil.

"First of all, it's not something that can be done overnight," he said, seeming to regain his objectivity. "The club is worth a lot of money. Not many buyers are in the market for such an investment. A sale would take weeks at least. Secondly, but most importantly, I tell you, Dolly, she thinks to change me." He crossed his arms over his chest. "I recognize the signs."

"Not necessarily." Dolly sat back in her chair, surprised by his outburst. Did he refer to experience with another woman? The expression on his face was harsh and dour. No matter, she decided. This was no time to pick at old wounds. "In her place, I might have demanded the same thing. It would have little to do with reforming you. You may have saved her from Nolan's clutches, but you merit no better reward, Carson, not after putting that bizarre marriage and annulment proposal before her. Sale of the Respite is such an appropriate revenge, better than merely strangling you, dear boy."

His indignant frown deepened. "I offered a fair if unconventional proposal."

"There is surely some action you can take or a counteroffer you can make that would suit you both," Dolly suggested. "Have you let it be known that the Respite might go on the block? Selling might be simpler than you think. I don't know a lot about these things, but aren't there all kinds of provisions that can be written into a sale contract?"

The harsh, unmovable frown on Carson's face softened into a pensive scowl. "There is a myriad of ways to sell property."

"If not"—Dolly shrugged, careful not to meet Carson's gaze—"well, you still have the problem of how to entertain your mother. The simplest thing to do would be to tell her the truth. Your mother would be disappointed, of course, but you would be off the hook. But that still leaves Katherine vulnerable to Denver bankers."

That brought Carson's head up. A shadow crossed his face. "That is not acceptable."

Dolly scrutinized his troubled profile, but she read nothing more than displeasure in his expression. She poured herself more tea in an effort to appear as unconcerned as possible. If she could not change his mind, could she move fast enough to win over Katherine?

Carson rose abruptly. "Thank you for the tea," he said, taking her hand and leaning close to place a quick peck on her cheek. "I'll let you know what I decide."

"You'll have the wedding here, of course," she called after him. Carson waved acceptance and strode out the door.

Her butler appeared without a summons.

"Well, Hollis, I feel as though I've done a full day's work and it's not even ten o'clock," she said, gesturing toward the fruit compote, which sat on the table just beyond her reach. Without another word, Hollis hastened to serve up a bowl of the steaming fruit for her.

"I thought as much, madame," he said as he set the bowl in front of her. "It will be interesting to see what comes of this."

"Indeed," she agreed, spooning into the fruit, mildly annoyed with herself for not taking a stronger hand in things sooner.

Regardless of the silly sentiment that the best marriage matches were made in heaven, she knew better.

The best matches were made with a pinch here, a prod there—and a whole lot of pushing and pulling.

When the doorbell rang only minutes after Uncle Owen had left, Katherine thought it might be someone connected with Lily's tutor, Mrs. Evans. But the moment she heard the caller's voice, she recognized it.

A thrill dropped through her. Carson was back.

"Miss Katherine?" Mrs. D appeared in the study doorway. "You have a caller. Mr. Fairfax again."

"Please show him into the front parlor," Katherine said, trying to remain calm.

When she was certain he would be waiting for her, she went to the door, pinched her cheeks, smoothed her hair, and shook wrinkles from her skirt. This was it. In the next few minutes her fate would be decided. Either she and Lily would be looking for a new home—or by her birthday she would be Carson Fairfax's annulled bride.

She swallowed the lump of apprehension in her throat and reached for the doorknob. When she stepped into the front parlor Carson was standing in the bay window, his arms folded across his chest as he gazed out at the passing traffic.

Something strange, light, and breathless fluttered in Katherine's heart at the sight of his broad shoulders and clean, handsome profile. Whenever she was in the same room with him, she was aware of being unwillingly drawn to him. Something inside of her longed to be near him, touched by him, though instinct told her that she must not allow that. His touch would melt the reserve she'd built to protect herself from fortune hunters—like Nolan had turned out to be.

When he turned from the window, a smug smile played across his lips. "I won't waste time with preambles. I have taken time to consider your condition on the proposal I offered last night. I have come to a decision."

"So quickly?" she asked, afraid to guess what he might have decided. Nor could she imagine why he was so pleased with himself—whatever his decision.

Still smiling, he reached into his coat pocket, pulled out a half sheet of white paper, and unfolded it. With a flourish, he held it up for her to read. "Take a good look at this."

Puzzled, Katherine stared at the tall lettering on the paper: BILL OF SALE. She sucked in a startled breath. The significance of the document sent a shock and something akin to relief through her.

Heavens, he'd gone and done it.

"That's right," Carson said, studying her, his smile growing smugger by the minute. "This is the bill of sale for the Gentlemen's Respite. I found a buyer. Start making arrangements for our wedding today. There's no time to waste."

Impatiently Carson waited for Katherine to come to the full realization of what the bill of sale meant. Finally her gaze left the document and searched his face.

"Wedding?" she repeated, her voice small and unsure, her eyes wide. "Start planning today?"

"We've no time to waste," he said, taking great pleasure in her shock. He felt like he'd just called an opponent's bluff—

and won the wager of a lifetime. If she thought she could buffalo him with any more excuses or conditions, she had another thing coming.

Quickly he folded up the bill of sale and tucked it into his breast pocket. Now, a romantic gesture would be a good touch, he reminded himself. He took her by the elbows and drew her close. She yielded, her eyes still wide with astonishment.

"I won't patronize you by dropping to my knee to propose," he said. Her honeysuckle scent reached him, and she felt so soft and tempting with her body pressed against his that he almost forgot what he wanted to say. "Our marriage is a matter of practicality. But your acceptance of my plan means a great deal to me. How about a kiss to seal the bargain?"

"I suppose a kiss is appropriate," she said, her voice hesitant with confusion. Her gaze went to his mouth and she licked her lips in anticipation. The gesture stirred lust in him.

The toe of her slipper touched the instep of his boot. She stood so close, he could see the blue-green depths of her turquoise eyes. Her hands spread across the front of his shirt. The warmth of her palms seeped through the starched fabric. All of him came alive.

"It's more than appropriate," he said, his voice suddenly husky with desire. "It's required for an engagement."

Despite his intention to be deliberate and gentlemanly, he abruptly lowered his head to capture that seductive mouth of hers.

She pulled away. "Wait. Let me be sure I have this straight. You sold the Gentlemen's Respite?" she asked, still searching his face. Wonder and disbelief echoed in her voice. "The deal is final?"

"Of course," he said, guilt twitching in his heart. "I mentioned the possibility of selling the place to Jack Tremain. You know Jack. His days in the mines are finished, and he was ready to give his right arm to have a place like the Respite. So I am no longer owner of the most luxurious men's club west of the Mississippi. Jack Tremain is. Satisfied?"

"Well, yes, if Mr. Tremain is." The disbelief left her eyes. "How fortunate for all of us."

Then the sweetest, most devastating smile he'd ever seen curved Katherine's luscious lips. The warmth of her approval flooded through him like a draft of fine brandy. Certain parts of him were now on fire. "Fortunate, indeed," he murmured.

Lust threatening to turn into serious passion, he attempted to draw her close once more, but she pulled away.

"There is so much to be done," she said, gazing off into space as she crossed the room.

If she'd not been so obviously distracted, he would have thought she was teasing him. But he could see her concerns were racing ahead to wedding and Christmas preparations.

What should he have expected from his ice queen? With a rueful sigh, Carson postponed designs for a kiss. "Yes, there is much to be done. You have servants to hire. It's obvious that the Elms has been understaffed for some time. And you have those furnishings you sold to Mr. Moro to purchase back. Then there is the matter of your wardrobe, and Lily's. And the wedding."

"You know about the furnishings?" Breathless and overwhelmed, she turned to him, wide-eyed once more. "And, yes, a wedding."

"Dolly wants to have the ceremony at her house," he hurried on, wondering for the first time if not having a big wedding was going to be a problem. "It needs to be small and very private. I realize you probably hoped to have something more elaborate. But remember, Mother thinks we've been married almost a year. I have the newspaper clippings to show you later so you'll know all the details."

A change came over her face, a kind of understanding, acceptance, determination. Her eyes darkened. She pressed her lips together and nodded. "Yes, I'll do my part. And there is your portion—paying off the mortgage on the Elms and the agreement to not touch our Tucker inheritance."

"It's as good as done." His frustration was becoming more

difficult to hide, but he would never allow her to see it. "What else?"

"Lily?" she asked. "What do you propose we do about Lily?"

"She's your sister, and I will concede to handling her however you wish," he said. "Twelve may be a bit too young to understand a marriage of convenience."

"I agree." Katherine wrung her hands. "I dislike the thought of being dishonest with her, but I'm afraid she wouldn't grasp the necessity of this marriage."

"No one beyond the two of us, Dolly, and Randolph need know that we've embarked on this scheme," he began, touched by her concern for her sister but annoyed with being the means to an end. Yet wasn't he doing the same thing to Katherine? he reminded himself. "As far as Lily is concerned, I like her immensely, and I'm sure that Mother will, too. We'll do everything we can to make this a happy Christmas for her, too."

"Good," Katherine said, apparently relieved. "Then there is Uncle Owen."

"I'll take care of your uncle." He reached for her once more. This time she allowed him to draw her close, his hands on her arms, his thumbs gently rubbing the sensitive insides of her elbows. "Now, how about that kiss for your new fiancé?"

She blushed and looked away, the color rising in her cheeks. "Yes, of course, to seal our bargain."

"Precisely, to seal our bargain." Carson smiled in anticipation. *At last*, he thought. He was going to sample those luscious lips. He bent to take her mouth with his.

"Wait. There is one more thing I want to be clear about," Katherine said, pulling away—again.

Carson sucked in an impatient breath. Parts of him were absolutely tortured by now. "And that is?"

"We do understand each other about this being a marriage of convenience?" Katherine asked, gazing up at him, her eyes solemn. "It is for appearances only. Once the purpose of enter-

taining your mother is served, the union will be annulled. There-
fore there will be no, ah, we won't—there'll be no intimacy.
Am I right?''

"But we must put on a convincing front for our guests and
the rest of Denver," Carson said, unwilling to draw lines in
the sand.

"Of course, but we will not share rooms or—you know,
anything else," Katherine stammered, her gaze dropping to
study his shirtfront.

"You mean we will not sleep together," he clarified for her,
enjoying the rise of color in her cheeks. "But we will have
adjoining rooms for appearances' sake."

"Yes, for appearances' sake," she said, obviously too embarrassed to meet his gaze.

"Agreed, if that makes you feel better," he said, though he
suspected conforming to her hands-off policy might be more
difficult than she seemed to think—nature being what it was
between a man and a woman. "Now, are you ready to seal the
bargain?"

At last she looked up at him again, her gaze searching his
face for the truth.

Putting on his most charming expression, he smiled back at
her.

The hint of a smile touched her lips. "Yes, let's seal the
bargain."

She closed her eyes. He bent to take her mouth, those luscious
lips his at last. Just as his mouth was about to capture hers,
she offered her cheek. A tendril of hair tickled his nose as he
planted a sound kiss on the side of her face, just next to her
ear.

Disappointed, annoyed, and not to be thwarted, Carson
reached for her chin.

Katherine pulled free of him before he could prevent her
escape. She was stronger than he'd expected, and clearly more
determined.

"There, the bargain is sanctioned," she said, over her shoulder, from across the ten feet she'd so hastily put between them.

With more discipline than Carson had ever needed at the poker table, he forced a smile to his face. He could not afford to annoy her at this point. Not today.

"And so it is sealed," he agreed. Their bargain was near enough to the perfect solution to his problem that he would accept her terms—what was one more condition after the sale of the Respite? He could afford to be patient now.

But if, in her righteous, stiff-backed innocence, she thought to change him, had he not the right to change her, too?

Chapter Eight

Owen could hardly believe his ears. His stomach began to burn. "You want my blessing on your marriage to Katherine?"

Outraged, he rose from behind his office desk and stared at the dapper Englishman who lounged in the chair across from him.

Fairfax had called just as he was finishing his regular Monday lunch of a ham sandwich and an apple at his desk. He'd agreed to see the Englishman only out of curiosity. But with the man's shocking news, searing indigestion struck.

"Yes. I've already spoken with Dolly Green, Katherine's godmother." Fairfax calmly tapped his walking stick on the floor. "She gladly gave us her blessing. Under the circumstances, you are the only other person I know to whom I should speak about our intentions."

"On Friday, you say," Owen stammered, stalling for a few seconds to gather his wits. First Nolan Stewart had bungled things with Katherine, then disappeared, and now this. He rubbed his burning belly. "Did I hear you correctly?"

"Perhaps I was remiss in not informing you of my intentions

beforehand," Fairfax admitted without the slightest sign of contrition. "But it all happened rather quickly. I proposed on Saturday night and Katherine accepted on Sunday morning. And she is of legal age."

"But such a short engagement," Owen protested. If Katherine wasn't going to marry Stewart, he'd just as soon she remained single—at least until he could find another fool to influence her. Fairfax certainly didn't fall into that category. "Don't you think that rather unseemly?" he persisted.

"But why should we wait?" Fairfax asked innocently. "Katherine and I know what we want. Please draw up whatever papers you think necessary to protect her affairs. Or would you like for my solicitor to do it?"

That was an unexpected offer. "You're willing to sign a prenuptial agreement?" he asked, eyeing the Englishman closely. The man appeared perfectly sincere, but with Fairfax you could never be sure.

"Of course. I have no desire to take advantage of what Ben Tucker intended for his daughters to have."

"That's thoughtful of you." Owen slowly lowered himself back into his chair. The burning in his stomach subsided slightly. Perhaps not all was lost. "You know Katherine comes into the full fortune next May, when she turns twenty-five. Though there is little cash, there are a number of investments and properties involved."

"That's of little consequence to me," Fairfax said, with an astonishingly indifferent shrug. "I hope, for Katherine's sake, you will give us your blessing."

"Well, as you point out, she is of age," Owen said. "I had no idea that you and she had . . . I thought Nolan Stewart was courting her."

"Stewart has left town," Fairfax said, flicking an invisible speck of dust from his shirt cuff.

"Yes, so I heard." He looked down at the papers on his desk. He'd just heard the news himself. How did Fairfax come by it so quickly? "It was rather a surprise. Whitman Senior of

Whitman and Whitman sent word that Stewart is gone and that he himself has taken over Katherine's affairs. I'll speak to him this afternoon about drawing up an appropriate agreement. Will that do?''

"Nicely," Fairfax said, with that congenial smile of his. "I like old Whitman. A bit stodgy, but honest and incorruptible as the day is long."

"Yes, he is that." Owen studied Fairfax for a moment. Was that an indirect comment hinting that he or Nolan were corruptible?

"Is Katherine satisfied with the arrangement?" Fairfax asked, still all innocence.

"I'm sure she will be," he said, pondering the Englishman's motives. "If you have no interest in Katherine's fortune, then tell me, just what are your intentions toward her?"

"Why, to make her happy, of course," Fairfax said, obviously surprised by Owen's ridiculous question. "Isn't that what every husband intends to do for his bride?"

"Yes, I suppose so," he replied, sorry he'd asked. He busied himself with the documents on his desk. "I'll send word to Whitman and Whitman right away. The papers will be ready to sign on Friday morning."

"Splendid," Fairfax said, rising from the chair and extending his hand across the desk. "And your blessing?"

"Ah, well, yes, of course you have it," Owen said, rising again, his belly burning worse than ever. What else could he do? Katherine was of age. But this made a shambles of his and Ray's plans for the Amanda Leigh. "You just took me by surprise, you know. I'd never thought of Katherine with anyone but Stewart."

"Thank you for your blessing." Fairfax gave his hand a firm shake. "I'm a bit surprised by all of this myself."

The day of Katherine's wedding dawned fair but bitter cold. She stood in front of Dolly's mirror gazing at herself dressed in her favorite pale blue and ivory lace ball gown, altered to be a wedding dress, and holding her bridal bouquet of red and ivory roses. She appeared surprisingly rested, considering the succession of business meetings she'd been required to attend to square away the legal arrangements—and the shopping and fittings to prepare for the wedding.

Miraculously the seamstress had even managed to find matching lace to turn into a lovely veil. The vision created by gown and veil was feminine and demure. She liked it—except for the bright vitality of her red rose bouquet.

"Red roses for a bride?" She cast a questioning gaze at Dolly, who'd been a world of help throughout the meetings and preparations. "Shouldn't a bride carry white flowers?"

"A bride should carry whatever color flowers her groom sends," Dolly said, smiling and stepping up behind her to admire her reflection and to adjust the veil. "They do complement your dress. You look lovely, Katherine. There's nothing wrong with red roses. They stand for passion, you know. How like Carson to choose them for his bride."

Dolly was right, she decided. The vibrant roses did set off the soft blue and ivory of her gown. She'd discovered in the last few days that Carson had an uncannily accurate sense of what she looked good in. But why should he choose red roses for her? she wondered. There was no passion between them, and even the thought of it frightened her. Of course, Dolly didn't need to know that.

"The roses remind me that we must have our talk," Dolly said, putting the last touches on the veil. "We have a few minutes yet before we need to go downstairs. Sit down, Katherine."

"What talk?" she wondered aloud as she sat on a cushioned stool to avoid wrinkling her gown.

"I wish your mother was here." Dolly drew up a chair and sat down in front of her. "Not just because I don't know how to do this, but because I know she would love to see what a beautiful bride you are. However, because she can't be here, and we were friends, it is my place to explain to you about the duties of a wife.''

"I know how to run a house," Katherine said. She and Mrs. Dodd had already planned where Carson would sleep and how his shaving things should be arranged. "I've been running the Elms for years. I'm sure I can make Carson comfortable there."

"No, my dear, I don't mean just household duties," Dolly said, smiling gently. "Of course you can run the Elms well. I'm talking about what is going to happen between you and Carson when you go to bed tonight."

Katherine's back stiffened. Nothing was going to happen between her and Carson tonight, but that didn't keep embarrassment from burning in her cheeks.

"I know all about that, too," she said to forestall any further awkward conversation.

When she was twelve, her mother had told her about where babies came from. By then she'd already come to suspect some of what her mother had explained, but the facts, the visions it brought to mind, had outraged her. Her mother had smiled understandingly. But Katherine had run out of the house, vowing she'd never let a boy do that to her. Even for a baby. Put his . . . where . . . it didn't even bear contemplation.

As she'd grown older, as she'd observed young, happily married couples together, as she'd begun to observe her own mother and father more closely, she'd begun to think there might be something pleasant about the process. Something not obvious to the people outside the relationship. Still . . . she and Carson? No. Never!

"You must forget all about Nolan Stewart," Dolly continued. "It was a terrible experience. What happened to you with him is not to be compared to what you will have with Carson. I'm sure you've noticed he is a handsome man. A man of some experience—not a libertine, but a man of the world. I suspect you will find him a thoughtful, yet an exciting lover."

"I'm sure we will manage very well," she said, gazing

toward the window. She'd heard enough. Already she'd discovered the unsettling difference between Carson and Nolan.

Carson's nearness did things to her that Nolan's presence had never done. His mere closeness could make her skin feel alive in a way it had never felt before, tingly and sensitive to the slightest stirring. Even the touch of his breath when he bent near to speak to her in their business meetings could bring all of her to life—from the roots of her hair down to her little toe.

But she and Carson were not going to share a bed.

"With the right man, it is a beautiful experience," Dolly said. "Sometimes there is a little pain at first, but it will go away."

Pain? She abruptly rose to her feet. "Really, Dolly, this isn't necessary."

"You should know these things," her godmother said firmly. She grasped Katherine's wrist and pulled her down on the stool again. "There are those women who think a wife's duty should *not* be enjoyable. I think they're misguided prudes myself. Or perhaps their husbands are careless. Bill and I used to have a great time in bed, and I think your parents found pleasure there, too."

The heat in Katherine's face burned all the hotter. She definitely did not want to hear this.

"In any case, there's no reason for the marriage bed to be less than a thoroughly delightful place your first night together and for a lifetime of nights to come. Just follow your instincts and have faith in Carson."

"I shall make Carson a very good wife," she vowed, in an effort to reassure Dolly that all would be well.

"I know you will." Dolly reached out and took her hand. "And he will make you a good husband. But if you need anything, you come to me."

She nodded, eager to bring the discussion to an end. "Now, I think it's time we went downstairs."

At the foot of the stairs, Uncle Owen was waiting for her. As he offered his arm, she peered into the parlor, where she could see Cornish Jack Tremain and several other gentlemen she did not recognize sitting on the groom's side of the "aisle." Mrs. D, Lily, Aunt Edna, and Opal Shaw were seated where Mama would have sat if she'd lived to see this day—and it was probably best that she hadn't.

Butterflies still fluttered in her belly every time she reminded herself that she was to be given in a marriage of convenience to a saloonkeeper. It was not what every girl dreamed of—but she'd make the best of it.

"It's not too late to call this off," Uncle Owen whispered into her ear as if he'd overheard her thoughts. "Just say the word and I'll take you right out the front door and you won't even have to face Fairfax."

But it was too late for that. At the end of the aisle stood Reverend Blake and Carson, with Randolph standing up as his best man. Around them stood basket after basket of red and ivory roses. Where on earth had the man found all those flowers in November?

"You've already given us your blessing, Uncle Owen," she protested.

Carson met her gaze, smiling that incorrigible grin that was almost enough to make her believe they'd enjoyed a courtship and engagement during the past week instead of a rapid succession of business meetings and planning sessions. He'd been a great help to her as she and Uncle Owen waded through the financial details of the mortgage on the Elms. How could she back out on him now?

"Yes, but what was I to do?" he said, speaking softly. "You are of age. However, I've done some investigating myself, my dear. Fairfax owns a large part of two mines, the Aztec and the Summit. And Cornish Jack—did you know he's known as the best gold bloodhound and mining engineer in all the Rockies? Are you sure of the Englishman's intentions?"

The news jolted her. While Carson had been meticulous in his review of her affairs, he'd told her little of his. She glanced toward him at the end of the aisle again. Did he want something more from her than hospitality for his mother?

She shook her head. "He signed an agreement to touch nothing of mine or Lily's. What more do you expect of him, Uncle Owen?"

He gave a long weary sigh. "If you have any problems, Katherine, you must come to me and Edna. You're like our own. You and Lily. Feel free to come to us for help."

"Thank you, Uncle Owen."

"I do so love a wedding," Dolly whispered, bustling up from behind. She edged around them, the taffeta of her green ball gown rustling as she turned to take Katherine's hands in hers. "Do stow that frown, Owen. Katherine makes a beautiful bride and Carson is a fine bridegroom. And you should be grinning like an idiot for having the privilege to give this gorgeous lady away on her wedding day."

"Katherine, your hands are freezing," Dolly exclaimed with dismay. "But perfectly natural for a bride. Everything is going exactly as it should. Don't fret over a thing, dear. Here we go."

With the first notes of the wedding march she was off, marching down the imaginary aisle behind Dolly, who paraded with all the pomp of a matron of honor at a royal wedding. Her green silk taffeta whispered across the carpet and her five-strand pearl choker glowed pink in the wintry sunlight.

Thankfully, Uncle Owen said no more. Katherine concentrated on walking steadily with her head up and her gaze on the reverend.

Mama and Papa, how I wish you were here. How I wish it was your arm, Papa, that steadies me as I march down the aisle. How I wish this was my real wedding and the man standing next to Reverend Blake was the man I love.

She bit her lip but did not succumb to the tears of self-pity that ached in her throat. She had accepted that for her such stuff as a love match and a big wedding existed only in fairy tales.

In the real world it was better to be practical than romantic—and homeless.

A movement at the reverend's side made Katherine look at Carson. He smiled at her again—an encouraging smile.

A sense of the surreal overwhelmed her. He was incredibly handsome in his black formal clothes, a bride's dream of a groom. She noted for the first time that his boutonniere was a red rose like the ones in the bridal bouquet he'd sent for her.

As soon as they reached the corner of the room where Reverend Blake and Carson stood, the organ music subsided.

In the hush, the reverend opened his book and began the ceremony, his voice clear and distinct to all. But from the moment that Uncle Owen placed her hand in Carson's, she heard little.

When his large, graceful fingers engulfed hers, she looked up into his face and forgot everything that was going on around her. Uncle Owen's warnings and misgivings evaporated. Reverend Blake's droning held no meaning. She was only barely aware of Mrs. D's sobs and Aunt Edna's sniffling.

Carson's dark-eyed gaze held hers transfixed, sending a message of confidence and pleasure. Relief flooded through her. Why couldn't they make this work? Carson wanted success as much as she did—if for different reasons.

They could make a triumph of this marriage. That was the thought in her head—and her heart—as Carson slipped the most beautiful wedding band she'd ever seen on her finger: an intricately worked circle of ivy leaves crafted of three shades of gold and studded with tiny white diamonds.

It fit perfectly. The design suited her small hand, just as superbly as the red and white roses complemented her dress. The perfection of it all almost frightened her. Surreality whirled through her head once more, whispering that all this was ordained somewhere in a sacred book. With the ring on her finger, she'd committed herself to a destiny she'd never desired but had been fashioned for her nonetheless.

"I now pronounce you husband and wife," Reverend Blake

announced, snapping his prayer book closed with a finality that made her blood run cold.

"You may kiss the bride," the reverend added.

Still numb, Katherine allowed Carson to turn her toward him. But she couldn't bring herself to look into his eyes. What had she done by agreeing to this outlandish scheme?

"There's no escaping this time," Carson murmured, lifting the veil away from her face, then putting a finger under her chin. "We must make a good show for our wedding guests."

She glanced up at him, suddenly thinking of the things they had not settled in the last three days—such as their honeymoon. What would she call his mother? Would they breakfast together? How much starch did he want in his shirts? Was he an early riser or a night owl? So much to learn.

"Is the thought of kissing your bridegroom so daunting?" His grin twisted with sarcasm. She realized she'd disappointed him already. "Playact, sweetheart, if you must," he urged, "like you do in your theatricals."

She could do that. She lifted her lips to his and closed her eyes. A fiery blush stained her cheeks—probably as red as the roses. She could feel every eye in the room on them. Bracing herself, she prepared to appear to accept his husbandly kiss with the eagerness of a new bride.

But nothing could have readied her for Carson's assault. He slipped a hand around the back of her head, angling her mouth so that when his descended on hers she could not oppose him. When his tongue invaded her mouth, she froze instantly, shocked by the intimacy but powerless to resist. Did married people kiss like this—so deeply, so suggestively?

Sensations of shock and shame battled with a fiery, sweet heat that made her offer her mouth for more. Carson took it, a soft sigh of satisfaction growling deep inside him.

She leaned into him, vaguely aware of slipping her arms around his middle. Her heart beat frantically. She stretched up on her tiptoes, pressing her mouth against his, suddenly afraid that he would take this new, wondrous experience from her. He went deeper.

"Ahmm," Reverend Blake said, over the murmurings of the other guests. "Ahmmm. It's always a joy to bring a happy couple together in holy matrimony. Excuse me. Carson. Katherine. Don't forget your guests."

Just as the reverend placed a hand on her shoulder, Carson released her. Breathless, her lips moist, tingling, throbbing, she turned to their guests, her cheeks aflame with embarrassment—and something more—pleasure? She studied the carpet as Carson slipped an arm around her waist and pulled her against his side.

"Ladies and gentlemen," the reverend said, pride—and relief—in his voice, "may I present Mr. and Mrs. Carson Fairfax."

Laughter and applause echoed throughout Dolly's drawing room.

"Sweetheart, I think we're going to make a very good job of this," he murmured into her ear.

Katherine forced a smile to her lips despite her mortification. But, to her surprise, everyone was grinning as though they'd thoroughly enjoyed the display. Anything less would have been a disappointment. Why should she feel flustered? No one else did. The tightness inside her eased.

Then she saw Uncle Owen at the back of the drawing room. Amid the laughter and good wishes, he stood apart from the wedding guests, his brows drawn together into a single bushy white line, his mouth turned down in a bitter frown.

Chapter Nine

"People will expect to see us kiss from time to time," Carson said, unsurprised at being taken to task by his new bride for their wedding kiss. Katherine sat frowning at him from across the carriage.

Try as he might, he couldn't wipe the smile off his face. In the past she had always felt perfect in his arms when they had danced. Today, during the kiss, the feel of her against him had been just as satisfying. He'd thoroughly enjoyed their first real physical intimacy. And he suspected—with great pleasure— from her inexperienced response that she'd never been kissed like that before. What's more, he suspected there were other intimacies she'd never partaken of. If she responded to those as hotly as she'd responded to his kiss—well ... "We're newlyweds, Katherine. People will think it strange if we don't—what is that charming term? Spoon? I must say, you didn't seem to mind it at the time."

"Well, you don't see respectable couples doing that in public," Katherine said, turning to gaze out the window as Willis drove them toward the Elms.

The afternoon had ended with a champagne toast made by Dolly and a full tea. No dancing. No games. No tossing of the bride's bouquet or any number of other quaint customs that went along with a big wedding.

Carson studied his bride and thought about moving to sit beside her, a gambit to encourage a bit more spooning, but decided against it. He would be satisfied with the wedding kiss for today. From now on they would be sharing a house. No need to rush anything. All in all, he was pleased with the bargain they'd made. He hoped that someday she would be, too.

"Do you think Mr. Tremain and Mrs. Dodd will have gotten everything moved into the house?" she asked, still gazing out the window.

"They only left Dolly's an hour ago," Carson reminded her, wondering what she was going to think about the things Jack had moved into the Elms. Everything had happened so fast, there had been little time to warn her about the goods she would have to accept as though she'd lived with them for a year.

And there would be the adjusting he must do also, he reminded himself as he studied his bride. She stared pensively out the window, solemn, absorbed in thought, lovely—but without the glow one expected to find on a bride's face.

"I'm sorry there wasn't time for a big wedding," he said, longing to ease the pang of guilt that dragged at his conscience. He'd robbed Katherine of the thrill of a lavish society wedding—like the one Randolph had reported for the newspaper.

Strange how weddings were important to women. He remembered the disappointment his mother had written of. She'd been terribly sad about being unable to take part in his fictitious nuptials. "A splendid wedding is what every young woman dreams of, is it not, Katherine?"

"Not necessarily." She shook her head. Perhaps she did not glow like a bride, but she truly did not look disappointed. "It was a lovely ceremony, and Lily and our friends were there. That's what is important."

"I'm relieved you feel that way," he said, studying her more closely. "But it would have pleased me immensely to have waltzed you around in front of that blackguard, Nolan Stewart."

A small smile pulled at Katherine's mouth as she met his gaze, her eyes twinkling with mischief. "Yes, I admit that would have been satisfying. You know, I haven't heard from him since I sent that letter of dismissal to him. He never sent an apology. He didn't even call and leave a card. Nothing."

"I don't think he will be troubling you anymore," Carson said, feeling no need to go into the details.

They fell silent again as the carriage turned into the drive. Katherine looked out the window again, then gave a small gasp of dismay.

"What is it?" he asked, wondering what Jack might have left sitting on the front porch that might startle her.

"Mrs. Dodd, Lily, Jack Tremain, and all the staff are gathered on the porch to greet us," Katherine said. "They look so innocent and happy for us."

"Nothing surprising about that," he said, wondering why she was troubled. "This is as much a celebration for the staff as it is for us."

"I don't know if I can do this." Katherine frowned and shrank back against the coach seat. "I'm sorry. Maybe I'm not as good an actress as I thought I was. Deceiving innocent people like Mrs. D and Willis upsets me. Doesn't it bother you?"

"We are playacting, Katherine. Nothing about what we are doing harms anyone," Carson said warily. He'd wondered how her proper, Ladies' Moderation League conscience was going to deal with duplicity. She'd been doing well up until now. "As far as the staff goes, they all have jobs in one of the most prestigious houses in the city. Our getting married is the best thing that has happened to them in months. Be glad for them, Katherine, and show it."

"Of course you're right," she said, taking a deep breath.

Carson watched with amazement as she composed her face into an expression of soft happiness. The transformation was amazing. While her new countenance hardly glowed like a bride's, it would do.

He smiled at her. "Perfect, Mrs. Fairfax."

When the carriage pulled up to the front steps, he alighted, then turned to help her out. She was smiling as graciously as he could hope for. He took her arm and escorted her up the steps. The servants cheered and threw flower petals in their path. Lily's idea, he suspected.

Katherine smiled throughout the ordeal, shaking the new servants' hands and thanking them for the welcome. Grinning, Carson doffed his bowler and offered them a lordly bow, a gesture he knew impressed without fail. When he was certain that every individual had been greeted, he led Katherine toward the threshold of the Elms.

The door stood open for them already. He handed his hat to Mrs. Dodd and took Katherine's hand from his sleeve. She looked up at him in confusion. Aware that she did not comprehend what he was doing, he took advantage of the moment and swiftly leaned down to swoop her up in his arms.

The instant his hand reached behind her knees, she squealed in surprise and struggled against him. "What are you doing? Put me down."

He laughed. "I'm carrying my bride over the threshold. Isn't that what a bridegroom is supposed to do?"

He glanced around at the servants for their opinion. Katherine ceased her struggles long enough to peer over his shoulder at Mrs. Dodd.

"Yes, that's just what a bridegroom is supposed to do, Mr. Fairfax," the housekeeper said, nodding in grave approval. She was going to be a tough old bird to win over, Carson thought, but he could see growing respect in her eyes. "Just carry Miss Katherine right on into the house. That's as it should be."

Apparently at a loss for arguments, Katherine slipped her arms around his neck and glared at him. "I suppose this is part of the show, too?"

"Of course." Carson strode across the threshold into the

Elms. He paused in the hallway, turning slowly to admire the gleaming walnut stairway that stretched up to the third story of the house. And as he did so, he took pleasure in the pressure of Katherine's body against his and in her honeysuckle scent. He even liked the way her arms rested on his shoulders. "Care to kiss me now?"

"Not a kiss like the last one," Katherine whispered, casting a furtive glance over his shoulder at the servants once more.

"A wifely peck on the cheek then," Carson countered.

"All right." She brushed her lips against his cheek. "There." The servants applauded.

He set her down reluctantly. Mrs. Dodd bustled forward to take their wraps, fussing over them like a mother hen.

Carson gazed around the hallway once more, pleased to see that the Elms was just as grand as he remembered. Mrs. Dodd had put the new staff to work already. He could smell the lemon oil and the beeswax. The dark wood of the stairway gleamed rich and warm. The parquet floor was polished to a high shine. The sparkling glass gaslight chandelier hanging from the third floor cast welcoming rainbows of light. Perfect. No wonder Katherine would do almost anything to hang on to the place, Carson thought, turning to admire his bride as well.

Everything about her was right, too: from the lace-covered swell of her breasts to the elegant line of her throat right up to the pearl teardrops dangling from her ears.

His body warmed at the sight.

Things were working out very nicely. Very nicely indeed. He smiled at Katherine. Taking her hand, he led her toward the crackling fire he'd glimpsed burning in the family parlor. "We are home at last, Mrs. Fairfax. Home at last."

After supper, at Mrs. Dodd's urging, Katherine took her first look at the things Jack Tremain had moved into the Elms.

"I've unpacked the boxes in the dining room," the housekeeper said, stacking dirty supper dishes on her tray. "Everything is laid out in there."

She had set Katherine and Carson's supper table in the family parlor for a "cozy" dinner that had been a blessing to Katherine after the hustle and bustle of arranging a wedding in three days. She just wanted to relax. Carson seemed to enjoy the informality, too.

The house was quiet. The other servants had been given the weekend off. Lily had been bustled out the door to spend the weekend with her tutor, Mrs. Evans, an outing thoughtfully arranged by Mrs. Dodd. Upon hearing of the plans, Katherine had protested that there was no need for Lily to leave. But Lily was excited about the prospect of a weekend out. Then she realized the kindhearted women thought of this time as a honeymoon for herself and Carson. Unable to explain otherwise—and unwilling to disappoint Lily—she'd given in.

"I don't know why it's necessary for us to look at these things now." She glanced across the table at Carson, wondering for the first time what a bachelor would have to move into the Elms. Without answering her, he rose from the table and went to put another log on the fire. "What did you bring other than your clothes and a razor?"

He turned, wearing that poker-table face of his. "Let's see, shall we?"

His expression should have warned her she was in for a surprise. When she reached the dining room door the gleam of silver nearly blinded her.

"What's this?" she asked, staring at the gigantic tea service on the sideboard.

Though daylight was fading outside, gaslight from the chandelier reflected off the silver vessels brightening the room almost as well as sunlight. The size of the set left her nearly speechless. She'd never seen anything like it in design, brilliance, or craftsmanship.

A glimmer from the dining room table caught her eye. She turned to stare. Sterling silver flatware, shiny and bright, lay on the dark mahogany wood. Dozens of Venetian crystal stems gleamed. Wedgwood china that would be the envy of every Denver matron was set in stack after stack of dinner plates, soup plates, cups, and saucers, bowls, tureens, platters, gravy boats, silver baskets for cut-glass cruets, preserve dishes, salt cellars, demitasse cups and spoons. Epergnes and vases, silver wine buckets, glass dumbbell-shaped knife rests, butter dishes, and silver egg stands. Mother-of-pearl-handled cutlery, silver tongs, pointed jelly spoons, and an array of silver ladles each for a special sauce or gravy.

"Did I mention that Mother sent us a few things?" Carson asked.

She could only stare. Papa hadn't struck it rich until she was eight years old—before Lily was born. She remembered well living in a two-room house in Georgetown through long, cold Colorado winters. She recalled vividly days before there was a bathroom in the house, before gaslights or coal-burning fire-places. She remembered breaking ice in the washbasin, sweeping bare floors, and setting a table covered with a threadbare theatrical cape of Mother's for a cloth and with tin plates and forks for dinner service and glass jars for crystal.

"There are table linens, too." Mrs. D joined Katherine and Carson in the doorway. "Irish linen. Belgium lace. Damask. Anything you can think of."

Katherine turned to Carson. "A few things?"

"Did I mention that Mother never does things by half?" Carson added. "All this has been packed away at the Respite since it arrived. Jack had one of the girls polish the tea service for us. It might be a good idea to use it when Mother is here."

"Did I write your mother a thank-you note?" she asked, still overwhelmed by the sheer magnitude of the gifts bestowed on her husband's bride. She was beginning to understand that there was a role already in existence that she had to fill.

"Yes, a lovely one, thanks to Dolly," Carson said, giving her shoulders a reassuring squeeze.

"It's beautiful, isn't it?" A look of pride glowed in Mrs.

D's eye as if the treasure was her own. "I've never seen the likes of that Greek key pattern. And look here."

Mrs. D entered the dining room, her firm footsteps setting the china and crystal on the table to dancing. She pointed to the letters entwined on each vessel of the set: the teapot, the hot water pot, the coffee pot, the chocolate pot, the creamer, the sugar bowl, the sugar tongs, and so on. All wore a *C* and a *K* entwined. "Your initials. Isn't it lovely?"

"But how——?" Dumbfounded by the intricately worked initials, Katherine followed Mrs. D. into the room. How could this be? All these things were engraved with *C* and *K*. She felt as though she was seeing her name on gifts meant for another woman. It was like peeking at someone else's life. Like infringing on someone's place in the world.

An eerie shiver coursed through her. "Set out dessert for us in the parlor, Mrs. D, while I look over the new things."

As soon as Mrs. D was out of the room, she turned to Carson. "How did your mother know your bride's name when there'd never been such a person?"

Carson casually shoved his hands into his pockets and leaned against the doorjamb. "She thinks your name is Kitty."

"Kitty?" she exclaimed, surprised to hear her father's nickname for her on Carson's lips. She'd never cared for the name except when her father used it. "*How unrefined.* Kitty! Like a dance-hall girl."

He never blinked. "It might have been worse. I could have named you Lucky."

"Would you care to explain how you came up with that?" she asked, folding her arms across her breasts. "Seeing as how you had no idea that we would be married."

"It's a long st——" Carson began.

At that moment a huge black blur appeared out of nowhere. It flew through the air and landed on the table beside her. Startled, she gasped and jumped back, bumping into the sideboard. The silver service clattered.

Perched on the edge of the table sat a huge black cat with

enormous blue eyes. It regarded Katherine with unblinking solemnity. Around it on the table silver rattled and crystal chimed.

Quietly Carson stepped into the room. "May I introduce Lucky? Don't say anything. Don't startle him."

His warning was unnecessary.

Speechless with surprise, she stared at the aristocratic feline. It was almost as big as Max, Lily's dog. He'd gone with his mistress for the weekend.

With a blink, the cat dismissed her, swiveling his head to study the table full of gleaming glassware and china. With his tail switching regally, the tom began to stroll the length of the table. His long back formed a sensuous *S*, first in one direction, then in the opposite one. His enormous paws adroitly picked their way through the shining flatware and the delicate crystal.

"Carson? Do something," she hissed. "Before . . . before . . ."

"Don't alarm him," Carson repeated. Neither of them took their eyes from the cat. "He's just showing off. Aren't you impressed?"

"No," Katherine managed to squeak.

Expensive Wedgwood chattered faintly. Costly glassware shimmered. Priceless silver rang—ever so softly. The cat's back twisted as he prowled—forever—from one end of the mahogany table to the other.

Unfamiliar with cats, Katherine could only watch in helpless silence. If either of them startled the feline, he might send crystal and china shattering to the floor.

The instant Lucky reached the far edge of the table, Carson swept the tom up and released him on the floor. "Sorry, old boy. This is the Elms. New house rules. No table walking."

The cat meowed, rubbed himself gently against her skirts as if he didn't mind the reprimand in the least, then stalked out of the room, clearly headed for more adventure.

"He likes you," Carson observed.

"A cat?" she cried, still mired in the disbelief of all the new and strange things in her house. "You didn't tell me about a cat. What kind of gambler has a black cat?"

"An unsuperstitious one," Carson said with a shrug. "But Jack takes it seriously. He refused to keep Lucky at the Respite. You're not superstitious, are you?"

"No, I'm not, but—" she began, suddenly thinking of additional complications the cat would create. "Lily's dog is going to love this. I won't have her upset by any Max versus Lucky squabbles."

"It'll never be a problem." Carson held up his right hand as if he was swearing an oath. "I promise. As soon as Lily and Max get back, I'll introduce the two animals myself. Lucky is very tolerant of other creatures."

"Wonderful." She flopped her arms at her sides, feeling defeated and beleaguered. "First I'm supposed to give up my Christian name—as well as my surname. My dining room is full of more china, crystal, and silver than we'll ever have room to store. Then a black cat invades. What else am I to discover?"

"Come now, the name Kitty is not as bad as that," Carson said, stepping closer to put an arm around her shoulders. "With a name like Katherine and your delicate features, someone must have called you Kitty at some time."

This time she bristled, fighting back tears. She pulled away from him. Even after two years, sometimes the pain of losing Papa descended on her when she least expected it. "If you must know, Papa called me Kitty. It was his special name for me and I've never permitted anyone else the privilege of using it."

"Ah." His smile disappeared, and he let his arm drop away from her. "I've trod into personal territory. I'm sorry. Would you prefer I call you Katherine?"

"Right now Mrs. Fairfax will do," she quipped, knowing she sounded petty and childish. She suddenly was as angry with Papa as she was Carson. If Papa was still here, none of this would be happening.

Carson made no protest. She could feel him studying her for

a long moment. "At an appropriate moment after Mother has arrived, I'll explain to her that Kitty is a very personal nickname and that you'd rather be called Katherine."

Ridiculous relief swept over her. His unexpected thoughtfulness only made her more tearful. She suddenly felt silly for showing such temper over a nickname. A tear slipped down her cheek. Swiftly she brushed it away. "I would appreciate that very much. That's very kind of you."

"Think nothing of it." Carson slipped his arm around her again and pulled her close. She allowed it this time, his nearness in the cold fall twilight oddly familiar and warming. "Now, let's have some of that dessert Mrs. Dodd has set out for us. And maybe a little more champagne. Then you can tell me which of the books on the parlor bookshelves you've read."

Katherine agreed, outwardly allowing him to distract her. But inwardly she could not shake the otherworldly sense that she'd somehow mistakenly stepped into another woman's life—the feeling inspired by the sight of the *C* and *K* entwined on the silver tea service. It hung over her, dark and sad, like a shadow.

How on earth was she ever going to fulfill her part of this bargain?

Chapter Ten

Over their wedding cake dessert, Carson entertained her with amusing stories about growing up in the English countryside: of sunny days playing mock polo games, rainy days playing card games with the grooms, and winter days skating on the ice of a nearby pond—usually with his brothers, John and Neville. It seemed like a happy enough childhood. At least he made it sound so. He spoke in a soothing voice and without seeming to expect any more from her than a laugh or a question.

"Am I boring you with my boyhood stories?" he asked at one point, smiling across the table at her.

"No, not at all." Katherine was quick to protest, eager to postpone going upstairs as long as possible. Though he was talking about himself, she did not believe he was thinking only of himself. Whenever their gazes met, she saw the watchful gleam in his eyes. "I know so little about you, it's nice to hear about you and your brothers."

He seemed satisfied with her reply and went on.

After another flute of champagne she relaxed, sinking deeper into her chair. The uncomfortable feeling that she was living another woman's life quieted. And she noted thankfully that Carson made no attempt to play the newlywed husband. He made no romantic speeches or gestures. The kiss at the wedding seemed to have satisfied him.

Regarding him over the edge of her champagne flute, she couldn't resist a smile. The man could be perfectly charming when he wanted to be. As he recalled his boyhood, he told the stories with animated expressions. She prayed he would never stop. Because when he did, they were going to have to go upstairs—together. Even if they had agreed that the marriage would be in name only, the situation was going to be awkward.

Perhaps they'd agreed that they would not share a room. But, as she studied Carson from beneath her lowered lashes, she couldn't help but notice how masculine he was. Refined, yet all male, strong, confident in every word and gesture. She'd liked the strength she'd felt in his arms when he'd carried her over the doorstep—and the scent of him. When he'd put his arm around her in the dining room, he smelled of spice and soap. And his wedding kiss—it hadn't felt like playacting to her.

Dolly hadn't mentioned it, but her friends whispered that men had urges, needs that they could barely control. Like Nolan in the buggy that night. Assaulting hands everywhere, bruising her. If she closed her eyes, she could still feel Nolan's fingers clawing up her thigh. But that had happened days ago. She was safe now.

And Carson was a gentleman. He could control his urges, couldn't he? His voice was so deep and soothing . . . and the fire was so warm . . . and the champagne made such a soft hum in her veins . . .

Suddenly the heat of Carson's hand engulfed hers.

"Here, let me have that," he was saying, slipping the champagne glass from her fingers just before she dropped it.

Mortified, she started and pulled herself up in the chair. "Gracious, I fell asleep. I'm so sorry." She glanced around the parlor, assuring herself that she was really quite safe. But the guilt of falling asleep—and of doubting him—made her heart hammer in her chest.

"It's time we go upstairs." Carson set the glass on the table and rose to bank the fire. "It's been a long day. And here I am boring you with old childhood memories."

"No, that's all right," she babbled, desperate to forestall the inevitable. "I mean, I'm sorry. Your stories aren't boring at all. I just—the champagne, you know. I'd love to hear another. Really I would."

"You're exhausted, Mrs. Fairfax." Carson took her hands and pulled her up from the chair. "You need your rest. We have a busy schedule ahead of us the next few weeks. We must be seen everywhere in Denver so that society is quite accustomed to thinking of us as a couple by the time Mother arrives."

"Yes, I know," she said. The four of them, she, Carson, Dolly, and Randolph, had planned a campaign of social rounds. "I hope this plan works."

"It will." Carson turned off the gaslight, then took Katherine's hand and led her toward the stairs.

As she walked, her head cleared enough for her to realize that they were on their way up the stairs—on their way to the bedrooms. With the proprietary air of the lord of the house, Carson turned off each gas jet as they passed it. (Mrs. Dodd had excused herself after serving dessert and Carson had promised that he and Katherine would see to turning out the lights for the night.)

"Your things should all be in Papa's room," she said, still overcome by the urge to babble. She fought it and failed. "I'm next door in Mama's room. I moved in there about a year ago. Their rooms are the nicest in the house. I think you'll be comfortable."

"I'm sure the room will be quite satisfactory." Carson seemed unconcerned.

Katherine continued to chatter, much to her dismay. "Papa's bed might be a little short for you."

She snapped her mouth shut, almost biting her tongue. Carson had no need to know that Papa's longer, custom-made bed had been moved into Mama's room years ago because Papa never slept in his room. He always slept with Mama. Occupying two bedrooms was just for proper appearances. Katherine had forgotten about the bed until now.

"I'm sure your father's bed will be adequate," Carson was saying as they reached the door of her room first.

She paused. What now? She didn't recall any lesson at finishing school that covered this situation. But it hardly seemed hospitable just to walk into her room and shut the door in Carson's face, leaving him to fend for himself. "Why don't I show you Papa's room first?"

She stepped to the next door and opened it, leading the way. Carson followed.

"See, quite spacious." She gestured to the room with a sweep of her hand. Mama had decorated it in masculine shades of burgundy and forest green. Beside the bed sat a green leather reading chair next to a table and lamp in the bay window. A pair of deep red velvet chairs flanked the black marble hearth, where a fire burned.

"Your shaving things are here," she observed when she saw his razor, brush, soap, and mug on the washstand by the window. So Mrs. D had indeed moved him in. "The sunlight is good there. That's why Papa kept his shaving mirror on that side of the room. And—what—?"

The sight of Lucky curled in the middle of Papa's bed as if the cat slept there every night brought her to a halt. "How'd he get in here?"

"Lucky seems to have made himself at home, hasn't he?" Carson ambled into the room, surveying the chamber from floor to ceiling with the air of a new owner. The presumption annoyed her—even frightened her a little. She glanced at him, suddenly seeing a stranger who'd moved into her house.

"I shall be quite cozy in here. And you'll be next door, all snug in your bed."

The mention of the sleeping arrangements made her cheeks burn anew. She grew even more vexed, this time with herself for being so easily embarrassed. "Yes, I'll be right over there."

She gestured to the door between the adjoining rooms, but she couldn't bring herself to open it.

Carson walked across the room and threw open the door, sauntering into her room as if he had every right to—as if he was her husband.

She swallowed her gasp—a stranger in her room—and hurried after him. "My room is just like yours."

He stood in the center of the carpet. "So I see. The mirror image of your father's room."

"Yes," she said, wringing her hands and praying that her undergarments were tucked away and out of sight. Husband or not, he was trespassing on her private domain—and the intrusion distressed her.

"I see Mrs. Dodd unpacked some things in here, too." He gestured toward the bed.

"She did?" She followed his gaze. Spread across her chintz counterpane was a white silk nightgown and peignoir so diaphanous, she could see the floral print of the chintz pattern through it.

"Really, sir." Embarrassed, she clasped her hands before her. A blush flamed in her cheeks once more. "I think you assume too much."

"It's a gift from Mother," he said simply. The twist of his smile made it clear he was enjoying her discomfiture. "I would be remiss not to see that you received a gift sent by your mother-in-law, would I not?"

"Yes, I suppose so," she stammered. What kind of countess, a white-haired, aristocratic lady with delicate sensibilities, sent a nightgown to her daughter-in-law? "You must admit it is an unusual gift for a bride from a mother-in-law."

"Mother can be a bit unconventional," he said, reaching for the gown. "So you see, I come by it honestly."

Then he held up the garment to her, as if judging whether

it would fit or not. Light streamed through the silk. Her wedding veil had been more demure. "I'm afraid Mother is eager for more grandchildren."

"Surely your brothers have provided—"

"Yes, of course." He waved a hand in the air as his smile became a bit devilish. "Three little Fairfaxes between the two of them, I believe. And Mother is quite pleased, too. But she seems to think the more the merrier. But don't let her urging trouble you. I don't."

"I won't." Katherine pressed her lips together in distaste. The varlet was enjoying her embarrassment. He was even playing on it. "But I shall make a point to thank her for the gown."

"And so shall I." Carson chuckled, still holding the garment up between them, eyeing it in a way that made her feel naked and exposed—vulnerable. "Does this embarrass you?" he asked. "You Yankees have the strangest notions of love and romance. So, ah, puritanical. Unresolved. Contradictory."

Cheeks burning with mortification, she snatched the gown from his hands. "Perhaps so, but we Yankees do have a sense of modesty."

Swiftly she turned her back to him, folded up the gown, and stuffed it into the dresser. The minute the drawer thudded closed, she felt safer.

Wondering if he knew how unsettled she was, she stole a glimpse at him in the dresser mirror. He was eyeing the bed. She forgot the gown. Drat, he wasn't going to notice that it was longer than his, was he? "Now, if you'll excuse me, Mr. Fairfax . . ."

"Yes, of course." Carson moved toward the door. "Get a good night's rest. I want my bride to look happy and satisfied in the morning."

Unable to think of an appropriate reply, she followed him toward the door, eager to shut him out. He paused on the threshold and turned to her expectantly.

"Shall we practice our kisses?" he suggested with that devilish smile.

At last her temper flared. "I thought we already had this childish conversation in the carriage."

Carson quirked a brow, but his eyes narrowed and his mouth thinned. "So we have, and you made your stand quite clear." His voice was harsh. "A nix on too much kissing. How could I have forgotten? Good night, then."

He turned, his shoulder obscuring his face. He pulled the door closed behind him—soundly.

He was angry. Feeling strangely rebuffed, she stood silent and alone in her room, staring at the doorknob. The click of the latch sealing them off from each other echoed in her ears.

She was married to the man on the other side of the door, the stranger whom she could hear moving around, preparing for bed. Despite spending an entire day with him, she had no idea who he was. Of course, she knew who he was, but she didn't really know him. Yet here he was, this stranger with a dashing smile and a strange accent, in her house, making ready to sleep within a few feet of her.

The thought sent a chill through her.

When she saw the key in the lock—a key she was certain neither her mother nor father had ever used—she turned it.

The bolt clicked into place, resounding through the rooms of the Elms.

Katherine stepped back from the door, a little startled by her action. She was being childish. Perhaps she didn't know him well, but he'd given her no reason to think he wouldn't be a gentleman—except that wedding kiss.

After a moment of silence, the floor on his side of the door creaked. The doorknob turned—only so far as the lock allowed.

Her heart beat faster. So he'd heard the lock and was testing it.

"Katherine?" came his voice, raised only as one might raise his voice to be heard through a solid wood panel. "Katherine, unlock this door."

He sounded reasonable.

"If you don't mind, sir, I'd like to have my privacy," she

said in her sweetest voice. Her pride would not allow her to go back on her deed. As she spoke her gaze fell on the key again, and she realized she'd better do something with it. "I'm sure you understand," she added.

"You may have your privacy," he called back softly, then his tone deepened. "But unlock the door."

"Why?" she asked, reaching to snatch the key from the lock. But before she grasped it, the thing jumped out of the keyhole and fell.

A cry of surprise escaped her. Helplessly she watched the key drop, tumbling end over end toward the floor. Toward the piece of Papa's stationery lying in wait for it. Where had the paper come from?

With instant understanding, her belly plummeted like the key.

"No," she breathed. Belatedly she stomped on the sheet to prevent it from moving. But the key clunked onto the stationery, and the stationery vanished beneath the door, carrying the key with it.

"Drat. Drat. Double drat!" she muttered under her breath. She stepped back from the door. The pounding of her heart began to thunder in her ears. How could she have been so stupid?

On Carson's side of the door, the key rattled urgently in the lock.

The door swung open. She stepped back, just in time to avoid being struck by it. The knob banged against the wall.

Carson towered before her, larger than ever, his brows drawn together, his mouth turned down in a forbidding frown. Anger swirled around him, a crackling energy in the air threatening to stir the draperies.

If she thought of him as a stranger before, now she truly saw an unknown man standing before her. Despite her urge to flee, her sense of dignity held her glued to the floor. She sucked a breath for courage.

"Let's get some things straight, Mrs. Fairfax," he began,

his voice dangerously low, barely audible. "Whether we're husband and wife or business partners, I detest locked doors. And key or no key, there isn't a door in this city that can keep me out. So don't you ever get it in your head to lock the door between us. It will serve no purpose. Is that clear?"

"Yes." She lifted her chin haughtily and prayed that her voice would not crack. "But I must insist on my right to privacy. I would appreciate a rap on the door before you enter." Then she added, as if it was a great concession, "Of course, I'll do the same for you."

"I shall expect no less," he said, slipping the key into his trouser pocket.

To her relief, some of his anger seemed to evaporate. A hint of that beguiling grin spread across his face again. He held out a hand in invitation to her. "I've changed my mind about the kiss. Come here and kiss me good night."

She hesitated. She realized her fearless stance had failed when he added, "It's only a kiss, Mrs. Fairfax, not a death sentence."

"I know that." She rubbed her perspiring hands on her satin skirt as she stepped toward him. He was right, it was only a kiss. "But, please, not like the one at the wedding."

His smile turned curious. "Why not?"

"Because, it was so . . . so personal," she finally admitted. The memory of his tongue in her mouth brought a blush to her cheeks.

"But that's what kisses are," he replied, reaching for her chin. "Very personal."

She tilted her face up to his and closed her eyes, bracing herself for another assault like the wedding kiss.

The heat of his nearness warmed her face as he bent close and brushed his lips across hers. That was it. No pressure. No invasion. No tasting, touching. Nothing like their wedding kiss. He pulled away, but only a little. Surprised and disappointed, Katherine opened her eyes and stared right up into his.

"But they are not intended to be frightening either," he said, his gaze searching her face. "You're not frightened, are you, Katherine?"

"Of course not," she lied, shaking her head for emphasis. She'd never been good at fibs, but she hoped this one was believable.

"Good, now go to bed."

After he was gone, the air in the room stilled. She retreated to the edge of the bed. Who would have thought he would become so outraged over a locked door?

Vague rumors about Carson came back to her—the stories hinting that it could be disastrous to cross him. Vague rumors about how people he disliked disappeared. Dime novel tales, she thought, when she'd first heard them, though she'd been as fascinated as all the other young ladies of Denver. Now she wondered, was there truth in them?

Suddenly her new husband seemed more an unknown than she'd thought possible. What if he decided to march into her room in the middle of the night and demand his husbandly rights?

She touched her lips. After that tender kiss? Katherine shook her head. She was letting her imagination run away with her.

Alert, she listened to the sound of his movements in the next room. Footsteps tread across the room from the fire to the dressing room. They sounded like the normal movements of one preparing for bed.

When her heart rate became normal, she quickly changed into her favorite flannel nightgown, turned out the lights, and crawled into bed. She lay back and pulled the covers up to her chin.

Though she heard nothing from the other side of the door, in the darkness she could see that the light still burned. She watched forever, it seemed, until finally the light went out.

Only then did she allow herself to sink into her mattress and close her eyes.

All through the night she tried to keep alert enough to wake at any sound—a knock at the door or a turn of the doorknob.

But she sank into dreams, rapid, illusive, spinning images of red roses, lace and blue taffeta, gleaming crystal. Uncle Owen's frown. Black cattails and *C* and *K* entwined, the letters struggling against each other.

Then she was dreaming of being kissed, a deep, probing, mouth-to-mouth experience that opened her up and made her feel all warm and melted. The man smelled like Carson, felt like Carson, his fingers trailing fire along her skin . . .

Suddenly sunlight fell onto Katherine's face, washing away the dreams. She opened her eyes, squinting at the light that flooded through the bay window. Struggling up on her elbows, she glanced at the door to see if it was still closed. It was. She sighed in relief. In the morning light her fear seemed groundless.

Yawning, she sat up and stretched. She felt oddly rested, even after all those dreams.

A movement at the foot of her bed caught her eye. With a start she peered over the folds of the counterpane to see Lucky curled there.

"How'd you get in here?" she asked, her gaze darting to the door once more. It was latched—but unlocked. She remembered distinctly that the last place she'd seen him was in Carson's room.

From his place on her bed, the blue-eyed tom cat purred in smug reply and flicked his tail contentedly.

Chapter Eleven

Three weeks later, Katherine sat in the Windsor Hotel dining room across from her husband, who—to her embarrassment—had twisted around in his chair to survey the clientele. Marriage was proving to be a more unique experience than she'd ever anticipated. She concentrated on spreading her napkin in her lap.

"No one of distinction is here today," Carson said, his sharp gaze returning to her at last. They had just ordered their midday meal and the waiter had departed. Since their wedding, Carson had made certain that they lunched at the elite hotel at least twice a week, in addition to the social calls they made and the invitations they accepted.

"No, there isn't," she agreed, smoothing, for the third time, a fold from the napkin covering her skirt. She hoped they would not see anyone they knew. Carson would make a great display of greeting their acquaintances and inviting them to join him and his new wife. She knew he was doing this to establish them socially, but the whole process was beginning to make her feel like an object on display.

Even so, she, too, ventured a quick glance around. The vast crystal-lit and walnut-paneled room was filled with four large tables of gentlemen doing business, and near the window sat two tables of couples, visitors to the Queen City of the Rockies, she speculated. "I don't see a single familiar face either."

"Then I have you to myself." Carson leaned forward, grinning like he could eat her up. *Like the Big Bad Wolf in "Little Red Riding Hood,"* she thought. And not unlike Lucky's expression when she'd found the tom sleeping at the foot of her bed at least a half dozen times during the last three weeks.

"So it would seem." Maybe it would be better if they did see someone they knew, she decided. If they didn't, he would do what he seemed to enjoy so much—sit across the luncheon table and make her laugh. It was a mystery to her why he so delighted in making a public spectacle of them (did he consider it part of their plan? she wondered).

But he would tell the most amusing stories, dropping names like Oscar Wilde, Andrew Carnegie, and Lillie Langtry. When she laughed, she always tried to be discreet; she hated making a scene. But he could almost bring her to tears. And everyone in the room eventually noticed them. Then he would sit back in his chair, a self-satisfied grin on his face and his chest expanding with conceit. The attention seemed to please him inordinately.

Beside the visibility of sitting in the Windsor dining room, the only other reason she could find for these lunches was that without the Gentlemen's Respite, Carson was bored to distraction.

She would have had to be a dunce not to see it. Ordinarily she would not have cared, but what if others saw it, too? Bored was hardly a condition one expected of a newlywed man. Could such a simple thing give away their charade? Worse yet, could such a simple thing make her look inadequate?

That thought made her fidget. She glanced at Carson, who was looking around the room again. "And what story do you have to tell me today, Mr. Fairfax?" she asked, encouraging him to display his wit, despite her discomfort with being the sole focus of his attention.

"Did I ever tell you about the hurricane I weathered when I was staying with friends in South Carolina?" Carson began.

"No," she replied, surprised once more by the variety in his stories. The man had been everywhere and knew everyone. "A true hurricane? What happened?"

And he was off with another diverting tale.

She'd done her best to keep him occupied. During his first week as lord and master of the Elms, she'd suggested that he see to the carriage house staff. And so he had. He'd hired grooms and stable boys. Then he'd purchased a team of flashy black hackneys and a new carriage. The Fairfaxes would travel in style. He'd also bought several riding horses and a white pony for Lily.

As pleasant as it was to see the carriage house filled and alive again, she had her doubts about the pony. It could never be more than a pet. Horseback riding was out of the question for Lily. However, what a pleasure it was to be able to order a carriage whenever she needed one.

But bringing the carriage house back to life had taken Carson only two weeks. After that, almost daily—graceful, observant, impatient but contained—like a wise caged lion, he prowled the house, the stables, the grounds. He tended to the new horses, supervised repairs to the carriage house, and directed the gardeners in shrub trimming.

Contrary to what you'd expect of a British aristocrat, she discovered that Carson was a social egalitarian. He took pleasure in speaking to every staff member. No one was beneath his notice. He knew each by name. In return they were too polite to work while he was talking to them.

Diplomatically—how was a wife to do these things without sounding like a nag?—she reminded him that the staff had jobs to do in preparation for the countess's visit. Time was growing short. Her list of things to do was long. He'd best not interfere with the staff's duties, she advised firmly.

He always listened and agreed with her ever so politely. Then, to her annoyance, he went on asking his questions of the staff, who stopped work to answer him with a smile. It was enough to make her tear out her hair.

"... so we started boarding up the windows," Carson was saying in the recounting of his hurricane tale. Now that she knew him better, she wasn't in the least surprised that he would jump into the work of saving someone's home from a storm.

"What happened when the hurricane struck?" she asked.

"I'll get to that." Carson smiled at her. "Patience, Mrs. Fairfax. Don't rush a good story."

Katherine fell silent. She was still learning her wifely cues. Being married was ever so much more complicated that she'd expected. Thank heavens she didn't have to sleep with him. What manner of new things would she have to learn then? Things like how to undress a man?

Her gaze flicked across the table toward him. What did he look like without all that fine tailoring? And that sprinkling of curly chest hair that she'd glimpsed one night when he'd removed his tie—what would it feel like between her fingers?

Lightness quivered in her belly.

One evening from the shadows at the top of the stairs she'd watched him on the way to his room. He'd pulled off his tie and unbuttoned his shirt. She'd seen just a sprinkling of springy hair that appeared to cover a broad portion of his chest and on downward . . . The intimate memory warmed her cheeks.

He paused in the telling of his hurricane story. "Is something wrong, Mrs. Fairfax?"

"No," she squeaked and shook her head, her ears absolutely burning with the impropriety of her lusty reflections. She re-aligned her fork on the table, unable to meet Carson's gaze. "Nothing at all, Mr. Fairfax. Please go on. You were saying about the darkness . . ."

"It was dark inside after we boarded up the windows, and we had to entertain two dozen people," he continued, "including the servants. Lamp oil was in short supply so we only had one lamp burning. And the dining room table was just big enough for . . ."

Katherine's thoughts drifted again, but she kept them from being too wayward this time. On several occasions in the last three weeks, Cornish Jack Tremain had come to visit. She assumed he and Carson had business to settle about the Respite. Tremain always seemed ill at ease, but Carson received him with pleasure, and they would retire to the study. Randolph Hearn dropped by from time to time, too.

Sometimes she caught Carson in the study looking at the books as if he wanted something to read. Once he'd caught her with Papa's journal, so she'd shown it to him. He'd seemed intrigued and spent an entire morning paging through the notes.

More than once she'd seen him sitting with Lily, flipping through a Braille tome and discussing her homework. Lily read to him sometimes. Katherine was pleased that a relationship seemed to be growing between her husband and her sister.

But the thing she saw him do most often was stand at the parlor window, gazing longingly in the direction of the Gentleman's Respite.

That was when the guilt struck her. If he still had the club to go to, he'd be out from underfoot and probably happy as a lark. But she steeled herself against her remorse. Tavern keeping was not a suitable pastime for *her* husband. He needed to find new ways to occupy his mind and energies.

So . . . what did a wife—a business partner—do with a bored former saloonkeeper?

Answer: She lunched with him at the Windsor Hotel whenever he invited her—and laughed at his stories.

"It turned into a three-day card game," Carson was saying, "one of the best I've ever played in."

"A three-day card game!" she exclaimed, before she realized she needed to keep her voice low. Heads turned in the dining room. She hunched down in her chair.

"What else is there to do while the wind blows?" Carson shrugged, but a mischievous grin spread across his face. "On the third day, when the wind stopped, we called the game and unboarded the door to look outside.''

She reined in her outrage. The gleam in his eyes told her that her shocked reaction only encouraged him. ''And what did you find outside?''

''The house had survived nicely,'' he continued, ''but the garden was awash with sand, and the yacht lying on its side near the front gate was quite beyond repair.''

''A yacht?'' Katherine repeated, spreading her hands on the table edge. ''But you said the house was a good mile inland.''

''Aren't you glad we live in Denver?'' Carson took a sip of his water.

''Indeed,'' she replied, unable to resist a wry smile.

The waiter arrived with the first course of their lunch. As the soup was served, she searched for a new topic of conversation. But Carson found it first.

''Tell me more about the Amanda Leigh and your father's journal,'' he said, appearing more intent on the salt and pepper than the topic of conversation.

''There's not much to tell about the mine,'' she said, uncertain what he wanted to know. ''But when it was producing, the Amanda Leigh was an exciting place to be. The thunder of the steam engine, the compressors and the hammers.''

''You were there?''

''Yes, Papa took me up to the Amanda Leigh and some of his other mines all the time,'' she said, suddenly swamped with nostalgic memories of mountainside buggy rides. ''In the summer Mama packed us lunch, and we had picnics on our way.''

''Your mother went too?''

''No.'' She shook her head. ''Mama always had something else to do. I don't think she liked the noise and the dirt, but I loved it. She allowed me to go, but only after making Papa promise not to take me into the mine. But sometimes he did anyway, if I asked just right.''

An irresistible smile touched her lips. "It was our secret. I never told Mama."

"And your father recorded events regarding the mine in the journal that you have," Carson said.

"Yes, he was a thorough note taker . . ." The vision of Papa's deathbed flashed through her mind, of his insistence that she keep the journal—as if she would ever let go of it—and the Amanda Leigh. She stared at her soup. Despite its excellent presentation, her appetite wilted.

"Were you there when the mine was closed down?" Carson asked, still seeming more interested in his food than her words.

"No, by then I'd gone away to school," she explained. *Would things have turned out differently if I'd stayed in Denver after Mama's death?* she wondered for the thousandth time. If she'd been there to comfort her father and give him the strength he seemed to lose with Mama's passing, would he have turned to drink and cards? She would never know.

"Closing the Amanda Leigh took a lot of heart out of Papa," she said. "It was the first of his mines to strike it rich, really rich. Then losing Mama was the last straw."

When she looked up from her soup, she saw Carson studying her. She tried to smile, but the expression would not come to her lips. "I'm sorry. I'm not hungry."

"It's all right." He nodded sympathetically and pursed his lips. "A gold mine really isn't appropriate luncheon conversation. How about when we leave here we go to that new florist and see about a few new plants for the conservatory?"

"Yes, that would be nice," she agreed, eager to leave sad, unchangeable memories behind.

Preparations for the countess's visit were going reasonably well. The house had been thoroughly cleaned: the crystal and brass chandeliers in every room had been polished, the woodwork washed, the chambers aired, the draperies cleaned, and the carpets swept or beaten. New china and glassware cabinets were purchased, delivered, and arranged for the new china.

Katherine and Mrs. Dodd had drafted menus and shopping lists to restock the kitchen's stores of flour, sugar, spices, nuts, candied fruits, and other condiments—all the things necessary for holiday cooking and baking. Carson offered to order the wine. She gratefully relinquished that task to him. What did she know about fine wines?

But the special stationery she had selected for the tree decorating party invitations was late in arriving. She was beginning to feel the pressure that comes when things are falling behind schedule. It was making her cross.

By the time the special paper arrived Katherine was feeling quite pressed.

That evening, as they left the supper table and strolled into the family parlor, she announced its arrival and her intentions.

"I plan to start writing the invitations this evening," she said, watching Carson take up his newspaper and settle himself in a large, comfortable chair.

The image of him sitting by the parlor fire seemed so natural to her that if he'd been wearing an ordinary suit, instead of the subtly flashy gambler's attire he continued to favor, he would look like any other extraordinarily handsome man of the house. Strong, reliable, benevolent. The sight sent a gentle thrill of pleasure through her, though she didn't know why.

"I'm glad it has arrived," he said, scanning the newspaper.

"Was it what you wanted, Katherine?" Lily was sitting on the floor by the fire petting Max. Lucky was nowhere to be seen. The cat often preferred Mrs. D's kitchen.

"Yes, it is," she said. "If you need help with your homework, Lily, you'll need to bring it into the study where I'll be. I know you spent all afternoon outside with Carson and the pony."

"Hominy knows me," Lily exclaimed with excitement. She lifted her face toward Katherine, joy written in her expression.

"That's her name. Carson told me. Hominy, because she's white. She eats out of my hand and her nose is soooo soft."

Katherine frowned at Carson, who still did not look up from his paper. Didn't he understand how dangerous a pony could be for Lily?

"I'll help Lily with her homework," he said without acknowledging her disapproving expression. "I took her away from her lessons this afternoon, so I should be the one to help her this evening."

"That would be excellent," Lily piped up. Max wagged his tail.

Was the poor man that bored? she wondered. Sharing his time with the horses and Lily was one thing, but spending the evening helping with a twelve-year-old's schoolwork? From the doorway, she studied Carson. He folded the newspaper and smiled back at her, his expression as innocent as an archangel's.

"That would be helpful," she said. "If you two do lessons, I'll have more time to devote to invitation writing. Thank you."

She was about to step out of the room when she heard Carson clear his throat.

"Katherine, before you go, there is something I wanted to ask you." He laid his newspaper aside.

She turned. "Yes?"

"About your father's journal that you let me look at earlier this week," he began, then hesitated, as if he was uncertain how to broach the topic. "The one about the Amanda Leigh."

"Yes, what about it?" she asked, remembering when he'd walked in on her paging through it, and she'd shown it to him.

"Would you mind if I let Cornish Jack have a look at it?" Carson stood, facing her. "You know how legendary the Amanda Leigh's vein of gold was. I think an old miner like Jack would find your father's notes of great interest. In fact, he could probably make more sense of them than either of us."

The request surprised her. It also made her apprehensive. "I've never thought about allowing someone outside the family to look at Papa's notes. Uncle Owen has seen the diary, of course, but he said there's nothing useful in it.''

"But the information would be of interest to another miner,'' Carson persisted. ''Your father was a real mining engineer, Katherine, and half geologist to boot. And his observations, while insightful and sometimes humorous, aren't of a personal nature. Jack could probably learn some interesting facts from them, and I'm sure he would be careful with the journal.''

"No, I don't think so,'' she said, suddenly uncomfortable with a stranger reading her father's thoughts—and with Carson's curiosity. ''Papa's notes are private.''

"But Mr. Tremain is very nice, Katherine,'' Lily said. ''Why not let him borrow the journal? I don't think Papa would mind. He was always willing to share his knowledge.''

"I just thought Jack might enjoy reading about how your father discovered the gold and set up the operation,'' Carson added. ''You know, one old miner to another. What harm could it do?''

"None, I suppose, if you don't mind, Lily,'' she finally agreed, realizing she was being overly possessive. ''All right, let Mr. Tremain have a look, then.''

"Good, thank you. I'll give it to him when he comes tomorrow,'' Carson said, glancing down at Lily. ''Now, let's get those lessons done, missy.''

When she left the parlor, Lily and Carson were pulling their chairs up to the center table with Lily's books laid out, ready for work.

In the study a fire was burning, just as she'd ordered, and the room was warm. She turned up the gas lamp, settled herself at the desk, and began writing. Starting at the top of her list, she decided she'd work as long as her hand was steady and her mind alert.

The invitations to the schools had already been sent out. She'd done that early and used her regular stationery. It was part of the Elms' tradition to invite the schoolchildren to come visit the house and see the tree after it was decorated. There would be cookies and punch as well as small gifts for every child and teacher.

Papa had begun the tradition because he wanted to share the holiday and the beauty of his home with as many people as possible. When Papa had been alive, they'd invited all of their employees, too, a practice not all of the elite agreed with. But she was glad to carry on the tradition. Papa's belief was hers. Christmas was a time to share—with everyone—not just your rich neighbors.

She worked for over an hour, moving down the list, until her hand began to ache. She put the pen down and wondered if hiring Opal Shaw as her secretary might be a good idea. Opal had a good hand and could be helpful with correspondence and other things around the house.

As she massaged her hand, she realized that the house was quiet—unusually quiet for eight-thirty on a weekday evening. Instead of the clatter of Mrs. Dodd closing up the kitchen and Lily's chatter as she prepared for bed, the house was filled with nothing more than the hiss of the gas jets.

Thinking that she hadn't heard anything because of her concentration, she sat back and listened. Nothing. What on earth was going on? Was something wrong?

She rose from the desk and hurried out into the hallway to investigate the silence.

Chapter Twelve

In the hallway, she stopped to listen. This time she heard the murmur of voices from the kitchen. Then it was silent again. After a moment, laughter erupted, hearty male laughter accompanied by feminine giggles.

For heaven's sake, what was Mrs. D allowing to go on in her kitchen? Katherine marched down the hallway. She took the turn through the butler's pantry and came up short.

The door to the kitchen was shut tight and latched. Mrs. Dodd never shut the kitchen door. She was always glad to have company. The door was usually open for anyone to wander in as they pleased. But tonight light streamed from beneath the door into the darkness where Katherine stood alone.

Another round of laughter broke out in the kitchen. The room echoed with unfamiliar voices. But she recognized Carson's chuckle and Lily's belly laugh.

"Shame on you, Mr. Fairfax," Mrs. D was saying, her voice high-pitched with excitement. "That's no way to treat your sister-in-law."

"I don't care, Mrs. D," came Lily's breathless reply. "Do it, Carson. Raise it, if you want. Do it."

She sucked in a shocked breath. Her good sense told her that they couldn't possibly be doing anything as wanton as the words sounded, but . . . but whatever they were doing, it wasn't lessons. She grabbed the doorknob and threw open the door. "I think that's quite enough."

The room went silent. In the bright glow of the gas lamp over the kitchen table, half a dozen faces turned toward her.

Carson and Lily sat across from each other. Filling out the group was Mrs. Dodd, Willis, one of the new grooms, and a gardener. A mound of copper pennies lay in the middle of the table. Everyone held a handful of awkward-looking playing cards.

Lily spoke up first. "Hi, Sis. Pull up a chair. Carson is teaching all of us how to play a good poker game. I won the last pot."

"Poker!" Katherine sputtered. "In my house?"

"Five-card stud with jokers wild," Lily explained, smiling from ear to ear. "It's great fun."

"I think we'd better call the game," Carson said, throwing down his cards and raking in the deck as the others did the same. "Mrs. D, return everyone's wager."

"Nooo," protested Lily, still holding her cards. "Katherine, are you going to lose your temper? Don't. Please, don't. This is so much fun."

The words, "How dare you?" finally blurted out of Katherine's mouth.

She couldn't take her gaze from Carson's face. When he glanced up at her again, she could see he had no intention of apologizing.

"We'd better do what Mr. Fairfax said." Mrs. D rose from the table and helped Lily with her chair. "Let's go upstairs and get you ready for bed."

"That's not fair," Lily complained, though she allowed Mrs.

D to lead her toward the door. "I did my homework. It's all finished."

Copper coins jingled as Willis and the others shoved money into their pockets. Chairs scraped the floor and boots scuffled as they jostled their way out the back door, all bolting for safety at once.

"Don't you get angry with Carson," Lily called from the doorway. "I started it. My cards. What about my cards?"

"I'll take care of them, Lily," Carson said, never rising from the table. "Your sister and I will settle this."

As soon as Lily was out of the kitchen, she unleashed her fury on him. "After the agreement we made about the Respite, you dare to bring gambling into my house?"

"It was a game for pennies," Carson said, his tone even. "Only pennies."

"Maybe pennies don't mean a great deal to you," she said, seizing a handful of the cards from the table and shaking them in his face, "but to people like Willis and Mrs. D, pennies mean a lot. And to corrupt Lily in her own house . . ."

"It's a game, Katherine," Carson said, without looking at her. "Just a game."

"And you purposely hid this from me," she said. "You waited for me to go into the study to do this."

"Well, we all agreed that you might make a fuss about it even though it's just an innocent pastime."

"Innocent indeed." She shook the cards in his face again as she searched for the words to express her anger. But she could find no words. Instead, the strangeness of the playing cards in her hand drew her attention. They were oversized and their texture was rough, unlike regular slick cards. "What on earth are these?"

She drew them back to take a closer look at them. They were larger than ordinary playing cards and were covered with bumps as well as printed with the usual large spades, hearts, clubs, and diamonds. She ran her thumb over the bumps again. "This feels like Braille."

"It is Braille," Carson said, holding out his hand to take the cards from her. "May I have them?"

"But where—?" Astonished, she looked up into Carson's face.

"Lily's tutor helped me find them." Carson held out his hand again. "May I?"

"Yes, of course," she stammered, surrendering the cards and feeling a bit deflated. Somehow he'd gotten Braille cards for Lily.

Poker or no poker, obviously he'd gone to some trouble to do it for her sister. This man who'd lied to his mother, who had run a gambling club that bilked innocents out of their money, and who liked to be the center of attention. He'd gone out of his way to learn about Braille playing cards and purchased a deck for Lily.

At a loss, she waved her hands in the air. "Couldn't you have taught her something less, uh, less risky? Something genteel, like solitaire?"

"I did," Carson said, carefully slipping the cards into a box. "But she learned so quickly, we had to go on to something more exciting."

"I hardly think poker falls into the exciting category," she quipped, her anger threatening to return. "Immoral is more like it. I'll thank you not to corrupt my sister."

"I fail to see how a friendly card game corrupts your sister." His face stony, Carson ceased putting the cards in the box and looked up at her from his seat at the table. "The fact is, you overprotect her."

"I what?" Shocked, Katherine stepped back from him.

"You fuss over Lily too much," Carson said, sounding as if he was warming up to a speech. "She should be in school with other girls and boys her own age. She should be exploring new things like horseback riding if she wants to, and what about going to the opera? Why haven't you taken her? She loves music."

"She's only twelve," Katherine protested, too staggered by his accusations to say more in her own defense.

"She's on the verge of young womanhood," Carson said, "and she should be embarking on a whole new world. She's bright and energetic and her biggest limitations seem to be the ones you've imagined for her."

Katherine glared at him. "How dare you presume?"

"At least let her enjoy the playing cards," Carson said. "With these she can sit at a card table and enjoy a game with anyone."

Confused by her warring emotions, she bit her tongue. Was there truth in what he said? Was she holding Lily back? "I don't try to keep Lily from accomplishing what she wants to do."

"Of course not," Carson said. "Just give her a little more freedom to show you what she's interested in."

"Like playing cards?" she asked. "I think she gained her interest from you."

"By the way, Mother loves to play cards," Carson continued, as if he'd not heard her. "How about Lily and I restrict our card playing to games that she can play with Mother? Fair enough?"

"The countess likes to play cards?" she repeated weakly. Of course the countess played cards. She herself had often played while she'd been visiting in London, harmless group games played all in fun.

Carson nodded. "Everything from solitaire to whist. But I'll admit, she doesn't play poker as far as I know."

"I suppose it wouldn't hurt for Lily to learn a few respectable games," she relented. Card games were an entertainment she'd never thought of offering her aristocratic visitor. "However, I must ask you to refrain from encouraging the staff to gamble."

"I'll agree to play for matchstick wagers," he said slowly, eyeing her as though he suspected she would ask more of him than he could grant.

"I would appreciate that," she said, her head still too full of his remarks about Lily to realize she'd lost the round. Then she took a deep breath, her anger and confusion slipping away. "And thank you for thinking of Lily. Most people just want to hear her play her music or for her to stay out of sight."

"It was a selfish enough gift," Carson admitted, glancing up at her with a disarming grin. Then he bent over the cards, finishing his task. "I've missed being at the card table myself."

"Yes, I supposed so," she agreed. As angry as she wanted to be with him, his honesty was endearing. She studied the top of his head as he completed his task, something dragging at her heart. Was being married to a near stranger as confusing and awkward for him as it was for her? she wondered.

The shininess of his curly dark hair, thick and vibrant, took on a strange fascination for Katherine. Compassion warmed her insides. What a unique man he was, thoughtful, yet independent and forceful in his own way. The urge to caress his head, to feel the texture of his hair between her fingers, came over her.

She was surprised to find that her hand had come up and hovered over the appealing cowlick at the back of his head. She halted. What was she doing? This man, her husband or not, was still a stranger to her. Instantly she withdrew her hand, tucking her fingers into the fold of her skirt. Thankfully, he had not seen her movement.

"Well," she stammered, "I'm certain Lily appreciates your thoughtfulness."

She turned on her heel and forced herself to walk out of the kitchen without saying more.

The day of the Countess of Atwick's arrival dawned cloudy and cold—the best weather the Mile High City had to offer in the first week of December, Carson thought with relief. Everything was in place for her visit, except the train schedule.

"At last, Mother's train is arriving on track four," he said when he reached the table in the Union Depot restaurant where

Katherine and he had been waiting for the last forty-five minutes.

He'd just gone out to the desk to double-check on the train's arrival time. When he'd reentered the restaurant, he found Katherine occupied in conversation with Randolph Hearn. *Count on Randolph to move in on a pretty lady when no one was looking,* Carson thought with annoyance as he wove his way between the tables.

Katherine was looking exceptionally good in a peacock blue suit with a feathered felt hat of the same color that highlighted the turquoise of her eyes. He especially liked the way the spotted veil came down over her face, just covering her lips, to make her look like a woman of mystery.

He'd expected living in the room next to her to pose some difficulties, but nothing like the frustration he'd faced in the past five weeks of marriage. While she'd responded to him during their wedding kiss, since then she'd put on a damned good show of being completely immune to his charms. A difficulty he'd never faced before. Until now his problems with women had been more along the line of having them hand him their room keys, not locking their doors, as Katherine had attempted to do.

He could probably save himself from a lot of pain and grief if he ceased prowling her room at night. Why did he need to know that she slept on her back with her left arm thrown back over her head? In the moonlight her gown stretched across her body, revealing the shadows of her nipples, her navel, and the thatch of dark hair between her legs. Why did he torture himself with that knowledge? Because the unlocked door was there, and why shouldn't he use it?

Being her husband and keeping his hands off her was proving more tedious than he'd expected.

Then her interruption of the card game with Lily reminded him that she was out to change him. That made him think again about his duties as a husband. Wouldn't her life be improved if she understood passion better? He liked that idea—better now than when he'd first thought of it. It gave him a new view of his playacting marriage.

At times Katherine was a delightful and intriguing companion. They'd spent two days buying her clothes for his mother's visit, things suitable for a Denver society matron to wear in the company of the countess. Selecting clothes for her had been one of the easiest tasks he'd ever taken on. The only problem had been that everything looked good on her small-waisted, full-bosomed figure. Ball gowns, shirtwaists, tea dresses, and braid-trimmed suits. He'd finally told her to order everything that pleased her. Limiting the choice was impossible. She'd made some fine selections.

She looked so good today that there wasn't a man in the depot restaurant who hadn't glanced in her direction.

"Randolph, what brings you here?" he asked after he'd delivered the good news about the countess's train.

"He just dropped by to say hello," Katherine said, rising from her chair.

Hearn scrambled to his feet and offered his hand to Carson. "I was just visiting with your lovely wife about the details of the countess's arrival. You've been pretty mum about it after that initial telegram."

Feeling oddly vexed and possessive, he reached for Katherine's arm and drew her around to his side as he laid payment for their coffee on the white cloth. "Mother said she'd prefer a quiet arrival. She's not one for formality or fuss."

"I could have had a photographer here," Randolph said, clearly disappointed. "I'd run it on the inside front page. Discreet, but visible. Denver loves royalty."

"You and a good deal of Denver will meet the countess at the reception tomorrow night," Katherine said, smiling and offering Hearn her hand. "You will be there, won't you, Randolph?"

The newspaperman grinned at Katherine, puppy-dog adoration shining in his eyes.

Carson frowned. Why hadn't he noticed Hearn's fondness for Katherine before?

Randolph seized her hand. "Wouldn't miss it for all the news stories in the world."

Carson crowded between them, forcing Randolph to release her. "We'll see you tomorrow, then, Hearn." He ushered Katherine out of the restaurant.

"Is something wrong?" she asked as they threaded their way through the hustle and bustle of the train station. "No problem with your mother's train?"

"No, nothing like that," he said, realizing that she'd misinterpreted his irritation with Randolph for annoyance with her. "Mother's train was delayed in loading goods and fuel along the line somewhere. Nothing serious."

The sprawling train station was crowded and noisy, voices echoing off the lofty ceiling and air thick with the excitement and tension of travelers off on holiday journeys. The grit of cinders crunched under their feet.

At this moment in front of the depot Willis was wiping mud off the new carriage. The Elms looked perfect, thanks to Mrs. D and Katherine's hard work. With Dolly's help they had scheduled a variety of tours, entertainments, and receptions to make his mother and her entourage feel welcome. The countess's retinue—a countess never traveled alone—included his brother, John, John's wife, and their eleven-year-old daughter, Sylvia.

Suddenly he stopped, realizing that Katherine was lagging behind him.

He turned to her. "What's the matter?"

When she looked at him, her smile faltered. He saw the uncertainty in her eyes.

She drew him near a column out of the flow of people. "Do I look all right?"

Carson stared at her, unable to understand how she could ask such a ridiculous question. She was the most beautiful woman in the train station. But apprehension glimmered in her eyes. Compliments weren't what she wanted.

"You look exactly right," he said, remembering the things they had discussed in the last week. They'd studied Randolph's newspaper accounts of their wedding.

He'd reviewed her knowledge of the British peerage, which he'd found to be adequate. He'd filled her in on the highlights of the Fairfax family history. They'd talked about how Carson's mother enjoyed informality. Lady Elizabeth delighted in novelty and would probably find American straightforwardness charming and quaint.

While he'd been instructing Katherine, she'd seemed to absorb it all without a hint of fear. But now, at the last moment, she obviously had stage fright.

"You look exactly how my wife would look," he said, taking her gloved hands in his and squeezing them. "Everyone in Denver is convinced. You walk and talk exactly the way an American Fairfax would. You know everything you need to know to be Mrs. Carson Fairfax, the daughter-in-law of the Countess of Atwick."

"What if I let something slip?" she said, glancing nervously at the crowd.

"You won't," Carson said, bringing her hands to his mouth and kissing them lightly. "If something comes up you don't know how to handle, just improvise. You can laugh it off or call me in. And as far as my family is concerned, no one except Father would be surprised or offended if you didn't know the details of the past seven earls of Atwick. And you don't have to worry about him. So take a deep breath, or whatever you do to shake off stage fright."

"Stage fright?" Katherine frowned at him, clearly surprised and indignant. She pulled her hands from his grasp. "You are talking to the daughter of Amanda Leigh Tucker, one of the great ladies of the Colorado stage. I don't get stage fright."

"Of course not," he said, amused and relieved. "How can I have? Forgive me, sweetheart, for such a foolish assumption."

"I just want to be certain that we've thought of everything," she said. "I don't like leaving things to chance."

"We haven't," Carson assured her. "Just remember, Mother is so delighted I've married at last that she would never say a cross word to any woman who agreed to share my life. When she sees you, she's going to be so impressed, you'll win the day without saying a word."

Katherine bridled and swatted lightly at his arm. "Don't patronize me, you varlet."

She'd used that name for him once before—during the episode with Lily and the playing cards. But today she was smiling.

He grinned back at her. "Ready, Mrs. Fairfax?"

"Just one more thing."

"And what's that?" he asked, glancing down the platform toward track four.

"Why did you leave England?"

He frowned and released a breath of sudden irritation. There were so many reasons why he'd left England, he hardly knew where to begin. Not all of them made sense to him and few of them would make sense to her. A simple answer seemed best. "Because my father invited me to."

"But why?" Katherine persisted. "Because of your gambling? I understand it's prevalent among the lords and ladies."

"But not with my father," he said, glad she'd supplied him with an answer. "Gambling about sums it up."

"Then your family will be glad to know that you've sold the Respite," she said.

"They will be very pleased with your influence on me," he assured her. "Now, are you ready, Mrs. Fairfax?"

"I'm ready, Mr. Fairfax," she said, taking his arm and matching her stride to his. A confident smile played across her lips.

At track four, the train conductor was just setting the step down at the door of the private car that the Countess of Atwick was traveling in, a car lent to the Fairfaxes by a New York acquaintance. The curtains were drawn, so it was impossible to see anyone inside. But at the other end of the car, luggage was already being unloaded. Carson had directed Willis to see that it was loaded onto the wagon they'd brought along for the purpose.

He was about to climb up to the car door when it opened and John stepped out. They recognized each other immediately.

But Carson hesitated to call out a greeting. He hadn't realized until that moment how uncertain he was about how his brother would receive him. Feelings had been strained when he'd left England ten years earlier. John and Neville had always taken their cue from Father in their treatment of him. Despite the way he'd made it sound to Katherine, sometimes things had gotten pretty rough among the three of them—when Mother wasn't around. Recriminations had been hurled back and forth and his actions misunderstood and resented. He wasn't certain how his brothers felt about him now.

But when John saw him, he never hesitated.

"Carson, old boy," he cried, pleasure shining on his face as he swung down the steps from the train car and enveloped him in a hearty embrace.

Katherine spotted Carson's brother immediately. The resemblance was unmistakable. John had the same sharp, intelligent features and dark hair as Carson, though John's was straight and graying at the temples.

The pleasure on his face as he greeted Carson was so genuine that Katherine forgot her stage fright and smiled. She stepped back to allow the brothers to greet each other.

John was of a narrower build than Carson and shorter, but he moved with the same economy of motion, though with a more formal bearing.

"What a sight you are to see," John said, holding Carson in his embrace. After a momentary hesitation, her husband returned his brother's embrace.

She smiled at him over John's shoulder. When she'd asked

Carson how John and he had gotten along, he'd replied that they got on as well as any brothers do. Never having had a brother, she had little idea of what that meant. But this appeared to be a warm greeting.

"Looks like this cursed big country agrees with you, little brother," John continued, releasing Carson at last. "I tell you, we liked to think the train ride would never come to an end."

"John, you haven't changed a bit," Carson said, standing back to hold his brother at arm's length. "As short and impatient as ever."

John slapped Carson on the back. "Don't start with me, brother. My impatience doesn't begin to match Mother's. She's been dressed and ready to arrive in Denver since early this morning. Can't imagine what's keeping her."

But instead of looking toward the train, John immediately stepped up to Katherine. "And you must be Mrs. Fairfax. Forgive my brother. He was always slow to introduce ladies to Neville and me."

"For good reason," Carson muttered.

Katherine laughed and offered her hand. John took it and bowed.

"You haven't come to create trouble for me with my bride, have you, John?" Carson asked, hovering at his brother's side.

"No, never," John said, his gaze sweeping over Katherine. "I won't tell a single story about your infamous years at university. I say, Mrs. Fairfax, Carson has done quite well for himself."

"Oh, but it is I who have made the catch," she said with a modest smile and just the right flutter to her eyelashes.

From behind his brother Carson gave her a surprised but appreciative nod.

That was when Katherine knew they were going to make it as husband and wife. This wasn't just the wishful thinking she'd experienced on her wedding day. This was she and Carson on stage. John believed they were husband and wife as clearly as Denver did. A wave of triumph swept over her. She could do this—act the part of the spoiled, pampered, witty wife of a rich man.

When she glanced at Carson again, she could see that he knew it, too. They would be a great success. At that moment she would have gladly brushed a victory kiss on his lips— almost as deep as their wedding kiss, if he wanted.

"What a clever answer to my compliment." John squeezed her hand and laughed. "You have done very well indeed, Carson. Though Neville and I were just saying we wouldn't put it past you to bribe some sweet thing into being your doting bride."

Chapter Thirteen

Katherine sucked in a breath of surprise and guilt, but she never let her smile waver. She glanced toward Carson. His smile had turned unnaturally pleasant. Control of the situation must be taken and taken now, or the doubt could linger.

"My lord, you offend me," she said with a mock frown, withdrawing her hand from John's grasp. "I'm not easily persuaded to speak other than my true mind. Not even by your handsome brother."

John laughed uneasily and glanced from her to Carson and back again. "Call me John, please. We don't stand on ceremony in this family, at least, we don't when Father isn't present. And I assure you, I meant no offense. If I did, Carson would be calling me out. 'Tis merely a jest. You can say anything you like about my brother. I certainly won't disagree with you."

"Then, John, we should get along famously." Katherine forced a smile to her lips, mentally berating herself for being oversensitive. Of course John had no idea about the agreement she and Carson had made. She could not go through the next month jumping at every gibe and wisecrack made about married couples, suspecting that the speaker knew more than he or she could possibly know.

She lifted her chin and declared, ''I always speak well of my husband, John, unless Carson gives me reason to do otherwise.''

Carson also wore a strained smile. He clapped a hand on his brother's shoulder. ''You see what a threat I live under, John.''

''Yes, don't all we married men, little brother, don't we all,'' John said, clearly relieved and turning toward the train. ''Ah, here come the ladies now.''

All three of them turned to the car platform expectantly.

''Carson?'' The soft, excited voice came from a petite, white-haired lady dressed in the height of fashion who emerged from the train car. Other women followed her, one in a white maid's cap and another in a dark traveling suit.

But clearly Carson only had eyes for his mother.

She grasped the balustrade of the platform and leaned over it, looking down at those awaiting her. Her peaches-and-cream complexion glowed with expectation. The ribbons of her plum-colored hat, which matched her traveling suit, fluttered in the breeze. A smile touched her lips.

''Mother.'' Carson's expression softened, the apprehensive lines of his face melting into a loving smile that made Katherine's heart ache for him. He did love his mother.

He started toward the train, but John moved ahead of him.

''Right here, Mother.'' John lifted his mother, the Countess of Atwick, down from the train platform. ''Carson and his wife were waiting when I opened the door.''

''Carson!'' The moment the countess's feet touched the track platform, she threw her arms around the son she hadn't seen for ten years and sobbed.

Carson wrapped himself around her, holding her close, nearly pulling the poor woman off the ground.

Tears welled in Katherine's eyes, knowing all she did about the trouble he'd gone to in anticipation of this perfect moment.

John and the younger woman—probably his wife, Marie—stood back and smiled.

Carson and the countess were obviously so glad to see each other that the woman wearing a maid's cap sniffled and Marie touched her eyes with her handkerchief.

Katherine had to glance down to blink her tears away.

If she'd had any doubt about whether she should help Carson with this charade to please his mother, it dissolved at the sight of them holding each other. She was glad she'd agreed to be part of bringing his family back together. And she silently vowed to do her best to make the visit a happy one—not just because she got what she wanted for doing it, but because it was the right thing to do for the Fairfaxes.

Finally, the countess pushed Carson away and stepped back to look him up and down, just as any mother would, taking stock of her child—counting his limbs, tugging on his coat sleeves, reaching up to smooth back a lock of his hair that had fallen across his brow.

Carson stood still, head bowed, a dutiful son submitting to his mother's affection.

"You've grown," the countess pronounced her findings at last. Her hat had been knocked askew, but no one seemed to notice.

Everyone laughed, including Carson.

"Mother, I was nineteen when I left," he said. "I had reached my full height."

"No, I don't mean that," the countess protested. "You've matured. I can tell. It's in your face and your voice. It's good."

Carson looked askance at John.

John shrugged. "Only Mother can see these things."

"Where is your wife?" the countess demanded, looking beyond Carson at last. "Is this Kitty? I mean Katherine? But, of course, aren't you lovely?"

She opened her arms, and before Katherine could even think to offer a hand to shake or a cheek to kiss, she found herself enveloped in the arms of the tiny but formidable countess. She smelled of roses.

"Welcome to the family, Katherine, dear," the countess said, giving her a peck on the cheek before releasing her. "We're so glad to have Carson married and respectable at last."

"Yes, she's made me quite respectable." He pulled Katherine to his side.

"We're so pleased that you could join us for the holiday season," Katherine said.

"And we are so pleased to be here, especially after that long train journey," the countess said. "And we have a surprise for you."

"What's that, Mother?" Carson asked.

"We brought your brother Neville and his family, too," the countess said, turning to the railroad car. "You'll have room for all of us, won't you? Of course, they can get a hotel room if necessary. I know it's rather an imposition, but at the last minute we thought we all should be here for Christmas together."

"Neville is here, too?" Carson said, surprise written all over his face but pleasure in his voice.

"But of course we have room," Katherine said, struggling to think where she'd put these extra people. She'd planned for the countess to take her old room. John and Marie would have the guest room, and their daughter, Sylvia, would sleep in Lily's room. It all seemed to be worked out perfectly. But where would they put extras?

Carson slipped an arm around Katherine and added, "Neville and his wife can take my room. I'll just double up with my wife. That will work, won't it, sweetheart?"

He gave Katherine a squeeze.

John gave a hearty laugh, slapping Carson on the back again. "Won't mind that much, will you, little brother? What with being newlyweds of only a year."

Everyone laughed except Katherine.

* * *

That night, about midnight, Carson was staring at the blankets, sheets, and pillow piled on the fainting couch in the dressing alcove of Katherine's room.

"I had a few extra things in the bottom drawer of my wardrobe," she said from in front of her dressing table mirror. "So I didn't have to say anything to Mrs. D. No one needs to have a clue that you're sleeping on the couch."

"Good," Carson said, unable to keep the sarcasm from his tone.

The house was quiet. His mother was comfortably ensconced in her room. John and Marie were in the guest room. Their daughter Sylvia, who had taken a great fancy to Lily, was settled in Lily's room. Neville and Hortense and their two small youngsters, Willie and Eunice, were already quiet in the room next door—Carson's room.

And here he was in Katherine's room. He glanced around, unable to shake off a hemmed-in feeling. The place was a feminine clutter of satin pillows piled in the boudoir chair, lace hanging at the windows, fringed velvet decorating the mantelpiece, and roses on the table. The scent of dried rose petals was a definite counterpoint to the leather bouquet of his room.

He frowned at the bed linens. Sleeping on Katherine's fainting couch wasn't exactly what he'd had in mind when he'd given up his bed.

"It seemed the only hospitable thing to do at the time," he said. Katherine had been the perfect hostess despite the surprise guests. And it was good to see Neville, too, and his brood. "I couldn't offer to take in one brother and not the other."

"Of course not, but you know what we agreed upon," Katherine reminded him from the other side of the room.

"I remember," he said. Though he knew it was the honorable thing to do—to agree *not* to sleep with a woman he was going to leave in a few months—he disliked being reminded of their arrangement. At the moment it seemed ridiculous, this vow of chastity between two people who, under other circumstances, would probably find each other quite attractive. And nature taking its course ... well ... Carson cast an admiring glance in Katherine's direction. She'd removed her suit jacket. Her shirtwaist and narrow suit skirt admirably revealed her hourglass figure.

She stopped in the midst of removing her earrings in front of the mirror.

"But you have to admit we were good together," she said.

Her admission surprised him. She was standing in profile to him. As she reached for her earlobe, the lace of her shirtwaist pulled enticingly across her breasts

His body tensed.

"We bantered exactly like newlyweds, don't you think?" she was saying. "Your brother and mother seemed quite convinced."

"Didn't I tell you it would work?" he said, deciding to dispense with the sheets, and the blankets, too. In fact, maybe he should just go outside and stand in the cold mountain air until he could control his reactions to her.

He glared at the couch again. Everything had gone so well today that it seemed a shame to end it sleeping on a piece of furniture intended for a fainting woman. "Do you ever use this thing?"

"What?" Katherine walked to his side and stared at the couch, too. "Of course not. I don't swoon."

"I didn't think so," he said. "Just like you don't get stage fright. So why do you have it in here?"

"It was Mama's," she said. "She used to lie on it and read stories to Lily and me."

She studied the couch a moment longer. "Sharing a room does cause some problems I hadn't anticipated."

"Such as?" he prompted, thinking of problems like a fainting couch about a foot too short for him to sleep on. But he suspected the difficulties she foresaw might be different from his.

"For one thing, Lily usually helps me with the buttons," she said, glancing over her shoulder at the row of buttons down her back. "She did them this morning. But right now it would look awkward for me to go running down the hall to ask my sister to unbutton me, wouldn't it?"

"I can manage that," he said. "Why didn't you ask before?"

"Because Lily has always done it," she said. "But . . ."

"Turn around," he ordered, unable to resist smiling and hardly able to believe that she was actually asking him to help her undress—not Miss Katherine "Ice Queen" Tucker.

She obeyed.

"I never suspected I'd neglected my wife these past few weeks." he stared at her long, graceful neck for a moment, admiring the way tendrils of chestnut hair lay curled against her smooth white skin. His mouth went dry. He thought about kissing the sensitive skin there, that translucent skin just below her ear where she would be susceptible to his touch. He leaned closer, spotting the pulse beating just below her earlobe.

"What are you doing?" she asked, turning to speak over her shoulder.

"Just admiring my wife's neck," he said, before he reached for the tiny pearl buttons parading single file down her narrow back. "But I remembered that we aren't playacting at the moment. So I lost interest."

"Oh," was all she said, almost as if she was disappointed. But she said no more.

It had been a long time since he had unfastened a lady's garment. It was a task he'd never expected to forget how to do, but suddenly his fingers were all thumbs. But he persevered, quickly forgetting his ineptitude as the lace and linen parted to reveal a white back that narrowed to a tiny waist. He finished the task all too soon, too easily. He gave in to temptation and touched the back of her neck with one finger, drawing it slowly—oh so caressingly—down her back over the contours of her backbone, along the silky bare skin, down across the thin linen of her camisole, then her corset.

"Oooh," Katherine sighed, leaning her head to the side. He could see that her eyes were closed. She did not pull away.

"All finished," he whispered close to her ear without touching her again. "Is there anything more I can do for you, Mrs. Fairfax?"

"Uh, no, I don't think so." Her eyes snapped open. She seemed to shake herself, then she stepped away from him. But she would not meet his gaze. "Thank you. As soon as I put on my dressing gown, I'll help you make your bed."

She disappeared behind the black-lacquered Chinese screen that obscured one corner of her room.

"Don't worry about it," he said, turning back to the hapless couch again. The room suddenly seemed terribly hot. He'd taken off his coat earlier. He grabbed his tie and began to yank at the knot. If living next door to her had been torture, sharing a room was going to be pure hell. How in the devil was he going to sleep a few feet away from her, watch her dress and undress day after day and not go mad—or seduce her?

When his gaze fell on the couch again, he knew there wasn't a chance in purgatory of him being able to sleep on it. Lust aside, the damned thing was at least a twelve inches too short for him.

"There." Katherine emerged from behind the screen wearing a burgundy satin dressing gown that put a blush into her cheeks. "Now, let's get your bed made. We'll have to clear it up every morning, too—"

"So no one will suspect that we're not sleeping together," he finished.

Katherine stopped midway across the room. "I take it from your tone that you're not very satisfied with this arrangement."

"And why should I be? My feet are going to freeze hanging off the end of that thing."

Katherine studied him for a moment before she looked at the couch again. Then she moved closer, scrutinizing his prospective bed. "Well, yes, I can see that it might be a little too short."

"Hmph, a little?" he said. "If it was any shorter, I'd be sleeping with my feet on the floor."

She put her hands on her hips. "Then I'll sleep on the couch and you take the bed."

"I have a better idea," he said. "Let's share your bed."

"We have an agreement." She glared at him.

"And I have no intention of breaking it." He followed her step by step into the center of the room. "I'll sleep on top of the covers with one of these blankets on my side. You'll sleep under the counterpane on your side. And in the morning you won't have to worry about clearing the couch."

She continued to glare.

"Nor will we have to explain to Mother why I can't dance at the Christmas ball because my toes froze off," he added, studying her face to read her reaction.

"We certainly wouldn't want you to freeze off anything important," Katherine quipped. Then realizing her double entendre, she colored bright red. "I mean . . ."

He grinned. "I appreciate your concern, Mrs. Fairfax."

"Carson, don't make this any more awkward than it is," she fumed, her pretty face so distressed he knew she was actually considering the idea. He held his breath.

She was silent for a moment longer. "It might work, if you remain dressed and you sleep on top of the counterpane."

"Agreed," he said, softly releasing his breath and marveling how every time he started to make a deal with her, she ended up with it on her terms. "Which side do you want?"

"I like to sleep in the middle," she said, glancing toward the bed.

"I know." The moonlit image of her lying on her back with her arm thrown over her head was still clear in his memory.

"How do you know?" she asked, inspecting him again.

He shook his head. "Why don't you sleep on the left, and I'll take the right? How does that sound?"

"All right." Katherine began to loosen the sash of her dressing gown; then she looked up at Carson. "I'll get into bed as soon as you turn out the lights."

"Whatever you like," he said, already reaching for the gaslight. As soon as it was out, he heard her climb into the bed. "My turn?" he asked.

"Yes," she said.

He sat on the edge of the bed and pulled off his ankle boots. Then he loosened his collar buttons, laid back on the counterpane, and pulled the blanket over him. Stretching out, he discovered his toes just barely touched the footboard. Strange. Her bed was at least six inches longer than her father's. "This is much better than sleeping on the couch," he said.

"I'm glad to hear it." She sounded almost as if she cared. "Are you going to be warm enough?"

"Yes, quite cozy." He could tell from her voice that she was lying on her back, staring into the dancing shadows cast by the street lamp onto the ceiling above them.

"You're really glad to have your mother here, aren't you?" she asked, her voice soft with gentle curiosity and the onset of sleep.

"I'd rank this as one of the best days of my life," he said honestly. He lay in the dark feeling surprisingly whole and complete for the first time since—he couldn't remember when.

His entire family was under one roof and happy, except for Father. His father did not signify. Even Katherine was near and his, too, after a fashion.

He took a deep breath and closed his eyes, content—for now—to feel the weight of her body on the mattress beside him.

Chapter Fourteen

"Casino," little Sylvia shouted, throwing her cards into the air so that Katherine finally had to laugh.

"My lovely niece wins the game," Carson declared, also tossing his playing cards onto the pile in the middle of the dining room table. Everyone cheered—Lily the loudest. They'd only played three rounds of the countess's favorite card game, and all—including the girls, his brothers, their wives, and the countess—except Katherine were excited about the game. But she had to admit that nothing about it seemed like gambling. They were having a good time.

"That's some luck you have there, Miss Sylvia," Carson added.

The pretty, dark-haired, apple-cheeked child blushed with pleasure.

Katherine found herself gazing fondly across the table at her husband. She wasn't exactly certain what had just happened. The subtleties of card play were beyond her, but she had the uncanny feeling that Carson had engineered his niece's victory. Just as she was certain that he'd done something to help Lily win the first game of the evening. And the countess had won the second.

What a rogue he was—making people think he was a cool, hard-nosed gambler when he could control the play around the table.

He met her gaze and smiled at her briefly as he began shuffling the cards again, his big hands deftly handling the large, awkward Braille playing cards. His fingers were agile, capable. Though his hands bore no calluses, she knew they were firm, warm, and sure.

"All right," Carson said, flipping the cards through a series of maneuvers that were more akin to slight of hand than mere shuffling. "Everyone ready for the next game? We can't have Sylvia get too confident, or Lily either."

Everyone at the polished mahogany table (little Willie and his sister, baby Eunice, had long ago been tucked into bed by their nanny)—the countess, John, Marie, Neville, Hortense, Lily, and Sylvia—agreed they were "in."

The clock in the hall chimed two in the morning. The house smelled pleasantly of the Christmas cookies Sylvia and Lily had baked while the adults were out at the theater. Between all the socializing, Katherine had been working to pull together the last details of the tree decorating party. She was becoming tired, but Lily's energy seemed boundless.

She stifled a yawn but nodded that she was also "in."

She'd never seen the likes of this family. In the past four days they'd attended one reception that she'd hosted, a formal dinner hosted by Dolly, a musicale presented by the church choir, and spent one entire afternoon shopping. Nearly every entertainment had lasted into the wee hours of the morning. The lot of them would come home, ready to sing to Lily's piano playing, organize a parlor game, or play cards with Carson as dealer. She'd never dreamed having a large, extended family could be so exhausting. But she loved it.

Slowly she began to pick up her cards as Carson dealt them

out. She stared at the symbols, diamonds, spades, her eyelids growing heavy.

Suddenly she felt a nudge against her instep under the table. Thinking that she'd stretched out into someone's foot space, she drew her feet back and picked up another card.

There was the nudge again, this time firmer, more insistent.

She blinked and looked up to meet Carson's gaze. Devilment glimmered in the depths of his eyes. The nudge again, but this time it was more like a long, slow, intimate caress.

What on earth was he trying to do? She glared at him, pulled her feet back under her chair, and studied her cards with renewed concentration. She didn't care much whether she won the game or not, but she didn't want to appear disinterested in her guests.

Carson tapped his cards on the table when he finished dealing, giving her the distinct feeling he wanted her to look at him. When she did, he shook his head ever so slowly, as if he was terribly disappointed. Then she felt his foot tap the floor across from her. She met his gaze again, realizing that he wanted to play another game. Or maybe he was just trying to help her stay awake. Whichever, Katherine set her feet out under the table again and passed on her turn to bid in the game.

"I must compliment you, Katherine," John began as the game progressed. "I understand from what Mrs. Green was telling me—that is her name, isn't it, Dolly Green? That remarkable lady with the pearl choker—she told Mother and me that you've single-handedly reformed Carson."

Carson immediately placed the toe of his boot between Katherine's feet. She could feel the heat begin to rise into her cheeks.

"John, darling, it's not our place," cautioned Marie, a sweet, round-faced matron with luxuriant brown hair that she always wore coiled at the back of her neck. "And there are children at the table."

"I know all about it," Lily piped. "Carson told me."

Katherine glanced up at her husband, then quickly looked

down at her cards again and replied, "I would hardly say that I've reformed your brother."

"But you made him sell the Gentleman's Respite, didn't you, my dear?" the countess asked, fingering her cards. She smiled at Katherine.

She returned the smile. The countess had been an unexpected delight—not that she hadn't expected to like her. In spite of all Carson had told her, she had expected the lady to be more formal, stuffy, with high standards—or expectations, depending on how you looked at it. Instead she was sweet, curious, accepting, and completely delighted with each new situation presented to her. In addition she was considerate, energetic, and warm. No wonder Carson was willing to move heaven and earth to please her. Realizing it was her turn to bid, "I pass," she said.

Carson wiggled his foot, working it deeper in between her feet. She tried to frown at him, but there was such a twinkle in his eyes, it was impossible. She liked having the secret contact with him. She liked the camaraderie, the intimacy.

"The Gentleman's Respite is a very respectable and successful men's club, Mother," Carson said.

"Then you should have made a very nice profit on it," John said. Marie elbowed him. "Ladies, please excuse us for discussing business," he added.

"Profit enough," Carson said, winking at Katherine. "But I wouldn't have sold it for anything less than marrying Katherine."

"There's nothing quite like the love of a good woman," Neville said, smiling fondly at Hortense. Unlike John, Neville was short and stout, and fair complected with a gentle face, like their mother's. Hortense, his wife, was tall, dark, sallow, and thin, with a tendency to be sour-faced. But a kind word from her husband always brought a smile to her lips.

"Indeed," Carson replied, meeting Katherine's gaze across the table again. "There is much a man will do for the love of a good woman."

How clever he was, Katherine thought with a frown. No one at the table seemed to note that Carson had never once said that he loved her. Why should he? Declaring his love—even as part of their playacting—would be going too far. Nevertheless, the omission unaccountably hurt her feelings. She tucked her feet back under her chair again.

An easy companionship had sprung up between them during the past week. Everywhere they went with Carson's family, they were received as a married couple. Everyone expected to see Katherine at Carson's side or Carson at Katherine's side. He had every right to put his hand on the small of her back as they greeted people and moved through society. She had the right to put her hand on his arm or feel the warmth of his hands on her shoulders when he helped her with her wrap.

Every night since his first night in her bed, they'd grown accustomed to lying in the darkness and evaluating the day, the success of each event, the countess's reaction to it, their hostess's resourcefulness. Without violating his agreement to sleep on top of the counterpane, their conversations sometimes drifted into things about his brothers and his homes in England, which had consisted of a couple of manor houses, a castle in ruins, a summer house in Brighton, and a town house in London. She found herself telling him about the winters in Georgetown and the rollicking performances in the local theaters where her mother had performed.

They were beginning to know enough about each other to anticipate the other's reaction to things. But what she had found most touching was Carson's obvious pleasure and happiness in having his family close. It was almost contagious.

She was glad she hadn't insisted on making him sleep on the fainting couch. What a silly prude she'd been to think that he couldn't be trusted. The sound of his voice in the dark was soothing and the feel of his body next to hers was becoming familiar, comforting. Just that morning she'd awakened to find him sound asleep, lying on his side, facing her, with his arm thrown across her body. It had seemed almost natural to lie so close. She'd lain there for some time, watching him.

He'd looked very young in his sleep, almost boyish, innocent. Hah! If they only knew what he'd been doing with his feet under that table.

"And what do you have in your hand, Katherine?" Carson was saying to her across the dining room table. His gentle tone made her realize that she'd been woolgathering and should return her attention to the game. "What do you bid, sweetheart?"

"Ah, let me see." She blinked, straightened in her chair, and forced herself to concentrate on her hand. Suddenly the card symbols leapt out at her and she saw that she had a winning hand. Her sleepiness vanished. Delight coursed through her. Victory at last, after all the dull hands of cards.

"Casino," she cried, throwing down her hand on the table to prove it.

When she looked up, she saw Carson grinning at her, a charming expression, warm and teasing, intimate, a look meant only for her.

The heat of it made her belly flutter. So she'd been his chosen winner this time. She wanted him to know that she knew what he was doing. She rubbed her feet on either side of his.

Surprise flashed across his face before he hid his expression in gathering up the cards once more.

Marie, John's wife, was the next winner, and the victory made her giggle in a manner that pleased everyone at the table. Then they broke up for the night, several of them stifling yawns as they rose from their chairs and bade each other good night.

Alone in their room, Katherine went to her dressing table mirror and began to take off her earrings. Carson closed the door softly, then stole up behind her and slipped an arm around her waist. She allowed him to pull her against his body. She'd become accustomed to his familiar, sometimes playful physical contact. They stood looking at their reflection in the mirror.

"Just what was that little game under the table all about?" he asked, almost crooning in her ear.

She laughed. "I don't know. You're the one who started it."

"I was afraid you were going to fall asleep right there at the table," Carson said. His hand spread across her belly was warm and strong. Katherine leaned against him, feeling secure in the circle of his arms.

"You're exhausted," he continued. "You're working too hard at being a good hostess. It comes to you naturally. Don't try so hard."

"But there are still so many details to see to for the tree decorating party," she protested, continuing to melt against him.

Carson turned her toward him and she lifted her face to his. He brushed his lips across hers lightly.

"And they will all fall into place in good time." He kissed her again, longer this time. She closed her eyes, her face still lifted to his. She savored the tender, intimate sensation. He kissed her eyelids, her cheeks, her nose; then his lips settled on hers again.

His embraced tightened, yet his mouth forced nothing fiery on her. She relaxed in his arms, tasting him. Then, before she knew what he was doing, he'd enticed her lips apart and lured her mouth into accepting his tongue. He stroked inside leisurely. Instead of shock, pleasure swept through her. She relished each caress of his tongue, though she knew she shouldn't. Why should she tempt herself—and him—into something that could never be, something that they'd agreed would never happen? Yet it was so wonderful.

Her knees became weak and a strange weightlessness lifted through her. Attempting to seduce him to continue, she made herself more accessible to him.

His hands spread across the small of her back and one slipped down, pressing her bottom closer until she could feel his hardness against her. His scent filled her head, tangy, spicy—Carson. She didn't want what he was doing to cease.

She slipped her arms around his neck so he couldn't escape.

A low, needy groan rumbled from him. He deepened the kiss. Katherine whimpered and attempted her own intimate forays into his mouth.

Finally they both had to surface for air.

Eyes still closed, she could only lean against his chest, breathless and boneless.

"Your ice is melting, Queen Katherine," Carson murmured, his lips pressed against her forehead.

She wondered how he knew that her breasts were tingling, that there was an aching wetness between her thighs, and that her bones had indeed turned to liquid.

"Let me help you with these buttons," he added, his fingers already working on the buttons at the back of her gown.

He'd helped her fasten and unfasten her clothing on many occasions over the past week, but her good sense told her that allowing him to undress her tonight could be dangerous. She turned anyway, allowing him to reach the buttons more easily. He'd only unfastened a couple when a soft rap on the door interrupted.

"Katherine? Mr. Fairfax?" Mrs. D called softly through the door.

"I'll get it," he said, dropping a quick kiss on the back of her neck before going to the door. "Yes, what is it, Mrs. D?"

"I wouldn't bother you at this hour, but there's a letter that came for you earlier," Mrs. D explained. "I promised Jack that I'd make sure you received it today."

From where she stood, Katherine couldn't see her housekeeper, but she saw Carson accept a white envelope. "Jack seemed to think that it was important that you have it today," Mrs. D added.

"Thank you," Carson said, studying the letter with that

bland look that she had come to know as the expression he wore when he was hiding his feelings. "Good night, Mrs. D."

"What is it?" she asked, hurrying to his side, worried that it might be bad news. Without thinking, she reached for the envelope.

"Nothing important, just business," Carson said, clearly wanting to dismiss the issue, putting the letter in his inside coat pocket, but not before she caught sight of the return address.

"It's from San Francisco," she said, puzzled. The flamboyant handwriting was unfamiliar. "Oh, that's where you're going to set up your new club."

"Yes, it's from Alice Johnson, my San Francisco partner," he said, his tone dismissive. "Nothing for you to be concerned about. It's probably just an update on how arrangements are going. Jack mistakes how important these things are to me."

"Of course," she said, suddenly chilled. The effects of their passionate kiss vanished, sizzling to nothing, like cold water on a hot griddle. She backed away from Carson, glancing up into his face. Instead of seeing her husband, the grinning man who had made certain she won at cards, she saw a stranger, a cold, insensitive man who invested in gambling casinos and men's clubs without regard for the welfare of families. She saw a man who'd promised her a quick annulment and a speedy departure from Denver. No wonder he'd sold the Respite so readily. He was intending to leave all along.

"Katherine, let me finish with your buttons." He reached for her.

Suddenly she couldn't bear the thought of him touching her. "That's all right. You unfastened enough that I can reach the rest."

Feeling like a fool, she retreated behind the Chinese screen. Thankful that the screen hid her from him, she sank onto her boudoir stool and took a deep, shaky breath.

How could she forget herself like that in the man's arms? How could she forget why he was here? How could she forget who he was?

She'd permitted him to kiss her—really kiss her—and hold her, and to start to undress her. And she had liked it. Really liked it. Drat. Drat. Double drat. With the back of her hand she covered her mouth to stifle a groan of mortification.

On the other side of the screen, she could hear him moving around, removing his coat—boots dropping to the floor, bedcovers being arranged.

"Katherine, I'm going to put out the lamp," he finally called. "Is that all right?"

She gulped, trying to rid herself of the tightness in her throat. No tears, she silently ranted at herself. She spoke up, trying to sound as normal as possible. "Yes, put out the lights."

The room went dark and she heard the bed springs creak as Carson laid down.

Fortified by the darkness, she awkwardly began to unfasten the last of the buttons at the back of her gown. She quickly slipped out of her clothes and into her nightgown and wrapper. Finally she crept out from behind the screen. She could tell from Carson's breathing that he was awake.

When she reached her side of the bed, she glanced at his side, but she could not see well in the darkness. She paused and cleared her throat. "You are on top of the counterpane, are you not?"

"Yes, I am." His voice was toneless. It sounded as if he was lying on his back.

"Fine," she said, feeling safer. She'd been afraid that he'd pursue the advantage he'd had earlier. She untied her wrapper, slipped out of it, and tossed the garment across the foot of the bed, where she knew she'd find Lucky in the morning. Then she slipped under the covers, careful to stay on her edge of the bed.

"Katherine?" Carson's voice came out of the darkness again. "Yes?"

"The letter—it's only business, you know," he said. "It doesn't have anything to do with us."

"I know," she said, the bleakness of their future relationship settling over her in the darkness. ''That's precisely the point, isn't it? It's only business.''

She didn't sleep a wink that night, and she didn't think he did either.

Take 4 FREE Books!

We created our convenient Home Subscription Service so you'll be sure to have the hottest new romances delivered each month right to your doorstep — usually before they are available in book stores. Just to show you how convenient Zebra Home Subscription Service is, we would like to send you 4 Kensington Choice Historical Romances as a FREE gift. You receive a gift worth up to $24.96 — absolutely FREE. There's no extra charge for shipping and handling. There's no obligation to buy anything - ever!

Save Up To 32% On Home Delivery!

Accept your FREE gift and each month we'll deliver 4 brand new titles as soon as they are published. They'll be yours to examine FREE for 10 days. Then if you decide to keep the books, you'll pay the preferred subscriber's price of just $4.20 per title. That's $16.80 for all 4 books for a savings of up to 32% off the cover price! Just add $1.50 to offset the cost of shipping and handling. Remember, you are under no obligation to buy any of these books at any time! If you are not delighted with them, simply return them and owe nothing. But if you enjoy Kensington Choice Historical Romances as much as we think you will, pay the special preferred subscriber rate of only $16.80 each month and save over $8.00 off the bookstore price!

We have 4 FREE BOOKS for you as
your introduction to
KENSINGTON CHOICE!

To get your FREE BOOKS,
worth up to $24.96, mail the card below
or call TOLL-FREE 1-888-345-BOOK
Visit our website at www.kensingtonbooks.com.

Take 4 Kensington Choice Historical Romances FREE!

YES! Please send me my 4 FREE KENSINGTON CHOICE HISTORICAL ROMANCES (without obligation to purchase other books). Unless you hear from me after I receive my 4 FREE BOOKS, you may send me 4 new novels - as soon as they are published - to preview each month FREE for 10 days. If I am not satisfied, I may return them and owe nothing. Otherwise, I will pay the money-saving preferred subscriber's price of just $4.20 each... a total of $16.80 plus $1.50 for shipping and handling. That's a savings of over $8.00 each month. I may return any shipment within 10 days and owe nothing, and I may cancel any time I wish. In any case the 4 FREE books will be mine to keep.

Name _____

Address _____ Apt No _____

City _____ State _____ Zip _____

Telephone ( ) _____ Signature _____

(If under 18, parent or guardian must sign)

KNOH0A

Terms, offer, and prices subject to change. Orders subject to acceptance by Zebra Home Subscription Service, Inc. Offer valid in the U.S. only.

4 FREE
Kensington
Choice
Historical
Romances
are waiting
for you to
claim them!

(worth up
to $24.96)

See details
inside....

||..|..|||...||||..|||.||..||.|..||.|..||.|..||.|..|||..|

KENSINGTON CHOICE
Zebra Home Subscription Service, Inc.
P.O. Box 5214
Clifton NJ 07015-5214

Chapter Fifteen

Putting on as cordial a face as he could muster, Owen Benedict ambled up to the Englishman standing in Dolly Green's library. "Marriage seems to agree with you, Fairfax."

It had been almost six weeks since the wedding and longer since he'd had a word alone with the gambler. Katherine and Fairfax's marriage had been such a shock that he'd been paralyzed—for a time. Still uncertain about his next move, he'd begun to fear that he'd waited too long to move ahead with his plans. But first, he needed to know how things stood.

"Benedict." Fairfax's smile was sociable, but not especially friendly. Though they traveled in the same social circle, the Englishman had never been particularly friendly. Owen had always assumed it had to do with them being associated with rival banks. Apparently his marriage to Katherine had changed nothing.

"Fine supper Dolly served up," Owen said, offering a casual conversation opening. They were standing in the corner of the library, where Fairfax was seemingly scanning the books on the shelf. The other male guests had gathered by the fire, lighting up their cigars, while the ladies had moved into the drawing room to chat.

"Fine dinner," Fairfax agreed, an element of distraction in his tone.

The afternoon had been filled with a sleigh ride and ice skating, then topped off with supper in the society matron's grand dining room. During the entire time, Fairfax had been constantly surrounded by his mother, his brothers, Dolly, or his wife.

Owen had noted that the Englishman and Katherine had been treating each other with studied civility all afternoon and throughout the dinner. He had absolutely no idea what their behavior toward each other meant, but he had no more time to waste.

And now that the moment alone with Fairfax was here, he didn't want to misstep. The problem was, how did one sway a man who was not vulnerable to the usual strategies—bribery, violence, or extortion?

"Your mother's visit seems to be a great success," Owen began, turning to watch the chattering women through the open doors as Fairfax was doing.

"Yes, it is going well," the Englishman said, his tone almost wistful. "Katherine is a charming hostess. My family is enjoying Denver immensely. They like the American West and Katherine, too."

"Fortunate for her and you that you discovered each other when you did," Owen said, trying to figure out how to get to the topic that was really foremost on his mind. "You saved the Elms for her and she opened the place to your mother and brothers."

To his surprise, Fairfax swung around and nailed him with a cold steely glare. "Yes, it was fortunate. Is there something you'd like to say about that?"

The Englishman's vehemence made Owen mentally backtrack. "No, no. I only wanted you to know that it has not escaped me that Katherine and Lily appear to be getting along well since you and Katherine wed. They seem to be happy."

"And . . . ?" Fairfax's hard expression eased into a poker face, but Owen didn't believe for a minute that he was off the hook.

"I want to apologize if I appeared to be suspicious of you before the wedding," Owen finished, nearly choking. He hated making apologies, but he wasn't going to get anywhere with Fairfax if the man thought he was still under suspicion.

"As Katherine's guardian, you were doing your job." Fairfax's face did not change. "I'm glad you see that I don't mean Katherine or Lily any harm."

Encouraged, he nodded. "I'm sincerely glad you feel that way. I think it's in the girls' best interest if we work together to maintain the estate for them. Of course, Katherine only has another five months before she comes into full control of the Tucker fortune, but this is no time to relax our vigilance. The shifting economic current can undermine even the most carefully managed fortune these days."

Fairfax nodded. "True, and I think it is important that Katherine be kept well versed on her affairs."

"Naturally." Owen covered his disapproval of the Englishman's misguided belief in Katherine's right to know. "But she is a woman, and serious financial matters—you know, those beyond the daily ins and outs of running a household— are far too complicated for the nurturing female mind."

"I find Katherine has an amazing grasp of things she needs to know," Fairfax said, his expression as unrevealing as ever. "What aspect of her affairs troubles you?"

"Well, it's the Amanda Leigh," he said, aware that he was stepping onto thin ice. "Of all the Tucker assets, it is the most depleting. The equipment sitting there is modern. That steam-powered compressor is one of the best ever made. It's still in good shape. Why not sell it off, and the mine, too? The Amanda Leigh produces no income and the equipment will only lose value as it ages."

"Who wants to buy a worthless mine?" Fairfax asked.

"Actually, there is a firm offering a fair price, I think," he said, pleased that Fairfax was interested enough to ask questions.

"Who?"

"I don't recall the name," Owen said, feeling like a fisherman attempting to set the hook in his quarry's mouth. "They approached the bank about it. I did not pursue the matter because I knew that Katherine would say no."

Fairfax nodded. "She is devoted to her father's wishes."

"For purely sentimental reasons, I'm certain," he said. "It was his first strike, you know. The mine he attributed his fortune to."

"And you have no feelings about the mine?" Fairfax nodded again, then added, "I thought you and he were partners."

"Not in the Amanda Leigh," Owen said, a bit surprised by the question. The strike at the Amanda Leigh had become something of a legend, and for that reason it was difficult to give up his connection with it. "Actually Ben and I were partners in several mines in the beginning. I still own half of the Clementine with Katherine. I'm embarrassed to admit that I gave up on the Amanda Leigh. I didn't think it would ever turn a profit. So I sold out to Ben."

"Is that so?" Fairfax asked with casual interest.

"Tucker wasn't the hero he liked to act, you know." Suddenly he could almost see the love of his life in his mind's eye. "Amanda Leigh, Katherine's mother, confessed to me that she sold her theatrical costumes and what little jewelry she had so Ben could buy me out."

"You and Amanda were close friends, then?"

"Close? I almost married her, until Ben came along." He snapped his mouth shut, annoyed with himself for bringing up unhappy memories. He realized Fairfax was watching him with a sidelong curious gaze. "But you're not interested in ancient history," he said, brushing away old memories that still had the power to hurt him.

"On the contrary, I find stories of the old days interesting." Fairfax sipped nonchalantly from his drink. "Too bad you didn't remain Ben Tucker's partner. Your fortune would have been made, too."

"I made my fortune soon enough," Owen said, bridling at the implication that he'd lost out. "My strike came only six months later."

He cleared his throat and marshaled his thoughts back to his purpose. "The point is, you can see why Tucker was sentimental about the mine. When he was down to nothing and even his wife had to give up her last baubles, the Amanda Leigh paid off for him. It was pure luck, of course, but he hit the vein that made him a multimillionaire. He could have just as easily struck nothing and been left starving with his family like hundreds of others who came to make their fortune in Colorado in Fifty-nine."

"And you are asking why Katherine should threaten her fortune because of her father's sentimentality?" Fairfax finished for him.

"Exactly," Owen said. At last he was getting somewhere. "I'm glad you take my point. You see, we both want the best for Katherine and Lily."

Laughter from the ladies in the drawing room drifted into the library. Fairfax turned to watch the women again.

For a fraction of a second, Owen glimpsed an unguarded softening of the Englishman's expression when he caught sight of Katherine. Was it possible? he wondered in astonishment. Perhaps theirs was a love match. The saloonkeeper and the reformer? After all, Fairfax had given up the Gentleman's Respite for her, token sale though it was.

Owen forced a tolerant chuckle. "Katherine is a willful young lady. I don't know that it's possible to change her mind. But with a few words of advice from you, we might be able to make her see the wisdom in the sale."

"You know I signed an agreement not to touch my wife's fortune," Fairfax said.

"And an admirable gesture that was, too," Owen said, uneasy with Fairfax's evasiveness. "But advising your wife is hardly the same thing as using her money for your own purposes. I'm merely suggesting you use your influence in her best interest."

"Just the same, I'm not inclined to encourage her to do something that she is set against," Fairfax said with a shrug of indifference. "If she wants to keep the Amanda Leigh, I'm willing to see her do so."

"But do you think that wise?" He took a deep breath to quell his growing impatience. "Just when she needs cash on hand, you encourage her to hang on to assets that could serve her better?"

"She doesn't need to worry about available cash," Fairfax said offhandedly. "She has mine."

"Yes, so she does," Owen said, smiling though the Englishman's arrogance angered him. He sipped his drink to hide it. "Think about what I said. You're in a position to keep her from making mistakes that she might regret where the Amanda Leigh is concerned. Ah, here comes Dolly. I'm afraid the peace of the evening is at an end. Thanks for your ear, Fairfax. By the way, Edna and I are looking forward to having you and your family at our New Year's Eve ball."

Not feeling in the least cordial but intent on keeping up appearances, he held out his hand and prayed Fairfax would accept it. To his satisfaction, the Englishman took his hand and shook it firmly.

"Yes, we plan to attend," Fairfax said.

Owen walked away disappointed and befuddled, but he forced another smile onto his face. So Fairfax was not going to cooperate. The fool was going to let his wife do what she wanted. Who would have thought one of Denver's richest men would become a henpecked husband? It still troubled him that he did not understand why Fairfax had married Katherine. If the Englishman was willing to keep his hands off her money and he was willing to allow her to make her own decisions about her money, why had he tied himself to the spoiled, snobbish chit? Merely to acquire a good hostess for his mother? Surely there was more to it than that. Lust? Katherine was attractive enough. Love?

Owen mentally shook himself. Not love. Whatever Fairfax's motivation, it didn't matter. The fact remained that there were now two people standing between him and Ray Jones and the Amanda Leigh—Carson Fairfax and Katherine.

As much as he disliked the idea, both would have to be eliminated.

Carson watched Benedict saunter away, then he drained his whiskey glass. He'd never trusted the man. Sell off the Amanda Leigh and its equipment, indeed. There was only one reason why any company would be interested in the Amanda Leigh. Someone thought there was gold in it—still. Undoubtedly, Ben Tucker had thought so, too. Sentiment? Hardly. Tucker had believed in the Amanda Leigh right down to his final hour. The man had been too successful through the years to be a foolish old sentimentalist. There was something in that mine, and he was willing to wager that Owen Benedict knew it, too.

Carson caught sight of Katherine following Dolly into the library. Her hesitant smile—the first since the arrival of that bloody letter from San Francisco—brought an answering smile to his lips.

She deserved to know if the mine had anything to offer. As soon as his mother and brothers were on their way back to England, he intended to make a trip into the mountains to find out just what allure the Amanda Leigh held for Benedict.

As the day of the annual Tucker tree decorating party neared, the excitement at the Elms grew. Everyone was pressed into service.

Carson was surprised to find even his brothers as excited as boys. They helped Willis and the deliverymen carry the gigantic Christmas tree Katherine had ordered up the front steps through the double doors and into the parlor. It had been a complicated task, five men maneuvering the fourteen-foot-tall tree into the hallway, around into the front room, then setting it upright so its top just grazed the ornate ceiling. All under the supervision of Katherine, of course.

They'd been so pleased with their accomplishment that they'd broken out the fine Scotch whiskey that John had brought and toasted the tree, the house, Denver, and the ladies.

As the fresh pine tree filled the house with its tangy scent, the ladies had set about performing a number of final chores. The countess and Katherine put the finishing touches on the plants in the conservatory. In the kitchen—even though vast quantities of food were being brought in by a caterer—there were still specialties only Mrs. D could make to be created with the help of Marie, Hortense, Sylvia, Willie, Eunice, and Lily.

When Lily and Sylvia weren't in the kitchen, they were in the music room at the piano, where Lily practiced carols and hymns. The Elms was filled with the most delicious fragrances and the most delightful sounds.

Finally the day of the tree decorating party arrived. The food was made and stored. The decorations where in place, rich and colorful. The tree stood naked but expectant in the parlor, where Willis had started a fire.

Most everyone had retired to dress for the party and the house was momentarily, if deceptively, quiet. Carson paced through the candlelit, garland-decked rooms, pleased with all that he saw. Satisfied, he jogged upstairs to put on his suit.

"There you are, Carson," his mother said, when he reached the top of the stairs. She was standing in the hallway, already dressed for the party in a rich, understated dark green gown, with her white hair piled high on her head. She looked lovely and as excited as a schoolgirl. But uncertainty was written on her face.

"Do you need something, Mother?"

"Only a moment to say what a wonderful time I'm having." She grasped his hands and gazed up into his face. The pleasure and love glowing in her eyes warmed him. "I have my boys together for Christmas. There was a time when I despaired that would ever happen again."

"I know, Mother."

"If only your father—"

Carson shook his head. His brothers, himself, and his father under one roof—that would never happen.

"Well, he's a stubborn man," the countess added, her voice quavering with emotion. "We won't let that dim our happiness. Katherine is a delightful girl. You made an excellent choice. I'm elated to see you settled and happy."

Carson's heart ached with the sight of her pleasure. It was enough. He didn't give a damn what his father thought. He had nothing to prove to the earl. But his mother's happiness made all of the lies and deceptions worthwhile.

"I'm glad, Mother." He accepted her loving hug. With this vital, energetic woman in his arms, he could hardly believe that only a year ago he'd feared for her life.

"Now, as to why I'm up here . . ." she said, releasing him and standing back, ready to get back to business. "We have a tree decorating party to get underway. This is so much fun and such a fine tradition for Katherine's family to have. I love helping with it. Anyway, Mrs. D was wanting to know if Katherine wished to use the Irish linen or the Belgian lace for the dining room table tonight." Mother gestured toward the door at the end of the hall. "I thought to ask Katherine, but she is in the bath."

"Oh." He glanced at the bathroom door. Now that his mother mentioned it, he could hear the water running in the tub.

When he turned back to her, she was smiling ever so wickedly. "Mrs. D is rather eager to get on with setting the table. Perhaps you'd be so kind as to ask your wife which linen she'd like to use this evening."

"Now?" Carson asked, glancing at the door again. Since the night of their game under the table, the night Alice Johnson's letter had arrived, things between he and Katherine had been cool—when they weren't playacting. Obviously they'd been convincing enough in public to have his mother and his brothers believe that they were happy newlyweds. But in private he might as well be sleeping on the fainting couch for all the closeness Katherine allowed him.

"Surely Katherine won't mind if you interrupt her bath ever so briefly," the countess said. "I mean, it's really not my place to disturb a lady at her bath. But you're her husband . . ."

"Yes, well . . ." he said, seeing no way to refuse his mother—and intrigued by the challenge. "I'll just see what I can find out for you."

When Carson reached the door, he rapped on it soundly and turned the doorknob. "Sweetheart, it's me."

To his relief, the door was unlocked. "Mother has sent me with some questions for you." Without waiting for Katherine to object, he opened the door and slipped in. The steaminess of the bathroom immediately closed around him and the scent of honeysuckle filled his head.

"What the—?" Katherine gasped, and water sloshed as she sank down in the tub into water up to her chin.

He put his finger to his mouth to silence her. Then he whispered, "Mother is outside and she is listening."

Katherine turned off the water, pressed her lips together, and glared at him. "You'd better not be fibbing about this," she whispered.

Undaunted, he grinned at her and started across the bathroom toward the tub. "Yes, sweetheart, I'd love to scrub your back for you," he said, in a voice loud enough for his mother to hear. "But first I have a question for you."

"That would be lovely, dearest," Katherine replied in equal volume. But her arm shot out of the water to hold him at bay. "Don't you dare come a step closer," she whispered.

Grinning at the sight of her bare, shapely arm, Carson halted and raised his voice again. "Mother and Mrs. Dodd wanted to know whether you wished to use the Irish linen on the table tonight or the Belgian lace."

He reached for the back brush lying on the stool next to the tub.

"The Irish linen, I think," she replied, loud enough for his mother to hear. Then she frowned at him, her eyes narrowing, and she shook her head. "Don't you come an inch closer to me with that brush," she hissed under her breath.

"Right, the Irish linen it is then," he said, waving the brush above her. She stretched to fend it off. Steamy water lapped in the tub, exposing her shoulders and one delicious pink-tipped breast.

Carson's body reacted painfully. "Just let me get this one last spot for you, darling. There, how's that?" he asked.

"Wonderful, dearest," Katherine crooned, with a sigh that almost made him toss the brush aside and drag her out of the tub to be ravished.

He swallowed the tightness in his throat and forced himself to ignore the ache in his loins. "I'll tell Mother about the Belgian lace."

"Irish linen." Katherine glared at him. "I want the Irish linen."

"Right, Irish linen." He dropped the brush and went to the door, opening it just a crack. How was a man supposed to think straight with a lovely body like that just soaking there in the water? "Mother?"

"Yes, I heard, dear." His mother was grinning. "Irish linen. I'll tell Mrs. D. Thank you, dear. Back to your wife. Don't let her take a chill."

Carson shut the door and turned back to Katherine.

Chapter Sixteen

"Is your mother gone?" Katherine asked, once again submerged up to her ears in bathwater. Dewy steam clung to her eyelashes and strands of chestnut hair lay plastered to her jaw. Carson burned to have her.

"Yes, she's gone," he said, studying his wife's flushed face. The room was stifling hot. He unbuttoned his collar and walked toward the tub again. Why had he ever agreed to go through with this charade of a marriage without bedding her? And after tasting the passion in her wedding kiss . . .

"Well?"

"Well, what?" he asked, sitting down on the stool.

"If your mother is gone, you can leave," she said, eyeing him warily.

"Since I'm here, why don't you let me scrub your back?" he said. "It does seem the husbandly thing to do."

"Very nice of you to offer, but I've scrubbed my back already," she said. "I'm finished with my bath, and I don't need your help. If you would be so kind as to leave . . ."

"No, I can't do that." He rose from the stool and pulled the towel off the shelf. "Mother is right, you know. As your husband I can't have you taking a chill while getting out of the tub."

"I can manage very nicely myself, thank you," she said, reaching for the towel. Water surged around her shoulders. The soft swell of her breasts came into view, only making Carson's desire more painful.

He stepped back from the tub, holding the towel just barely beyond her reach. "Are you sure?"

"Stop that." Katherine looked up at him but didn't move. Her charms remained immersed in soapy water. "Carson, you're overstepping our terms."

"I don't remember any caveats about bathing." He shook the towel. "I'm just offering my assistance as your husband. We live under the same roof and sleep in the same bed. I've seen you in your nightgown. You've seen me in little more than my trousers. These intimacies are bound to happen when two people share a room, even if it *is* playacting."

She eyed him for a long moment, her head cocked to one side. "Are you trying to talk me into getting out of the bathtub in the all together so you can—?"

"Admire your charms? Indeed I am," he admitted, unable to keep the lecherous grin from his face. "A husband's prerogative, don't you think?"

Katherine huffed. "If you were my husband, you'd offer me the towel and avert your gaze in a gentlemanly fashion."

"You mean you don't think your husband would feel passionately enough about you to desire a good long look at your beauty?"

"Well, of course my husband would be passionate," Katherine stammered, clearly torn by conflicting ideals. "But he would understand my desire for modesty, too."

"Umm, and you'd have no desire to give him what he wanted," he taunted, gently, softly. He leaned closer. "You'd have no desire to indulge his urges? This man who would be the love of your life. You wouldn't be willing to give him that?''

Katherine glared at him, clearly resentful of his probing at her confusion.

"I'm just saying that I'm not sure your husband would be able to give you both," he argued as innocently as he could manage. "Passion and privacy. The two are a contradiction, are they not?"

"How so?" Katherine asked.

"Passion requires the shedding of all pretenses," he said, a little surprised by his own words. He understood what he was saying, but he also knew that he'd never practiced what he was preaching with a woman. "It requires the revelation of our true selves, of all that we really are. The offering up of your whole self, unguarded, vulnerable, exposed. Naked, if you will, physically and emotionally. Body and soul."

"A very pretty speech." Katherine seemed to consider his words. Then she looked up, meeting his gaze. Amusement glimmered in her eyes. "Mr. Fairfax, I think you missed your calling. You shouldn't have been a saloonkeeper, you should have been a snake-oil salesman. Naked and exposed? Body and soul? You're as full of flimflam as any sideshow huckster."

"Snake-oil man. I'm wounded, Mrs. Fairfax." He released a long breath of exasperation—and frustration. He'd been short-sighted. Maybe he deserved this. He'd proposed a marriage of convenience and then accepted the ridiculous terms—selling his club and no lovemaking. "Remind me. What did you say your husband would do?"

"Hold up the towel and avert his gaze, like a gentleman," Katherine said, smiling sweetly at him.

Carson held up the towel and turned his head away. "I shall take nary a peek."

"Promise?"

"I promise," he vowed, crossing his fingers.

After a moment's silence, the water sloshed and he heard her rising from the tub, the water sluicing off her body.

Then he looked, watching through barely opened eyes as his Venus rose from a bathtub seashell, her back to him. Water coursed down her fine white skin, caressing her, gleaming along the delicious curves of her body, her shoulders, the curve of her back, the fullness of her breasts, hips, thighs.

He could not muffle the groan that rose in him.

Katherine reached for the towel, but he refused to relinquish it. He insisted on wrapping it around her, then pulling her against him so her bottom pressed against his arousal and his arms supported her cloth-covered breasts. Just within the reach of his lips was her damp neck, crying out to be nibbled. He buried his nose in the silky mass of hair piled on her head and began to kiss her neck.

"Carson," Katherine said in a breathless voice. She struggled a little, just enough to excite him even more.

The weight of her breasts against his arm was divine. He stroked her body from her ribs down over her belly to the juncture of her thighs. She clutched at his stroking hand, but she did not pull it away. He tasted her neck, allowing her damp hair to tickle his nose and her clean, feminine scent to fill his head, his mouth. Then he found her earlobe.

"Carson," she whispered on a sigh. "We must be ready to receive guests in an hour."

The thrill of his name on her lips only made him harder. "I know, dammit. But there is later."

"No." She shook her head imperceptibly. "You agreed . . ."

"Damn the agreement," he grumbled, leaving her earlobe. "We're two healthy people who lie side by side every night, so close our breaths mingle. And we are husband and wife."

"But only temporarily, you varlet," she said, but she made the epithet sound like a pet name. She attempted to shrug him off without facing him. "Wasn't that the bargain?"

"Ah, that's what troubles you," he said, feeling the magic of the moment slipping away but not discouraged yet. He knew the truth. Her body had quickened in response to his touch. He'd heard the passion in her sigh and glimpsed sultry desire in her eyes when she'd glanced at him over her bare shoulder. He knew making love to her was going to be an extraordinary experience. And it would happen, arrangement or not. "That part of our deal was your idea, that silly chastity vow between us that you insisted upon. I'd like to propose another pact."

"Oh, no," Katherine said, turning to face him. He allowed her to pull away this time, but she was still standing thigh deep in bathwater with only a towel clutched around her. "No more tricks."

"No tricks," he said, putting on his guileless face. But he was beginning to realize that there might be something else on her mind, too. "Just listen to me for a minute."

"All right, Mr. Snake-Oil Man," she said, skepticism in every sweet angle of her face. "I'm listening."

"I think it's safe to say that we're a man and a woman who find each other attractive," he began.

Katherine closed her eyes and shook her head. "Purely a matter of familiarity."

He paused, exasperated by her stubborn refusal to see the truth. "All right, call it familiarity if you insist, but an attraction does exist between us. Will you grant that?"

"Yes." Katherine rubbed her ear with the towel. "I fail to see how that changes anything."

"Let's see what happens, sweetheart," he said, taking her face between his hands. He struggled against the urge to kiss her. "Think about it. That's all I ask. And remember when it happens, it won't be anything like what happened with Nolan."

Then he dared to kiss her, quick and sweet. "Nothing, I promise."

"Promise?" she repeated, her tone soft, questioning, awed, suspicious. He wasn't sure which.

"I promise," he vowed. Then, with all the strength he had he forced himself to turn away without taking in one more eyeful of Katherine, flushed and pink, naked beneath the towel. He left her, closing the door solidly behind him.

He stood in the hallway for a minute, wondering whether

he was a fool for leaving his wife like that. He'd just stroked her body with only fabric between his palm and her fragrant skin. He'd glimpsed yearning in her eyes. He'd seen the flush of desire on her bare flesh. Maybe she wasn't an ice queen. But he was beginning to suspect he would die of lust before she admitted it.

"Sir, what are you scribbling in that reporter's notebook of yours?" Katherine demanded, sneaking up on Randolph in the hallway in the midst of the Christmas tree decorating party.

Festivities were in full swing. Piano music drifted from the music room and conversation and laughter clamored from the drawing room. She had just returned from the kitchen, where she'd instructed Mrs. D to start setting out supper. That was when she found the newspaperman in the hallway, obviously stealing a moment to jot down something important.

Randolph started at the sound of her voice, then turned to grin at her. "I'm writing that the Christmas tree decorating party at the Tuckers'—sorry, at the Tucker-Fairfaxes's—was another success, and a jolly good time was had by all."

"Well, I should hope so," she said, proud and happy with the way the party was going. The event was always a success. From the first year her mother had organized it, the Tuckers' annual holiday party had been the talk of Denver, the highlight of the holiday season. But this year, with a house full of her new family as well as distinguished guests, it seemed especially outstanding. The golden glow of merriment lit the house and warmed the rooms.

"And I'll thank you to mention by name all the Denver notables here," she added. "From the governor to the Countess of Atwick."

Randolph acted as though he was scribbling more. "Duly noted, ma'am. Mayor. Senator Smith. Mr. and Mrs. Owen Benedict. Mrs. Dolly Green. Let's see, who else?"

Katherine laughed.

"And a fine party it is, too." Randolph tucked his pencil behind his ear and seized her hand. As he bent to kiss it, his pencil dropped to the floor. He reached for it with his other hand, nearly dragging Katherine over with him.

"Well, damn and blast," he muttered. He straightened and his face reddened. "Sorry, Katherine. How does your husband make it look so elegant to kiss a woman's hand?"

"He's had a lot of practice, Randolph," she said, amused and touched by his effort to impress her. "Don't try to compete with a worldly gambler. You don't need to. Are you having a good time? Do you need anything?"

"Hardly," Randolph said. "Everything is wonderful, as always. But your husband was grousing about cookies in the drawing room."

"Then I shall see to that," she said, taking Randolph by the arm and leading him into the front room, where the Christmas tree stood nearly decorated.

Carson's mother was charming everyone, lady and gentleman, with kind words and holiday wishes. Carson's brothers quickly fell into conversation with the Denver men about railroads, horses, or hunting. Their wives, Hortense and Marie, loved discussing fashion with the local ladies.

Dolly was on hand, performing as the grande dame as always, delighted to engage the countess in conversation.

The children had great fun with the tree decorating, the carol singing, and the sampling of cookies. The house was strewn with crumbs—soon lapped up by Max or Lucky—and Christmas litter, ribbons, pine needles, and tinsel crunched underfoot.

Laughter filled the rooms. Katherine loved the chaos. She thought the constant murmur of conversation and the tinkle of china plates and crystal punch cups the music of a triumphant party. But the highlight for her was Carson.

He played the gracious host and the master of the house with aplomb, as if he'd been doing it for years. Yet, beneath his smooth manners lay a contagious youthful delight. If she didn't suspect him of playacting, she would think he was truly happy. Oddly, his happiness, real or not, pleased her.

"We're not out of those molasses cookies, are we?" he murmured in her ear when she retrieved the empty platter from the drawing room fireside. He slipped an arm around her and drew her close enough to make her blush. "Little Willie likes them."

"No, sir, we are not out of them," Katherine said with a reluctant smile. "I think it's Willie's uncle who is eating all of them."

"Guilty," Carson said with a grin.

She smiled up at him, her ear tingling from the warmth of his breath. Playacting like this in front of people had become routine. Earlier, when he'd interrupted her bath, she'd been shocked, but she hoped they'd acted that scene through to his mother's satisfaction. And she'd appreciated that he'd been a gentleman—in that devilish way of his. She was beginning to like him better than she wanted to. If she could make herself forget about Alice Johnson's letter from San Francisco, she might almost enjoy their married couple playacting.

But he'd certainly given her something to think about today. He'd been a gentleman and deferred to her wishes when she'd voiced her reluctance, but would it always be so? How long before her feelings for him were too evident? Next time when things warmed between them, he might not be so willing to walk out of the room. She might not want him to.

"What do you think of the tree?" he was asking.

Katherine grinned at him, reminding herself to play her part. "The tree looks wonderful. What is left to do?"

"We are ready for the finishing touch, I think," Carson said, surveying the tree from top to bottom. "The candles."

"Good," Katherine said, admiring the fourteen-foot pine that was covered in tinsel, painted glass balls, ribbons, and garlands of popcorn and berries made by the children. "I'll just slip this plate into the kitchen so Mrs. D can fill it for us directly. I'll be back with the candles."

"Don't take long." Carson pressed his lips to the top of her head.

His solid warmth and spicy scent was so pleasant, Katherine allowed herself to lean against him for a moment.

"I won't," she assured him, pulling away, conscious that the countess had glanced at them and smiled. A blush warmed Katherine's cheeks as she hurried out of the drawing room into the privacy of the hallway, where the air was cooler.

She paused for a moment to take a deep breath and to wait for the blush to subside. In the music room she could hear the children giggling about something under the supervision of Mrs. Evans. In the dining room the voices of the ladies trilled over the food. Satisfied that her guests were momentarily content, she turned toward the kitchen at the back of the house as the doorbell rang.

She halted. Who could that be? Through the oval etched glass of the door she could make out a tall black form against the white snowflakes that had begun to fall about half an hour earlier. All the guests had arrived long ago. With all the noise in the house, she doubted that Mrs. D had heard the bell. The hired serving girls were busy in the dining room, setting up for the midnight supper.

With the platter still in one hand, Katherine went to the door and pulled it open, fully expecting to come face-to-face with some guest who'd been delayed. But the face she greeted was both familiar and strange.

Her heart skipped a beat. She knew exactly who it was: the Earl of Atwick,

An older version of Carson, dressed in black, stared back at her. He had the same build: broad shouldered, slim hipped, and long legged. The same arrogant, aristocratic features. The same sharp, cold blue eyes. The only difference she could see in the porch light was that the older man was a little heavier and his hair had gone silvery gray. And perhaps something more; unlike Carson, there was a twist to this man's mouth that she did not like. Her spine stiffened.

Carson wasn't going to like this and nor did she. Her first impulse—silly as it was—was to slam the door in his face and pretend he wasn't there. Maybe he would take the hint and leave. Disappear.

But it was too late for that. With the house packed with guests, she could hardly act as if no one was at home.

"It's cold out here, miss. Perhaps you'd be so kind as to fetch the Countess of Atwick," the older version of Carson said, his tone edged with condescension. "Tell her that her husband requests her presence."

Katherine's dislike of him deepened. But he'd crossed an ocean and half a continent to arrive on the front porch of the Elms. She could not deny the man the company of his wife. She stood back from the door. "Won't you come in?"

A blast of cold air carrying snowflakes blew into the hallway, fluttering the peacock feathers in the vase on the table and robbing the warmth of the house.

"I will not. I'm Edward Fairfax, the Earl of Atwick," he said, removing his top hat. "Would you be so kind as to inform your mistress that I'm here and fetch the countess for me?"

Katherine raised her eyebrows. She set the platter down on the hall table and turned to face the earl.

"I am the mistress here, sir," she announced. "If you'd like to come in before we have all of Colorado's cold in the house, I will ask your wife if she wishes to speak to you."

Surprise and a hint of embarrassment flickered in the earl's eyes. He was not as adept as his son at hiding his emotions, she noted with malicious pleasure.

"My mistake," he said, inclining his head ever so slightly. "I'm unaccustomed to your informal ways here in the West. Then you are . . . ?"

"I'm Carson's wife," she said, unable to keep the harshness from her voice. No doubt he'd expected someone more accustomed to a gaming hall than a fine house. She stood aside so he could enter. "I was told you had chosen not to join your family for Christmas."

''Ah, well,'' the Earl of Atwick had the good grace to sputter as she closed the door behind him. ''I was forced to reconsider my decision. And here I am. It was rather a spur-of-the-moment change of heart. I apologize for any inconvenience. I have taken rooms at the Windsor Hotel, and I won't stay long.''

At that moment Marie, John's wife, stepped into the hallway.

''There you are, Katherine,'' she said. ''Mrs. D is setting out the pudding and the cold meats for sup—''

The earl's expression brightened at the sight of a familiar face. ''Hello, Marie.''

Marie's eyes grew wide and she paled. ''Oh, my lord. I mean, my lord.'' She dropped a quick curtsy. ''I'll fetch the countess,'' she volunteered and disappeared into the drawing room.

In the awkward silence that followed, all Katherine could think of was how she was going to tell Carson his father was here. How was Carson going to react? She knew from the hard glimmer in his eye when he spoke of the earl that there was no love lost between the two. She'd assumed that was why the earl had not accompanied his wife. ''May I take your cloak, my lord?'' she finally offered.

''I am not staying,'' the earl said.

''But surely, since you came all this way . . .'' she began.

The countess swept into the hallway, followed by Marie and John. ''Edward,'' she gasped at the sight of her husband. She was breathless with surprise, and Katherine didn't think the woman quite believed her eyes.

Thankfully, Carson did not appear. Katherine wracked her brain for a way to tactfully warn him of this unexpected development.

''Father,'' John stammered, casting an uneasy glance toward the drawing room. Obviously he was thinking the same thing. What was Carson going to say?

''It truly is you?'' the countess said. A sudden awkwardness seemed to come over her. She did not close the distance between them immediately.

"Yes, 'tis me." The earl glanced uncomfortably from Katherine to John, Marie, then back to his wife. He cleared his throat. "I looked around the drawing room at Atwick and saw that . . ."

"We'd all left you?" the countess finished for him with a soft smile on her lips. "But you know, it is what we thought you wanted, dearest, or we wouldn't have come without you."

The earl cleared his throat again. "But it was just not like Christmas without you there, dearest." His voice took on an odd gruffness. "So I booked passage on the first ship out of Liverpool."

Katherine studied the formidable man standing in her hallway. What courage it must have taken for him to back down on his refusal to accompany his family. Her heart softened— a little.

"I traveled so fast, I didn't even bring my valet with me," he added.

"I'm sure we're all glad that you reconsidered, my lord," Katherine said.

"Yes, indeed we are," the countess said, rushing forward to throw herself into her husband's arms at last. "I'm so glad you're here."

Katherine stood back, startled by the old earl's subdued smile as he embraced his wife.

"Katherine, where are those candles?" Carson strode out of the drawing room and into the hallway. "And aren't we about to serve . . . ?"

He halted at the sight of his father and mother in each other's arms. His face went stony cold. The air in the hallway turned coldly brittle.

She knew she had to act fast. "I think this would be a good time for all of you to exchange greetings in the family parlor," she said, taking the earl by his arm and gathering the others in front of her. "Marie, would you be so kind as to invite Neville and Hortense to join us."

Marie did as she was asked, glancing over her shoulder. John followed her. The countess lingered.

Carson never budged. He and the earl locked gazes.

"Carson?" the earl said at last, refusing to be urged forward by Katherine's tug on his arm. His voice was cold and hollow, his jaw set in a belligerent line.

Katherine glanced at her husband. "Sweetheart, look who has come to visit."

"You're not welcome here," Carson said, his voice snarled with emotion—his tone cold, final, and resolute.

Chapter Seventeen

"You think it pleases me to be standing at your door?" the earl replied, his tone as cold as his son's.

"Gentlemen, please." Katherine frowned at her husband, but Carson hardly seemed to notice. His glower was for the earl alone. She had to do something before their anger spilled over into her party, disrupting her guests' pleasure and making the Fairfaxes the target of ugly gossip—or worse. Randolph with his notebook was just in the next room

"Let's retire to the parlor, please." She tugged on the earl's arm again. The earl did not move. Neither did Carson.

"I'll not stay where I'm not wanted," the earl said, his gaze still locked on his son.

"Carson, please," she pleaded. "Let's not disturb our other guests."

"Katherine is right." The countess moved to Carson's side and slipped her arm through his. "Come, let's settle this in private. Come along, Edward."

Finally, Carson's gaze shifted to his mother. She smiled

encouragement at him. Only then did he turn and walk toward the parlor.

Katherine tugged on the earl's sleeve once more. "Well, my lord, after you've come all this way, the least you can do is speak to your son," she said.

"I enter only to settle this matter," the earl replied icily.

In the family parlor, Neville and Hortense had also gathered with Marie, John, the countess, and Carson. As Katherine closed the door, the countess left her son's side to hurry into her husband's arms. She kissed the earl soundly.

"Edward, you're cold," she exclaimed, placing her hands on either side of his face. "It must be freezing out there."

"Indeed, it is, Bess," he said, obviously using a pet name. He smiled down into her gentle face with an expression disarmingly like that of a bashful boy. "But I've found that I need you to warm me."

In a gesture that almost brought tears to Katherine's eyes, the earl seized his wife's hands and kissed them.

John and Neville chuckled. Marie and Hortense smiled.

Carson's glower deepened, and he made a scoffing sound.

Hearing it, the earl stepped back and cleared his throat. "I was just telling Katherine that I've taken rooms at the Windsor. I'd like for you to join me there, Bess."

"But you must stay here, Edward," the countess said, still holding his hand. "We can't have you travel halfway across the world to be with your family, then stay in a hotel, can we, Carson?"

"Certainly not," Katherine said before Carson could respond. Her heart began to pound heavily.

She couldn't have the Earl of Atwick staying at a hotel while the countess stayed at the Elms. What would Denver say? Worse yet, what if the countess went with him to the Windsor? Rumors about the hospitality at the Elms would fly. And there was her truly selfish reason—what would the countess's defection do to her bargain with Carson?

"Your invitation is very kind, ma'am," the earl said. "But the fact is, I will not stay under my son's roof."

"Edward!" the countess exclaimed, drawing out her husband's name.

The earl started, as if he'd just received a set down.

"No offense intended, Mrs. Fairfax," he said, giving Katherine an apologetic bow clearly prompted by his wife.

"But I am offended, my lord," Katherine said, throwing caution to the wind. "Whatever your quarrel is with my husband, you would refuse your daughter-in-law's hospitality? How else am I to feel but affronted?"

"You see the difficulty, Edward," the countess said, throwing up her hands in helplessness. "There is nothing to do but stay now that you're here. Carson was merely expressing his surprise, weren't you, Carson?"

The earl looked askance at his son.

Everyone else in the room turned to Carson.

He glared back at each of them, his lips pressed in a thin line, his back rigid, his face harsh.

Katherine turned her back on everyone in the room. Only Carson could see her face. The anger and outrage in his usually cool blue eyes shocked her, but she knew that the success or failure of his mother's visit rested in his decision. "Do this for your mother," she mouthed.

His gaze flickered over her mouth, clearly reading her words. After another eternal moment, he gave a nod. "Stay."

"It's settled, then," Katherine said before more unfortunate words could be spoken, before more denials were spit out. She was already thinking ahead, wondering where she'd put the earl. Perhaps Lily and Sylvia could be moved to the third floor.

"Perfect; you'll sleep in my room, of course," the countess said, almost as if she'd read Katherine's mind. The countess took her husband's hand and smiled fondly up at him. "You won't mind, will you?"

Under her gaze, the formidable earl's expression softened and his formality melted away. Katherine blinked at the astonishing change. It was like watching an amazing transformation. The earl smiled, a warm, youthful expression. "If you say so, Bess."

"I'll send Willis around to the Windsor to cancel your room and bring back your luggage," she said, glancing once more at Carson. He had turned away, refusing to look at his parents, but he uttered no objections.

Relieved, Katherine smiled at the earl. "Welcome to the Elms, Lord Atwick."

By the time Katherine softly closed the door to their room, the landing clock had long ago chimed two o'clock. Only a lamp at the bedside burned. Carson stood at the window, his back to her. He stared out into the snowy darkness. She could see his unhappiness in the stiff angle of his shoulders, in the rigid line of his back. This was no playacting. He might have allowed her to welcome his father into the house a few hours earlier, but he wasn't pleased about it.

"The tree looked beautiful when all the candles were lit," she said, moving into the room and hoping to distract him out of his mood.

"You should have called me to the door at once," he said without turning.

"Why?" she said. "So you could send your father away? And how would you have explained that to your mother later, when she found out, as she was sure to do?"

"I don't want him here," he said, as if he hadn't made that plain enough.

"You did the right thing by allowing him to stay," she said. "He was a great success with the party. I thought the governor was going to fall over himself when I introduced him to your father. There's nothing like an English earl to impress people."

"There is nothing humorous about this, Katherine," he said, turning from the window. His brows were low and knit together. Lines of anger scored his handsome face. "That man, my father, tried to keep me from my mother's side when she was ill. That man told me he never wanted to lay eyes on me again the day my ship sailed.''

Katherine sucked in a stunned breath. ''Such a harsh thing to say to a son. Because you gambled?''

Carson gave a short, humorless laugh. ''No, actually, not so much because I gambled, I think, but because I would not be what he wanted me to be.''

''I don't understand.'' She joined him at the window to stare out into the black night, all downy with white snowflakes, fluttering like goose feathers from the sky. She wanted to understand his bitterness, his pain. Maybe if she could make some sense of it, she could do something about it. ''What was it he wanted you to be?''

''A clergyman.'' Carson stared at the darkness, too.

''You?'' blurted out of her mouth before she could stop herself.

''Yes, me. You see the problem,'' he said. ''Actually, it took me a long time to understand that. He'd assigned a niche for me to fill. Like John. As heir, all he had to do was learn how to become an earl.''

''And Neville, the military?'' she asked, studying her husband's troubled face.

''It's customary for a son to go into the military,'' he said. ''So it was Sandhurst for Neville. And he did some years in India. I believe that's where he met Hortense.''

''And for you, your father chose—?''

''My father chose the clergy for me,'' Carson finished for her.

''And is that customary?'' she asked, trying to recall whether she'd noted this custom when she'd visited England. But she couldn't recall meeting many aristocratic vicars.

''In the days of knights and dragons, perhaps,'' he said ruefully. ''But this is the nineteenth century. No, there's more to it than custom. After being dismissed from one gloomy church-related school, then another, and refusing to be an altar boy, it finally dawned on me that Father wanted me to go into the clergy. I wasn't trying to be obtuse. It just wasn't my nature to sit in a musty library studying texts by candlelight when good company and fun could be had at a gaming table."

"I see," she said, recalling her first impression of the earl as she met him at the door. His appearance had made her think of a black-clothed preacher right out of Nathaniel Hawthorne.

"The Atwick Manor library is full of scholarly texts on the Bible and biblical history," he continued. "Maps of the biblical world. And a collection of old Bibles. There's a Wycliff translation, one of the first translations from Latin into English, and even a Gutenberg Bible. Father was always trying to interest me in reading them. He'd lecture me on their merits for hours."

"So as third son, he thought you should go into the church," she said, the exact nature of the conflict growing clearer for her. "And you rebelled."

"Precisely."

"How betrayed he must have felt to have a son who liked playing cards instead of studying scholarly tomes of Greek," she mused.

"Let's not feel too sorry for the old man." He gave a bitter laugh. "Why couldn't I have had a father who didn't give a damn if I lost a few pounds at the gaming table? I had friends whose fathers found their sons' peccadilloes amusing, almost something to be proud of."

"So that's why you didn't think your father would come to Denver," Katherine said. "He does not approve of you."

"A lot of things were said and done in anger before I left England," he said. "I took him at his word when he said he never wanted to see me again. Except when Mother was ill . . ."

"But he's here," she said, squeezing his hand. "Don't you see that means something?"

"It means he missed Mother," he said, dismissing the importance with a shrug. "Whatever my father is or says or does, I will give him that. He truly loves my mother."

"Umm," she agreed, her mind racing ahead. "But he's here

now. He traveled across an ocean alone and he agreed to stay at the Elms. It's a good thing, Carson."

"Katherine, all I ask of you is to help me make my mother's visit an enjoyable one," Carson said, turning to her. "Placating my father was never part of our deal and I don't want you to worry about it."

"No, I do understand, honestly," she protested, realizing how much it must hurt to grow up knowing that you were not the kind of person your father wanted you to be. To know you could not win his approval. To be unaccepted—what torment! "Part of making your mother's stay enjoyable will be making your father happy, too."

She studied Carson's profile, her heart aching for him, for each line of pain that she saw etched on his face. She moved closer and slipped her arm around him, wishing she knew how to heal his wound. "Lily and I were very fortunate that our mother and father approved of anything and everything we did. They were absolutely doting parents. We were protected and spoiled."

"Your father was a good man," he agreed, turning slightly from the window. "You were fortunate and I'm glad for you and Lily. You deserved that."

"Every child deserves that." She let him slip his arm around her and pull her to him. They stood so close, the length of their bodies touched. Even in his pain he was hard and warm. She looked up into his face to see uncertainty written on his features. She also saw his need to be accepted for himself—his need to be loved.

With no other thought than to comfort him, she slipped her arms around his neck and offered her lips up to his.

Without hesitation, he slid his hand around the back of her neck, dipped his head, and laid his lips against hers. His mouth was cool and firm yet soft, so many wonderful things to experience all at once. She surrendered herself to soaking up all the newness of it. The hint of stubble brushed against her skin, but with tenderness and firmness. She sighed against his lips.

Then his tongue teased the corners of her mouth and stroked her lower lip. Willingly, her lips parted, allowing his tongue to dip inside, nimble and clever. She was surprised by a sudden aching sensitivity in her breasts and a melting warmth in her belly. She yielded to the pleasure of his thrusting tongue and the feel of his hands gripping her shoulders.

Finally he released her, but only enough to allow her to regain her breath. He continued to brush kisses across her face; light, feathery, hot kisses that tickled and tingled and warmed her nose and cheeks. His lips burned a mysterious trail down deep into her middle until something uncoiled, burgeoned heavy and urgent, then blossomed into the need and desire to give him anything he wanted to make him forget.

His caresses grew bolder. His hand stroked down over her breast, molded it against his palm, massaging gently. She closed her eyes, savoring the heat inside her that stretched and spread, stealing the strength from her legs, making her as weak-kneed as she'd been on her wedding day. She whimpered softly and let her head fall back, encouraging him to kiss her throat. He did, planting passionate kisses all the way down the hollow.

She gasped as the heat began to simmer inside her. Her fingers twisted through his hair and slipped down to his shoulders, seeking to explore his body as he was exploring hers.

He raised his head and pulled away slightly. "Let's undress and go to bed."

"Uh-huh," she mumbled without opening her eyes. She was unable to think of anything except the need to hold him close— and to be held and touched.

Even when his fingers began to work at the buttons down the back of her lace and velvet gown she did not open her eyes. She didn't want to leave this magic place in his arms. She didn't want to escape from the thrill of his touch. A sigh escaped her as she felt her gown slip away. He pushed it down over her hips and helped her step out of the yards of fabric.

As soon as she was free of the gown and her petticoats, she could feel his gaze on her, intense and hot. She should have been shy, but she wasn't. He'd glimpsed her in her camisole and petticoat before. He'd even seen her in nothing more than her nightgown—or a towel. What was there to be modest about now?

"Lovely," he whispered. Taking both of her hands, he drew her to the bedside. He sat down and pulled her close until she stood between his knees. "Take down your hair for me," he said.

She smiled and lifted her arms to do as he asked. She pulled the pins from her tresses, which were piled high on her head. He watched her every move. Instinctively she pulled one tendril down first, dropping the pins to the floor and allowing the long curl to lie along her throat and against her collarbone.

"More," he demanded, his voice husky.

She obeyed, pins plinking to the carpet as she released more curls, shaking them down around her shoulders. Carson stared, resting his arm between her breasts to stroke her chestnut locks.

She was glad to see that the angry bleakness his father's arrival had brought to his eyes had disappeared.

Afraid to break the spell, she put her hands on either side of his face and bent to kiss him again. Suddenly his fingers were busy with the ribbons of her camisole, then with the hooks of her corset.

Abruptly reminded of where all these lovely sensations were leading, she broke away, covering herself with her hands.

"We shouldn't . . ." She drew a shaky breath. "This isn't supposed to happen."

"But it *is* happening." He stood and pulled her closer, encircling her with strong arms. His half smile was beguiling, intriguing, promising. "Have you considered that what you ask of us is unnatural? A man and a woman, together. Husband and wife, yet separate?"

"Carson, you know the reason for that," she said, her emotions tangled and confused. How could she defend a perfectly logical decision made at a perfectly lucid moment with him nibbling at her ear?

Her knees turned to jelly. She clung to him. She tried to speak, to protest, but nothing seemed to come out of her mouth but nonsensical monosyllables.

"Let me make love to you tonight," he said, tending to her other ear. "We'll worry about the agreement again tomorrow."

"Carson . . . ?"

"Sweetheart, you have my name and my promise of protection," he whispered as he kissed her brow, then her eyelids. "Let me share my passion with you."

There seemed to be no sensible answer to that. Nothing she could think of. She could think of nothing but the burning touch of his hands on her body and the sweet power of his kisses.

When his fingers found the hooks of her corset again, she refused to let herself think of how he knew so much about the unfastenings of women's garments. Taking a deep breath, she let him move down her throat again.

She felt her corset fall away, freeing her breasts. Carson's mouth sought one nipple and his hand the other. The hunger of his mouth stole away everything but the sensation of his suckling. While his tongue caressed one achingly sensitive nipple, his thumb teased the other. The passionate assault tore a gasp from her, but she did not pull away.

No man had ever touched her like this. It was what she'd longed for yet hadn't known she wanted it. And this was her husband. This was the man who should introduce her to the rites of the marriage bed. The man who'd lain beside her night after night without asking more of her even though he was entitled.

Entwining her fingers in his hair again, she offered herself to his mouth. And he took her, making love with his tongue to one nipple, then the other, then her navel, and tasting the smooth, sensitive skin of her belly.

His hands held her on either side of her waist. Soon he'd freed her from her drawers. Cool air struck her bare skin. She was naked and didn't care. Ardently his hands traveled the length of her body, his gaze nearly as feverish. She realized that in the lamplight she could hide nothing from him. But the admiration in his sultry-eyed scrutiny left her with little desire to hide herself. He released her only long enough to pull back the counterpane.

"Under the covers, quick, before you catch your death of cold," he whispered. "I'm right behind you."

As soon as she'd wriggled between the cold sheets, he impatiently stripped off his coat and shirt. She stared, amazed at his beauty. He looked ever so much more interesting and touchable than the David statue she'd seen in Italy.

Just as he began to unfasten his trousers, he bent to the bedside lamp and blew it out. But even in the darkness she could see the sculpted beauty of his chest and shoulders. The strength and the power. The dark dusting of hair across his chest that she'd been so curious about—and tapering downward toward his belt and lower.

As soon as he'd divested himself of his trousers, he put one knee on the bed and reached for her. The shadows hid what she'd never seen, a man in full arousal.

"You're not frightened, are you?" he asked, his voice husky and soft.

"Only a little," she admitted. "It's just that I've never—"

"I didn't think you had," he said. The mattress sank under his weight as he settled down beside her—under the covers with her this time. "We'll go slow."

He cupped her chin in one hand and leaned over to kiss her again.

She forgot about her momentary doubts. Despite the weeks of sleeping under the counterpane with Carson sleeping on top, the warmth of his naked body pressed against hers seemed right and natural and the most wondrous thing she'd ever experienced.

The cold sheets quickly warmed from the touch of their bodies.

* * *

Carson rose up, straddled Katherine, and pulled the covers up over them. Then he devoted himself to making love to her. Holding her, touching her, smelling her, drove away his pain. There was nothing to know but the passion of her mouth and the heat of her skin. Nothing else mattered but the fragile line of her collarbone, the sound of her sighs. He explored the texture of the excited buds of her breasts with his tongue and tasted the sweetness of her mouth again and again.

He moved downward, allowing his aching sex to press against her belly, the juncture of her legs, then her thighs, enjoying yet suffering in his need for her. She was the only real thing for him at the moment. He would find release soon enough—but he didn't want it to be too soon. He wanted this moment to last for a long, long time, for her and for himself. He would do his best to make it easy for her. Taking virgins wasn't something he was experienced in. He knew he was being selfish, but at the moment he didn't care. All he wanted to hear was the sound of her sighs of fulfillment and to experience the thrill of his own release.

He moved downward, exploring with his lips and stroking with his hands. The feel of her fingers in his hair was all the encouragement he needed. His lips brushed the undersides of her breasts, her ribs, her navel again. When he reached her belly, he began to stroke her thighs—the outsides first, then he stroked inward. Under his hands, she relaxed, her thighs parting slightly. He kissed the thatch between her legs.

"Carson!" she gasped and pulled at his hair.

"It's all right," he reassured her, rolling to his side. He could hear the fear in her voice. "Just let it happen. The more we prepare now, the better it will be later."

"But—"

He moved up quickly and kissed away her protests—her misgivings. "This is what a man does for a woman, sweetheart. This is right. You'll see."

She quieted and kissed him back. He took advantage of the moment to find the spot between her legs that made her writhe in passion. When she opened herself to him again, he rested his cheek against her stomach, stroking whimpers of pleasure from her with his fingers. He would be content with that for now. He would teach her more about intimacy in the nights to come.

When she was ready, he buried himself in her. He made it quick, her maidenhood giving way instantly. She stiffened a moment, crying out in pain. Carson prayed that the main discomfort was over quickly for her.

He braced himself on his elbows and stroked a strand of hair from her forehead. "Are you all right?"

"Yes," she whispered. "I think so. It's not over, is it?"

Struggling for control, he smiled against her shoulder. Dear God he was buried in her, inside heaven, silken, tight, and fiery sweet. "No, it's not over," he panted.

"Good," she murmured against his ear. "It's going to get better, isn't it?"

"I don't know if I can stand it, if it does," he confessed, seeking her mouth. Capturing it, he began to move again. She moved with him, her arms around his middle, her action instinctive, astonishingly uninhibited. He could hardly believe she was so totally his. Holding him, being held. Whispering sweet encouragement in his ear. He'd known she was naturally sensual. He'd known having her was going to be good—but nothing this exquisite. Only when he heard her gasp in fulfillment did he allow himself to find release.

In giving pleasure, he took pleasure—secretly understanding that he had changed her—and given something of himself to do it.

When he rolled to his side, he pulled her with him. They fell into an exhausted, blissful sleep, her head pillowed against his chest and their legs still entangled.

Chapter Eighteen

Katherine awoke with a start. Soft winter sunlight filtered through the lace curtains. Suddenly remembering their passionate lovemaking, she looked toward Carson's side of the bed, but he was gone. The sheets were cool. Only the imprint of his head remained on the pillow. The knock sounded again. She realized that it was the noise that had awakened her.

"Katherine?" The door latch clicked and Mrs. D peeked in, carrying a tray. "Mr. Fairfax said you were tired after the party and would like breakfast in bed this morning."

"That would be nice," she said, trying to make her eyes open wider than just the squint that was all she seemed able to manage. What a thoughtful thing for him to suggest. When she sat up, she realized she was as naked as a jaybird. She yanked the covers up to her chin.

Mrs. D smiled knowingly. Setting down the tray on the bedside table, she fetched Katherine's robe from behind the Chinese screen. "And so it appears to have been a late night."

"Yes, well . . ." she muttered. As she struggled into her robe, her memory danced with dreamlike images of Carson's lovemaking. His hands warm and gentle, teasing and knowledgeable. His body hard and powerful. Her body was already warming at the thought of his touching her where no one had ever touched her before.

When Mrs. D turned away to fuss over the teapot, she peeked at the sheets. Bright red spots of blood stained the white cotton. She was truly his wife now. What would this do to their annulment agreement?

"Is something wrong, darlin'?" Mrs. D picked up the tray and set it across her lap. "I brought you some tea and scones, made from that recipe that Lady Hortense gave me."

"And the others?" Katherine asked, forcing herself to set thoughts of last night aside and think about her duties as hostess.

"Mr. John and his missus and the little girl have gone with Lily and Mrs. Evans for a drive," Mrs. D said. "Mr. Neville and his missus and the little ones are still abed. But the countess and her husband are up and at the breakfast table with Mr. Fairfax."

"What?" Sudden visions of war breaking out across the dining room table leaped into her head. Katherine shoved her breakfast tray at Mrs. D. "Here, take this. I don't dare leave Carson alone with his father. I have no idea how those two will treat each other and I can't have them battling their final falling out at the Elms."

She was almost out the door when she realized how she was dressed—or not dressed. She halted and turned around.

"Well, I didn't think you wanted to go down like that," Mrs. D said, clearly disapproving of her haste.

"Where is my old morning gown?" she asked, rushing behind the Chinese screen to find the loose gown she wore when working around the house.

"I have it right here," Mrs. D said, holding it out to her.

"Yes, there it is." In another few moments, she had donned the dress and pulled her hair back with a ribbon. As she hurried down the backstairs, her feet clad only in slippers, she could hear the sound of men's voices coming from the dining room.

They were raised in disagreement. Heavens, Carson and his father were at it already. She could not make out the words, but the tone was angry and belligerent.

She dashed across the kitchen, then slowed down when she reached the butler's pantry. The shouting had stopped and she could hear the countess's voice—soft but sharp, ringing with annoyance. Katherine put her ear to the door and listened.

"What on earth are the two of you bellowing about?" Carson's mother demanded. She'd entered from the front hallway, so none of them had any idea Katherine was listening in the pantry. "I could hear you before I started down the stairs," the countess continued.

Silence.

"Well?" she demanded once more.

"We were discussing your illness," Carson said, a rebellious note in his tone.

"It didn't sound like a discussion to me," the countess said.

"You have a headstrong son, Bess," the earl said.

"He comes by it honestly, Edward, directly from a long line of headstrong Fairfaxes," the countess said. "Shall we sit down and enjoy this nice breakfast that Mrs. D has prepared for us?"

Katherine heard the muffled scraping of chairs on the dining room carpet, and the threesome seated themselves at the table.

"And how is Katherine this morning?" the countess asked.

"Very well, thank you," Carson muttered. "The tree decorating party and all the preparations have left her a little worn out, so I encouraged her to sleep a bit longer."

"Excellent idea," the countess said. "It was a lovely party, and all the better now that I have my entire family under one roof."

"No thanks to Father," Carson said.

"Don't you start on that—" the earl replied.

She heard crystal and china clatter. She could envision the earl rising abruptly from his chair, then Carson jumping to his feet to glare across the table at him.

"Start what?" Carson said. "She doesn't know, does she?"

"Know what?" the countess asked. "Sit down, both of you."

"Nothing important," the earl said.

"He never told you that he forbade me to come to you when you were ill, did he?" Carson demanded.

Katherine bit her lip. No child wanted to be forbidden from coming home—ever.

"There's no need to go over this now—" the earl began.

"Is that true, Edward?" the countess asked with disbelief in her voice. "Did you tell Carson not to come when I was ill?"

"You were very sick, Bess," the earl said, a slightly pleading note entering his voice. "Carson couldn't possibly have arrived at your bedside in time—"

"For what?" Carson demanded. China and silverware rattled again. "In time to be with her during her recovery?"

"Your presence would have upset her," the earl said. "Look how you're upsetting her now."

Katherine put her hand on the door, preparing to march in and put an end to this embarrassing display of hostility between the two men.

Something thumped on the table. "Now listen to me," the countess ordered, her voice only slightly raised, but the authority in it unmistakable.

Both men fell silent.

Katherine hesitated. Perhaps this wasn't the moment to walk in.

"I would have liked very much to see Carson," the countess said in a softly imperial tone. "I am most unhappy about what happened a year ago, but the past is the past. Here and now, I don't want to hear anymore bickering."

The only noise to be heard was the passing of a carriage in the street outside.

The countess spoke again, quietly, but Katherine could almost hear the attentiveness of her audience. "Carson and his wife have been gracious enough to open their lovely home to us, and for the first time in ten years I have my whole family together. This has given me great joy. I will not have anything spoil that.''

Katherine smiled to herself. *Yes, tell them, Countess, tell them.*

"What's more," the countess continued, the volume of her voice rising ever so slightly, "I think it's extremely rude for the two of you to carry on with your grudges in the presence of your ladies and in the season of love and joy, too. Whatever the two of you are unable to agree upon, put it away for now. I want peace this Christmas. Do you hear me? Peace!''

A long moment of silence stretched out again. Then low mutterings reached Katherine, sounds that she took for the men's embarrassed, reluctant agreement.

"That's better," the countess said, sounding more like herself. "Now may I try the apple butter over there? Please pass it, Carson. It was so sweet of Mrs. D and Katherine to find imported marmalade for us, but I do love this apple butter.''

"Of course, Mother," Carson said, his voice normal, as if he passed his mother the apple butter every morning.

"Would you like to try some of this ham, Bess?" the earl added. The sounds of three people taking their breakfast together drifted through the door.

Katherine straightened and sighed with relief. *Score one for the countess,* she thought. She prayed the cease-fire the lady had established would last—and she vowed she would do her part to make certain it did.

After the initial disruption of the earl's arrival—and his clash with Carson—the Fairfaxes's visit settled back into the harmonious chaos of family amusements and social activities. Secretly Katherine was proud of Carson. The tension between him and the earl was hardly noticeable—to anyone who did not know that they would be at each other's throats in an instant if it wasn't for the countess.

She spent the remainder of the day so absorbed in being a

hostess, in seeing that the earl was entertained, comfortable, and enjoying himself, that she had little time to reflect on the change Carson and her intimacy would bring to their relationship.

Vaguely, part of her hoped that she and he would return to the old sleeping arrangement, with him on top of the counterpane. Her heart would be safe that way.

The honest part of her knew there was no going back. He would never allow it. Nor, she admitted, did she really want him to.

She also knew in her heart that after her sensuous night with Carson—after seeing his pain—she cared for him. Their arrangement took on new meaning.

If she successfully entertained his mother, no doubt it was even more critical that his father be coddled as well, for Carson's sake. She was determined that whatever happened, no aspect of the earl's visit was to be neglected. She would dedicate herself to making everything as perfect as it had been before the earl's arrival.

After a long day of showing the earl around Denver, lunching with the entire family at the Windsor, then dining at the Elms, Katherine undressed for bed slowly behind her Chinese screen, wondering if Carson was going to be waiting for her in bed.

"Katherine, what's taking you so long?" he called, a certain light, warm impatience in his tone.

After the clash with his father that morning, he'd been grim and distant all day. He seemed older, the planes of his handsome face hard, his words almost grudgingly spoken. There'd been no time for the two of them to be alone, to discuss what had happened between them. At first she'd thought his shift in mood had to do with his father. But as the day wore on, she'd begun to fear he regretted their night together. What a relief it was to hear something of his old taunting self again.

She listened, thinking he sounded as if he was near the bed.

"Why don't you wear that pretty silk gown Mother sent you?" he added. "You know, the sheer one."

She closed her eyes. Yes, she knew the one. No, there was no going back. She found the gossamer-thin gown and put it on.

When she stepped out from behind the screen, she sucked in a deep breath of surprise. He lay on his side in bed, bare chested and looking heart-thumpingly virile. She could only imagine he was just as naked beneath the covers. It was almost enough to make her blush.

"I've warmed the sheets for you," he said, propping his head on his elbow. His eyes dark with hunger, he grinned and patted the empty side of the bed next to him. "The gown looks perfect on you."

His invitation made her insides weightless.

"Carson," she began without moving, "what about the annulment?"

"There are all kinds of reasons for an annulment," he said, studying her face. "Whether we shared a bed is the least of them. You didn't seem to mind the new arrangement last night, sweetheart."

"But that was different." She waved her hands uselessly in the air as she attempted to explain. "You were ... We were upset."

"And you slept with me out of pity?" he asked with a skeptical lift of his brows.

"No," she said, avoiding his hungry gaze. She was almost certain that he knew exactly why she'd slept with him, and he wouldn't be satisfied until she admitted it—at least part of it. "I—we—you—because I cared and because your touch feels—it makes me feels so—I like it. There, is that what you wanted to hear?"

He laughed softly. "It's what you had to confess to yourself." He stretched across the bed, the covers falling back enough to confirm her suspicions. He was naked and ready for her to come to bed. He turned out the bedside lamp. "Come to bed, my queen,'' he invited. ''I'll show you how right my touch still feels.''

She went, knowing she and her heart were lost.

In the week that followed his father's arrival, Carson learned that he had more self-control than he'd ever dreamed. Every time he entered a room where his father was, he could feel the man's hackles rise. And his did the same. Yet they remained civil to each other, enabled to do so by the unspoken agreement between them. The last thing either of them wanted was to make the countess unhappy, to risk her health. They'd almost lost her a year before. Nothing, not even their dislike for each other, would make them risk that loss again.

Often Carson found himself on edge. Then he would make himself seek out Katherine. She became the bright spot in all the turmoil. He wished she wasn't driving herself so hard to make his father happy. She smiled at the earl, laughed at his jokes, waited on him hand and foot. She was up early before anyone else to fuss with Mrs. D over breakfast, and she was up late after everyone had gone to bed to make certain things would be ready for the next day. It was enough to make Carson brood, but then night came. Then—

Then she came to bed with him. They kissed, and for an hour or so, nothing else in the world existed but the two of them in each other's arms. She was warm and passionate and amazingly willing to be tutored in the more exotic arts of lovemaking. With a little encouragement, she soon lost her shyness about exploring his body. Just the memory of her hands and her lips was enough to make him groan aloud—and his body react.

He'd discovered that if there was one person who could destroy his self-control, it was Katherine. When she took him inside her, he knew nothing else mattered in the universe but the two of them, made one in that fleeting, vulnerable moment of union—and ephemeral, primal pleasure.

Knowing they would be together each night made each day of dealing with his father a little easier. It also made him sensitive about how his father treated Katherine. The earl had always been polite to his daughter-in-laws, but neither Hortense nor Marie were the wife of the family's black sheep.

However, neither of them was as adept at taking care of themselves as Katherine was.

One evening all three brothers and their families and the countess and earl were seated around the supper table, all of them together after a day of shopping for the ladies and horse buying for the gentlemen. Christmas Eve was only a day away. The mood at the table was relaxed and happy, at least as relaxed and happy as it was going to get with him and his father in the same room.

Little Sylvia was dishing mashed potatoes onto Lily's plate.

"There, Lily, you have mashed potatoes at two o'clock on your plate," she said.

"And the roast beef is at six o'clock?" Lily asked, tapping the meat with her fork.

"Yes, you have it exactly right." Sylvia smiled with unabashed admiration. The ten-year-old had become an adoring companion to twelve-year-old Lily and the girls were inseparable. They played the piano and sang together. They rode Hominy together, with Willis at hand to handle any problems. There'd even been some talk of Lily going to England to visit Sylvia, talk that had made Katherine frown. But Carson thought it was a good idea. The experience would be a great opportunity for Lily. He intended to press Katherine for her permission when the time was right.

"I swear, Lily, I don't know how you do it," Sylvia said, obviously marveling at how well Lily managed her food. "Not just eating, but everything."

"Don't swear, please, Sylvia," Marie scolded.

"Well, you know what I mean, Mama," Sylvia said. "I

can't manage half as well, and I can see. Sometimes I try to close my eyes to learn what it would be like. But I can't imagine what it would be like to have to count the steps to each place I went.''

"It's not hard," Lily said. "In fact, it becomes second nature.''

"But wouldn't you be more comfortable in a place with others of your kind?'' the earl said, speaking directly across the table to Lily.

Carson watched in surprise. His father rarely deigned to speak to children—even his grandchildren. Youngsters were the women's domain.

"Surely you've given this some thought, Katherine,'' the earl added.

Everyone at the table froze. Then heads turned in Katherine's direction. Carson glanced down the length of the table to see her head come up. He knew trouble was brewing when he saw her coolly polite expression.

"Father, I think Lily and Katherine are content with their current arrangement,'' he said, to head off any sharp comments from his wife.

"Of course they are,'' the earl said. "But I understand there are fine schools for the blind, well equipped to teach and help those affected with a loss of sight,'' the earl went on. "You could board there, Lily.''

Confusion clouded Lily's pretty face. "I like being with my sister.''

"We are quite content, my lord,'' Katherine said, her voice studiously even. "Lily could go to the School for the Blind and Deaf in Colorado Springs. But we prefer to have her here with us. Mrs. Evans is formerly of that school's staff. We feel fortunate to be able to have her tutor Lily.''

Carson was about to change the subject when Katherine continued speaking, clearly with a purpose.

"Lily's loss of sight is a challenge at times,'' she admitted. "Sylvia, you said you've tried to imagine it. There is a better way to understand the experience. Are you interested in learning more about being blind? It's a kind of experiment, a game of sorts. Lily can be your guide for a change. Would you like to try it?"

"Yes, I would," Sylvia said, bouncing up and down on her dining room chair. "Can we do it now?"

"After dessert." Katherine glanced toward Marie, "If it's all right with your mother."

"Of course," Marie said.

"And what about you, my lord?" Katherine's gaze, direct and commanding, had fallen on the earl.

Everyone at the table went still again. Heads turned toward him expectantly.

The earl, realizing he was under scrutiny, cleared his throat.

Carson put down his fork and his eyes narrowed as he met his father's gaze. As much as he wanted to give his mother the peace she sought, he would not allow his father to be rude to Katherine. Not after she'd worked so hard to make his unexpected visit pleasant.

"I'd like to take part," the earl said, turning away from Carson to smile at Katherine. "In the game, I mean. The experiment. It would be useful to know more."

"Wonderful, my lord," Lily said, smiling sweetly in the earl's direction, clearly unaffected by his aristocratic status. "It is a fun game."

"Good," Katherine said, any pretense of warmth gone from her face. She took up her fork again. "I'll have Mrs. D serve coffee in the dining room and I'll explain the game to you then."

"This should be entertaining," the countess said, amusement in her sidelong glance at her husband.

The steely annoyance flashing in Katherine's eyes was difficult to miss. Carson had no idea what kind of game she had in mind. Briefly he again considered interfering, but then, the man had had the nerve to suggest—when it was none of his concern—that she send her sister away. How like Father. Carson settled back in his chair, toying with the stem of his wineglass and smiling maliciously to himself. His father deserved whatever Katherine had decided to do with him.

Chapter Nineteen

After coffee had been served and they were all gathered around the drawing room fire, children and adults, Katherine began to have second thoughts about doing what she'd suggested.

When several of Lily's friends had expressed the same curiosity in the past, she and Mrs. Evans had shown them this little game that they found amusing and insightful.

But now she was dealing with a peer of the British realm. The earl had been polite, though aloof and distant, since he'd arrived a week earlier. His sudden declaration of his thoughts about Lily's condition had been a surprise and an irritation. She was uncertain how to proceed. He sorely needed a lesson in being less judgmental, but he was Carson's father. She didn't want to make things more tense than they already were.

"Katherine, do you want to explain the game to them, or shall I?" Lily moved to the center of the room, her pretty face shining with the pleasure of being the center of attention.

"I'd like to join in, too," Hortense said, much to Katherine's surprise. "If I may."

"Of course," she said, thinking that the more who partici-
pated, the less the earl appeared to be singled out for the lesson.
"I'll explain the game. First, Sylvia, would you be so kind as
to go ask Mrs. D for three clean napkins. It's very simple really,
but I think you'll find it interesting. I'm going to tie the napkins
over your eyes like a blindfold. Then you are going to explore
the house. Thank you, Sylvia. You will have Lily as a guide.
I'll be your guide, my lord. Carson, will you help Hortense?"

She cast a quick glance in Carson's direction to see if he
was having second thoughts now that they all knew what the
game was. He said nothing.

"It will be a pleasure to have you as a guide, my dear," the
earl said, stepping forward, obviously prepared to submit to
being blindfolded.

She folded the napkin and handed it to Carson. "Please, put
this on your father."

She did the same for Hortense, handing the folded napkin
to Neville to tie over his wife's eyes, and tying the last one on
Sylvia herself.

"Can you see anything?" she asked, moving from Sylvia
to Hortense, then the earl, inspecting their blindfolds. "It's not
fair if you can peek below the cloth. That's why I folded them
long."

"I can see some light and shadow," the earl said, turning
his head toward the chandelier, then away. "But that's all."

"That's all right," she said, touching the folded napkin to
be certain it was tied firmly in place.

"I see some light and shadows," Lily explained as she took
Sylvia's hand. "Sometimes I see movement, or maybe I sense
it, but I see no colors or shapes. I can tell a lot by smells, too.
Every room smells different."

"Is that so?" the earl said, his voice full of skepticism. "I'm
ready to start, if you are."

"Where do you think we should go first?" she asked Lily.
"This is the game you are expert at, Lily. You take the lead."

"If this was a real game of blind man's bluff," Sylvia said, "you would turn us around three times to be sure that we lost our bearings."

Lily laughed. "But the point of this game is to find your bearings, not lose them. Isn't that right, Katherine?"

"Exactly," she said.

"I have my bearings and I have my guide," the earl said, groping thin air for her hand. "We are standing in the middle of the drawing room. I'm ready to begin my adventure with the best guide in the house at my side."

She reached for his hand, large and fine like Carson's. He latched onto her immediately, clearly uneasy with his new sightlessness. She couldn't resist smiling at his apprehension.

Everyone laughed nervously. She gave Carson a reassuring nod and motioned away his brothers, who were hovering protectively near their father.

"My lord, I think you will find that it is more effective for you to place your hand on my forearm as we walk," she explained, freeing herself from his clutch. "You will be able to sense more by my movements that way—when I turn or step up or down."

"Like this?" he asked, grasping her as instructed. "Yes, I see—I think you're right."

"Let's go, then." Without hesitation Lily started off, bearing to the right around a side table and chair and into the adjoining family parlor, then around into the hallway. Katherine followed, with the earl firmly attached to her right arm. Despite what Lily had said, she was trying to mix them up. Katherine decided to let her sister enjoy the game, too.

"We are in the hallway," Hortense announced. "I can feel the cooler air here and the scent of the outdoors."

"Very good," Katherine said.

"Yes, yes, I feel it, too," said the earl, his tone light with surprise. "And I can hear the wooden floor creak beneath my feet."

Thump.

"Ow," Sylvia cried. "What did I stub my toe on?"

"The bottom step of the stairs." Lily stopped to turn toward her friend. "Are you all right?"

"Yes. Let's go on," Sylvia said, shaking Lily's hand with impatience. "Do you ever stub your toe there?"

"Hardly ever." Lily reached for the banister. "We're going up the stairs now. You can hold on to the banister with your right hand and onto your guide with your left. There are fourteen steps up to the landing. Then you take three steps across the landing and turn right. Then there are five more steps up to the second floor hall."

"Fourteen steps to the landing, then three steps across the landing," the earl muttered to himself, as if reciting magic numbers.

"Then five more steps up to the second floor," Katherine finished for him. "Lily and Sylvia are going first. Then you and I."

Katherine led him around so that their toes were against the bottom step. "Feel that?"

"Yes. I am ready to go up the stairs?" the earl asked, his right hand searching for the banister.

"We are ready," she said, lifting the hem of her skirt to take the first step. "Here we go."

They began counting. She watched the earl, amused at the frown of concentration on his face as he counted the steps upward.

"Twelve, thirteen, fourteen," he said. "Am I there?"

"Yes, now around to your right three steps," she directed. She glanced around behind to see how Carson was doing with Hortense. They seemed to be doing very well. But her movement startled the earl.

"Is something wrong?" he asked. "We're on the landing, aren't we?"

"Yes, we're fine," she said. "I was just looking to see how Carson and Hortense are doing. You do trust me, don't you, my lord?"

"Of course. To the right, one, two, three," the earl said.

The toe of his half boot struck the bottom step of the short flight. "Up five more steps."

"Exactly right, my lord," she said, smiling at his earnest efforts. "You are doing very well."

"You are a most trustworthy guide, my dear." He came to a stop at the top of the stairs. He grinned, an expression amazingly like Carson's. "We made it. You know, I didn't intend to give any offense when I brought up schooling for Lily. I just thought, you know, she seems to be such a bright girl, I thought you'd be interested in the best for her."

"Indeed, I am concerned," she said, moved by the earl's attempt to apologize. "Lily, is leading us down the hall. Around this way."

"How many steps to the end of the hall?" the earl asked, his frown of concentration returning.

"I'm not certain, but I am sure Lily could tell us," Katherine said. "Keep your hand on my forearm, and I will tell you when we reach the end."

"Thirty-one steps to the end of the hall," Lily called over her shoulder.

Suddenly the earl's head came up. "We've just passed the bathroom," he said, clearly astonished with the discovery.

Hortense giggled.

Katherine had to bite her lip to keep from doing the same.

"Well, I can smell the dampness and Bess's rose of attar soap," the earl stammered. "I'm merely applying Lily's observation that every room has its own odor."

"Excellent," Katherine said, sharing a smile of amusement with Carson, who had come up close behind her with Hortense at his side. Sylvia and Lily had started on down the hall toward the back of the house.

The rogue took advantage of the moment to bend close, kiss her ear, and whisper, "I don't know what you're up to with my father, but I suspect it is very clever, sweetheart."

The kiss and the compliment spread tingles from her ear down through her toes, and she smiled at her husband.

"Let's follow the girls on down the hallway, shall we," she said.

Soon they reached the end of the hall, the earl counting under his breath every step of the way. She was amazed at how thoroughly he devoted himself to an experience that was meant to be little more than a parlor game with a lesson attached. The man was opinionated and single-minded—nearly as much so as Carson. No wonder the two had butted heads. But he was also a willing pupil.

"We've reached the backstairs, my lord," she explained. "They are very narrow. But it's the same number of steps down and you can put your hands on both walls at once to steady yourself. Yes, like that."

"Seven, eight, nine," the earl counted. Suddenly he halted. "I don't hear anyone in front of me. Heavens, I feel as helpless as a baby."

"You're all right," she said, following close behind him. "The way is clear."

"Are we in the kitchen?" the earl asked, his foot extended to find the lip of the last step. His voice was filled with victory and wonder. "I smell Mrs. Dodd's fine cooking."

Mrs. D stood in front of her sink, where she was supervising the washing up. She braced her fists on her ample hips. "What is this, Katherine?"

"Just a game, Mrs. D," she said, smiling at her weary, overworked housekeeper. "Bear with us."

"Where to now?" the earl asked, reaching for her arm again, his grasp less urgent this time and more trusting.

She took his hand and placed it on her forearm. "Lily is leading us on a merry chase, my lord. Out of the kitchen we go."

She had a good idea of where Lily was headed next and she was right. Lily led the way through the hall around into the drawing room again and headed straight toward the conservatory door.

"I'm opening the door for you," the countess said as Lily and Sylvia neared. "How are you faring, my dear?"

"Tolerably well," the earl replied to his wife. "But I don't know how Lily deals with this day in and day out. Such courage."

"Thank you, my lord," Lily said, and led Sylvia into the darkened conservatory. Steam heat kept the glassed-in room warm in the winter months, but it was not lighted unless a lamp was brought in. The darkness hardly discouraged Lily.

"Where are we now?" the earl asked, turning his face toward the new room they'd entered.

"It's the conservatory," Sylvia cried. "I can smell the flowers."

"And the damp earth," the earl added, amazement in the curve of his lips. He drew in a long, deep breath. "I never realized how rich it smells before. And sweet, that must be from the plants."

"It's a different experience when you can't see it, isn't it?" she asked, smiling at the earl's discoveries.

"Yes, but no less a feast for the senses," the earl said. "Just a feast for the nose—and my skin. It's moister in here."

"I love to come out here," Lily said, smiling into the darkness. "Especially when the sun is out. Of course the steam heat keeps it warm out here, but I love to feel the sun warm my face."

"I can smell the lavender growing in the corner, Katherine," Hortense said. "Yes, this would be a pleasant place to come on a sunny day."

"This plant has a thick leaf," the earl was saying as he fingered a succulent. "Here is a fern. And what is over here?"

"Whoops." Katherine grabbed his wrist. "That one has thorns, my lord. It's one of my few cactus plants."

"Oh, thank you for saving me from my own enthusiasm," the earl said with a rare chuckle. "Can we take off our blindfolds?"

"Yes, of course." She noted that Carson had already helped Hortense remove hers, and they were walking back into the drawing room. "I hope you found the game instructional," she added.

"I did find it so, my dear." The earl whipped off the blindfold and absently stuffed the napkin into his coat pocket. He took both of her hands and drew her closer, an unexpected gesture of sincerity. "It was a fitting lesson for an old man who was too quick with his judgments. Forgive me for speaking so thoughtlessly. I can see why Lily does not want to leave you and why Carson married you. You are both gracious and wise ladies."

"Forgiven, my lord," she said, in spite of her reservations about the man. There was hope for him. He was humble enough to admit when he was wrong. "You flatter me. I only wished to help you understand Lily's world better."

"And so I do now," he said. "But please do not hesitate to call on me or Bess if we can do anything to be of service to you or your sister."

"Thank you, my lord," she said. "Shall we return to the drawing room?"

When the earl released her hands, she turned toward the conservatory door to find Carson standing there, a frown on his face. "Is there some problem?" he asked.

"No problem at all," Katherine said, suddenly uneasy with the tension that had sprung up in the conservatory. "Your father was telling me he enjoyed our little game, our experiment."

Carson's eyes narrowed and he locked gazes with his father. "Is that so?"

"And I also told Katherine that I thought you had chosen your wife well," the earl said, his pleasant expression gone.

The two men glared at each other.

With growing dismay, she looked from one to the other. "Gentlemen, I think—"

"It's all right, Katherine," Carson said at last, his gaze shifting to her, but his expression remaining cold and unyielding. "I think Father and I have found at least one thing we agree on."

"Indeed, we have," replied the earl. He offered his arm to her and smiled down at her. "Shall we join the others?"

"Yes," she said, taking the earl's arm hesitantly. When she glanced to Carson again, he gave her an ever so slight nod of approval.

Then he stood aside as his father escorted Katherine past him and out of the conservatory.

Early the next day, Christmas Eve, Cornish Jack called at the Elms. Carson was up already, reading the *Rocky Mountain Sentinel* and sipping his first cup of coffee at the study desk.

Sweet as lying next to Katherine had been, he'd awakened restless and clear eyed, ready to meet the day. He'd taken a few moments to study her sleeping form, naked, flushed with sleep—with passionate lovemaking. The way she'd handled his father the night before had made him bloody proud of her. She deserved whatever rest she could get. He'd lightly kissed her forehead and left her to dream a bit longer.

No one else was up yet when he heard Mrs. D greet the retired miner at the front door. Because Jack was a frequent visitor, Mrs. D showed him right into the study and took his hat with little fanfare. Jack stood in the study doorway with a large brown envelope in his hand and Ben Tucker's battered journal under his arm.

"Morning, Captain," he said, using the same address miners used for their favorite shift boss. "You told me you wanted this as soon as it was ready. I brung it over myself to deliver it with my own two hands. I didn't want to get Mrs. D in trouble like I did last time, with the letter from Alice."

He slapped the envelope down on the desktop.

"You didn't get Mrs. D into trouble," Carson said without taking his gaze off the envelope. "Her delivery of the letter was just unfortunate timing."

He laid aside his newspaper and picked up the envelope. "Is it what I think it is?"

" 'Tis," Jack said, dropping down in the chair in front of the desk.

Hastily, Carson ripped open the envelope. Unfolding the lengthy document, he scanned the words, though he knew what the document contained. The processing had taken long enough. Too long. But here it was at last, in writing. He felt more than just the victory in possessing the document; he felt relief in knowing what comfort it would give Katherine.

This piece of paper would erase the furrow that formed between her brows when she fretted over Lily's future. He smiled to himself. For some odd reason knowing he'd eased her burden pleased him immensely—better than anything he'd done in a long time.

As he looked over the paper again, Mrs. D slipped into the study and handed Jack a steaming cup of coffee.

"Thankee," was all Jack said, though he craned his neck to eye the housekeeper with an admiring gaze as she left the room.

"Mind your manners, Jack," Carson said when Mrs. D was gone. Satisfied with the document's contents, he folded it, replaced it in the envelope, and tucked it into his inside coat pocket. "It's exactly what I wanted. Thank you for bringing it over."

Jack nodded.

"How are things going at the Respite?" Carson asked, knowing what the answer would be.

"Quiet, what with the holiday and all." Jack sat in the chair and rested one ankle on his other knee. "The gents are busy with their women folk and families. Less willing to drop money on the table this time of year. The charities get it now. Ye know the way of it. Is there something ye want me to do about it?"

"No," Carson said. Business at the Respite was the least of his worries. "Any word from Alice Johnson about our San Francisco venture?"

"Nothing." Jack shook his head. "And nary a thing from

Nolan Stewart either. What did ye expect to learn from that scoundrel anyway?''

"I'm not sure." Carson leaned back in his chair. He was beginning to wonder if Stewart was going to keep his word about finding the name of the company Benedict had talked of. "What'd you think of Ben Tucker's journal?''

"Pretty interesting." Jack brightened. Carson knew a number of retired miners. Some had worked the mines to strike it rich—and often left disappointed. Some had worked the mines because the money was good and they didn't mind the discomforts. But some truly loved the rocks and the mystery of the dark holes in the ground. Jack was one of those. He was one of the miners who thought of mines like women, with beauty, foibles, whimsy, and heart.

"Ben Tucker was a smart man. He knew rock," Jack explained. "But he didn't let his knowledge get the better of his instincts, like some overeducated gents do.''

Carson nodded, partly because Jack's nodding was contagious and partly to encourage the miner to keep talking. He always knew more than he shared. But eventually he would spill the goods.

"Tucker thought the vein of gold was still there," Jack continued. "Or maybe some isolated pocket of it was undiscovered. These things happen.''

"But in slate? That's never happened before. And they dug into the slate layer several feet, if I understood what I was reading.''

"But ye know, 'tis an old saying, but true," Jack said, wagging his head. "There's a first time for everything that ever happened. I would have to see the mine. Do some digging. The vein could be there but have shifted. You know how the rock layers slide against each other. This is good coffee.''

"Mrs. D's is the best," Carson said, turning over Jack's information in his mind. "You're saying the vein could still exist, but above or below where it had been deposited in the rock?''

"Maybe they didn't look hard enough, or they missed the signs of it," Jack said. "The slate strata would make the vein hard to read. And there is still some mill-grade ore there. Ben talks about it. The question is if there's enough to make it financially feasible to run the mine. The so-called experts told him no. But he thought otherwise. He just couldn't prove it."

"And by that time Tucker had other holdings that were more profitable, so they closed the mine," Carson continued the line of thought, sorting through the options Ben Tucker must have contemplated. "But that doesn't explain how this other mysterious company might know about it—unless they sent somebody in to find it."

"The place is locked up, ain't it?" Jack asked.

"Yes, from what I understand," Carson said, thinking how a mine isolated back in a mountain ravine could easily be explored by anyone who had the desire to do so.

"Or somebody might be able to get into it from a neighboring mine," Jack offered. "Those mountainsides are honeycombed. You know, a drift tunnel accidentally intersecting a shaft. Something like that."

Carson sat up. The possibility had merit. "Any way you can learn more about the neighboring works?"

"I'll ask around." Jack gave a smart nod. "See if I can find some miners who worked up there. Weren't but a few years ago it was closed? Four or five years?"

"Sounds right," Carson agreed. "I'd be interested in what else you learn."

"Sure enough, Captain," Jack said, rising from his chair and reaching for his coffee cup. "Don't mind if I go back to the kitchen to speak to yer housekeeper, do ye?"

Carson tried to hide his smile. Jack was sensitive about his relationships with women and took offense at any comment about them. He happened to know that though the old miner wore clothes just on the respectable side of near ragged, he had a healthy bank account. And he'd seemed to take a fancy to Mrs. D. And the lady seemed to warm up to ol' Jack enough to send him away with a napkin full of cookies.

"Not at all, Jack," Carson said, returning to his newspaper as nonchalantly as he could manage. "I'm sure Mrs. D will be glad for a visit."

Jack left, turning down the hallway toward the kitchen carrying his coffee cup.

Carson patted his coat pocket, just to assure himself that the brown envelope was still there. He smiled to himself in anticipation. He could hardly wait to see the expression on Katherine's face when she opened it.

Chapter Twenty

Carson had been watching her like a hawk all day—like a hawk with a sly smile tugging at the corners of his mouth. The attention was beginning to unnerve Katherine. Even the presence of his father in the room hadn't prevented Carson's gaze from following her wherever she went. She could almost feel it touching her, and it'd made the day—Christmas Eve—most bewildering.

There'd been so many things to do in a house full of Christmas secrets. Everyone seemed to be conspiring—in the jolliest spirit, of course. She was loving every minute of it. What fun it was to have a family under the Elms' roof again, with all the associated noise and clamor, whispered confidences, closed doors, and hasty hiding of gifts. She loved the smiles and the secret pleasure of anticipating a loved one's reaction to a special present.

For a man who had confessed a certain amount of ambivalence about Christmas, Carson seemed to be joining into the festivities with interest. If only he would stop following her every move with his gaze.

There was laughter around the dining room table at mealtime and much hustle and bustle as last-minute errands were run. Mrs. D was busy at work in the kitchen, making the dining room smell of cinnamon and vanilla. In the hallway hung the piny scent of garland draped along the banister and the Christmas tree in the drawing room.

There was even the merry sound of Christmas carolers to enjoy, then treat to Mrs. D's eggnog and rum cake and Sylvia and Lily's sugar cookies. The girls had a great time making them. In the midst of it all Katherine tried her best to ignore Carson's unsettling attention.

But now, as they dressed for Dolly's Christmas Eve ball, it was becoming more difficult.

"Have you seen my black worsted wool suit?" Carson asked, leaning toward his shaving mirror as he prepared to draw the razor down his cheek. "I didn't see it among the clothes returned by the cleaners."

"No, I haven't seen it." She slipped her arms into the ivory lace sleeves of her ball gown and emerged from behind her screen. She crossed the room and presented her back to Carson. Even now he seemed to be following her every move by way of the mirror. "Is that why you've been watching me all day?"

"Watching you?" he asked. "Have I been watching you?"

"You most certainly have," she said. "You're going to wear your tuxedo tonight, aren't you? Dolly's affairs are always formal dress, though the atmosphere is casual."

"Yes," he replied. "I was just wondering about the suit."

"Would you button me, please?" she asked over her shoulder. "I know all these little buttons are the height of fashion, but they are so tedious."

"On the contrary, I think these pesky buttons are most enchanting." He put down his razor and dropped a kiss on the back of Katherine's neck. "Oh, sorry, I left some lather on you."

He wiped it off with his finger. She was unable to resist the shiver that coursed through her. Even after a week, his touch never failed to stir her. "I don't mind these buttons at all," he added, his fingers already at work.

The heat of his touch burned deliciously along her skin. Katherine sucked in a breath and closed her eyes. She tried to ignore the sensation. Maybe it would be easier to forget if she made small talk. "This ball is the perfect setting for showing off your father," she babbled. "Everyone he met the night of the tree decorating party will be at Dolly's."

"I don't give a fig about the ball," Carson whispered in her ear. "I'd rather stay here with you. Sit by the fire. Enjoy a glass of champagne to celebrate a special occasion."

"What special occasion?" She immediately wondered if it had anything to do with the reason he'd watched her all day.

"I'll show you in a moment," he said, continuing to whisper in her ear. Her body wasn't ignoring him at all. "As soon as I finish these blasted buttons."

The moment he was done, she turned to him. "Well?"

He stepped back and assessed her from head to toe.

She couldn't resist the cue to preen, turning first one way, then the other so he could see the gown, a new confection she'd had made for the ball—with the hope of inspiring that particular hungry glint that could come into his eyes before he made love to her.

The sheer lace fit like a glove from her throat down to her bustline. Puffy sleeves and a skirt of blue satin accented with ivory lace godets finished the dress. "What do you think?"

"Nice, but it covers too much," he said. "However, since we're going to be out in public, that's all right. Your pearl earrings, I think, and your mother's rope of pearls."

"Good suggestion," she said. "Now, you must tell me why you've been watching me all day like a cat stalking a mouse."

He laughed. "I had no idea I was so transparent. I must work on my poker face. I have something for you."

"It's too early for Christmas gifts," she reminded him.

"This isn't a Christmas gift," Carson said, the low seriousness of his tone warning her that he was not teasing. "But I think it's the right time for you to have it."

He walked across the room to the chair by the fireplace where his coat hung and reached into the pocket. He held up an envelope. "I wanted you to have this sooner, but . . . well, Jack brought it over today. It's yours now. Though it is not a Christmas gift, I hope it makes your Christmas a little merrier, sweetheart."

"What—?" She stared at the envelope, puzzled, a bit fearful. "Is this why you've been watching me?"

"It is," he admitted. "I was hoping for a moment alone, but when it didn't come, I decided I'd wait until tonight. Open it."

She took the envelope with impatient hands and pulled out the long document, which she recognized immediately. The sight of it was so unexpected, she felt as if someone had knocked the wind out of her.

"The deed to the Elms!" she finally gasped, hardly daring to believe her eyes.

"In your name, just as we agreed." He pointed to the appropriate line in the document. "It's always been yours, really. No surprises. This is what we agreed to. But I wanted you to have it in your hands as soon as all the paperwork cleared the bank and the courthouse."

"I knew it would take some time," she began, her hands trembling with joy and relief. The Elms was hers again, hers and Lily's. She turned toward him. "I'd assumed you would keep this until our deal was complete—until your family returned to England."

"No reason to wait," he said with a negligent shrug.

"Thank you," she said, still breathless with surprise. "I can't tell you what a scare Uncle Owen, Nolan, and Ray Jones at the bank put into me when they started talking about calling in the mortgage. I had some sleepless nights."

"I know." He took her by the shoulders and pulled her closer. His expression of pleasure strengthened his whispered words. "No more of those, not on account of the Elms, anyway."

She threw her arms around his neck and kissed him firmly—on the mouth. "I'm glad, too," she said, brushing her lips against his freshly shaven skin. He smelled of soap. She realized he was holding her tightly, his arms snugly around her waist. She savored the taste of him. Her body warmed. Her satin skirt would be wrinkled from the tight embrace, but she didn't care. "Oh, so glad," she murmured against his lips.

She took his mouth again, offering him a real kiss this time. A kiss that was deep and passionately grateful, yet full of the tenderness she felt for this man who—in spite of his emotional wounds—could be gentle and generous.

When they finally released each other, nearly panting for air, she was the first to speak. "But I don't have anything to give you. I mean, there is the gift I put under the tree today, but—"

He put a finger to her lips. "This was not a gift, sweetheart, remember. I owe it to you. I don't deserve anything in return. But I will ask one thing."

"What's that?" She laughed softly in her happiness. "You snake-oil man. You know I'll grant you anything."

"Promise me you'll never risk the Elms again," he said, holding her just far away enough from him to eye her pointedly.

"Never, never again," she vowed, amused by his unexpected request. She gazed up into his face. Spying a spot of shaving soap, she brushed it from his cheek. How different he was from the man she thought had taunted her from the Respite's window. "What a curious request from a gambler."

"Ah, but foolhardy as we are," he said, kissing her forehead with a tenderness that melted her insides, "even we gamblers know to hold some things sacred."

Dolly Green's Christmas Eve ball was a great success. Katherine looked stunning. So much so that Carson danced nearly every dance with her—except four. He danced once with his mother and once each with Marie and Hortense, and with Dolly. He was even reluctant to allow Katherine to dance with his brothers. The sheer lace of her gown barely revealed the smooth whiteness of her throat and the shadow of her deep decolletage. She looked prim and proper, yet incredibly sexy. But he relented. She danced once with each of his brothers and Owen Benedict.

And when she danced with the earl . . .

"Stop grinding your teeth and glaring at your father," the countess said as Carson swung her around out onto the dance floor. She smiled up at him with understanding in her eyes. "Your father likes Katherine. He will be gracious with her. Please pay me heed."

"Sorry," Carson said, chagrined at how visible his reaction was to seeing Katherine smiling at the man who'd made his life miserable. He was glad she'd won his father over, he told himself. He really was.

"In fact, I'd say you improved your standing with him by marrying such a sweet, strong girl," the countess said. "I know he had his doubts about a Fairfax marrying an American. But he thinks Katherine is a treasure, and I agree."

"I'm glad to know that, Mother." His gaze rested on Katherine again.

"You really must bring her and Lily to Atwick Manor for a Christmas," the countess was saying as they whirled past the earl and Katherine on the dance floor.

Carson misstepped, then recovered smoothly. His mother's invitation shook him out of his preoccupation with his wife. Here was a turn he'd never seriously considered. "Do you think Father would agree to that? When I left Atwick last, I was told he didn't care to set eyes on me again, let alone have me under his roof."

"For Katherine, I think he might be persuaded to forget his words," the countess said with a smile. "Of course, I'm the one to work on making that happen. It shall take some time, but I think it's possible."

Splendid he thought, the realization slowly dawning of the quandary he'd dragged himself and Katherine into. When he'd hatched this plot with Dolly and Randolph's help, he'd never anticipated that his father would turn up—nor all of his brothers. What's more, he'd always thought his mother would return to England, where he was unwelcome. He and Katherine would go their separate ways after the quiet annulment and that would be the end of it. Now the question begged: *How would his mother and father, who'd come to profess their affection for Katherine, take his annulment from her when the time came?*

His simple scheme was becoming unbelievably complicated.

"Is there a problem, dear?" his mother asked. A frown of concern crossed her face as she gazed up at him.

"No, not at all," he said, shoving away thoughts of complications only to realize with mild surprise how much he'd like to take Katherine to England. He could squire her around the sights of London—treat her to shopping for herself and the house—take her to the theater, entertain her with tea at the Savoy, show her Atwick Manor, escort her to balls and soirees.

He frowned and glanced unhappily across the ballroom to reassure himself that she was there, dancing with his father. The problem was that she and he had this damned arrangement. When this scheme had been played out, she was going to Europe and he was going to San Francisco. His future was in the Bay City. She would be free to marry again and have the family she wanted, once the scandal died down.

"Of course, we'd especially be delighted if you brought a new little Fairfax with you," his mother added, beaming up at him now. "How glad I would be to see you start your family at last. Are you certain nothing is wrong, son?" his mother added. "You're frowning so."

"No, I'm not," he lied, forcing a smile back onto his face for his mother's sake. Fatherhood was definitely not in his picture of the future. "I'm sure Katherine and Lily would love to spend Christmas in England. But I can't make any promises, Mother. We'll just have to see what the future brings."

                            * * *

   The ball ended in the wee hours of Christmas morning, leaving the grown-up Fairfaxes just enough time to play the part of Santa, as Katherine called it. Amid yawns, they arranged the toys under the tree for the children. A hoop for Willie. A doll for Eunice. A large picture book for Sylvia. A music box for Lily. Then they retired to their beds before first light.

   Dawn barely glowed on the horizon when the children— Willie, Eunice, Sylvia, and Lily—padded their way down the stairs to discover the surprises under the tree.

   She heard them. She'd been so excited and pleased about having family in the house for Christmas, she only dozed for a couple of hours, her ear cocked for the sound of the children. The moment the sounds of soft giggles and little feet on the carpet reached her, she threw back the covers, surprised to find that Carson was gone. How had she missed him leaving their bed? Grabbing her robe, she followed them down the stairs.

   Mrs. D could be heard at work in the kitchen. She'd already fixed coffee; Katherine could smell it. She knew the house-keeper would be rubbing pepper and lemon onto a ponderous tom turkey. After that, she'd be up to her elbows in stuffing him with oyster dressing so he could be steamed for the Christmas feast.

   She followed the sound of the children's *oh*s and *ah*s into the drawing room. They were gathered in the center of the room, admiring the tree.

   "Uncle Carson is lighting the candles, Aunt Katherine," Willie unnecessarily informed her as she entered. Sylvia was chattering away with a description of the tree for Lily.

   "So I see." She grinned at the sight of Carson.

   Wrapped in his robe and his hair uncombed, he was down on his knees, his eyes still heavy with sleep. But with a steady hand, he was lighting the last of the candles on the tree. For someone who had started the season ambivalent about it, he'd certainly done his best to join in the spirit. A flood of love coursed through Katherine for this man who was always up to the unexpected.

"It's truly beautiful," she said, thinking more of the sight of him than of the tree.

He finished and got to his feet to join her in the center of the room. "It is beautiful, isn't it?" he said, slipping an arm around her waist.

In the watery light of the wintry Christmas morn, the myriad candle flames burned bright, lighting up the drawing room with a cheery glow as well as any chandelier could.

"I've never seen a tree so big." He pulled her closer. "Nor a lady of the house so lovely on Christmas morning."

Too late, she put her hand to her hair, thinking how unkempt she must look. But it didn't seem to matter to him. He pulled her into his arms and planted a kiss on her lips, right there in front of the children.

"Happy Christmas, Mrs. Fairfax," he murmured.

She waited to feel a blush burn in her cheeks, but it didn't. This felt so right, being here in the drawing room in his arms with the portrait of Mama and Papa looking down on them and all of Carson's family together. "Happy Christmas, Mr. Fairfax," she replied with a smile.

"Okay, you two, enough of that spooning stuff," Lily said, her hearing obviously as sharp as ever. "What did Santa bring us? What's in our stockings?"

"Yes, what's in the stocking?" little Sylvia echoed, already peering into hers to discover the sweets, nuts, and prizes.

One by one, garbed in robes and with eyes heavy from lack of sleep, the adult Fairfaxes gathered around the Christmas tree in the drawing room to watch the children descend on the gifts like locusts on a wheat field. Their squeals of delight filled the air.

With everyone in the room, there was a shortage of chairs. Carson pulled Katherine over to sit on his knee. She rested there tentatively.

"This is a little familiar, don't you think?" she muttered

under her breath, casting a glance in the direction of the earl and the countess.

Carson shrugged. "They don't seem concerned."

Lily cooed in delight over the gift she'd just unwrapped, Braille music for a song she'd been wanting. She'd already discovered she could change the music scrolls on her new music box.

There was a gold-headed ebony walking stick for the earl, and for the countess there was a Colorado gold, ruby, sapphire, and pearl choker. Beaded bags for Marie and Hortense. Fine doeskin gloves for John and Neville. For Carson the countess brought three English-made monogrammed dress shirts.

"From your favorite London shirtmaker," his mother reminded him.

"I remember." He grinned at her.

During the preceding days, as the children took inventory of what was under the tree for them, Katherine couldn't help noticing that there was no box for her from Carson. She'd tried to tell herself that it didn't matter, even when she'd placed her special box beneath the tree for him.

After all, she had the deed to the Elms, thanks to him.

"I can't believe how generous your family is being," she whispered to Carson.

"And why shouldn't they be?" he replied

"Here is another one for Uncle Carson," Willie cried, who'd appointed himself the official Santa's helper for the morning. With a box almost larger than he was, Willie trotted across the drawing room to hand it to Carson.

"What could this be?" Carson asked, looking from the box to her.

"Something special just for you," she said, suddenly nervous about whether he would like the gift. She'd given its selection much thought. But now, remembering how he'd handed the deed to the Elms over to her, she wondered if she would have been wiser to select something she was certain he wanted.

Something a wife would be expected to give to her husband. Something worthy of a man who'd been so generous with her.

Carson studied her for a moment, then began to pull at the ribbons and wrapping. Soon he had the box bare.

"No hint?" he asked, offering her a last chance to warn him.

She realized with dismay that he'd read her uncertainty. She bit her lip and shook her head. *Oh, dear heavens, I've made a mistake.*

Slowly, with drama, Carson set the lid aside, parted the tissue, and lifted out an elegant black silk top hat. His gaze met hers over the conventional hat. His eyes narrowed ever so slightly, but only for a fraction of a moment.

Her heart sank. No matter how expensive or how perfect the hat's fit, it was a mistake. She didn't understand exactly why, except that he had a perfectly good gambler's bowler, and he was content with it. She knew that. Yet here she was trying to change his ways, to remake him.

After all he'd done for her her gift of a top hat was a betrayal.

"It's very handsome and fashionable, too," the countess said, moving across the room. "Carson, you must try it on."

Katherine slid off Carson's knee and backed away as he good-naturedly submitted to his mother's attentions. She prayed no one in the room could feel the schism that suddenly yawned between them.

"Makes you look very respectable, brother," John said with a laugh.

"Quite," the earl agreed.

"In a chapeau like that, Carson, one would hardly know you were a saloonkeeper," Marie agreed.

"I think that was the idea," he said with a rueful smile that chilled Katherine. "Now, wife, I have something for you."

He pulled a small box out of his robe pocket. "Go ahead. Unwrap it. No need to stare at it as if it has fallen out of the sky."

She tore at the paper, revealing a jewelry gift box. She

couldn't imagine what he might have chosen for her. She glanced at him long enough to realize with some relief that the gift was one that the playacting Carson was giving to his playacting wife. It wasn't as if these gifts were supposed to have any actual meaning.

She knew whatever it was, she would smile, laugh, and deliver a little speech of gratitude. Whatever it was, it would not be a true gift to a wife.

"Don't stop, sweetheart," he said.

"Open it." Sylvia and Lily had come to stand at her shoulder, soaking up all the vicarious pleasure children so adored at Christmas time.

"What is it?" Lily asked. "Describe it, Sylvia. What is it?"

Katherine opened the box, expecting something like a pair of diamond earrings or a cameo or some such thing that would be appropriate for a husband to give his wife. But what she found was so different, so beautiful and—in a strange way—meaningful, it left her momentarily speechless.

"It's a key," Sylvia crowed to all the adults, who were curious but could not see what Katherine was bent over. "It's encrusted with lots of diamonds and gold. Oooh, pretty. Why a key, Uncle Carson?"

"Aunt Katherine knows," he said, without looking at her.

"It's the key to his heart, of course." The countess smiled fondly at Katherine.

"It's beautiful," she said, knowing that the countess was wrong. She lifted the necklace with its delicate gold chain from the box and held it up so all could see. The diamonds of the first water gleamed in the candlelight, casting rainbows across the room.

"Do you like it?" he asked, in a tone that nearly sounded like that of an anxious husband.

"Yes," Katherine replied with the kind of enthusiasm she thought appropriate from a delighted wife. She wanted to ask what it meant for certain, but she swallowed her questions—for the moment.

"Let's go to the hall mirror and I'll help you put it on," he offered, towing the two of them away from the rest of the family.

In front of the hall, facing the mirror, she permitted him to latch the necklace around her neck.

The diamonds sparkled brilliant and pure with a life of their own.

Carson stood behind her, his new top hat shoved to the back of his head, the way he liked to wear his bowler sometimes.

They made a totally mismatched pair. He didn't look right in a top hat. And she didn't deserve to be wearing diamonds. Suddenly Katherine wanted to cry because it was all wrong and she didn't know why. With determination, she swallowed the lump in her throat.

"Your mother doesn't understand," she said, watching their reflections in the mirror. "This is the key to the door between us, isn't it?"

Carson shrugged. "Take it for whatever you like."

Then, putting his hands on her shoulders, he leaned closer and added, "But know one thing, sweetheart. You can't change me with a hat. I'm a bowler man. A top hat won't take the saloonkeeper out of the man."

Chapter Twenty-one

By the night of Owen Benedict's New Year's Eve ball, as much as Carson loved his mother and as pleased as he was to share her company, the Earl and Countess of Atwick's visit was wearing thin.

"John? Neville? I was just pouring myself a brandy while we wait for the ladies to come down," he said when all four men, dressed in tuxedos, had gathered in the drawing room. "Father?"

More precisely, his father's presence was wearing damned thin. He had to admit, until Christmas Day—until Katherine had given him the bloody top hat—the visit had gone remarkably well. But once they'd all been reminded of what he preferred to do for a living, the uneasy truce his mother had demanded began to deteriorate.

His brothers accepted his offer of a brandy.

"Father, may I pour one for you?" he asked, to be polite.

"Not for me," the earl said, casting a disapproving frown in his youngest son's direction. His kind words were reserved for Katherine or John or Neville. Carson reminded himself he was almost thirty-two years old—much too old to be troubled by his father's reproach—but it still smarted.

"To the new year," he said, lifting his glass in a toast.

"Hear, hear," John and Neville chorused, doing likewise.

"Don't you think you ought to save that for midnight?" the earl said.

Carson turned away and drained his brandy snifter in one long gulp.

Fortunately the week between Christmas and New Year's had been too full of events and entertainment to allow him and his father to be alone together. Nevertheless, he found himself contemplating some scheme to get his father to leave soon, while his mother stayed to enjoy the visit.

"I don't think there's a limit on how often one can toast the new year," Neville said equitably. John agreed.

Father said nothing more.

Carson contemplated pouring himself another, but decided against it even though it was going to be a long evening. Life could be worse. Despite the odd rift that had sprung between he and Katherine since the gift exchange—he'd put the silk top hat high on the back closet shelf; she'd made no objection—he'd had the solace of her in his arms each night.

As far as Carson knew, this was the first New Year's Eve ball the Benedicts had ever hosted. Because they lived in a rather modest home—though they could afford better, Edna had refurbished the house several times and refused to give it up—the ball was held at the Windsor Hotel. The benefit was twofold: they could invite as many people as they liked and out-of-town guests could stay in the hotel.

The guest list was impressive. The governor was present along with a host of congressional figures, railroad and mining tycoons, and rich merchants. If Carson had been pressed to speculate, he would have guessed that Benedict had developed political aspirations.

The New Year had rung in, good wishes made all around, toasts drunk, and breakfast was about to be served when the ladies excused themselves to go freshen up. Noise filled the gaily festooned ballroom. The orchestra was on break.

Out of idle curiosity, Carson ambled into the neighboring smoking room, where some of the male guests were intent on a game of poker. He'd merely wanted to see who was at the table, what game they were playing, and how high were the stakes. He never noticed that his father had followed him in.

Benedict was observing the game from across the smoke-filled room. When he saw Carson, he rose from his chair and made his way around the table.

"Fairfax. Atwick," Benedict greeted with a respectful nod. That was when Carson realized his father had followed him. "Care to join in? They'll be calling this pot soon. I'm sure there will be a place at the table for either or both of you."

"Not tonight," Carson said, nodding greetings to several of the men around the table. He'd sat across from most of them more than once at the Respite.

"I'm not a gambler myself," the earl said, the sour twist of disapproval on his lips that Carson was so familiar with.

"You're not, sir!" Benedict raised his eyebrows in surprise. "And I thought Carson must have learned his card sense from you."

Carson saw the back of his father's neck go rigid.

Benedict continued, "I can tell you, my lord, that your son is among the best card players there are. It's great sport to sit across the table from Carson Fairfax. And there are those who rue the day he sold the Gentlemen's Respite and gave up his place at the card table."

"Hear, hear," cheered one of the men at the table.

Another man cursed sharply and threw down his cards. Mutterings and laughter broke out. Several men rose to leave. One remained to rake in the chips.

"Come on. Sit down, Carson," Ray Jones the banker called. "I'm one of those who has missed playing against you."

"No, thanks." He wasn't even tempted. As a card player Jones was a cheater—when the banker could pull it off—and a poor loser. He'd often wondered if the man ran his bank the same way. But what concerned him more was his father's reaction to what Benedict had said. He would hear about it later.

He did.

When they returned to the Elms, the Fairfax men had just gathered in the family parlor for a nightcap when the earl started in on him.

Thankfully his father had waited until Mother and the ladies had gone upstairs to bed.

"I knew it all had to be a myth," the earl began after refusing the nightcap.

John and Neville blinked, mystified by what their father was talking about. They turned questioning gazes on him. He braced himself.

"What are you talking about, Father?" John asked.

"That tour of the bank and the insurance offices Carson took us on," the earl continued, glaring at him. "Pointing to buildings as we drove down the street and claiming ownership. It's all a story to impress your mother, isn't it?"

Carson glared back, full to the gullet of his father's silent disapproval. "No, it's not. And I'll thank you not to utter that slander in front of Mother."

"Humph, slander, indeed," the earl said, pacing the length of the room in his agitation. "Just what was that Mr. Benedict said about that place, that gambling hall, the place where you gambled with all those men? The Gentlemen's Respite? That's the business you own, isn't it? That's what you've made your fortune from. Then you married a sweet but conveniently rich girl like Katherine and set yourself up as some kind of respectable citizen."

Carson could feel his hold on his temper slipping away, not because of what his father said about the Respite, but because of the implication that he was taking advantage of Katherine.

"Whatever quarrel you have with me as your son, you lay it at my feet. Do you hear? Blame me! But leave my wife out of it."

"Father? Carson?" John attempted to step between them. "This is not the time or place—"

"By God, it is the time and place to let your brother know that I understand exactly what he is up to," the earl said, shoving John aside. "You boys stay out of this."

Neville and John fell silent.

"And just what is it you think I'm up to?" Carson demanded, setting his jaw in defiance. Nothing he'd ever done in the past had satisfied his father. Had he really expected to do so now? "There are contracts, agreements, and deeds proving that I own over fifty percent of that bank and eighty-five percent of the insurance company. Those buildings I pointed out—they're mine, free and clear. And a nice little income producer they are, too. Are documents the proof you want to see?"

"No, they are not."

"Good, because I don't intend to show them to you," Carson said, slamming his glass down on the table. "I've shown you all I intend to show you. You can bloody well take my word for it."

"I don't give a damn about those holdings," the earl said, his voice low and angry. "What I want to know is how you financed the Respite. I've heard all the stories. The fanciest men's club in town. How did you manage to build a place like that within a few years of coming to Denver? From your winnings as a gambler? Or did you have a little seed money?"

Instantly, Carson understood, though the accusation grated on him. He'd built the Respite from his own efforts, not from anything his father had given him. "I'll repay you for what I did, if that's what you want."

"You think a few ill-gotten dollars will make up for the way you flouted my generosity?" the earl demanded, his hands balled into fists at his side. His voice raised an octave. "You think there is a way to repair the damage done to tradition and family reputation?''

"Reputation. For God's sake, Father," Neville said with impatience. "It isn't as though Carson murdered anybody.''

"But he did his best to humiliate the family name," the earl insisted.

"Nonsense." Carson gave a harsh laugh and brushed the charge aside with the back of his hand. "If I'd wanted to embarrass the family, I would've gambled those estates away, not sold them.''

"Don't even sug—'' the earl began, shaking a finger in Carson's face. He was about to grab his father's hand and thrust it back in his face when the whisper of the countess's quilted silk dressing gown announced her arrival.

The earl fell silent. He and Carson stepped away from each other, neither able to meet the countess's gaze.

"What's going on in here?" she demanded, studying each man's face.

John and Neville looked at their mother, guilt written in their expressions even though they had nothing to do with the argument. Carson remained silent. His father could defend himself.

"I could hear you at the top of the stairs," she scolded, her face stern, her tone laced with irritation. "You woke the children with your wrangling. I thought I had an agreement for peace.''

"Go to bed, Bess," the earl said, running his fingers through his gray hair. "We have things to settle. We'll be up to bed . . . eventually.''

"You'll come now," the countess said, tenacity flashing in her eyes.

"No, this has to be settled tonight." The earl spoke directly to Carson.

"I want it settled, too," he agreed. They'd been tiptoeing around each other long enough.

Katherine appeared in the doorway. She glowered at him,

then at his father. If they thought the countess looked determined, Katherine looked thunderous.

"Go on up to bed, Elizabeth. I'll arbitrate this discussion," she said.

"This thing between the two of them has been festering for almost twenty years," John warned her gently. "I don't think it is going to go away tonight."

"I have a few things I want to say to them," Katherine said, her expression as solemn as he had ever seen it. "And what better way to start the new year than to take the steps toward a settlement?"

"This doesn't involve you, Katherine," he said, thinking of all the sordid details he did not want her to know.

"If Katherine can get the two of you to listen to each other, then I'm willing to leave it in her hands," the countess said.

"It doesn't matter whether Katherine is involved or not," the earl asserted, "I don't believe Carson can ever say or do anything to satisfy me."

"There!" Carson said hardly believing what he's just heard. "He's admitted it."

"Hush, both of you." Katherine stepped into the room, her mouth pinched in irritation. There was no brushing her off now.

"This is my house and I'll have no more of this," she continued. "Jumping at each other's throats like back-alley dogs. Disturbing the children."

She pointed a shaming finger at Carson. "You're upsetting your mother."

She glared at the earl. "And you, distressing your wife. Shame on you. If this thing is so terrible that you feel you have the right to upset everyone you love, then let's give it an airing."

"Bravo." The countess clapped her hands. "If you'll excuse me, I will go to bed now. I'll leave them in your capable hands, Katherine. In the morning I'm looking forward to a leisurely, peaceful breakfast with all my family."

Without another word she kissed the earl on the cheek. Then she went to Carson and kissed him on the cheek. She smelled of roses as she always did. She touched his face, her fingers warm and loving as they'd always been, even when he was a boy. He was overcome with a desire to please her, to settle this and give his mother what she wanted: peace.

"Good night," she murmured, then ushered Neville and John out of the room.

As soon as they were alone, Katherine braced her fists on her hips and raked them with a demanding glare. "Just what is the matter with you two? You've lived here under this roof for three weeks and done very well, thank you. What is the matter now? Just what is it that is so all fired awful the two of you can't put it behind you?"

The earl pressed his lips together in a surly pout. "This is a waste of time. Carson has thrown everything I've ever tried to do for him back in my face. There is nothing anyone can say to repair the damage."

Katherine's brows went up. "I don't have to do the repair work. You do."

Confusion settled on the earl's face. "I think we should call it a night," he said, casting Carson a silent appeal for help.

He folded his arms across his chest and waited. "Let's hear her out."

Katherine stepped between the earl and the door. "Let me tell you something, my lord. You have enjoyed my hospitality. You owe me the respect of your attention."

"That's so," he conceded.

"Then listen carefully. Both of you." Katherine cast her scowl at Carson as well. "Sit."

He and his father found chairs across the room from each other. She sat down facing them.

"Lily and I lost our mother seven years ago when I was barely eighteen." She paused, seeming to struggle with her emotions. "We lost Papa two years ago to an unfortunate accident. Our grandparents on both sides are gone, long ago. For two Christmases we've been alone. Oh, yes, we have many friends—kind, loving people like Dolly Green and Uncle Owen—but we only have each other for family.

"I can tell you from experience that there can't possibly be anything on this earth—short of murder—that is so terrible you can't forgive each other for it. Nothing is so awful that a family should be divided, shouting recriminations at each other. Not if you truly try to love each other. Because when the final separation comes and you know you will never be able to say all the things you wanted to say—when there is no second chance—you'll realize how small all those arguments were."

Carson stared at Katherine, his own problem momentarily forgotten. How painful losing her parents must have been. She'd been so young, and she'd had no one to rely on—except Dolly. When she gazed back at him, then at his father, there was no self-pity in her expression.

He gave his father a sidelong glance. Did the earl feel as much of an ingrate as he did?

Katherine went on, her eyes clear and her voice matter-of-fact. "Here you are, fortunate enough to have each other still on this earth. Fortunate enough to be able to travel to see each other. Then you spend the time laying blame at each other's door for something that happened how long ago?"

"Ten years since I left England," Carson admitted, feeling the heat seep out of his anger in the face of her great loss.

"Ten years ago, last June," his father corrected. The earl wasn't going to relinquish his outrage easily.

"What happened?" she asked, folding her hands in her lap. "Tell me. I warn you, I'm expecting a story full of murder and mayhem, you know. Something as terrible as Cain and Abel at least."

"I'll admit it's nothing that dreadful," the earl grumbled, his chin lifted in a resentful line.

When his father didn't continue, Carson began the story, telling it the way he wanted it told. There would be no mention of locked doors or the like. He didn't want to upset Katherine. But he didn't intend to let his father off lightly either. "The final straw came when one of the university fellows complained that I was trying to make a science out of cards and probability. Father pulled me out of university and tried to make a farmer out of me.''

"I tried to give you some responsibility," the earl said. "I thought you needed to meet new people. I thought if you had some responsibility, you'd reevaluate your life and see what a mistake you were making with your talents. Then you'd hear your calling.''

Puzzlement crossed Katherine's face. "Calling?"

"Carson was meant for the pulpit," the earl said.

Katherine blinked at his father, then turned to him. "Yes, he told me you'd hoped he'd go into the church. Did you hear this calling, Carson?"

"Nobody spoke to me."

"Don't be irreverent," the earl scolded, clearly offended. "Being a man of God is an honorable life."

"Of course it is, my lord," Katherine said. "But for Carson?"

"He should have felt blessed to have the freedom to pursue a life in the clergy," the earl said. "Look at me. I was forced to give up a scholar's life and take up my place as the family heir, as your brother, John, is forced to do."

"John will love being the earl when the time comes," he said, determined to make his father see the truth. "The pompousness of it thrills him."

"Carson!" she warned.

"I'm trying to explain." He went on, "If ever a man was made for the military, it was Neville. I was forever ducking his cavalry charges when we were boys."

"Did you seek out religious study?" Katherine asked.

"Never."

"He just didn't realize what that life held for him," the earl insisted. "He was always good at his letters and sums. He could remember numbers and do arithmetic like no child I've ever seen. The tutors frequently remarked on it. The scholarly life was just what he needed. I sent him to the best church-related schools.''

Carson leaned toward Katherine to confide, "I was dismissed from all of them. He never seemed to be able to get the hint.''

"I offered you the opportunity of a lifetime." The earl pounded his fist on his knee. "I would have given my right arm if I'd had the same opportunity.''

The earl's words rung in the air. Carson's heart stopped beating. He stared at her father, wondering if he'd heard what he thought he'd heard. His father wanted to be a clergyman. "What did you say?''

"You heard me. I said, I would have liked to have had the opportunity when I was young," the earl said, turning to him, suddenly animated with the desire to make his son see the truth. "Don't you see what it offered? You could have spent your life in the pursuit of spiritual truth. You could have spent your days exploring the biblical texts, sharing your insights with the less fortunate. A quiet life of contemplation and study. Sundays dedicated to the ritual of worship. Mornings spent in prayer. Don't you see the beauty of it?''

"But perhaps he never wanted it," Katherine said.

Carson glanced at her. She met his gaze only long enough for him to know that she too had heard what his father had truly said.

"He would have, if he'd had the sense God gave a goose," the earl said, aiming his barbs at Carson. "Yes, of course I would have liked to live a more scholarly life. I would have liked to become a member of the clergy. But it was not to be for me. However, I could give that opportunity to my son.''

The confession astonished Carson. Speechless, he stared at his father. In the place of the harsh controlling man, instead of the monster who'd shut him behind locked doors, he saw a stranger, a disappointed soul—a sad and frustrated man.

A long, low, slow breath of astonishment escaped him. The revelation changed everything he'd assumed about his father.

He opened his mouth to speak, but Katherine stayed him

with a small wave of her hand. "And a generous offer it was, my lord, but Carson is not a man of the cloth. Think about it. Where did you find him as a boy when he went missing? In the library? In the chapel?"

"In the tack room playing cards with the grooms," the earl said, without a moment's hesitation. He glared at Carson. "More than once I found him there. His mother did, too, but she would never admit it, not to me, at least. We argued many a night over you, Carson."

He knew that and it had only made him all the more resentful.

"Didn't that tell you anything?" Katherine asked.

"Only that he didn't have the good sense to understand his position in life," the earl said, staring at the floor, clearly unable to forgive his son.

Katherine turned to Carson. He felt her steady gaze probe him. The intensity of it made him straighten in his chair.

"Now, husband," she began, "tell me just what was this terrible deed you committed for which you must offer repayment?"

Chapter Twenty-two

Carson eyed Katherine and wished to high heaven that he'd never allowed this discussion to get started—much less permitted her to become involved. This was between himself and his father. This was a man-to-man issue. Even his mother didn't truly understand.

"Yes, Carson," his father goaded, his gaze fastened on him, too. "Explain what you did. Your wife has a right to understand fully the issues here."

"I'm not proud of it," Carson began, looking at Katherine and truly regretting for the first time what he'd done. Not because he'd infuriated his father, but for the childish public display of pure, bad temper. "I was barely nineteen."

"And he'd been sent down from university," the earl added. "I signed over two long-held family estates to him in the hope that responsibility and duty would help him see his place in life. One of them, Somerton, included a nice vicarage. I had hopes that the old vicar, Mr. Brooke, would provide an example for Carson."

"I knew that and I resented it," Carson admitted. "Why do you think I sold the estates off as soon as I could?"

"You sold two family estates!" Katherine cried, clearly as astonished as his father was angry.

"Pure bloody rebelliousness and ingratitude," his father snapped back. "If you'd minded your p's and q's you could be a bishop by now."

"But I never wanted to be a bishop," Carson said. "Or a Bible scholar. Can't you see that? A bishop is what *you* wanted to be."

The truth spoken aloud—acknowledged—for the first time burst into the air between the two men like a swarm of gnats.

"Then what did you want?" the earl asked, his tone demanding but his voice weakened.

"To be exactly where I am." Carson turned to Katherine and held her gaze. "Where a man is respected for what he does and how well he does it, not for his position in life or his family name. Here, where a man builds his own reputation. Right here with a lovely wife and a comfortable home."

Katherine met his gaze, a blush rising in her cheeks. He hoped she understood that there was no playacting in that speech. "I'm sorry that I cannot fulfill your ambition," he continued, with heartfelt sympathy for a man who gave up his aspiration to take over an earldom he never truly wanted.

The earl rose and waved the apology aside.

"My lord, why not make your life into what you want it to be?" Katherine asked, also rising. "Surely John could take over some of the responsibilities of your position."

"I'm too old," the earl said, his voice weaker still. "Too much water has passed under the proverbial bridge."

"I will repay you for the sale of Somerton and the other estate."

The earl brushed the offer away. "No need. I'm going to bed."

At the door he stopped and turned to Katherine. "I promise to be on my best behavior for the remainder of the visit. You have been a wonderful hostess, my dear. I would not have my differences with Carson spoil our stay at the Elms.''

He left the room. In silence Katherine and Carson listened to him climb the stairs with the slow steps of a spent man.

''I will make arrangements with Father's business manager,'' he said. ''He won't be so indifferent to a matter of repayment for the estates I sold off.''

''I think that's a good idea,'' she said. ''I'm not certain that we resolved anything, but at least you both understand the conflict.''

''Yes, I understand many things better now,'' he said, filled with affection for this woman, the likes of which he'd never felt for anyone in his life. He rose, took Katherine's hand, and drew her toward the stairs, toward their room. ''Many things are clearer now.''

The last three weeks of the Earl and Countess of Atwick's Denver visit was comparatively uneventful. They continued to enjoy the best socializing society had to offer, in addition to sleigh rides, ice skating, shopping, and parlor games.

To Katherine's pleasant surprise, the frost seemed to disappear in the courtesy Carson and his father showed each other. In its place developed an awkwardness, an uncertainty, a tentativeness in the way they dealt with each other. A carefulness not to offend. But it was a vast improvement over the chilly veiled tension that had settled on a room when the two of them confronted each other during the earlier weeks.

Carson said nothing more about his father and their confrontation. The household schedule continued as it had: breakfast as each rose, luncheon frequently out, with everyone gathered around the table for supper. There actually were moments when she could let herself pretend that it was all real: that they were, indeed, a family visiting over the holidays, enjoying each other's company, sampling each other's life, sharing the joy of the season. Even the dog and cat adopted everyone as family.

One morning, when she encountered the countess alone in the upstairs hall, the woman threw her arms around her and crushed her in a spontaneous embrace.

"Thank you, Katherine," the countess said. "The breach may not be mended, but it is at least defused."

"I didn't do anything," she said, hugging the countess in return. "I think they just understand each other a little better."

"Yes," the countess said, and they giggled with joy and relief and intimacy—like a pair of schoolgirls.

Katherine pressed her cheek against the countess's, realizing how much she was going to miss her company. She wished that the lady was going to be her mother-in-law forever, along with her sisters- and brothers-in-law, nieces and nephew. How good it would be for Lily, too, to have relatives.

When the day came for the Fairfaxes to board the train, her heart was heavy, though she forced a smile to her lips. She could tell from the tight grip of Lily's hand in hers that her sister was just as sad as she was to see their English family leave. Carson remained stoic.

The parting was tearful for the ladies. The men shook hands all around. Carson and his father even shook, an exchange that had not happened the night the earl appeared at the front door of the Elms, she remembered. It was a small thing, but it was another sign of healing, she hoped.

There was a flurry of loading luggage and three food baskets well packed by Mrs. D. Blankets and pillows, though everyone knew the private car was well equipped for any need. Then the engine whistle blew—the last signal for all aboard.

The countess grasped Katherine by the arms and kissed her on the cheek. "Take care of him, dear, and of yourself and Lily. As sorrowful as parting is, I rest assured that Carson is at last happy and loved and cared for as he deserves to be."

The undeserved words of praise brought tears to Katherine's eyes.

"And you must let us know as soon as there is news of a

baby," the countess continued. "Telegraph. Don't waste time with letters. They take too long. Good-bye, dear."

Katherine nodded, then stood aside so the countess could say farewell to Carson. She had no idea what his mother said to him, but he hugged her tight before he helped her board the train. They stood on the platform waving good-bye to their family until the private car was out of sight.

"Well, that's that," Carson said, turning to her with a satisfied expression.

"Yes, it's over," she said, feeling oddly out of sorts. His cheerfulness annoyed her.

He offered his arm.

Out of habit, she took it, and they began to walk back through the depot. Lily held her other hand.

With a subtle, breathless panic, she realized she was walking out of one life and into another. So was Carson. She glanced at him. He was strolling along as if nothing had changed.

She tried to follow his example.

When they stepped out onto the street, the wagon that had carried all the luggage was gone, but Willis and the carriage, plus the hired buggy that had carried them all to the station, were waiting at the curb. The day was cloudy and cold, the wind sharp.

She guided Lily to Willis, who helped the girl into the carriage.

Then she turned to Carson.

"What now?" she asked, wondering how long annulments took.

"I promised the president of my bank that I'd stop by and look over some investments he's been looking into," he said, as if it was just another workday.

She studied him, trying to understand what he was saying.

"Go home and rest." He patted her hand on his arm. "You've been playing hostess for almost two months. You deserve to take it easy."

A profusion of clean-up chores flooded into her mind. "I have to help Mrs. D set the house to rights," she protested.

"Do what you feel up to," he said. "I'll be home for supper."

She blinked at him. No mention of moving out of her room? Out of the Elms?

"But—there's no need to playact," she said, lowering her voice so the people rushing around them could not overhear. She knew they all saw a husband and wife standing on the street, discussing their plans for the day. But the truth was so far from that. "What about San Francisco?"

"This is the end of January," he said, clearly incredulous that she would mention travel westward at this season. "Trains get snowed in for days in the high passes. No, I'm not striking out for the west coast now, if that's what you're thinking. I'll be home for supper, as I said."

To her surprise, he leaned forward and bestowed a quick, husbandly kiss on her lips. She realized she'd forgotten to put on her gloves when the fine linen of his monogrammed shirt moved like silk beneath her bare fingertips.

"Have Willis drive you home," he directed, reaching for the carriage door. "I'll take care of the hired buggy. See you tonight."

As Willis drove off, Carson waved to her with his silver-headed walking stick, a smile on his face and his bowler set back on his head the way he liked it.

Katherine spent the afternoon putting the house back into order after almost eight weeks of guests. But because he had said nothing about his things, she left them in her room, as they were.

Though she kept her hands busy, her mind wouldn't let go of the future. What if he didn't come home? It was all over, just as he'd said on the platform. There was no need for him to walk through that door again.

But not long after the street lamplighter had been around, Carson walked in the door. He tossed his hat onto the hall tree as if he did that every evening. He greeted Lily with a quick hug and a kiss on the top of her head.

When Katherine appeared, her heart fluttering in her throat like a schoolgirl's—she'd been so uncertain about what to expect—he wrapped her in his arms, kissed her soundly, and asked what was for supper.

They sat at the supper table recounting their day, laughing at humorous gossip and sharing reactions to news. It was all so ordinary, mundane, and commonplace. The precious humdrumness of it almost brought tears to her eyes.

Was he playacting? she wondered, because she could no longer.

That night Carson undressed her in front of a roaring fire in their room. He wrapped a silk-fringed shawl over her shoulders. Then he undressed himself. As always—except for their first night together—he took a moment to protect her with a condom, a marvelous device to prevent babies she'd never known about until he'd explained it to her.

Before the leaping flames, he began to teach her the thrilling technique of making love with her astride his lap. She moved as he urged her to, aware with wordless satisfaction of his penetration moving deeper inside her than ever before. She spread her hands across the small of his back. Sighing against his ear, she held him tight, inside and out, savoring his heat and his sounds of pleasure. His hands grasped her waist as they rocked together. The pleasure of their movement became her world, her existence, and her goal.

When he nuzzled her throat, then her collarbone, she leaned back, still clinging to him with her hands at his nape. He suckled her breasts, first one, then the other. The sensation shot liquid fire through her and brought a soft cry to her lips. She arched her back, basking in the pleasure. The sudden movement released the wave of ecstasy that rocked them both, again and again.

For a time she remembered nothing. When she became aware again, they were both in bed, limbs entangled. Carson asked her if she was all right and she nodded, too replete to speak. All she could do was silently offer thanks that her charade family would last a little longer at least.

Dolly set her teacup down and looked across the Windsor Hotel private parlor at the broad back of the handsome young man staring out the window.

"Why did you invite me and not Randolph here today, Carson?" Dolly quipped. "To impress me with your indifference to my company and to celebrate your victory? Surely Randolph deserves to be here, too."

"Sorry." Carson turned long enough to bestow an apologetic smile on her. But he did not leave his place at the window. "He sent a note saying he was called away to cover a story at the last minute."

Dolly wondered what it was going to take to get him to forget what was really on his mind and sit down with her. He'd sent around the invitation to tea the day before. She'd assumed, at first, that Katherine would be there, too. But upon greeting her, Carson had spun some tale about Katherine being out helping to organize the next amateur theater project.

"So we're not going to take this private moment to congratulate ourselves on a triumphant piece of deception?" she asked, aware that once again she had to speak carefully, to choose each word, to measure her tone. He seemed to be brooding about something. She couldn't tell if he'd called her here to share it with her or for some other reason. "It is no small thing, you and Katherine successfully convincing your family that she is your wife and that you are a happily married couple."

"We did that, indeed," he agreed, still at the window.

"Are you watching for someone?" she asked, to the point this time.

Carson turned at last. "No, just thinking how exquisitely perfect Katherine was. And it wasn't always easy. Willie ate too much candy on Christmas day and proceeded to get sick all over the drawing room rug. The dog chased Lucky through the dining room and up the tree the day after Christmas. We nearly lost a crystal chandelier and I thought we were going to have the tree go through the window. Katherine never lost her temper. She frowned. I know she bit her tongue more than once, but she was patient. My whole family took her to heart.''

She allowed his observations to drift through the quiet of the tiny parlor. He'd had tea and little cucumber sandwiches served. She wasn't particularly fond of cucumber, but sometimes it was fitting to pretend that she was. A fire had been lit even though the rare winter sun was pouring through the window. ''And they all climbed on the train and left, almost a week ago. So, now what?'' she asked at last.

Carson shoved his hands into his trouser pockets and shrugged.

Dolly took a deep, impatient breath. What was the man thinking? ''Surely you and Katherine discussed this eventuality?''

''We did,'' he admitted. ''At length, before we were married. Katherine made a number of stipulations.''

''One of them being the sale of your beloved gentlemen's club,'' she reminded him.

''Yes, but we came to other terms, too,'' he said. ''We made an agreement.''

''Well, there you are,'' she said. When he said nothing more, she realized she was going to have to state the obvious. ''Is there some problem?''

''It's just that I'm having second thoughts about that bloody bargain,'' he said.

''Ah, the annulment provision rears its ugly head.'' She struggled against betraying her delight. So walking out on Katherine wasn't going to be as easy as the poor, besotted boy had thought. With great effort she endeavored to arrange her expression into one of sincere regret. And it had to look good. She was, after all, dealing with the best poker player in Denver. ''What has happened?''

"Some things have changed since we made that deal," Carson said. "If I'd known things would get this complicated, believe me, I would have gone along with Randolph. We would have just killed off my fictitious wife."

"You don't mean that," Dolly scolded. "Look how happy you made your mother. And then your father came so far to be with his family. I know your mother was thrilled to have all of you together. This was a Christmas she will never forget. She is such a dear."

"And she even took Katherine into her affections," Carson said.

"Of course, and what about you? Do you have feelings for our Katherine?" she ventured at last, successful with her facial expression but unable to keep the hopeful note from her voice.

"I do," he said with astonishingly little hesitation.

His ready admission brought her up in her chair. The arm bumped the tea table and liquid sloshed from her cup into the saucer. She was too interested in Carson's admission to notice.

Without prompting, he continued, "Think how easy it would be to go on with this charade, assuming Katherine was willing. Assuming she wouldn't go on trying to remake me. There would be no awkward explanations to make to my family."

"So true." Once again she schooled her expression as she asked the obvious. "Have you talked to Katherine about how you feel?"

"No," he confessed. "And I certainly have no idea whether she would be receptive or not. She has what she wanted from our bargain. The house, money, and respectability, since I sold the Respite."

"Ah, yes, I forgot about Katherine's tendency to reform," she muttered. "She has not given up on that?"

"For now she is silent on the issue," he said. "But there have been indications that I am not what she would wish me to be."

Dolly wondered what the poor, misguided girl had done.

Katherine's heart was good, but where liquor and gambling were concerned, she had a blind eye.

"On the other hand," he went on, "I see certain advantages in remaining married to Katherine that I believe she does not see."

"And what would they be?" Dolly asked, completely lost. This conversation had not taken the direction she had hoped.

"Her birthday," Carson said, returning to the window.

"Birthday?"

"She turns twenty-five in May," he said. "She will fully inherit all the assets her father willed to her. I can't put my finger on it, but I think there is security in her remaining married to me until then. There's something dangerous in the air for her during the next few months."

"Like what?"

"For one thing, no fortune hunter will approach her as long as she is married," Carson said, in a cool, logical tone. "With a little guidance from me, once she comes into the fortune and is independent, I don't think she will be easily swayed by anyone."

The wisdom of his observation settled over Dolly. "I agree. Katherine has a respectable sense of herself. Owen is the one who is shortsighted and given to being influenced by fortune hunters."

"My point exactly," he said. "Yet what business do I have thinking about marriage?"

He held out his hand, palm up in a gesture of appeal. "Her reformation urges aside, if we remained married, certainly she would want children. She was so good with my brothers' little ones, and with Lily, too."

"So?" Dolly asked, surprised. "You appear to be able. Dare I say, willing? Surely that part of the bargain doesn't trouble you."

"That's not what I mean." Carson strolled across the room, looking directly at her. "Children mean fatherhood, Dolly. Fatherhood is not for men like me."

She groaned, mildly surprised by this dilemma, yet annoyed with herself for not anticipating it. "But I thought you enjoyed Lily. She certainly speaks of you with great fondness. She was even teaching me card games when I last called."

Carson nodded. "Lily is a good student. She has a thirst for knowledge. She doesn't need me to teach her. Dealing with her has nothing to do with being a father."

"Poppycock!" Dolly considered his words for a few moments. "One of the advantages of being a rich old woman is that you can say whatever you like and no one dares to scold you."

"I've never known you to hold back," he said. "Out with it."

"Does this disinterest in fatherhood have to do with your relationship with your own father?" she asked.

"That's not really any of your concern." Carson turned away and shrugged. "But consider—what kind of a father would I be? I spent my childhood dismissed from school after school, locked up a good deal of the time, constantly existing under a cloud of my father's disapproval. No, I'm not taking on the responsibility of shaping a child."

"There's no logic in that," she said, rising from her chair in exasperation. Heavens, if it wasn't one thing with this boy, it was another. "I suspected it was thinking like that that forced you into this damn mess in the first place. Don't forget, I've met your father. He is a charming man in his British way. But beyond a certain family resemblance, you and he are not in the least alike."

"Think of the mistakes I would make," Carson persisted. "Think of the unhappiness I would inflict."

"Poppycock again." She huffed in frustration. "That's not what you fear."

"Of course it is," he said. "I am not going to be responsible for ruining an innocent child's life."

Her patience evaporated. "You've got it ass backwards. And I think you'd better figure it out soon. It isn't just your future children's happiness that you risk. It is yours and Katherine's, Lily's, your mother's, and—Dammit, Carson, I gave you credit for better sense than this. Much better. If you can't see what this is truly about, then I wash my hands of it.''

She made a great show of gathering up her gloves and handbag, allowing silence to hang in the room. Then she added with as much drama—and sting—as she could bring forth, ''Maybe Katherine really would be better off without you.''

Chapter Twenty-three

"Glory, married life seems to agree with you," cooed Opal Shaw, Katherine's Ladies' Moderation League companion, as the two of them stepped out of the storefront building that the amateur theater group had called home for the past three years.

On the walk, Katherine turned and waited for Opal, the group's treasurer and keeper of the key, to lock the door.

"You really think so?" she asked, surprised that the change in her feelings for Carson—and toward their marriage—was so obvious.

"Oh, yes," Opal said, grinning mischievously and pocketing the keys. "It has put roses in your cheeks and a perpetual smile on your lips. Mr. Fairfax must be a most satisfactory husband."

They'd just attended their first meeting for the spring production of *The Tempest* and it had gone on an hour longer than she had expected, but she wasn't terribly concerned. Carson had said he had some additional accounts to review and that he would be home an hour later than usual. She still had time to get home and check on supper before he returned.

He'd been dividing his time between the bank and the insurance company, spending the day at work almost like a normal man of business. She loved the amazing domesticity of it.

Though a little embarrassed, she couldn't keep from smiling. "I didn't realize it was so obvious."

"Only another young lady would notice, I'm sure," Opal added as she pulled her hat down over her ears.

Beneath overcast skies, darkness was falling. The street lamps had yet to be lit.

"I'll walk you as far as Colfax," Opal offered, clearly no more thrilled about walking alone than she was.

"But that's out of your way," Katherine objected, almost sorry that she'd refused the offer of a ride from Cynthia Whitman, the daughter-in-law of Nolan's former legal partner. She'd caught the curiosity in Cynthia's eyes. She was certain the young woman would ask awkward questions about what had happened between her and Nolan. Questions she preferred to avoid. So she'd declined, virtuously citing her desire for fresh air and exercise. She smiled to herself ruefully. For her virtue she was sure to get a bone-deep chill and chapped cheeks.

"It's not really out of my way," Opal said cheerfully. "I'm going over to my aunt's house, so I'm walking in your direction."

"Let's get moving, then," she said, shoving her gloved hands into her coat pockets. She started off down the street with Opal at her side. "Let's keep that cold wind at bay."

"Or we'll freeze off our toes trying," Opal said with a laugh.

They trudged down the snow-lined street, exchanging a few remarks about whom they expected to read for which roles and what they might use for costumes and scenery.

The supper hour was growing near. Few people were on the street, walking or driving. At one point Katherine thought she heard the heavy steps of a man behind them, but when she glanced over her shoulder she saw no one.

At the corner, the icy wind whipped viciously at their coattails. She and Opal exchanged hasty farewells. Then each, with shoulders hunched against the cold, strode off in her respective direction, head down to avoid the brunt of the wind.

She was only a block and a half from the Elms, near enough to see the faint glow of the gaslights from the front window and the smoke driven horizontal by the wind as it escaped the chimney. Close enough to anticipate the warmth of the fire and the tantalizing aromas drifting from Mrs. D's kitchen when she again heard the footsteps. Rapid this time. Running steps.

When she looked over her shoulder, she saw a man rushing up behind her, a broad-shouldered and lean-hipped figure as familiar as Carson. With his head bowed against the wind, she couldn't see his face, but he was wearing a bowler and carrying the familiar silver-head cane.

She halted and turned to call over the wind to him. "Carson? What are you doing out here? I thought you rode to the bank today."

He did not answer. He did not raise his head. He did not offer a greeting or answer her question—but he continued to close the distance between them—with alarming speed.

Her instincts leaped to life. Surely he'd heard her. Something was wrong. Her heart began to beat with a panic she did not understand but knew to obey.

"I'll meet you at the house," she called, unwilling to be discourteous to her husband. Yet—she turned and trotted toward home.

She'd almost entered the safe circle of light cast by the Elms's gaslight postern, when she heard his steps practically on her heels.

Before she could turn up the drive, something crossed her vision with lightning speed. It crushed against her throat. The force of it hauled her backwards. Her feet swung out in front of her. Her breath was choked off before she could scream. Wheezing and in agony, she clutched futilely at the rod cutting off her air.

Momentarily she felt herself dragged backward. She kicked at her assailant. Her feet struck only air. Abruptly she was released, only to have powerful arms surround her and tow her deeper into the shadows—away from the house, away from help.

Away from the light, but she managed to get a gulp of air. The scent of Carson's cologne filled her head, the spicy oriental sandalwood fragrance of the imported brand that he had to special order. The smell that had once excited her now sickened her.

Once in the deep shadows, the thing—his silver-headed cane, she realized—was at her throat again, suffocating her, making her vision go dark, then star-studded. There weren't any stars to see. She struggled against the stick; weakly, she knew, but she struggled.

His strength was superior, but his hold on the cane loosened. When she managed to catch another breath, he gave her a violent shake. Her teeth rattled in her head. Then he renewed the pressure on her throat. Her breath was cut off again. Her head swam with shock and disbelief.

"Be still," he rasped, his lips pressed near her ear. But his pressure on the cane never diminished.

There was no logic in obeying his orders. She closed her eyes and fought. Summoning the last of her strength, she resisted his hold with every shred of might she possessed. She called on every ounce of fury she could wring from her body.

Her thrashing made him hiss a string of profanities.

Suddenly the pressure of the cane ceased. She sucked in a gigantic breath, choking, coughing. A strong arm still held her by the waist. Then she was released. Her knees almost gave out when he shoved her away. She staggered a few steps but remained on her feet. Then she heard the ring of metal against metal—the sound she'd heard once before.

The hair on the back of her neck stood on end. She turned to face him. The rapier had been freed from its innocent-looking ebony sheath. In the darkness she could not see his face, but she knew he was going to skewer her.

She tried to scream. Only a hoarse noise came out of her

mouth. Astonished, she put her hands to her throat. It was like an awful nightmare. She had wind now, but no voice. All she could do was watch in silent horror as the rapier blade glimmered in the faint light.

He had turned her loose in preparation for running her through. With a presence of mind she could only attribute to a guardian angel, she stood her ground.

His features were still obscured by shadow, but from his build, his size, and the proportions, it had to be Carson. Her mind reeled. But she knew that to turn her back on him and run—on wobbly legs—would be fatal. He'd lance her from back to front with little difficulty. She would die a slow, agonizing death.

He stepped back to gain room to thrust the rapier. She followed him to give him as little room to maneuver as she could. But as she did, she stepped sideways, making as small a target of herself as possible and holding her arms in front for protection.

Realizing what she was doing, he cursed, his voice still too raspy to be recognized as Carson's. Despite her defensive stance, he lunged. The razor-sharp edge lashed across her arm. She heard the soft shearing of wool, then felt the sting of steel slicing through flesh—hers. The pain made her suck in a sharp breath. But she had foiled him—his first charge, at least.

He roared in frustration this time and started toward her. Her legs had regained some strength. She staggered backward, just beyond his reach, nearly tripping over her long skirt. He gave up pursuing her and pulled back the rapier, readying to strike again.

"Here, what's going on out here?" Willis called from just beyond the reach of the darkest shadows. The sound of his beautifully gruff, no-nonsense voice was sweet to her ears. She uttered a hoarse noise of relief. His approaching footsteps crunched on the gravel drive.

Once more Carson hesitated, listening, his ear turned in the direction of Willis's footsteps. But he made no move to retreat.

Renewed terror stole away her relief.

He wouldn't kill her alone. He would kill Willis, too.

She wanted—needed—to scream in bloody horror, to warn Willis. Not a sound came out of her mouth. The poor man had no clue that Carson's walking stick was a rapier in disguise. He had no idea an armed man waited in the darkness.

Blade poised in midair, Carson faced the sound of Willis's voice—and waited.

She could have turned and run. Yet she knew with a terrible certainty that he would follow. He would murder them in the drive before anyone in the house realized what was happening. She had to do something. The only defense she could imagine was some unanticipated act.

Desperately she gathered what was left of her strength and lunged at Carson's chest. She squeezed her eyes shut and willed her weight to send him crashing to the ground, to stun him, to disable him—or, at least, knock the blade from his hand.

The impact of her shoulder against his breastbone elicited a grunt of surprise. Of pain? She didn't knock him off his feet, but she knew the satisfaction of hearing his breath hammered out of him.

His unbuttoned coat parted. She stumbled on his foot and lurched back to right herself. Her injured arm briefly brushed against the fine linen of his shirt, smearing a trail of blood. He staggered backward, arms pinwheeling, seeking balance. The rapier fell.

She heard it strike the frozen crust of the snow.

"Miss Katherine, is that you?" Willis called, still walking in their direction. "What the devil?"

Carson regained his balance just enough to shove her away from him, nearly sending her to the ground. Then he took off, running down the dark street, nothing to be seen of him but his back, his bowler, and his flapping greatcoat silhouetted against the white snow.

"Mr. Fairfax?" Willis called, having caught sight of her

fleeing attacker before he saw her. He stepped out into the street to watch the fleeing man.

"Willis," she rasped, still voiceless. She staggered out of the shadows on unsteady feet. Then he saw her.

"My God, Miss Katherine, what happened?" Willis immediately put an arm around her to prevent her from sagging to the ground. Her strength was gone. The trembling began. She shook with cold, with relief, with fear, and with weakness. Willis hurried her toward the house. He muttered reassuring words that she could make no sense of over the chattering of her teeth, but every syllable sounded good.

Once more Carson shuffled through the letters and invoices that had been sitting here waiting for him in his apartment over the Respite. There was a letter there from Alice Johnson of San Francisco, but he was looking for a letter from Nolan Stewart. A second sorting turned up nothing.

What the hell was Nolan up to? he wondered. In disgust, he dropped the stack of mail on the desk blotter and turned toward the window. Surely the lawyer had managed to turn up some information by now. If someone planned to make a play for the Amanda Leigh while Owen Benedict had influence over Katherine, they would do it soon. Her birthday was only three months away.

Jack appeared in the doorway. "Here's the inventory of the wine cellar, Captain. I need help with what to order."

He turned from the desk. "Of course. I'll take it. Anything else? How is the stock of the chef's pantry?"

"The chef is taking pretty good care of that," Jack said as he strolled across the half parlor/half office where Carson had always conducted the Respite's behind-the-scenes business. "And Newt, the bartender you hired, has done a good job at the bar, but the wine cellar is a mystery to me."

"What happened to Phipps?" Carson asked. "He's the wine steward. He should be able to do the ordering."

"Phipps left, at my invitation, two weeks ago," Jack said. "Didn't I tell ye? I caught him sipping more than his share of the cellar's stock. Decanting and sampling, he called it."

"I see," he said with a nod. "Yes, I do recall you telling me. I'd suspected he might be sampling a bit too much. I see the Ladies' Moderation League is still standing on the corner, trying to get more signatures. So how do you like being a saloonkeeper?"

"I like it well enough, Captain," Jack said, shoving his hands into his pockets in a way that contradicted his words. "But I'd sell the place back to ye in the blink of an eye."

Carson smiled. "I thought as much. Anything more you'd like me to tend to while I'm here?"

"No, Captain," Jack said. "But I'd appreciate it if ye took a look at those bills and let me know if ye have any concerns about them. If not, I'll have the bookkeeper pay 'em."

"Certainly." He allowed his gaze to fall on the stack of mail once again. The puzzle of no word from Nolan annoyed him. "I'll take care of it right now."

Jack left. Carson sat at his desk to work. He went through the bills with a shrewd, experienced eye. He signed off on all but one, on which he scribbled a note requesting more information. Then he sat back and opened Alice's letter. He scanned her report of what she'd achieved in setting up a gentlemen's club in the Bay City.

But his mind drifted back to Katherine—to the sweet, searing heat of her as she'd ridden him last night. His concentration vanished. The letter fluttered to the desk.

She'd straddled him on the bed, all molten heat, holding him, her breasts swaying in the firelight, her nipples tight and rough, tempting his mouth, her body milking his of passion, bestowing shattering pleasure, banishing barriers. If he closed his eyes, he could almost smell the scent of her hair, the womanly musk of her body, the familiar sweetness of her mouth. And how she could move, driving him mad, then gratifying him. The memory was enough to make his body react.

For the first time he understood what it truly was.

In those intimate moments with her in his arms, with their bodies so entwined that it was difficult to know where his body ended and hers began, he could almost believe—he longed to believe—that they were truly one.

The passionately profound thought abruptly interrupted Carson's delicious fantasies. He sat up straight. Was that feeling, that oneness, the thing that his mother had wanted him to have? Did his parents know that emotion?

Since he was a boy, he'd avoided the thought of his parents making love when, of course, they had to. They had three sons. They'd slept in the same bed the entire six weeks of their visit at the Elms. Did his father and his mother know not just the ecstasy of the act, but that deep, passionate river of oneness that could flow through a man and a woman? They must.

He'd never dismissed his mother's desire for his happiness, but he'd never truly understood it either. This sense of union he was experiencing must be it—this abiding knowledge that the two of you belonged together, that you were joined, whether physically entangled or by an invisible link. It was love. What an inadequate word for such a mighty emotion.

Last night Katherine had whispered those astonishing words in his ear.

They'd still been wrapped in their intimate embrace, the thrill of its climax just subsiding.

"I love you," she'd whispered, her luscious lips pressed against his ear—her breath already exciting his sated senses. "I love you, Carson."

He'd been so amazed, so humbled, he hadn't had the courage to confess his feelings to her. But he had made love to her again.

He released a slow breath, almost a whistle, of astonishment. He and Katherine? Of course, he'd always been attracted to her, even though he'd refused to admit it in the early days.

Was his love for Katherine what Dolly had been trying to get him to see? He shook his head. No, Dolly had been getting at something else, though he'd be bloody damned if he could figure it out.

"Captain?"

Carson looked up to see Jack standing at the door again.

"There's a policeman downstairs asking for ye," he said. "Something has happened at the Elms, and he says yer to come as quick as possible."

Downstairs at the back door where deliveries were made, Carson greeted the waiting Officer O'Hara who, to his frustration, would give him no details beyond that his presence was required immediately at the Elms. He grabbed his hat and reached for his walking stick. It was gone. He remembered he'd been unable to find it this morning in the umbrella stand where he usually put it. He'd left the house without it. Then he forgot the missing cane when he realized he was staring at a bare coat tree.

"Where is my coat?" He glanced around at Jack.

Jack stared at the bare tree, too. "I don't know, Captain. I saw you hang it here when you came in. But then I got busy."

"Well, it's gone now," he said, pulling on his hat. There wasn't time to worry over a missing coat or cane. "Let's go."

The policeman opened the door and Carson strode out, intent on reaching home as quickly as possible.

An hour after the attack, Katherine was still shivering—but only in fits and starts—despite the roaring fire Willis had built in the family parlor and the weight of Mrs. D's warmest shawl on her shoulders. The doctor, police, and Uncle Owen had been summoned, and Lily had been sent off with Mrs. Evans.

"But you never managed to get a clear look at his face?" Uncle Owen asked for the third time. He was bent over her with Carson's cane in his hand, the rapier safely tucked away inside the ebony. He spoke in loud, exaggerated tones, as if she had a bruised brain instead of a bruised larynx.

"Let her rest, Owen," Doc Hughes advised, repacking his

black leather bag. He'd just finished stitching up her right arm and swaddling it in enough bandages to make her look like a war veteran. The pain she'd hardly noticed a half an hour earlier was now an angry throb.

She was losing patience with Uncle Owen and the police chief, who was standing on the other side of her. Because her right arm was so painfully injured she couldn't write and had to communicate through informal sign language. She'd told them all she knew.

"Where's Carson?" she asked once more, mouthing the words. None of them seemed to understand that she had to talk to her husband.

"He wasn't at the bank where he told you he would be," Chief Kelly pointed out. "They said he'd left around two o'clock. If he's anywhere in Denver, my men will have him in custody before the night is out."

She closed her eyes against the dark doubts. There had to be an explanation for why he'd left the bank. Something ordinary and mundane. There had to be a reason he had followed her down the street. . . .

"Drink some of your tea." Mrs. D attempted to put a cup in her good hand, but she waved it away.

"I never saw his face, neither," Willis said. He was standing in the corner of the room, being questioned by one of the police chief's men. "But I didn't need to. Besides swinging that stick that Mr. Fairfax always carries, the man wore the same kind of bowler hat and greatcoat. Same build he was, too. I can't imagine who else it could have been. But I don't know why he'd want to hurt Miss Katherine. They're newlyweds and all. I ain't never seen them exchange a cross word."

Uncle Owen, who'd obviously been listening, looked down at Katherine. "We know better than that, don't we?"

She blinked and looked up at him. "What?" she mouthed.

"Carson's motive for attempting to murder you," Uncle Owen said, speaking quietly for the first time. He was neatly dressed, as though he'd been prepared to go somewhere when

Willis had summoned him with the news of the attack. "As your husband, Carson Fairfax stands to inherit a great deal."

She opened her mouth to object.

"You must rest that voice box, Katherine," the doctor warned. "The easier you are on it, the faster it will heal. No attempting to speak for at least a couple of weeks."

She shut her mouth and made a gesture like signing something.

"The prenuptial agreement?" Uncle Owen asked. "He can easily protest it in court. It's only as good as the judge who backs it up or sets it aside. The money to be gained is definitely worth the risk of filing a lawsuit, if you're a *gambling* man."

She shook her head and frowned. She would not believe what Uncle Owen was implying. Learning the truth was simple.

To do that she had to see Carson face-to-face. Only then would she know if he'd been her attacker. His guilt or innocence would be written in the line of his mouth and the angle of his head. He might be the best bluffer in Denver, but she would know the truth when she looked into his eyes.

Uncle Owen knelt down by her chair, and the police chief was suddenly leaning over her, too. "You said yourself the attacker smelled of Fairfax's pomade," Owen persisted. "It's an unusual fragrance."

She nodded, sorry that she'd made that detail known.

Chief Kelly shook his head. "I'm afraid the truth is, we need to ask your husband some serious questions, Mrs. Fairfax."

So did she, she thought. As much as she hated to put any credence in Uncle Owen's accusations, she remembered only too well a time when she'd thought it impossible for Nolan to have nefarious motivations, too.

At the sound of the front door bursting open, everyone in the parlor fell silent and all heads turned toward the hallway. She caught her breath and listened intently, praying Carson had arrived at last.

His voice rang out clearly, demanding, urgent. "Where is she? I want to see Katherine immediately."

Mrs. D hurried into the hall. "We're in the family parlor, Mr. Fairfax."

His solid, sure footsteps started down the hall.

As if there was some silent agreement, Uncle Owen and the police chief took up positions in front of her and facing the door.

She could barely catch a glimpse of Carson when he appeared in the doorway, his face grim, his brows knit together.

"Benedict? Chief?" Carson's steps slowed as he entered. "Where's my wife? Your man O'Hara wouldn't tell me anything." At last he spied her behind the men. "Katherine? Sweetheart?"

Uncle Owen and the police chief moved shoulder to shoulder.

"Gentlemen?" Carson's voice was low and strained. From what she could see of his face, he was an unhappy man.

An internal voice spoke up. *But if he'd attempted murder and failed, he'd be an unhappy man, wouldn't he?*

"What's going on here?" Carson demanded. "Would you kindly stand aside so I can talk to my wife?"

"We have to ask you some questions, sir," the police chief said.

"You have a lot of explaining to do, Fairfax," Uncle Owen announced.

"I'll tell you any bloody thing you want to know as soon as you let me see my wife," Carson said with deadly calmness. With lightning speed, he shoved his arms between the two men, parting them forcibly like a heavy curtain. They stumbled aside.

She clutched the shawl close to her throat, and at last she gazed up into her husband's face—and searched for the truth.

Chapter Twenty-four

Carson scrutinized Katherine, her chestnut hair loose, her face pale, her mouth tight with pain, the shadows of fear lurking in the depth of those beautiful turquoise eyes. Dear God, what had happened?

Everything inside him turned cold. Blood drained from his face.

Drawing on all his gambler's skill, he set his fierce emotions aside. The woman he loved looked small, fragile, and wounded. He did not want to alarm her with his violent reaction. Someone had hurt her, and he hadn't been there to stop it. All he could do was clench his hands into fists at his sides—and remain calm.

"Katherine?" He stepped closer, holding out his hands to take hers. She remained in her chair, looking up at him in silence. He would give anything to banish those haunting shadows from her eyes.

Benedict and Police Chief Kelly reached for him, but he shrugged them off, parting them like so much dust in the air. Kneeling in front of her, he only had eyes for her bleak face.

He was vaguely aware of the two men hovering close by, and of Doc Hughes standing behind her chair. But their presence was of little interest to him.

He spoke in as even a voice as he could manage. "Sweetheart, tell me what happened."

She shook her head.

"Her voice box is bruised," Doc Hughes explained.

Silently she allowed him to take her hands.

"It's all right, sweetheart. Rest your voice. My God, your hands are like ice," he gasped, shocked by the chill of her fingers. Yet, at the feel of her slender hands moving in his, something inside him eased. Doc Hughes's words meant little to him. He could see for himself that she was all right.

He'd imagined all sorts of horrible things on his way to the house. It was so good to touch her, to reassure himself that she was alive, that she was well enough to sit in her own parlor— beyond that, his mind refused to grapple with what had taken place. He just wanted to hang on to her for the moment, to banish the terror she must have known, to surround her with safety and solicitude—to kill the bastard who dared to touch her. "You're trembling. And what's this? Your arm is bleeding."

"She was cut with this blade," Benedict said, his voice full of accusation. Carson ignored the man. As her guardian, Benedict had to be almost as upset as he was.

"Are you all right?" he asked, gazing up into her somber face. He longed to take her into his arms, but she seemed remote, reluctant—probably in shock. "Did you see who it was, Katherine?"

Benedict tapped Carson's shoulder. "This is yours, correct? Everyone in Denver has seen you with it at one time or another."

"If you'll excuse me, sir, I'm talking with my wife," he snapped without glancing in the man's direction.

"Admit it was you, Fairfax." This time Benedict shoved

something within his view. "Confess you tried to kill your wife with this."

The silver-headed cane he'd misplaced practically struck him in the nose. Startled, he glanced at Benedict. "That is mine. It was missing this morning. Where did you find it?"

"At the site of the attack," Benedict said with triumph.

Cold understanding began to seep into Carson. He looked at Katherine. She stared back at him, still detached and unnaturally calm. Now he knew why. She was too frightened and confused to know who to believe—him or Benedict. His heart ached for her.

"You tried to strangle your own wife," Benedict taunted.

He looked around the room for support, but everyone was staring at him—as if he might, indeed, be the attacker.

"I did no such thing." Battling to maintain his calm, he turned away from Benedict. "Katherine, surely you don't believe any of this."

"She really shouldn't talk," Doc Hughes reminded him.

This time the doctor's words brought understanding. He realized things were worse than he'd dreamed. "Katherine? I want to see your throat."

He reached up to pull away the shawl. Her eyes widened with fear. To his surprise, she lurched away from him. Dismayed, he withdrew his hand, reminding himself that she'd been through a bloody bad experience.

"Show me," he urged gently.

Then, studying him, she unwrapped the shawl herself.

At the sight of the angry wine-purple bruise across her throat, his gut twisted into a cold, painful knot. "Dear God," hissed from him.

He was on his feet in an instant, reaching for Chief Kelly. He caught the man's arm.

"You think I did this to my wife?" he demanded and rounded on the rest of the crowd in the room. Benedict. Willis was there, and two other police officers. Mrs. D in the doorway and the doctor behind Katherine stared at him as if he were mad. "You would believe that of me?"

"It happens more often than you think," Chief Kelly stated. "Husbands attacking their wives. Wives attacking husbands, sometimes."

"You think that is the case here, or are you too lazy to find out the bloody truth?" Carson challenged. "Why aren't you searching for the man who attacked my wife?"

"Because you're the man who attacked her," Benedict said. "Everyone knows your history with business partners. How they disappear, like that fool you started your first club with, what's his name—"

"Dan Raily?" Carson said, growing incensed with their inability to see the obvious. "We made a settlement. Raily went back to Chicago to start a shipping business of his own. Check it out with the Chicago police. As far as the cane goes, anyone could have picked it up and left it at the scene. What do you want to take some action? A reward? All right, I'll offer a reward. Ten thousand dollars to the man who brings in the villain, if I don't find and kill the bastard first."

"Nice move, Fairfax," Benedict said. "Just what an innocent man might do, offer a reward. Take the light of suspicion off yourself."

"If I act like an innocent man, it's because I am," he vowed, trying to be a voice of reason in a parlor of people gone insane. He looked each person in the eye.

Mrs. D pursed her mouth in distaste, "I sure don't want to believe it myself, Mr. Fairfax."

Willis glared at him but shuffled his feet. "I was there. It looked to be you, sir, your bowler and all, but I admit I didn't get a good look at your face."

It was like a blow to the belly. *Splendid,* Carson thought, *the one eye witness besides Katherine couldn't help him.* Then the most damning thought of all struck him.

His heart went still. He turned to Katherine.

Slowly he knelt down once again. Her hands reached for his

this time, and she squeezed his fingers. His heart fluttered with hope. "Katherine? Do you believe me? You must have seen your attacker."

She shook her head. With a sinking heart, he realized she wasn't any more certain about the identity of who'd accosted her than Willis was. She actually thought he might have been the villain who'd done this to her. He released a long, weary sigh. "After almost three months together, don't we know each other any better than this?"

She made no reply.

"Let's see what other evidence we have," Chief Kelly said, seemingly unrattled by the scene. "Tell me where you've been since two o'clock."

"Where have I been?"

"Your people at the bank told me you left about that time," the police chief said. "Where did you go? Who saw you?"

He took a deep breath, met Katherine's gaze, and willed her to forgive him. If anyone in this room knew his history for telling lies, unfortunately Katherine did.

"I was in my rooms over the Respite," he said, his words clear and distinct. She was going to hear the truth now. "I go there once or twice a week to check my personal mail."

She sucked in a breath of surprise and her eyes grew wide. That worrisome little furrow formed between her brows. He cursed silently, but he refused to let her look away from him or pull her hands from his grasp.

"Did anyone see you there?" the police chief continued.

"Jack saw me come in. We spoke about some inconsequential matters and I went through my mail," he said. "Jack is right there in the doorway, behind Mrs. D. He'll vouch for me."

The chief turned toward Jack.

The Cornishman stepped into the room. "It's true, I saw the captain come in at a little after two and we talked."

"Did you see him after that?" the chief asked.

"Not until the officer came asking about him," Jack admitted.

"And when was that, Mr. Tremain?"

"About five o'clock," Jack said. "I remember hearing the clock chime the hour."

"But you didn't see him from about two until then?" the chief asked.

"No, sir, I didn't," Jack said. "But I don't think he went out."

"You can't accept that as an alibi," Benedict objected. "He didn't see Fairfax for almost three hours. Besides, Fairfax owns the Cornishman. Everyone knows it."

"But when Officer O'Hara called," Jack protested. "I found the captain at his desk right where I left him."

"Mr. Benedict is right," Chief Kelly said. "Mr. Fairfax could have gone out and come back without you knowing the difference."

"And after the story circulated about Fairfax and that sham of a sale of the Respite for a dollar," Benedict said, his malicious gaze on Katherine. "Nobody is going to believe a word you say, Tremain."

At the mention of the Respite's sale, Katherine's hands became claws in Carson's hands. Her fingernails scratched across his palms.

"What?" she croaked, trying to rise from her chair. "Respite?"

"Did Fairfax lie to you about the Respite, Katherine?" Benedict asked, clearly delighting in being the bearer of bad news. "I thought as much."

"Do we have to go over these questions in front of Katherine?" Carson demanded, succeeding in avoiding her indignant gestures. He seized her arms and pulled her down into her chair again. When he looked into her eyes, this time he saw disillusionment.

How would he ever make her believe him now? With every fiber of his being, he restrained himself from landing a blow in Benedict's face. "Let's go into the study to answer your questions."

"We can take your statement at city hall," the police chief said.

"Then let's go," Carson said, suddenly eager to get Benedict away from Katherine before the man could plant any more unpleasant ideas in her head.

"Fine," the chief said. "Benedict, you come along, too. Let's clear this matter up to your satisfaction."

"I'd like nothing better," Benedict replied. "Let's go."

Carson stood. "I'll be back soon, sweetheart. Rest. Then we'll have time to talk, and I'll explain everything."

Katherine's eyes narrowed when she looked at him, but she nodded.

Only then did he start out of the parlor. He'd have time with her later—alone—to explain what he'd done. He could take the time to remind her of all they'd shared. Of the way things had changed from the beginning, when she'd demanded he make that ridiculous sale.

But just as he reached the hallway, the front doorbell rang.

He halted in midstride. "Were you expecting someone else?" he asked of the chief, who was right behind him.

"Possibly. I sent a couple of officers out to check for evidence. Who is it?"

Mrs. D admitted two police officers. They followed Carson and the chief back into the parlor. Each carried a bundle under his arm. Carson had never met either of them. They were breathless and ruddy-cheeked from the winter cold. Their faces were animated with excitement as they strode into the parlor.

"Let's have it," the chief said, turning to them without preamble.

"We found this." The tall officer held up a black greatcoat. "It was in the rubbish heap behind the Gentlemen's Respite."

Carson stared at the garment in surprise. The coat looked suspiciously like his. An unpleasant misgiving began to take form in his head. "Someone must have taken it from the coat tree by mistake," he said, aware of how lame the story sounded.

"And they didn't return it when they discovered the mistake, but threw it into the rubbish heap?" Benedict taunted. "A likely story."

"Anything else?" the chief asked.

"This is the best part," the smaller officer said, gloating in his voice. Then he hesitated. "Do you want me to show you here, in front of the lady?"

"Yes," Katherine managed to say, nodding her head vigorously.

Carson's unease grew.

The chief gave a nod, and the shorter officer pulled a white bundle from under his arm and unfurled it. "We found this on the rubbish heap, too, wrapped in the coat."

The shining white garment ballooned, sleeves flopping in the air. Across the shirtfront slashed a wide smear of fresh blood.

Mrs. D gasped, and her hand flew to her mouth.

Willis muttered a rare profanity under his breath.

"There's a monogram here," the policeman said, pointing to the fine stitching on the shirt. "See. *CRF.*"

Carson's initials. His blood ran cold.

"You'd been struck with the blade when you shoved your attacker that last time, is that right, Mrs. Fairfax?" Chief Kelly asked.

Katherine seemed hypnotized by the shirt, but she nodded slowly, touching her wounded arm. She started to shiver again.

"Take it out of here," Carson ordered. How dare the idiot flap the gory thing in front of her? He strode across the room to grab the bloodied shirt out of the man's hands, but Benedict reached it first.

"No, you don't. Let me see that monogram." Benedict seized the garment and turned away to examine it under the lamp. He bent close over the white-on-white stitching. "*CRF.* Carson something Fairfax?"

"Carson Rhys Fairfax." He saw no reason to be evasive. "It was a Christmas gift from my mother."

"So you admit this is your shirt, sir?" Kelly asked.

"It is." Carson scrutinized Katherine, willing her to meet his gaze again.

But when she did, her eyes were wide with horror. She turned away from him, obviously unable to look at him any longer.

He'd lost her—as surely as if she'd been murdered. The thought sucked the breath out of him. He raked his hand through his hair and surveyed the room full of people who'd suddenly become his adversaries.

"How'd your shirt get into the trash behind the Respite?" Kelly asked.

"I have no idea," he said, his voice low, crisp, and angry. He understood what was going on now. Someone was trying to hurt Katherine and frame him.

The bastard wasn't going to get away with it. He put on his poker-table face.

"You hadn't missed it?" Kelly pressed.

"The washerwoman comes in twice a week," he said, glancing at Mrs. D for confirmation, but she only stared coldly at him. "I assumed it was in the laundry."

"Another likely story," Benedict said. "What more proof do you need to make an arrest, Kelly? I demand you arrest Fairfax for attempted murder."

"Yes, I should say so," said Mrs. D, who so seldom spoke an opinion about family affairs. "I'll not have the villain under my roof."

"So it was you, sir." Willis pointed a finger at Carson. "I should have known from that fine coat, and him in the bowler and with that fearsome cane. It was him."

When Carson looked to Katherine again, she was staring at him as if he were a stranger.

"I'm placing you under arrest for the attempted murder of your wife," Kelly said. "If you'll give me your gentleman's word you'll not try to escape, we'll forego the cuffs."

"Cuff him," Benedict demanded. "The man is a danger to everyone in this room."

"Shut up, Benedict," Carson snapped. "I give my word, Kelly. All I ask is to talk to my wife privately before we go."

Everyone in the room went silent.

Benedict glared at him, then glanced at the chief.

"Fairfax isn't going anywhere, Owen," Kelly said as he turned to Katherine. "Are you willing to talk with your husband, Mrs. Fairfax?"

Carson waited a terrible moment during which he thought she might refuse. But she agreed with a reluctant nod.

"I'll be watching from the doorway," Chief Kelly said. "Let's go, everybody. You too, Owen. Give the man a moment with his wife."

As people filed out of the room, Carson turned to Jack. "Fetch Mrs. Green. Tell her what has happened and ask her to get over here as soon as she can."

"Aye, Captain," Jack said and disappeared.

Carson turned back to Katherine, knowing he could trust Jack and Dolly to do the right thing, but he had to make Katherine understand, too.

When only the chief stood in the doorway, attempting to light his pipe, Carson pulled a chair up and sat in front of Katherine. She refused to allow him to take her hands. He tried to look into her face, but she avoided his gaze.

"You don't believe any of this, I hope," he said, scrutinizing her, memorizing every detail of her face to sustain him while he was in jail, which wouldn't be long, though any time in jail would seem like forever—he knew from experience. "I know the evidence looks bad, but you must know I would never harm you."

"You have," she mouthed, her eyes growing tearful. "The Respite. True?"

"Yes, true." Unable to refute that accusation, he bowed his head and cursed silently. When her body quaked with sobs, he ached to take her in his arms and soothe away her pain, but he couldn't. He knew she would never allow it. Instead, he seized her hands again, refusing to allow her to pull free this time. With his free hand he reached up and stroked her hair, still longing to kiss away her tears.

"Katherine, I know what you're thinking," he said, his voice husky. "It was a childish thing to do on my part. All I can say in my defense is that it was over three long months ago. Everything was different then. Many things have changed. Can you understand that?"

Katherine met his gaze, her eyes shiny with tears. She made no effort to hide her anger. Holding his gaze, she pulled a hand free to gesture to her bruised throat.

Carson understood instantly. "No! Dammit! Never. I did not attack you."

"Here now, sir," Kelly called from the doorway. "Are you all right, Mrs. Fairfax? You just give me the high sign and I'll have him out of here."

Katherine shook her head, but she continued to refuse to meet his gaze.

"Think of me what you will," he continued at last, willing to have her think the worst if she would heed his warning. "The important thing for you to remember is that whoever did this was unsuccessful. That means they will try to harm you again."

Her head came up and she blinked at him. He was relieved to see that for the moment her tears had ceased.

"You are still in danger," he said, glad that she seemed to be listening. "Do you understand? When Dolly gets here, have her stay until we know who is behind this. In fact, have her send for some of her stable help. Arm the experienced men. Keep a guard posted every night, all night. One in the front of the house and another in the back. Whatever you do, don't go out without an escort. Go nowhere without Dolly and an armed man with you at the very least. Do you understand?"

Katherine eyed him sullenly. He wasn't certain whether she was taking him seriously or not.

He stroked the back of her hand with his thumb and carefully planned his next words because he knew she would not like them. "Don't announce your trips or plans to anyone other than Dolly, not even to Owen Benedict. Am I clear on this?"

Katherine narrowed her eyes.

"He knows too many people," Carson explained, without going into more detail about his growing suspicion of her guardian. "Owen might let something slip, and it could get back to the wrong person. It's important. Promise me."

Katherine gave him a reluctant nod.

"Good." He glanced over his shoulder at the police chief. "I believe Dolly will understand what's going on. If you need to get word to me, send Jack around. Despite what they say, he's as solid a soul as there is in this gold town."

For the first time since this nightmare had begun, he caught her nodding as if she agreed with him.

"Then you believe him about me being at the Respite?" he asked, a kernel of hope growing inside him.

Katherine studied him for a long time. He could feel her gaze roaming over his face, touching the planes of his countenance, searching his eyes for the truth. He held still as he would if Lily was exploring his features with her fingertips. Katherine was seeking his honesty. He held his head up and met her gaze, praying that she found the truth she needed to see there.

But at last she sobbed, covering her face with her hands and turning away. With a shake of her head, she shrugged her shoulders and whispered, "Truth. Not simple. Not simple at all."

Chapter Twenty-five

Katherine stared out the family parlor window into the black night of this endless day—and fought back another wave of nausea. It was almost a welcome distraction from the hollowness she felt inside, the emptiness, the void. Carson's betrayal—be it attempted murder or lies or both—was impossible to comprehend. Her mind would not grasp the reality. She was numb—and sick.

From the hallway she could hear the drone of Uncle Owen and Dolly Green arguing. If they thought they'd lowered their voices so she couldn't hear, they were mistaken. She eavesdropped detachedly. Nothing seemed to matter now that she knew Carson had lied to her about the Respite. And what about the murder attempt?

Everyone was so certain it had been him. There was the shirt. The walking stick. She wasn't so certain, but she knew she'd been betrayed.

"I'm Katherine's guardian," Uncle Owen was saying out in the hallway. "It's my place to be here when she needs me."

"Well, I'm her godmother," Dolly said, "and I think she

needs the care of a woman. I've posted guards outside, and Chief Kelly has agreed to have a beat officer pass by frequently. There's no need for you to stay here at the Elms.''

''Why all these precautions?'' Uncle Owen asked. ''The culprit is in jail. I saw the chief turn the key in the lock myself. Katherine is as safe as a baby in its mother's womb. All she needs is comforting.''

''That's exactly why I'm here,'' Dolly said. ''She is badly frightened. She needs the reassuring company of a woman to ease her through it. A few guards outside the house can't hurt a thing.''

Katherine sighed, glad to have her aunt fighting her battles for her for the moment. Uncle Owen was in such a dither over this attack, if he stayed at the Elms he'd only drive her to distraction.

''I'll tell her you came by to offer your company,'' Dolly added. ''I'm staying the night with her, or longer if needed. She'll have every comfort. But she needs her rest. Randolph, my dear, how nice of you to call.''

Surprised at the arrival of another caller at the Elms, Katherine turned her head toward the hallway to listen more carefully.

''What are you doing here, Hearn?'' Uncle Owen demanded. ''I don't want to see this on the front page of the *Sentinel*. Katherine doesn't want this kind of notoriety.''

''I'm here in an unofficial capacity,'' Randolph said. ''I just heard the news about the attack—and about Carson. Katherine is all right?''

''I was just telling Owen that she is fine, but in need of rest,'' Dolly said. ''But I must talk to you about something. If you'll excuse us, Owen? And please give my regards to Edna.''

Katherine heard Uncle Owen make his farewells and the door close. Another wave of nausea washed through her. She covered her mouth with her hand and took a deep breath, fighting the sick feeling off as she had before. If she was persistent with her deep breathing, it went away, or it had for the past week. Sometimes it came in the morning, too. She wanted to tell herself that it was from the shock of the attack, but she knew better. She'd been suffering from this malady for too many days to be able to blame it on her physical injuries.

"... and I don't care if you have to get Tippet out of bed," Dolly was saying, out in the hall. Tippet was the name of her godmother's attorney. "Tell him I want him down at City Hall and this mess cleared up pronto. Tell him to work with Carson's lawyer. Got that? Find out who the judge is. If it's Miller, he owes me a favor. If bail or bond money is needed, or whatever, tell Tippet he's authorized to sign it over. I'm not going to have Carson sitting in jail. This is a frame-up."

Randolph muttered something. She only heard part of the statement. "... after that talk we had back before Christmas, back before all this started. Remember? I'd never have thought—I didn't mean real murder."

"Of course you didn't, dear boy," Dolly said, her voice full of comfort. "You're no more guilty of anything than Carson is. Go. Do as I say. We must get Carson out of jail as soon as possible so he can get to the bottom of this. Tell him that Katherine is well guarded. Go."

Dolly seemed certain of Carson's innocence. Katherine closed her eyes and wished she could feel so sure of it, too. But Dolly hadn't felt the walking stick pressed against her throat. She hadn't smelled Carson's scent on the greatcoat. She hadn't seen the blood-smeared shirt.

Then to discover his deception concerning the Respite ...

Shaking her head, she drew in a long breath. She should have known. Suddenly she could see herself and Carson reflected in the hall mirror on Christmas day as he put the key around her neck, with that drat top hat she'd given him set back on his head. *You can't change me*, he'd whispered to her.

She put a hand to her throbbing throat. Was this the price she must pay for daring to hope that he would give up saloonkeeping? Or was it a husband's greed, as Uncle Owen had implied? Or was Carson right—and Dolly, too? He was being set up by someone.

She turned to stare out the window again. How she longed to believe in his innocence. But the truth was proving more difficult to discern than she'd thought it would be. How foolish she'd been to believe she would discover his guilt or innocence in his eyes. How foolish she'd been to believe she truly knew Carson.

She should have known something was amiss when he had returned the morning after proposing with the bill of sale. She should have known he would never give up his life's work in Denver just because she'd asked it of him. The so-called sale was a sham. Jack Tremain had put on a show for her benefit so Carson could get what he wanted.

On the other hand, he'd generously handed over the deed to the Elms long before he'd had to.

Every night his lovemaking had been exquisitely tender and incredibly intimate. Before they were married, she never would have believed the sensual secrets she'd learned and practiced with him. Secrets about her own body and his. The sensations a man's hands can create in a woman's body. The joy of being locked together in the ultimate act of union.

Longing sighed in her belly. She didn't know what to think. The throbbing in her throat tightened and she blinked away tears of sorrow, of shame, of self-pity. She'd given Carson her heart and her body. She'd even whispered words of love to him, only last night. Had she been a fool?

"Miss Katherine, you haven't touched the soft egg I made for you," Mrs. D fussed. "You haven't eaten since lunch and it's near midnight. We must get some food down you. You need your strength."

Katherine started, wondering when the housekeeper had entered the room. With her fingertips, she tried to wipe away her tears without the notice of Mrs. D, who was bending over the tray of food.

She put her hand over her stomach and shook her head.

"Are you sure you're not hungry?" Mrs. D asked. "I can fix you anything you want. How about some hot cocoa?"

Katherine shook her head.

"Now, how is our suffering heroine?" Dolly demanded, sweeping into the room with purpose written on her face. Katherine knew she was going to get taken care of whether she liked it or not. "She's not eating, I see."

"I've offered her anything she likes," Mrs. D said, wringing her hands with worry. "I have custard baking in the oven right now, but it'll be another three-quarters of an hour before it's done. That's her favorite, you know, with rum sauce."

Rum sauce suddenly sounded like the most noxious stuff in the world. Katherine shook her head. She had no desire for food. She didn't think she could sleep; her nerves were strung as tight as a violin string and her brain was as busy as a beehive. She just wanted to sit in the dark and think. She wanted to find where things went wrong. She wanted to know what she could do to set at least some of it right.

"What can we do to get her to eat that custard when it comes out of the oven?" Dolly was saying, eyeing her speculatively. The two older women turned their backs to her, put their heads together, and began to plot.

Suddenly she knew what she wanted. Sitting up in her chair, she tried to get their attention. Finally, snapping her fingers caught Dolly's eye.

"Yes, are you ready to eat—" Mrs. D asked, a hopeful smile tugging at her mouth.

Katherine shook her head and reached for the paper and pencil on the tea table next to the chair. With her left hand she scribbled out the name. It wasn't in her usual pretty hand, but Dolly could read it.

"Jack?" Dolly asked. "You want to see Jack tonight? Now?"

She nodded.

Dolly's eyes narrowed shrewdly. "If I bring Jack here, will you eat?"

She rolled her eyes in exaggerated exasperation. If that was what she had to do, she would eat, and pray she didn't throw everything up. But she had to talk to Jack, ask him questions, learn what he knew. She nodded to Mrs. D and Dolly. Then she'd hope she suffered from a stomach disorder and that she wasn't really with child.

"Is this where the attack took place?" Carson asked, signaling Jack to slow the horse as they drove past the Elms. He'd just been released from a sleepless night in jail—on bond, with a charge of attempted murder against him—and warned by Chief Kelly to stay away from Katherine.

But his wife—and the attack on her—had been all he'd been able to think of through the night. With the morning light he wanted to see for himself where the crime had been committed. He also wanted to be certain that she was secure.

"That's the place they said," Jack said, reining the buggy horse to a walk. "Right there at the postern. Then the bastard dragged her back into the shadow of the bushes. See the tracks?"

Muddy footprints scarred the week-old snow.

Carson scrutinized the area with careful detachment. It was clear from the disarray of the prints that Katherine had put up a respectable fight. If he thought too deeply about what had happened there, he'd personally take an ax to the bushes. Then he'd start swinging at the first suspicious-looking man he saw.

Just the thought of the terror she must have known, the pain, the struggle, made him break out in a cold sweat, and his breathing quickened. He'd never been a violent man, beyond the practical ability to defend himself required by his profession. But now he knew what it was to want to do cold, ruthless, brutal violence against someone for the horror inflicted on a loved one.

"I want the blackguard," he whispered under his breath.

"I know the feeling," Jack said. "It's not nice to think of cruel hands on Mrs. Fairfax. Ain't no fate too bad for the slimy lowlife, whoever he be. See, there at the corner of the porch is a guard. Mrs. Green hired a couple of Pinkertons.''

''Good,'' Carson said, relieved that Katherine and Dolly had taken his advice seriously. ''I wonder how Katherine is feeling.''

''She looked a mite peaked when I saw her last night after you was carted off to jail,'' Jack said, his gaze suddenly focused on the back of the buggy horse.

''You saw her later?''

''She sent for me,'' Jack said, seeming ready to say more but uncomfortable with it. ''She made signs with her hands, you know. Asked a lot of questions. She don't believe everything that's told her, I don't think. Then she gave me some of your clothes and your shaving kit. Said she thought you'd need it when you was released.''

''Moving me out already, is she?'' Carson said as lightly as he could, trying not to betray the cold, sinking feeling in his gut. What had he expected? Even if she was willing to believe he was innocent of murder, she would not forgive him for the Respite. Not Katherine the reformer. There was only so much acceptance or forgiveness one could ask, even of love. He of all people knew that.

''Appears she is, Captain,'' Jack said, urging the horse on with a slap of the reins. ''Appears she is. But I do have some good news. Ye know that letter ye been looking for from that Stewart lawyer fella? It came this morning. I put it on yer desk.''

''That's the best news I've heard for a long time,'' Carson said. Slapping Jack on the back, he added, ''Let's get that horse moving.''

When they reached the Respite, he bounded up the stairs, taking two at a time, to his rooms. He found the letter the Cornishman had spoken of and ripped it open. It was lengthy and detailed. Stewart might have taken his time about it, but the lawyer appeared to have done a thorough investigation. As he read, he lowered himself into his desk chair. The investigation had not been easy, because the men involved were shrewd, experienced, and influential. But Stewart had found them out. This was exactly what he'd been looking for all along. This proved exactly what he'd suspected.

He reread portions of the letter, rubbing his day's worth of beard, mentally sorting through the details to his satisfaction, slotting them where they belonged. All the pieces of the puzzle were falling into place. The truth was, Katherine had been in danger all along; they just didn't know enough to realize it.

Carson folded the letter, hastily rose, and began to strip so he could wash and shave. As he was, he couldn't present himself to anyone, not even his wife. Though the jail cot he'd been assigned had appeared to be free of fleas, he wasn't certain he could say the same for his cell mates.

He didn't expect a warm welcome at the Elms. Regardless of what Katherine thought of him, regardless of the attempted murder charges, he hoped she'd hear him out on this. She wouldn't like what he told her, but tell her he would, and the sooner the better.

"Katherine? Carson is out of jail and he's here to see you," Dolly said from the doorway of the family parlor, a questioning look on her face. "Do you feel up to receiving your husband?"

She looked up from the book she'd been pretending to read. Carson, here? She'd heard the front doorbell ring, but she'd thought it was just another note from a well-wisher. After that scene last night, after the way she'd turned from him, Carson was the last caller she'd expected at her door.

"He is very eager to see you," Dolly continued when Katherine made no reply. The grande dame stepped into the parlor and tipped her head as though to speak earnestly, as though she feared Katherine might turn him away. "I know you're still in shock, and I warned him that the last thing you need is another upset. He promised he would not distress you. He seems to think he has some important news."

Truth be known, in spite of the attempted murder charge, Katherine had worried about Carson all night. Was there a clean place for him to sleep? Was he warm enough? While he wasn't a fussy, fastidious man like Uncle Owen, he did seem to create a kind of orderliness wherever he went. He was hardly the sort of man who'd take well to being locked up with Denver's unshaven, bedraggled riffraff.

When she'd finally fallen asleep, thanks to a prescribed dose of laudanum, she had dreamed about him—a tortuous night filled with sweet dreams of lovemaking and hideous nightmares of black canes and suffocating pain and helplessness. The torment of knowing she was going to die and could do nothing to save herself.

She'd bolted awake in the first light of dawn, longing for Carson to be next to her, for him to comfort her, to hold her and murmur soft words of reassurance. How could the deepest part of her being need the man who'd tried to murder her? Unless he wasn't the murderer and that deepest part of her knew it.

Now here he was on her doorstep.

"May I bring him in?" Dolly asked, peering into her face. "I'll stay in the room with you, though I'm sure he'll be a perfect gentleman."

She hesitated before she nodded. Maybe in the light of day she'd be able to see the truth.

When Carson walked into the room, she was immediately reminded of the moment the night before when he'd walked in and his face had gone white as a sheet at the sight of her. Could a man playact that well? Well enough to make the color drain from his face as though he'd had the shock of a lifetime?

He met her gaze immediately, his eyes roaming over her. When he seemed satisfied with what he saw, a smile of relief spread across his face. "Katherine, you look much better this morning."

She nodded, thinking the same about him. Unbidden, a smile

came to her lips. Freshly shaven, wearing a clean shirt, tie, vest, and suit, dapper as always, he looked incredibly good.

It was all she could do to keep herself from running to him and whispering all her fears in his ear. How she was afraid someone was going to attack her again as he warned, how she feared that he was going to leave her. She longed to throw her arms around his solid body and press her cheek against his shirtfront, soak in his warmth and listen to his heart beat, steady and sure.

But dark doubts remained. She stayed in her place on the settee.

"Why don't you have a seat there, right next to your wife," Dolly invited, gesturing toward the vacant place on the settee next to her.

"May I?" Carson asked before sitting.

She nodded. He never took his gaze from hers as he sat beside her. When he spread his hand on the brocade between them, she suddenly realized that he wanted to touch her.

The questioning in his eyes was so touching that, in spite of her doubts, she hesitantly offered her hand. He seized it, his grip crushing her fingers, and an incredible light of relief brightened his countenance.

She knew he was not her attacker—regardless of the bloodied shirt and silver-headed cane. No man could fake that expression of utter relief. Her heart could not long for a man who would try to murder her with his own hands. The realization washed over her like a fresh breath of spring.

She squeezed his hand in return.

"I'm so glad to see you looking well this morning," he said, heedless of repeating himself. He studied her hand in his, then pressed his other hand over it.

Her heart melted. "You, too," she managed in a hoarse whisper, then added, "I believe you."

Carson looked into her eyes, a glimmer of hope in the depths of his gaze. "You mean that?"

She nodded.

With the secret smile of a conspirator, Dolly settled in a chair across from them.

Carson turned to Dolly, seeming to regain some mastery of himself. "Thank you for arranging for the guards. I think I can explain why I was concerned. It's not especially good news, but I think you should hear it. It does explain some of the strange things that have been happening."

Dolly nodded. "Do you want to hear it, Katherine?"

She nodded. *What could be worse than being told your husband has attempted to murder you?*

With reluctance, Carson released her hand and pulled a letter from his pocket. "I had a talk with Nolan Stewart after our confrontation here at the Elms, before he left town last November."

"You and Nolan . . . ?" she asked. She'd always wondered if Carson had had something to do with her former suitor's hasty departure from Denver.

"Let's just say that he and I came to an understanding about the awkwardness of him remaining in the city after what had happened. As a gesture of apology to you, he agreed to investigate the company that has been offering to buy the Amanda Leigh and its equipment. Owen Benedict seemed so hazy on the specifics, and I thought it was important to know more about them. After Benedict took me aside and asked me to convince you to break your promise to your father and sell the Amanda Leigh, I thought it was important to know more about who was offering how much for what."

"Owen tried to get you to influence Katherine." Dolly nodded, with a sidelong glance at her. "Curious, indeed. Did Nolan find out anything?"

Katherine gestured for Carson to go on.

"Indeed he has," he said, unfolding the lawyer's letter. "The details are all here, but the gist of it is that a company called Eureka was formed last year in Georgetown, with the officers being the same officers of a bank in town, but the principal stockholders are . . ." Carson hesitated, glancing at Dolly.

"You know I don't take any pleasure in this, but it is important that you both understand what is going on."

Cold apprehension settled over her, but she gestured for him to go on.

"The principal holders of this company are Owen Benedict and Ray Jones," Carson said. "It's all here in the letter. Do you understand what this means?"

Unfortunately she did understand, but she didn't like it. Carson reached for her hand again and she withdrew it. She'd long been aware that Uncle Owen benefitted from the management of her fortune, but she'd thought of it as his due; fees for management, if you will. But Carson was hinting at something more sinister. She shook her head and turned away.

"I know it isn't pleasant to accept that someone who is practically family is working against you," he went on. "But I'm afraid that's what's happening. Benedict had hoped that you'd marry Nolan, and together they would influence you to sell the mine. Why? There has to be profitable ore in there, just as your father claimed there was."

Dolly leaned forward in her chair. "Do you think there is a connection between this effort to buy the mine and the attack on Katherine?"

"I believe there is a connection between Katherine's reaching twenty-five in May and coming into her inheritance and the attack," Carson said, holding her gaze. "I believe there is a connection between you being married to me and this attack."

"No," she shouted in a whisper. She understood very well. What he was implying was that Uncle Owen wanted her dead. "No."

"Think about it, Katherine," Dolly urged. "Carson makes sense."

"If something happens to you, God forbid," Carson said, taking her hand again, "the estate goes to your husband unless he's hanged for murder. Then the estate goes to Lily. As Lily's guardian as well as yours, Owen Benedict remains in control."

"Don't like it," she said, without a care for her injured

voice. The plot he outlined was unthinkable. "Uncle Owen would never do this."

"I don't like it either, Katherine," Carson said. "But you see the practicality of it." He stopped and took a deep breath. "If you had died, I would be hanged for your murder and Lily would be the sole beneficiary of the Tucker estate. With Lily not even of majority age, Benedict would manage things as he saw fit. He could sell off the Amanda Leigh and reap whatever profit the mine would bring."

"Carson, you're assuming the mine is worth something," Dolly pointed out. "What's more, you're accusing someone who's been a respectable citizen of some pretty nasty stuff. I've never liked Owen Benedict much, but he's never been known to be a dirty dealer. And he's a longtime friend of the Tuckers. Some say he was in love with Amanda Leigh. He'd never do her daughters harm."

"I know," Carson said, his gaze on Katherine again, though she refused to look at him. He turned back to Dolly. "Here's another angle to consider. I've heard the rumor, too, that he was in love with Katherine's mother. Think how he might feel about *Ben Tucker's* daughters. How does he feel about the children of the man who took the woman he loved away from him? For that matter, how much influence do other people have over him? What do you know about Ray Jones? Have you noticed the company he's been keeping lately? I'd say he has political aspirations, and those cost money, maybe more than Owen Benedict has."

Dolly sat back in her chair. "These are valid points, Katherine."

Katherine still refused to look at either of them. "Proof?"

"What proof do I have?" he repeated. "I've discovered the Elms's washer lady has suddenly and mysteriously come into money and left town. But I want more substantial proof than the testimony of one poor woman who's merely trying to survive.

"Presently all I have is Nolan's record of an investigation of the suspicious front company, Eureka. It's not an illegal setup. Yet the fact it exists raises a lot of questions. The most important one being, why does it want to purchase the Amanda Leigh and just how much is the Amanda Leigh worth?''

Dolly raised a skeptical brow. ''And how do you intend to find out?''

''I'm going to Georgetown tomorrow,'' Carson said, folding up Nolan's letter and tucking it into his coat pocket, each movement cool and efficient. ''Jack is going with me. I think we ought to be able to tell what the mine is worth as easily as any of Benedict's or Jones's men could. But to make everything aboveboard, I'd like to have your written permission to enter the mine.''

Carson's cool, businesslike manner sent a chill down Katherine's back. She could see the hard gleam of his eyes. He was setting out to prove something—his innocence and Uncle Owen's guilt—no matter the cost.

''I want to see,'' she rasped, despite the pain in her throat. She seized Carson's hand. ''I want to go.''

He frowned and shook his head. ''A letter of permission to inspect the mine is all I need in the event a local law officer should ask what I'm doing. I agree you have a right, Katherine, but now is not the time, not with what you've been through and in this winter cold. Besides, I'm accused of attempting to murder you. Remember? You shouldn't go anywhere with me. Tell her why she can't go, Dolly.''

''Father took me when I was little,'' Katherine said, in a longer speech than she'd made since the attack.

''I know. You told me,'' Carson said, with a maddeningly condescending smile on his lips. ''But you're not going.''

''I've been more times than I can count,'' she persisted. Though her voice was dwindling, she would have her say. ''I know as much as Jack.''

''You're not going,'' he said, rising from the settee. ''Dolly, I could use some help here.''

Dolly folded her hands in her lap as if she was helpless. ''She seems determined, Carson.''

"She is not going."

Katherine stood up and faced Carson. "Can't stop me."

"Meaning?" Carson challenged.

She tried to speak again, but her voice failed her this time. She pointed toward the carriage house.

"She means, if you won't take her," Dolly translated, "someone will."

"I don't think—" Carson stopped, glaring at Katherine with annoyance. She knew he understood her. "You would, wouldn't you? You'd talk poor Willis into taking you to Georgetown, and Lord knows what would happen then."

She nodded. "I have keys."

"There's a good reason why she should go," Dolly said, clearly pleased as punch with that argument.

"I don't need keys, but I'll not have you go up there without me." Carson turned his glare on Dolly this time. "The train leaves early. Dress her for a long ride and cold weather. I'll talk to Randolph to see if he can come along. Another man with good powers of observation would be helpful."

"Not to mention that our Randolph isn't half bad with a gun," Dolly said. "A little-known, unsuspected fact that he prefers to keep quiet."

"There isn't going to be any gun play, Dolly," Carson said, frowning. "If I thought there would be, I'd be forcing you to help me lock her in the closet."

"You're serious, aren't you?" Dolly sobered and glanced at Katherine. She realized the older woman was reassessing the situation. "Maybe you'd better let the men go alone, Katherine. This is a bad time of year to be traipsing up and down a mountain and in and out of a mine."

Katherine shook her head. "Going to see for myself."

And she meant it.

Chapter Twenty-six

The train trip to Georgetown the next day was uneventful. Katherine was ready when Carson called for her early in the morning. He already regretted agreeing to take her. The only excuse he could think of for his lapse was that he'd been so blasted glad to hear her say she believed him innocent that he'd temporarily lost his good sense.

Jack did not like the addition of a woman to the party at all, and had made his objection known before they arrived at the Elms to pick her up.

" 'Tis bad luck to take a woman into a mine, Captain," Jack had complained. "Every miner knows that. I like Mrs. Fairfax, don't get me wrong. But I don't care if her pappy did take her belowground. Look what happened to him. Run over and killed by a carriage when he was drunk. 'Tis bad luck, I tell ye."

"Next you're going to tell me that we'll have to be careful of treading on the tommyknockers," Carson baited. He'd almost forgotten how superstitious the old miner could be.

"Don't you go making fun of the mine spirits," Jack said, clearly offended, his pale blue eyes wide with concern and his graying red hair bristling. ''If they take offense, they can turn mean. We don't need that.''

Carson held up his hand to stay any more talk on the subject.

Jack didn't seem to mind that Randolph was joining them, nor did he oppose carrying weapons. While a town's streets might seem civilized enough, confrontations in the isolated mountain ravines where few witnesses dwelled often turned violent.

That chance of violence was exactly the reason Carson decided to take one of the Pinkertons named Biggs with them. When they reached Georgetown, he would ensconce Katherine—and the Pinkerton—in the hotel before they went any farther.

For the moment she was sitting next to him, enjoying the black and white of the snowy winter landscape as the train chugged around the curve, bringing Georgetown, lying in the valley below, into view. At first she'd seemed to be under the weather, but as they neared Georgetown she'd begun to act more like herself. He'd felt like a schoolboy when he slipped his arm around along the back of her seat. But it was damned good to have her close again.

''Pretty town,'' Katherine struggled to say. ''Compared to others.''

She was wearing a flattering gray velvet riding habit with a divided skirt. The high lace collar of the habit hid the bruises on her throat. Her normal coloring had almost completely returned, making the pink of her cheeks a beautiful contrast to the rich gray velvet. Over her habit she wore a quilted tan duster and on her feet were thick-soled boots. He had to admit the lady knew how to dress for the occasion.

''Georgetown was also the site of a nasty mining feud about fifteen years ago,'' he pointed out. He didn't want to be a wet blanket, nor did he want her to fall into the misconception that this was a social outing. They were going to the mine on serious business.

Katherine's smile faded. He could see she knew the story.

"Yes, Papa talked about it. The Dives and the Pelican companies. Not the same."

"No, I hope not," he agreed, though he wasn't as sure as she seemed to be.

They'd spoken little during the train ride. Katherine was still resting her voice, but when she did speak she was sounding more like normal. Carson was content to sit with her for the moment. But he found himself turning over a number of things in his mind that he didn't entirely like.

"What made you decide on my innocence?" he asked finally, when Randolph, Biggs, and Jack were occupied with a card game. The five of them were the only passengers on the train.

She turned from the window and smiled, then touched his cheek. "White face," she said. "Can't playact that."

"I wasn't a happy man at that moment," he agreed, remembering the moment he'd turned cold and felt his blood drain away.

There was something else that wasn't making him very happy. What happened if they found what he expected to find in the mine? What happened when they discovered that there was more gold in the Amanda Leigh? What happened when she discovered that her uncle had misrepresented the situation to her? Katherine would have money again, and her problems would go away.

The thought wrenched Carson's gut. He resisted the urge to get up and pace the car. He studied her profile instead, admiring the clean line of her delicate nose and the slope of her cheek, and those sultry lips.

She wouldn't need him anymore. Wasn't that what he'd planned on? He pressed his lips together and looked out the window on the other side of the car. Wasn't that his plan in the beginning? he asked himself. To leave her when he'd gotten what he wanted? A damned sour plan it seemed now.

He wondered if Benedict knew Katherine had left the Elms with him this morning. He wouldn't be surprised if she was being watched. Obviously someone had been watching her the night she was attacked. Suddenly the idea of leaving her in Georgetown, even with a Pinkerton guard, didn't seem like such a good one. She'd be safer with four guards than one.

Ray Jones leaned across Owen's breakfast table the minute Edna left the room, leaving the two of them free to talk. "Did you know Fairfax and Katherine just left on the train for Georgetown this morning?"

"No, I didn't know that." Surprised, Owen set down his coffee cup. So that was what he owed this early morning call to. Jones had never called at his house before. He knew the reason had to be important.

"What are you going to do to salvage this mess?" the banker whispered across the table, with more agitation than Owen ever remembered seeing in him before. Was old Jonesy losing his nerve?

"Why ask me?" he asked. "You're the one who thought this husband-murdering-his-wife plan was the perfect answer."

"It would have worked if you'd hired someone capable of doing it," Jones accused. "I thought you said your setups had always worked before."

"I hired the man you said to hire, and he had a good record of getting the job done," Owen said, annoyed at having the blame cast on him but determined to remain calm. He'd be damned if he'd be the whipping boy for Jones's disappointment. The murder plan had not been his in the first place. From the beginning he'd disliked the idea of someone murdering Katherine. But when he kept the whole affair in perspective—when he reminded himself that Katherine was Ben Tucker's daughter—the picture took a shape, one his conscience could deal with.

Fortunately neither Tucker nor anyone else had ever been smart enough to realize how much he'd hated his partner for winning Amanda Leigh away from him.

"I saw Katherine immediately after the attack. Our man

made a good effort at it," Owen said, taking small pleasure in seeing Jones squirm for the first time throughout their long association. "Who would have thought a woman would confound a paid assassin?"

"Damnable bad luck, if you ask me." Jones pulled his handkerchief from his pocket and mopped his sweating brow, though only a low fire burned in the stove.

"Not only does the man botch the job," Jones continued, "Fairfax is bailed out by Dolly Green and his wife takes off with him to Georgetown the minute he's released. Now why is that?"

"To inspect the mine," Owen said, his mind already racing ahead to possible actions. The first murder attempt had been made. Now was not the time to get cold feet. He leaned forward, elbows on the table. "Did they go alone?"

"No, they took Cornish Jack with them, a Pinkerton guard who had been posted at the Elms, and Hearn from the *Sentinel*," Jones said.

"But anything can happen in a mine," Owen said, his mind already reviewing several possibilities.

"Exactly," Jones said. "You'll need some men and the speeder to get up there."

Owen frowned. Lord, he hated the speeder. No place to get warm in the little hand-pumped trolley. It would be a long, cold ride up to Georgetown, but they had no choice. There was only one train up and back a day.

"Take Brinkley and Harris with you," Jones said. "Brinkley screwed this up the first time. Make him get it right this time. The two of them know where to find the guns and dynamite. Yes, take dynamite with you. If the three of you take Fairfax and the others by surprise at the mine, you shouldn't have any problem. They'll die up there. Then poor Lily will be an orphan with only you to help her with the Tucker fortune."

"Where are Brinkley and Harris?" Owen asked, rising to his feet, wondering already if Katherine would be smart enough to search out the stopes. She knew more about the mine than a girl should.

"Probably at their usual saloon," Jones said, waving a hand in the direction of the corner tavern. "By the time you get to Georgetown, they should have sobered up enough to do their part."

"Right," Owen said with distaste. He disliked working with drunks, even sobered ones. No self-respecting man gave up his dignity to drink or cards. But then, no self-respecting man would hire on to do this kind of work. "If we're successful, I'll telegraph 'Job accomplished.'"

"I'll be looking forward to the message," Jones said, also rising. "Keep your nose clean. You've a lot to lose if any of these dealings go public."

Owen didn't need the reminder.

In Georgetown, Carson rented a buggy for the five of them and the box of tools and lighting supplies Jack had brought along. They ate lunch at Louis Dupuy's famous Hotel de Paris restaurant. He'd heard much made of the place, and it lived up to its reputation.

After the meal they headed up the mountainside toward the Amanda Leigh. As he drove, Katherine became more and more excited.

"Chimney rock," she cried loudly in childlike delight at the sight of the rock outcropping as they drove south out of town.

She pointed out many of the landmarks along the trail. The transformation was magical. Denver's leading socialite became an artless young woman enjoying a winter buggy ride into the mountains. The seriousness of their trip once more forgotten, she pointed out sites of picnics with her father along the way and the sighting of birds and deer. He didn't have the heart to remind her of the serious purpose of their trip. He let her enjoy the excursion back into the days when she rode with her father to the mines and mills, enjoying the beauty of the mountains and the camaraderie of the miners.

He began to understand how close she'd been to her father. What an influence the man had had on her. Naturally it'd been difficult for her to watch him destroy himself with drink after the death of her mother. Selling the Amanda Leigh would seem like selling part of her childhood. *Strange what a legacy fathers leave their children*, he thought

An hour later, they reached the Amanda Leigh, which appeared long deserted. The road was unused. The office, compressor house, and mill buildings, as well as the entrance to the main tunnel, were locked, the locks undisturbed and rusting in the thin mountain air.

"Compressor first," Katherine said, taking charge with an authority that surprised Carson. He followed her as she struck out toward the largest of the mine buildings, her father's keys jingling in her gloved hand. The other men took their cue from him.

"Boiler good," she said, to no one in particular, as she examined the giant tanks and vessels inside the building. They'd left the Pinkerton man to stand guard at the door.

"And the compressor, too," Jack added, looking over the huge gear wheel and pipe connections. "The hoses would have to be replaced."

"Yes." Katherine walked along the length of a hose and nudged it with her boot. "Equipment valuable. Mill equipment dated. New extraction method. Alkaline potassium cyanide solution."

"Aye, I've heard of it," Jack said, eyeing Katherine as if he was seeing her anew.

"Right," Randolph said, staring at the looming equipment inside the two-story building. "I've read it's being used with good results in Utah."

"Yes," Katherine said, stroking the side of a hydraulic shaft with a tenderness that almost made Carson jealous.

"Let's get a move on," he said. "It'll be dark in a few hours."

"Map in office," she said, leading the way out of the door to another building, where they found a map tacked on the wall. The diagram labeled tunnels and shafts, drifts, veins, and crosscuts. Katherine and Jack had no difficulty making perfect sense of it.

"Stopes." Katherine pointed to a crisscrossed area on the map. "Most likely area."

Reaching for the map, Jack agreed. "Let's take it with us."

They formed their plan and began to put on the equipment that Jack had brought. Without any fuss Katherine replaced her jaunty velvet hat with a miner's resin-stiffened, waterproof hat, with a tiny oil lamp mounted on the front. Then she donned an oversized oilcloth slicker. Carson and each of the men did the same.

Jack supplied each with a candle to carry in addition to their safety lights. "Just in case," he said, then he lit the lanterns and pulled a huge coil of rope over his shoulder.

At the door to the mine, Katherine handed the keys over to Carson, who soon had it unlocked.

The door creaked as he dragged it open. A great black hole yawned before them. Water dripped in the depths, each drip echoing against the stone walls. The unmistakable sound of scurrying creatures reached them. A musty breath of mold and things even more unsavory struck them in the face. Carson turned his head away. Randolph choked.

"I've smelled worse," Jack said, holding his lantern up to get a better view of the entrance. "You'd be surprised what garbage miners will leave behind."

In the rays of his lantern, the pink nose and white whiskers of a rodent were visible, then vanished.

"Well, the rats aren't deserting," Jack said. "That's a good sign. How long has it been since the mine was worked, Mrs. Fairfax?"

"Five years," Katherine replied, with no visible concern

about the rat or the stench. She gazed eagerly into the black tunnel.

"I'll stand guard here at the entrance," Biggs, the Pinkerton man, offered, backing away.

"Good idea," Carson said, wishing he had as good an excuse to remain on the daylight side of the door. He'd come to Denver to make money off business, not to mine. Exploring the bowels of the mountains held no appeal for him.

He glanced around in time to see that Katherine, carrying a lantern, had already stepped fearlessly into the mine. She was sashaying off into the darkness as if she was on a walk in the park, her boots splashing through puddles. He glanced around at Jack.

The old miner picked up his lantern and shrugged. "Hell, Captain, no offense, but she's no woman. She's half miner on her pappy's side."

"Fine, but I'd just as soon it wasn't my wife leading the way." Carson gestured toward Katherine, who was already several yards into the mine.

"I'm getting there." Jack trotted to catch up with her.

Despite his reluctance, Carson was not far behind, and Randolph was practically walking on his heels.

"I'm a newspaperman, you know," he said, looking back over his shoulder as the tunnel curved slightly and the mouth of the mine disappeared behind them.

"I know, Randolph," Carson said. "Think of the material this gives you. Now you know what a miner goes through every day."

"I can interview a miner to find that out, thank you," Randolph said. "I'm here for Katherine's sake."

The sound of her name on his friend's lips brought him a flash of intuition about Katherine's future. With unsettling clarity he could see what would happen. After the annulment of their marriage and an extended trip to Europe, she would return to Denver, beautiful and sophisticated. If some continental sort didn't snap her up during her tour, a Denverite like Randolph would be on her doorstep within a day of her return. Blast and damn, it probably *would* be Randolph. Flowers in one hand and a lovesick poem in the other.

Carson stopped in his tracks. Randolph walked into him. He whirled around and glared at the newspaperman.

"What?" Randolph asked, clearly at a loss about his friend's strange behavior. "What's the matter?"

Carson's eyes narrowed. He knew he sounded ridiculous, but he couldn't help himself. "Do you write poetry?"

"Poetry? Well, I turn my hand to it once in a while, but—" Randolph began. "Look, Carson, Jack and Katherine are practically out of sight."

He cursed, turned again, and started after his wife. He was being a fool, trying to second-guess the future. But he felt certain that whatever lay ahead, if they carried through with their bargain—if Katherine regained her fortune—it wouldn't be she who ended up alone.

"New stopes," Katherine said only half an hour later, when Carson and Randolph caught up with her and Jack in a large, high room off the main tunnel. She was holding her lantern up so she could get a better view of the walls. "Not on map."

"Did ye see the signs that someone has been in here recently at the Jefferson shaft?" Jack asked when Carson came up behind him. "I'd swear I saw the signs of a bucket having been dropped down there I'd say within the last couple of months. That's what they could be doing, coming from the shaft above and leaving the entrance undisturbed."

So that was what Benedict was up to, he thought.

"Yes, fresh drilling here," Katherine said. "Hand drilling. Exploratory."

"Yep, they're looking for the vein, all right," Jack agreed as the two of them walked along, examining the walls for signs that only they seemed to be able to read.

"You think old Benedict has been cheating Katherine and Lily all along?" Randolph muttered into Carson's ear.

"It's beginning to look like that," he said, watching Katherine and Jack carefully.

"Why? Just for the money?" Randolph asked.

"Or for the power?" Carson suggested, finally willing to share what he'd been speculating all along. "Heard him make any political noises lately?"

"He's been seen hobnobbing with Gill Shay of the Republican party." An expression of enlightenment brightened Randolph's face. "Say no more."

"Here," Katherine cried from the other side of the cavernous room. "Jack, look. Look, there. See?"

The old miner crouched down, bringing his lamp up close to the area she indicated. He and Randolph crowded behind them, peering over Jack's shoulder. As Carson looked closely, even he could see the glitter of gold in the rock—a bright, wide vein.

"That's it," Jack said. "That's got to be it. Don't know nobody who sees a vein like that would call this mine played out. It was here all the time. They just had to keep looking for it."

"I'll wager somebody in the Eureka company knows about it," Carson said. "What do you think, Katherine?"

"Not selling," she said.

"I'm satisfied," Carson said, noting that she was beginning to shiver. The cold dampness could penetrate almost any amount of warm clothing if a person was in the mine long enough. He reached for her arm and led her toward the stope exit. "Let's go. I'd like for us to be out of this mine and the ravine by dark."

"I'll be right with ye," Jack called over his shoulder. "I'm going to chip off a sample."

Swiftly they began to backtrack. Carson hadn't lied about being anxious to get away from the mine. He was holding his lantern up high and walking along fast enough to make Katherine almost trot at his side. They'd just reached the main tunnel when the blast hit them.

A wall of dust and sound slammed into them. It ripped the lanterns from their hands, the hats from their heads. Blackness. Carson tightened his grip on Katherine. He half stumbled into her and half shoved her against the tunnel wall to shield her from the debris.

Rock pummeled painfully his back. He shielded her as best he could. The ground beneath them quaked. Boiling clouds of dust rolled over them. A flood of earth roared into the tunnel—between them and the mine entrance.

Chapter Twenty-seven

As the roar died away, echoing down the long tunnel, Jack's cursing drifted from the stopes to Katherine's ears. In the sudden inky darkness—she wanted to curse, too, but the dust was choking her. When she coughed, she realized Carson's body was pressed heavily against her own. Her heart began to pound. Was he hurt?

"Carson?" she muttered, frantically trying to rouse him. Grit filled her mouth. Her head throbbed from being knocked against the rock wall, but she ignored the pain. Carson had been showered by falling debris. "Carson?"

He moved at last and cursed, also, an oddly reassuring sound, as he eased himself off her. But he grasped her arm as he moved, his grip firm. "Blast it, Katherine. Why on earth did I allow you to talk me into bringing you along?"

Light appeared in the tunnel behind them. Because Jack had still been in the stope, his lantern had survived the explosion. "Head count," the old miner demanded.

"I'm here, I think," Randolph said between fits of coughing.

"Are you all right?" Carson asked, touching her face with

a grimy hand. His hat was gone and his face covered in filth, just like hers, she could only assume. Mud caked their clothes. But he was in one piece and that was all that was important.

"Yes," she whispered, drawing in a deep breath of relief. Her heart began to beat almost normally again.

"Katherine and I are here," he called.

"What happened?" Randolph asked between more coughing. "Was that a cave-in?"

"Nope, it was a dynamite blast," Jack said. "Just who is the bastard dropping dynamite down the shaft? Captain, let's get Mrs. Fairfax back into the stopes. It's safer there."

"Right, come on." Carson helped Katherine up. When she reached for her hat, he brushed her hand aside. "Don't worry about it." Urgently he pushed her back in the direction from which they'd come. "Do you have your candle? Light it. Stay with her, Randolph. I'm going to go look at the damage with Jack."

"Carson, be careful," she warned, touching his sleeve, suddenly aware of the danger they were in. Aware of so many things she'd left unsaid. Terrified that he was going to get hurt because someone wanted her dead.

"Don't worry." He grabbed her by the shoulders and gave her a sound kiss. "Everything is going to be all right. I'm not ending my days in a dark mine. And neither are you."

He turned and started out of the stope with Randolph on his heels, but Jack blocked their way.

"Wait," the miner said.

"Why?"

"Just wait," Jack said. "I have a feel—"

Before he'd finished his sentence, another blast roared through the mine. Carson reached for Katherine again, but both were knocked off their feet before he could reach her. Dust rolled into the stope. Small rocks rained from the cavern's ceiling. She rolled over on her stomach and covered her head with her arms.

Again the roar echoed away down the tunnels, clamoring

like a train speeding into the cold bowels of the earth. Katherine became aware of all of them coughing in a cloud of dust.

"As I was saying," Jack choked out, "the bastard wanted to make sure he got the job done."

"That probably did the trick." Randolph crawled to his feet and looked around the underground room. "How much air do you think we have?"

"Ventilation shaft up the mountainside," Katherine said, as soon as she stopped coughing. "Villain might block it."

"If he knows about it," Carson said.

"If he knew about the Jefferson shaft, we have to assume he knows about the ventilation shaft," Jack said, glancing at the map. "It's on the map, and it's small and easy to block."

"We probably have air enough to make a good dint in digging out the rubble," Randolph said. "But we don't have any tools. Just the rope Jack carried in. Surely Biggs has gone for help."

"Not if he's dead," Carson said. "If our villain is willing to throw two sticks of dynamite to be certain he's finished the job, he isn't going to overlook a guard at the mine entrance."

Katherine listened with a sinking heart.

"I think we have to rely on ourselves," Jack said.

They all agreed. They rationed the candles Jack had given them. The men began to dig with their hands.

Katherine sat on a boulder, tending the candle and holding Carson's coat.

Several hours and two candles later, it had become painfully clear that enough rubble from the Jefferson shaft had dropped into the tunnel to make it impossible for them to dig themselves out without proper tools and bracing lumber.

The nausea that had subsided during the train ride returned. She leaned her head against the wall and took a deep breath, fighting back the waves of queasiness. Her feet were cold, but she hardly noticed. It seemed of little importance at the moment.

She watched Carson, Randolph, and Jack make another effort to dig through the rubble, but the hole they'd dug suddenly filled with fine rock again. They were right back where they'd started.

"We need another plan of attack," Carson said, standing back from the rock. Katherine could see that his fine hands were raw from digging. "What about the ventilation shaft?"

"It's not a likely escape route, with it being about two hundred fifty feet to the surface and only about a foot in diameter," Jack said.

She nodded in confirmation.

Despite the cold and wet in the tunnel, Carson worked in his shirtsleeves. Even with his grimy face, every move he made appealed to her. She began to wonder if she was being unfair by not telling him what she suspected, that she was going to have his baby. She didn't want to obligate him to her, but maybe he deserved to know. Even if they weren't going to survive, maybe he should know that their intimacy had begat a new life.

Would it matter to him? she wondered.

Or would it make him unhappy? He seemed so set against marriage and so determined to go to California.

Almost as if he'd heard her thinking about him, he turned to her and walked to her side. "We're going to get out of this. Don't worry. When we do, I have something I want to talk to you about."

She held her breath, foolishly hoping against hope that he would tell her that he loved her. That he'd heard her words uttered in passion a few nights ago and wanted her to know that he felt the same. Her heart went tight and still. "Yes? What is it?"

"We're going to have a talk about this agreement we have," he said, taking her hands in his bruised and scraped ones. "I never intended any harm."

"I know," she said, disappointment creeping over her. He wasn't going to speak words of love to her.

"That's a start," he said, solemnly. "Kiss me, sweetheart."

And she did, bestowing all her love without saying the words.

When they drew apart, he smiled at her, a truly happy smile. A smile that was almost enough to make her heart burst.

"We'll be out of here soon, you'll see," he said, patting her hands.

She nodded, knowing perfectly well that they were never going to dig their way out, not with the great mound of rubble blocking the tunnel.

Exhausted, she leaned her head against the rock wall and stared into the candle flame, watching it waver ever so slightly. In her exhaustion, she'd almost drifted off to sleep when she heard a small shower of rock fall behind her. When she turned to look for the source of the noise, she glimpsed a figure in a yellow and red shirt vanish in the darkness beyond the candlelight.

I'm dreaming, she told herself, turning back to the men. They hadn't made much headway since the last time she'd looked. She checked the candle to see that it had probably another half hour before it would burn out. Then she leaned her head against the mine wall again.

At first she was hardly aware of the noise. How long the tapping had gone on before it interrupted her thoughts about her baby she never knew. But suddenly she could hear the tap, tap, tapping in the rock wall. It sounded like a little rock hammer working away at the stone, regular and persistent.

She sat up, a strange, unbelievable hope fluttering in her chest. "I hear someone in the mine. Listen."

The men stopped talking among themselves, and turned to her.

"Where?" Carson asked, stepping closer to her.

"What kind of tapping?" Jack asked, thrusting his head forward, as if also listening.

"In the wall," Katherine said, beginning to doubt herself. She put her ear to the wall again. It was still there, but very faint. "Around the corner."

The impression was so strong, she rose from the boulder and

ventured down the tunnel and around the corner into one of the dark stopes.

"It faded," she said, disappointed to find the stope empty. She'd been certain there'd be someone in there or some sign of human habitation.

When she turned back, she saw Jack standing by the boulder with his ear pressed against the rock. "I hear it, too," he whispered, as if speaking would interrupt the tapping.

"Wow, that's great," Randolph said. "Someone has come to rescue us."

Jack straightened, his eyes wide with wonder and his expression light with hope. "Not someone. Some *thing*. It's the tommyknockers."

"I don't know about that," Carson said, his gaze on Katherine's candle. "Look at that flame. It's moving. That means there is more than one opening in the mine to the outside."

"That's what they're telling us." Jack pulled the rock hammer he'd taken the sample ore with and tapped on the wall. "There, they be answering me."

Katherine exchanged a skeptical look with Carson. She'd lived around mines long enough to know the stories about the two-foot-tall, colorfully clad spirits who haunted the dark underground, playing pranks on the miners and sometimes giving them warnings of danger. Her father had treated the stories like delightful myths, and that was how she'd always thought of the tommyknockers. None of the modern miners believed in them anymore. But the old miners, the Cornish and Welshmen like Jack, did.

"I hope they are tapping out directions in Morse code on how to get out of here," Carson said with a wry smile.

"The tappings lead in this direction," Jack said, ignoring Carson's humor. "Isn't that what you heard, Mrs. Fairfax?"

She nodded and cast Carson a frown. At the moment she was willing to believe in anything. "Yes."

"Let's go deeper then," Jack said, clearly committed to following the tappings.

"It's as good a prospect as we have here," Randolph said, following the old miner down the tunnel.

Carson reached for Katherine's hand.

"Coat," she advised, shaking out the garment and holding it up for him.

A smile of mild surprise crossed his face. "Yes, ma'am."

"Catch a fever," she warned, helping him shrug into his coat in a wifely fashion.

"My thought exactly." Carson took her hand and kissed it, a light, tender kiss.

Then he led them toward the glow of Jack's lantern, deep in the mine.

She glanced at the map, then prayed silently that Jack's little tommyknockers knew what they were doing. This part of the tunnel was unmapped.

The tap, tap, tapping led them to six unmapped stopes into the side of the mountain. Finally, in a stope where the candle flame danced like crazy, they found a shaft to the surface— high on the wall of an unrecorded underground room. In the darkness, with stopes and drifts angling off the main tunnel in all directions, they would never have spotted the shaft if they'd not had a clue to its whereabouts.

They stared up at the black, two-foot-wide hole in silence. The candle in Katherine's hand flickered enthusiastically. No one said a word.

No one was willing to make any disparaging remarks about tommyknockers.

"He ain't dead, just unconscious," Brinkley called up from the dark, rocky draw where the buggy and the Pinkerton man had crashed, according to Owen's plan. "Can't I just shoot him and get it over with?" the man asked.

"No. It must look like he was in a hurry to get help and accidentally drove over the edge of the switchback," Owen called down to the bumbling idiot. He was holding the buggy horse to prevent it from trotting off toward the livery stable. The longer it took for anyone in Georgetown to figure that there was trouble at the Amanda Leigh, the better it was for them. "If he's shot, the law will immediately begin to look deeper into every aspect of the mine and the deaths. Smother him."

"Ah—" Brinkley uttered an oath.

"Do it."

Owen turned his back on his henchman and started back up the road to the mine entrance to wait. He felt certain that by first light, if they'd heard nothing from Fairfax and Katherine, they could count their mission successful. Then they would release the horse. Once it turned up at the Georgetown livery stable—homing, as a loose hungry horse will—someone would be dispatched to see what was happening at the mine. By the time help arrived, it would be too late for poor Katherine, her meddling husband, and their unfortunate friends. A deadly cave-in would have done them in.

Owen tied the horse up in the lean-to beside the office, waved to Harris, whom he'd posted at the mine entrance, then went inside. A small fire he'd started earlier burned in the stove. The room had warmed considerably. He laid his rifle across the desk, wiped the dust off the desk chair, and sat down. Leaning back, he swung his legs up on the desktop and made himself comfortable. It was going to be a long, bitter, cold January night in the mountains. He didn't intend to suffer any more than he had to.

He must have fallen asleep because when he opened his eyes, he could see the pale hint of dawn brightening the peak of the mountains. The chair creaked as he sat up. Where the hell was Brinkley? The fool should have reported back by now. With a sense of urgency, he swung his feet to the floor and stood. His knees protested. On stiff legs, he reached the door and threw it open.

"Harris?" he called toward the mine entrance door.

In response, Harris opened the door enough to wave at Owen. Everything looked okay. "Any sign of survivors?" he asked.

"Nope," Harris said. "All clear."

"Good." Owen turned away, scanning the rest of the mine and mill buildings. Then where was Brinkley? Unease growing, he started down the road to the site of the buggy crash. When he reached the switchback where they'd pushed the buggy over the edge, he leaned over, searching the ravine for the wreckage and for the Pinkerton's body—or Brinkley. In the pale dawn light no bodies were visible. No Pinkerton man. No one.

Owen muttered a curse under his breath and backed away. He turned to look around at the mountainside, dark and colorless in the predawn light. The slope huddled above him covered in pines, big and silent as a hibernating bear.

If the Pinkerton man was alive, he could do much damage to their plans. Would he be on the slope above or would he be on his way to town?

Owen turned on his heel and started back up the road toward the mine office. If the Pinkerton man was alive, they still had a hell of a lot of work to do. And when it was done, he'd personally skin Brinkley alive.

Chapter Twenty-eight

Until Carson saw the rope drop down through the shaft as they'd planned, he'd imagined all sorts of unthinkable things that might have happened to Jack as the first out of the mine. But just as arranged, the old miner jerked the rope three times, signaling all clear and ready for the next one to climb out.

"Katherine?" he pulled her toward the rope. She looked wary and worn out, with dark smudges beneath her eyes, but she was not particularly frightened. Though her exhaustion and her injuries—her throat and arm—concerned him, he was proud of her strength . . . and glad of it. She was proving as sensible in a calamity as she was in a domestic crisis. "You're next, sweetheart. Remember to find cover as soon as you're above and stay put until Randolph and I are there."

She nodded and reached for the rope.

Carson heaved an audible sigh of relief when he saw the rope jerk three times to confirm Katherine's safe arrival on the surface.

Randolph said nothing, but he slapped Carson on the back

and shared a look of understanding. Then the newspaperman reached for the rope. Carson hoisted himself up last.

On the mountainside he was surprised to find morning dawning. Jack gave him a hand up. He took a deep breath of fresh air and glanced around to find Randolph and Katherine. They were waiting back in the shadows of the trees. No one said a word. They all knew how far voices could travel in the still, cold air. They all knew they weren't alone on the mountain. From the direction of the mine, smoke curled upward into the stillness.

Carson gathered them together under the pine trees. The men checked their guns to be certain all were in working order and to tally how much ammunition they had. Each man had a gun but only a few rounds. Only Katherine was without a weapon. He didn't like that, but it couldn't be helped.

He proposed they split up, with he and Jack going down to the entrance to learn who and how many their foe was. Katherine refused to be left behind. Randolph agreed with her.

"You can wager whoever it is down there is better armed and better prepared for a fight than we are," Carson reminded them. He wanted Katherine to understand why he insisted she be under cover when the shooting began.

But she shook her head and gave him that tight-lipped, stubborn glare of hers. There was no changing her mind, and they didn't have time for him to attempt it. He took her hand and led the way downward toward the mine.

From an outcropping overlooking the road and the mine office, they counted the horses in the lean-to.

"Three saddle horses and the black that pulled the buggy," Randolph said. "Where's the buggy? Where's Biggs?"

"Not where he can help us." Carson wished for a spyglass to better observe the mine entrance and the office. "There has to be a guard at the entrance."

Suddenly a door creaked and a tall, spare man carrying a rifle emerged from the compressor building. He appeared to be talking to someone behind him.

"Uncle Owen," Katherine gasped.

Unsurprised, Carson silenced her by putting his finger to his lips. She heeded him but continued to stare at the man whom she'd called uncle. Now she'd seen with her own eyes that Benedict was out to murder her. He knew she was shocked.

A man followed Benedict out of the building, a man with dark hair and about Carson's height and build.

The two men were arguing.

"You fool. You idiot," Benedict was shouting.

"What?" erupted from Katherine at the sight of the second man. She silenced herself with a hand over her mouth.

"Holy Moses," hissed from Randolph. "If you weren't sitting next to me, I'd swear that was you down there, Carson."

He frowned. So that was how it had been done. A lookalike. Not so much to fool Katherine; after all, she was supposed to die. But if she died muttering his name, so much the better. And anyone who witnessed the crime, as Willis had, would accuse him. With his cane as the murder weapon found on the scene, no one would suspect anyone else.

"I feel sick," she whispered, hiding her face in her hands. "I can't believe ... Uncle Owen ... he and Aunt Edna are family."

He pulled her close. "Don't think about it now."

Randolph elbowed him and gestured to the two men standing below. "They're watching something behind them, on the downhill side of the mine."

Without warning a shot rang out from the pine woods below.

Carson shoved Katherine down behind the outcropping, but he continued to watch. His look-alike hit the earth, obviously hit. But Benedict stood his ground, aiming down the mountain and firing twice. He had the advantage, with a rifle that had greater range than the six-shooters they carried. After firing, Benedict dashed for cover in the mine office.

"That must be Biggs," Carson said, feeling a sense of real

hope for the first time since he'd realized Benedict had two henchmen with him. "Katherine, stay here. Jack, stay with her. Randolph, cover the road. We're not letting these curs get away."

"I'll cover the road, but I'm coming with you," Randolph said, checking the cylinder of his gun again. "I want to be within range when I start shooting."

Carson didn't argue. With a nod, he moved out from their cover, down the mountainside to the open ground around the mine. At a distance on the road side of him, Randolph followed.

Katherine watched helplessly with her heart gone still. If she didn't lose Carson to the lure of San Francisco, she was going to lose him in a shoot-out over a mine. A shoot out with a man she'd thought of as family. A man who must have had something to do with the murder attempt on her life.

She didn't know whether to weep—or be fighting mad.

"Don't worry." Jack put a gentle hand on her shoulder. "The captain, he don't look it with the dandy way he dresses, but he's bloody canny in a fight."

"I know," she murmured. The memory of how efficiently Carson had managed Nolan on the front porch of the Elms was still fresh in her mind.

Holding her breath, she watched him edge his way along the mountainside embankment toward the mouth of the mine. Her dirty hair annoyed her and she shoved it out of her face. She was covered with dust and her clothes were caked with mud from crawling through the shaft—but only Carson's welfare mattered at the moment. She glanced at the look-alike to see that he was moving, every so slightly. His hand sought the rifle on the ground not far from him.

"Cover him, Jack," she cried, astonished to find that her voice had returned.

But before Jack could take aim, a shot rang out from the road where Randolph had stationed himself.

The wounded man's rifle jumped beyond his reach.

She sucked in a breath and looked in Randolph's direction. The newspaperman was crouched behind a tree beside the road. Smoke curled upward from the barrel of his six-shooter.

"Heavens, Randolph can shoot," she gasped. She'd never guessed he possessed such skill. When she looked back toward the mine entrance, she saw the door open and a rifle barrel appear. Carson lunged at it, seizing the barrel and going after the man holding the gun. The two disappeared into the black hole of the mine.

"Carson!" Frantic, she stood up to get a better look.

Jack pulled her down, nearly yanking her arm out of its socket. "I'll have none of that. I don't want to have to explain you getting shot to the captain."

"But I can't see what's happening," she complained.

"There's been no shot." Jack watched the entrance as keenly as she. "Wait."

Dear Lord, she prayed silently, *deliver Carson from this danger and I'll gladly see him off to anyplace he wants to go.*

"We ain't heard nothing from Benedict either," Jack said, peering down at the mine office. "I don't remember. Is there another door to the office?"

"No door. But there's a window," she said. "On the side where Biggs might be."

"Right." Jack studied the office building with a fiery glint in his eye.

Katherine could see he was as eager as she to get into the fight. Just at that moment Carson appeared at the mine entrance with a rifle in his hand. She let out a pent-up breath. Dear heaven, he was all right.

That left only Uncle Owen in the mine office.

"Let's go," she said, scrambling to her feet.

"Whoa. The captain said to stay here," Jack reminded her.

"Only until he was in control," she said, already moving out from behind the outcropping.

"Here, wait." Jack lurched after her.

She evaded his reach and started down the mountain toward the office. She had a few things to say to Uncle Owen.

A shot rang out, striking the ground at her feet. Instinctively, she flattened herself against the earth.

She heard Carson curse and the firing began. Rapid. Close. Deadly. It wasn't just Carson pulling the trigger. Shots came from the road and from the downhill side of the mine. Uncle Owen didn't have a chance.

When the shooting ceased, the gunfire echoed down the valley, smoke hung heavy on the air, and an oppressive silence settled on the mountainside.

Carson emerged from cover first, gazing up in Katherine's direction. He waved to her. "Don't move from there until I give the signal. Do you hear me?"

She waved in return and stayed where she was. She wasn't going to argue with that tone of voice.

Randolph came loping up the road, and Biggs materialized from the pine woods. He was hatless. The bruises on his face made her grimace. The Pinkerton man had taken quite a beating sometime in the last twelve hours. He stopped long enough to check the look-alike, sprawled on the ground. He seemed satisfied that the henchman was dead.

As she watched, Carson went into the mine office first. The other two men soon followed.

She was on her feet and most of the way down the slope before Carson appeared again. When he saw her, he shook his head, but he didn't bother to scold.

"Is he dead? Uncle Owen?" she asked when she reached him.

"He's wounded," Carson said. "But I think he will survive. The man at the mine entrance is tied up."

Randolph appeared next. "I'll ride for help."

"Bring the sheriff," Carson said.

"I want to talk to Uncle Owen," Katherine said, touching Carson's sleeve. Her heart had started to pound at the thought of facing the man she'd thought of as family. Her hands trembled.

"I thought as much." He took her by the arm and led her into the office.

Uncle Owen was propped up in the desk chair, blood oozing from his left shoulder. His face was gray, but his eyes were alert. Biggs stood behind him.

She kicked a path through the shell casings on the floor and sat down in a chair beside the desk.

"So what do you think of your ol' uncle now, Kitty, my dear?" Uncle Owen said, a cruel smile on his ashen face.

The sound of her nickname on his lips struck her ear like a profanity. She sucked in a shocked breath.

Carson frowned.

"Mind your manners, old man." Biggs tapped the back of the desk chair with the butt of his gun. "It's been a long, cold night in the woods. You ordered your man to kill me. I'm so weary right now, I'd sure hate for this extra gun I carry to go off when I wasn't looking."

The threat left Uncle Owen nonplussed. He stared back at her, his face hard.

"How could you do this to Lily and me? And to Carson?" she asked, searching his face for the clue, in his eyes, that she should have seen. A clue that something was terribly wrong. A warning. "Mama and Papa loved you, and Aunt Edna, too, as if you were family."

"I almost was your mother's family." The heartless smile twisted into an ironic smirk. "Amanda Leigh almost married me. I was almost your father. You didn't know that, did you? But your father stole her heart. Took her away from me. Once she saw him, I never had a chance."

"So this is your revenge?" Carson demanded. "Taking advantage of two innocent young women?"

"That's not how I saw it," Uncle Owen said, meeting her gaze across the desk. "I thought it was better to be Ben Tucker's partner and Amanda Leigh's friend than to lose your mother completely. But then she died. We both lost her, Ben and I. And ol' Ben couldn't hold it together anymore. But I could. Why shouldn't I have what he left?''

"But you had money from the Clementine," she said.

"Yes, and Ray Jones made me see a chance to have something your father never would have," Owen said, his eyes becoming brighter, with pain or delusion, she was uncertain. But the unnatural shine in his eyes sent chills through her.

"I had a chance at a place in the state house," Owen continued. "Who knows, maybe the U.S. Senate. All it takes is knowing the right people—and money.''

"Like the gold in the Amanda Leigh," Carson said for him.

"The perfection of it," Owen said. "Gold from the mine named for your mother. It seemed just. If I couldn't have the woman I loved, why shouldn't I have power?''

Katherine listened with disbelieving ears. Was this the man she'd known all her life? "And you would kill for that?'' she asked.

"Everything has its price," Uncle Owen said with a cynical smile.

She stared at him, the knowledge stealing over her that this man was not the person she'd once known. He was a stranger: a sick man, sick in his heart, sick in his head. He'd lost something—compassion, love, the ladder of reality that everyone uses to hang their life decisions on. And he'd likely never get it back.

Another shiver rippled through her. She was suddenly cold to the bone. And so weary. She wanted to put her head down on the desk and weep.

Instantly Carson's hand was resting on her shoulder. "Have you said what you wanted to say, Katherine?''

She nodded, and allowed him to lead her out of the office. A great sadness weighed on her heart. Outside, she turned to him. "He's mad. I see it in his eyes now. But when . . . why didn't any of us see it before?''

"I don't have any answers for you, sweetheart," Carson said, brushing a stray lock of dirty hair from her face. "The human mind and heart are wondrous things. I just know that it's over. You don't have to worry about your future any longer."

She let him take her into his arms, but she knew what he said about her future wasn't true.

Chapter Twenty-nine

After a bite to eat at the Hotel de Paris, they decided to go home rather than stay overnight, despite their dirty condition and exhaustion. Katherine curled up on the train seat and slept during the trip back to Denver. Carson sat across from her, longing to hold her but content with having her near. Satisfied with knowing that Owen Benedict was locked up in Georgetown until he was well enough to be extradited to Denver.

But a single thought tortured him. Katherine was for all intents and purposes a rich woman, with little need for a husband. The thought left him cold and hollow inside.

It was dark when they reached Denver. Biggs went on to the police chief's office to give Kelly the news about Owen Benedict's confession of conspiring to murder Katherine. He was confident the charges against Carson would be dropped. Randolph headed for the newspaper office to write the story. Jack went back to the Respite, muttering something about tommyknockers.

At the Elms Dolly and Mrs. D met them at the door. Katherine embraced them both. Mrs. D fussed about how dirty they were.

Dolly asked what had happened. Carson explained that it was Benedict who had masterminded the murder attempt on Katherine. But his real concern was getting his wife upstairs so she could rest.

"Is Lily still with Mrs. Evans?" she asked, going to the hall table where the mail always waited. "We'll send for her as soon as I've bathed. I have to explain to her about Uncle Owen, though heaven knows what I'm going to say."

She stopped long enough to glance at the missives lying there. Something made her frown. Her gaze darted unhappily toward him. Apprehensively, Carson ignored Dolly's additional questions.

"Let's get you rested before you worry about Lily or the mail," he suggested, reaching for Katherine's elbow. She pulled away.

"There's a telegram for you," she said, holding the message out to him. Just as he touched it, she began to sway.

"Dizzy," she croaked, staggering away from Carson and putting her hand to her head. Then she crumpled, collapsing against him only because he'd gone after her.

He was able to get one arm around her shoulders, then the other under her knees, and swing her up before she fell to the floor.

"Send for the doctor," he ordered, afraid to think how her injuries and the complications from the night in the mine might have endangered her health. "She's exhausted. I think that's all it is, but send for him now."

He carried her up to their room, gently laid her on the bed, and pulled off her boots. Then he threw his gloves aside and began to unbutton the tiny buttons of her habit. The livid bruises on her neck made him frown. What surprised him was to find, lying at her throat, close to her heart, the diamond-studded key charm that he'd given her for Christmas. The key to his heart.

"Sweetheart, will we ever understand each other?" Carson murmured, touching the pendant that was warm from lying against her skin.

Mrs. D appeared at his side and made no protest about him being under her roof or undressing his wife. "Willis is fetching the doctor. Is she come to yet? Gracious, you are both filthy. That's what you get for crawling around under the ground. I've started drawing a bath for you, Mr. Fairfax. I don't have a razor for you, but I found enough spare things for you to make yourself respectable. Go clean yourself up and I'll see to Katherine. Go on. Go."

As he rose from the edge of the bed, he realized he still held the telegram in his hand. He stared at it, seeing what Katherine must have seen. It was from San Francisco. From Alice Johnson, no doubt. His San Francisco business partner was the last person he wanted to hear from at the moment .

He bit off a string of oaths that made Mrs. D frown at him. Without reading it, he threw the cursed telegram into the fire and retreated to his room.

Katherine awoke as Mrs. D pulled off her jacket. "I fainted, didn't I?" she asked, humiliated. She'd never considered herself the fainting type, though it was rather fashionable to be so fragile.

"Nothing to worry about," Mrs. D said reassuringly. "You've been through a lot. Mr. Fairfax told us about Mr. Benedict. It's a shock to all of us. I can imagine how you must feel. You just rest easy. I'm going to have you cleaned up in no time. The doctor is on his way. He will check you over."

"Where is Carson?" she asked, the painful memory of the telegram coming back to her. Was he packing his bags already?

"He is cleaning up," Mrs. D said. "What did you do, Katherine? Your clothes look as if you've been crawling through tunnels like a prairie dog."

"Very nearly," she said, caring little about the state of her clothes. The telegram had only served to remind her what was important to Carson. San Francisco. What had she expected from him? San Francisco had always been in his plans. What was the surprise?

She'd known about Alice Johnson when she'd insisted on the agreement, when she'd made him sell the Respite. She'd been righteous and priggish. Why did she think he would change now?

Mrs. D began stripping off her underclothes.

Of course, they'd enjoyed a happy Christmas with his family. That was part of what she'd agreed to make happen. And they'd enjoyed a pleasurable physical relationship. She'd always heard that had little meaning to a man's heart. It hardly seemed enough of a reason to keep him at the Elms.

Mrs. D handed her a dressing gown. She accepted it without interrupting the flow of her thoughts.

Perhaps she should be looking at this from another angle. She owed him so much. He'd helped her: extended her cash for the Elms, helped her learn the truth about the mine, showed her how to be more relaxed with Lily. Whatever happened, she would have his baby. With the gold from the Amanda Leigh, she would have enough money to take care of them all. She and Lily would take that long trip to Europe and come home with a young Fairfax. By then Carson would be settled in San Francisco, doing whatever he wanted to do, and talk of the annulment—or divorce, if it came to that—would have died down. And she'd always have a part of him with her. She would ask no more of him than that.

I've been so righteous, too righteous, she thought. *Moderation means moderation. Not every man who walked into the Respite lost control of his life like Father did. I've been unfair to those who know how to temper their vices. I've been unfair to Carson.*

It was abruptly clear that she'd always taken from Carson and never returned anything.

But it wasn't too late to do something about that.

Suddenly she realized that Mrs. D was coming at her with a hairbrush. She reached out and took it. "I can do that, thank you. Send someone for Jack, please. I want to talk to him right away.''

Carson leaned against the stairwell banister outside their room, waiting. He'd been kept from Katherine first by Mrs. D, then by Dolly, and now by the doctor.

"Did you ever figure it out?'' Dolly asked when she left Katherine's room. "Did you ever realize what it is you have ass backward?''

"Of course I did,'' he lied. He'd had plenty of time to contemplate the questions that night he'd lain awake in jail, worrying about Katherine. Still he hadn't quite seen what Dolly was getting at, but he'd be damned if he'd admit it now. All he knew was that the woman he loved didn't need or want him anymore.

"Good,'' Dolly said as she swept away, down the staircase. "Then you're ready to talk to her and do away with this nonsense she's gotten into her head. She's ready to send you off to San Francisco, you fool.''

Carson cursed the telegram again under his breath.

Then Jack came up the stairs, acting embarrassed and mysterious. With an expression of apology he sidled past Carson into Katherine's room.

But then Doc Hughes came out of her room, smiling. At the sight of the doctor, Carson forgot about Jack. The doc's smile sent a flood of relief through him.

"Carson,'' Doc said, giving him a hearty slap on the back, "that didn't take you long, ol' boy. You've hardly been married more than three months.''

"Yes?'' he said, resisting the urge to grab the doctor by his coat lapels if he didn't make himself clear immediately. "She is all right?''

"Fine, especially considering what she's been through,'' Doc said, cheerful as a preacher at a church supper. "I promised I'd let her tell you the details. But I'm expecting some fine cigars from you, my boy. Yes, sir, some fine cigars.'' Doc laughed, jogging his way down the stairs, leaving Carson mystified but suspicious.

He turned back to the door to Katherine's room and frowned. Cigars? What did that mean? The obvious answer came immediately; everything inside him froze. Now that he thought about it, she'd not had a monthly flow the entire time they'd been together. He'd worn protection with her every night—except the first. That night had been so full: the party. His father's arrival. Katherine's unexpected sympathy. Her hesitation. Then the seduction.

Was it possible? Was he going to be a father?

He turned toward the banister. Hands gripping the rail, knuckles white, elbows braced, he waited for the terror of fatherhood to sweep through him. Instead, a tiny resonant hum of excitement grew inside. He and Katherine? Had they created a life? A shiver of fear threatened, but it wasn't strong enough to chase away the rising song of excitement. Of elation.

In that instant he knew what Dolly had wanted him to understand. He knew what he had ass backwards. He wasn't afraid of being a father. He was afraid of being *his* father.

But he *wasn't* his father. Hell, he wasn't about to force his son to be a gambler—though he'd made a decent card player out of Lily. What if the baby was a daughter? What if he and Katherine had a sweet little girl with chestnut hair and turquoise eyes? Lord, he'd have a little reformer on his hands. He stood, clapped his hands, and laughed out loud.

The sound of the door latch turning spun him around to face the door. Jack was standing in the doorway.

''Well, Captain, I'll be damned if I understand any of it,'' he said, appearing indignant and bewildered at once. ''But yer wife wants to see ye. And ye be nice to her, ye hear. I did what I thought was best, and I don't want to hear no more about it.''

Without waiting for Carson to speak, he started down the

hall toward the stairs. Then he halted. "Bye the bye, do ye think Mrs. D has any coffee made?"

"In the kitchen," Carson said, already wondering what Katherine had said to Jack. What did she have to say to him, after all these visitors?

"Aye, the kitchen." The Cornishman stomped down the stairs.

Carson walked softly into the room and shut the door.

Katherine was sitting up in bed wearing a delicate pink lace bed jacket. Her hair was loose, damp from washing, and brushed back from her face. Her color was still pale and the dark smudges still lingered under her eyes. But a healthy hint of pink was seeping into her cheeks. She gave Carson an uncertain, almost sad smile.

"You look better than you did when we stepped off the train," she said, absently stroking Lucky's back. The cat, who'd made himself a fixture in the house, had ensconced himself next to her on the bed.

"You look beautiful," he said, for want of the right word. There seemed to be none. Only a matter of hours ago they'd faced death. Here she was now, looking like an angel resting in their bed. Despite his own exhaustion, desire stirred in him.

"Did I thank you for everything you've done?" she began, her lips trembling. She avoided his gaze, her fingers combing through the tom's fur. "I'm afraid I've been terribly ungrateful."

"No need." He shook his head, not trusting himself to say more. Words were inadequate to express their good fortune. They were both alive. He walked to the bed and sat down on the edge near her feet. "Doc Hughes said you're all right, considering everything that's happened. Is there something more you'd like to tell me?"

She looked up immediately, annoyance crossing her face. "No. Did he say there was?"

"He said something about details." He rested his hand on the coverlet covering her ankle.

"Yes, well, I have something for you." Katherine pulled a piece of paper from her sleeve. She handed it to him. "Open it. Don't blame Jack for any of this."

With a frown, Carson took the paper and unfolded it to find a bill of sale for the Gentleman's Respite, purchased from Jack Tremain by Katherine Juliette Tucker Fairfax and signed over to Carson Rhys Fairfax.

"Jack said he'd have the deed recorded and sent along to you as soon as it's taken care of," she said, staring at her hands in her lap. "Don't misunderstand. I'm not asking you to stay in Denver. I know you have plans to move on. I'm doing it because it wasn't fair of me to ask you to sacrifice the Respite in the first place. I was trying to change you, and that was wrong of me."

As he stared in astonishment at the bill of sale and held his breath, she continued.

"I've learned there's little virtue in virtue. I've learned that from you. My righteousness made me cold and unreachable. Uncompassionate. It made me narrow-minded and small. I don't want to be that way anymore. I hope returning the Respite to you makes up for some of the unhappiness I caused."

Carson stared at the bill of sale a moment longer—it was about the last thing he'd been expecting to hold at that moment—then he raised his gaze slowly to her face. "Do you want me to go to San Francisco?" he asked. As much as he appreciated her confession, he wanted to know whether she was going to tell him about the baby or not. Did she feel so confident in her ability to take care of herself that she'd keep their child a secret? Or was she waiting for something from him?

"Honestly?" she asked, meeting his gaze at last. The bleak shadows in her eyes gave his gut a painful twist. She was afraid of losing him. "I want you to be happy," she whispered.

"Odd," he said, grappling with the suspicion that she might love him almost as much as he loved her. He moved closer to her on the edge of the bed—within kissing range. "You know,

I threw that telegram into the fire. If you'd asked me what I most desired for you, I would say the same thing. Your happiness. Because I love you."

Katherine ceased stroking the cat. Her head came up and her lips trembled again. "Don't say that unless you mean it."

"I mean it." He leaned closer. "I love you. I love you. Want to make a wager on it?"

A small smile touched her lips. "You varlet."

He took advantage of the moment to kiss her lightly. "I love you," he repeated against her lips. "Now, tell me about our baby."

"You know!" she cried, pulling away. "Doc promised he wouldn't say anything."

"He lied," he said, certain of himself at last. She loved him. Why in the world would he want to be anywhere but with her? "If you think you can get rid of me with the threat of fatherhood, you're wrong."

"I don't want you here because you feel obligated and trapped," she said indignantly. "Lily and I can take care of ourselves. We have the gold mine now, thanks to you."

"Of course you can take care of yourselves," he said, kissing her lightly again. "You are rich women. I swear I'm not staying out of obligation. I'm here because I'm your husband and I can't imagine a future without you. I'm here because I love you. I'm here because a baby just makes our future look all the brighter."

He framed her face with his hands and kissed her longer this time, savoring her warmth; the warmth she'd given him so freely when he'd needed it most. The warmth he knew she would give lovingly to their children. "About our agreement: The marriage stands, of course. That's legal and recorded. Let's just call the rest of it null and void."

She looked him in the eye, clearly weighing his words. "Agreed. The past is null and void. But our future is bright."

Carson laughed and kissed her again and again. Eventually he had to lock the door.

Epilogue

In September of that year, a daughter was born to the Fairfaxes, whom they named Amanda Leigh. She was a bright, dark-haired, turquoise-eyed child who was the apple of her father's eye and the delight of her mother's life.

The Amanda Leigh mine was reopened and remained productive for decades. Carson eventually closed the Respite and turned his talents to investing in hotels and mines—though he refrained from spending time belowground.

Eventually Amanda graciously shared her limelight with two brothers and a little sister. They enjoyed every other summer in England at Atwick Manor, as did Lily. She became an accompanist to an opera coach, whom she met in London and later married. She enjoyed a life rich in world travel and music.

Young Amanda became a staunch supporter of the women's suffrage movement and married a Denver banker. Carson and Katherine's older son became a Colorado rancher—enough of a gamble, to Carson's way of thinking. The younger son fell in love with his grandfather's Bibles, and the old earl finally had his clergyman. Their youngest, Bess, fell in love with a daring young man in a flying machine, a barnstormer. It was enough to give her parents many sleepless nights.

Katherine remained a supporter of the Ladies' Moderation League but turned her greatest work to supporting theatrical efforts in Denver. She never lost her fondness for playacting.

Every Christmas Lily returned with her husband, as did the children with their spouses, to the Elms. The house glowed with Christmas candles and the doors were thrown open to the high and humble citizens of Denver. All enjoyed tree decorating and carol singing to Lily's piano playing in the best loving spirit of the season.

Their life together was rich. Each night, as Katherine fell asleep in Carson's arms, she thanked heaven above that they'd found each other and had been granted a life full of passion and a love brighter than gold.

About the Author

Linda Madl and her family live in the Flint Hills area of Kansas and are frequent visitors to the Rocky Mountains. As author of many historical romance novels and stories, she loves to hear from readers. You may write to her c/o Zebra Books. For a response, please include a self-addressed, stamped envelope.